ADVANCE PRAISE FOR

THE COMPANY OF DEMONS

"The terror of the Torso Murderer returns in this gritty, Cleveland-centric tale. Jordan delights with crackling dialogue, true-to life characters, an intensely paced plot, and an explosive finale. A must-read for fans of Lecter, Dexter, and the Ripper."

—**John Keyse-Walker,** Author of *Sun, Sand, Murder* and *Beach, Breeze, Bloodshed*; winner of Minotaur Books/Mystery Writers of America First Crime Novel Award

"Michael Jordan brings characters and scenes to life in this emotionally gripping and compelling breakout novel. Brilliantly crafted."

—**Rick Porrello,** Author of *To Kill the Irishman* (adapted into a major motion picture), *Superthief!,* and *The Rise and Fall of the Cleveland Mafia—Corn, Sugar, and Blood*

a novel

THE COMPANY
OF DEMONS

MICHAEL JORDAN

GREENLEAF
BOOK GROUP PRESS

Published by Greenleaf Book Group Press
Austin, Texas
www.gbgpress.com

Distributed by Greenleaf Book Group

For ordering information or special discounts for bulk purchases, please contact Greenleaf Book Group at PO Box 91869, Austin, TX 78709, 512.891.6100.

Design and composition by Greenleaf Book Group
Cover design by Greenleaf Book Group

Cataloging-in-Publication data is available.

Print ISBN: 978-1-62634-451-8

eBook ISBN: 978-1-62634-452-5

Part of the Tree Neutral® program, which offsets the number of trees consumed in the production and printing of this book by taking proactive steps, such as planting trees in direct proportion to the number of trees used: www.treeneutral.com

Printed in the United States of America on acid-free paper

17 18 19 20 21 22   10 9 8 7 6 5 4 3 2 1

First Edition

For my parents,
William Thomas Jordan and
Luella Jean Wilson Jordan

1

There was never any trouble at the Tam O'Shanter, even on a rocking weekend night, even when one of the Tribe smacked a homer for a go-ahead run. Tim and Karen ran a tight joint, the perfect hideaway to lounge beneath faded posters of '70s rock bands and sip a cold one. So when Karen screamed from the seedy alley behind the bar, our little oasis was shattered. Tim bolted for the back door.

I rushed after him and squinted in the bright sunlight. Tim was cradling his wife in his arms. She stared at me vacantly, then broke away and retched. Huddled over the rough asphalt, in her thin T-shirt and faded jeans, Karen reminded me of a fragile little girl. The waste-basket she'd intended to empty lay near her, paper napkins and discarded receipts fluttering in the humid breeze. Tim waved a hand toward a Dumpster, its lid flung open, wedged tight against the crumbling brick wall. "Don't look."

But I did.

The sight of a naked body, sprawled across plastic garbage bags, was impossible to miss. Or part of a body, really, because the head was gone. So was everything below the waist. The hairy torso had been split down the middle, and I didn't need to be a pathologist to know that someone had scooped out the guts and the lungs and the heart. Flies droned incessantly, and in the summer heat, the stench of rancid meat wafted to me. I backed away.

We headed back into the Tam, none of us saying a word. I dialed 911 on my cell. The Indians' third baseman cracked a triple as I slumped onto a black vinyl bar stool, the announcer's agitated voice echoing from the worn paneled walls and yellowed tin ceiling. His enthusiastic play-by-play was a jarring accompaniment to Karen's quiet sobs. She was hunched over, a couple of stools from me, wiping her mouth with a bar towel. Tim, glancing at me or the walls or the floor, hovered close to his wife, rubbing her shoulders.

The 911 operator's initial skepticism turned to shock as I related what we'd found, and she assured me that a car was on its way. The Tam was in Lakewood, an inner-ring Cleveland suburb, on busy Detroit Avenue. The police wouldn't take long.

My beer tasted warm and bitter, but I took a couple of long swigs. Memories came back in a rush.

Karen turned to me, her face ashen and her lipstick smeared. "You just talked to that magazine about all those killings when we were kids."

"They were running the article whether I talked to 'em or not."

"Not one week ago and now this?"

Tim scratched his gut just below the orange Browns logo on his pullover and said, "Let it go, Karen."

A couple of unnaturally serene cops soon strolled in, a tableau of belts and guns and badges. Tim filled them in, and the uniformed pair walked toward the back door to the alley, past the vintage Wurlitzer and the pool table wedged into an alcove beneath a hand-lettered sign that read No Gambling. The dark side of me wanted to follow them, to see if they might go off script when they saw what someone had done to that body in the trash.

I studied my beer and wished that the interview with *Cleveland*

Magazine had never taken place. We were quiet for ten long minutes, pretending to watch the game, until the back door swung open and Bernie Salvatore, a detective on the Lakewood force, strode in. We'd played football together at Holy Name, and he dropped in at the Tam for the occasional beer. He was a burly man, a couple of inches taller than my six feet, with a nose that looked like it had been jackhammered to his face. Yet he went right to Karen and was surprisingly tender as he reached out and touched her shoulder. "You okay? Boys said you found him."

She looked up at him. "I'll never forget that."

Bernie shrugged, looking every inch like the classic dick from late-night detective shows. Tan slacks, a white button-down dress shirt, wrinkled gray sport coat. An Armani model he was not. "I can get somebody to talk to you, if you want."

"It's just like before, what the Butcher did to those people."

"No shortage on psychos, sad to say."

"Oh, God . . . " Karen crossed herself. "Don't let it happen again."

"There was a pair of pants folded up, real neat, under the body. Still had the wallet in it, cash, credit cards." Bernie's eyes roved over the three of us. "There's no easy way to tell you. It's Oyster. I knew from one look at his license."

I had raised my mug, but lowered it back to the bar without taking a sip. Oyster was another regular at the Tam, a guy who was always willing to grin and bullshit and make people believe, even after just one beer, that they had a friend. He'd roll those bulging eyes of his when I got all cranked up and bitched about the Indians. He was called Oyster on account of those eyes. Gelatinous—like plump shellfish glistening on a bed of shaved ice.

Tim slapped the bar hard, loud as a shot.

"Why the fuck would somebody do that? Oyster never hurt anybody." He was visibly shaking. "Cut off his fucking head."

"Take it easy, Tim," Bernie said. "We'll get this son of a bitch."

"Right. That's what they said about the Butcher. Or that guy before him, killed all those people." Tim raised a hand and fluttered his fingers. "The . . . fuck."

I filled it in for him. "The Torso Murderer." I was too young to have been around for those brutal killings in the forties—at least a dozen victims disemboweled—but I remembered all too well when the Butcher had struck one generation later and paralyzed the city.

"It's not the same. We've got better labs now, forensics."

"Bernie's right." I leaned back and nodded. "Don't blow this out of proportion, okay? We—"

"I was six when the Butcher left that body on the East Side, naked and strung up on a playground fence." Karen took a deep breath and leaned toward me. "Jesus Christ, I just found Oyster in the trash!"

She kept her face fixed on mine, and I had no response. The tension was broken when Bernie said, "We gotta ask some questions, Karen. Let me take care of . . . outside, and I'll come back later, okay?"

She shuddered and crossed her arms, drew them tight. Bernie looked at me. "John, can I have a word?"

It wasn't really a question. I followed him into the side room with the pool table and a whiff of stale beer. The Tam was a holdover from the old days when saloons with lax ID policies lined Detroit Avenue, and we'd carouse all night, giddy on misspent youth and shots of cheap tequila. Although a dive now, the bar had become my fond refuge from encroaching micropubs, coffee houses, and gluten-free bullshit places. Well, at least until I'd seen Oyster's corpse mixed in with the garbage.

"You okay?" Bernie narrowed his eyes. "I mean, that article, now this . . . "

"Somehow, I thought that reporter would be more sympathetic. 'The Price of Failure.' Nice title." And to think that I'd viewed my old man as a hero when they'd put him in charge of finding the Butcher. Thank God Bernie had been around when everything had happened; he'd stuck up for me when the other kids had ridden my ass.

"All those reporters, pricks. Fuck 'em. C'mon. Go home and spend a nice Sunday afternoon with Cathy and your kid. Give 'em a hug for me. Let's get coffee tomorrow. I'll call."

We walked out of the alcove, and Bernie turned, disappearing through the back door. I returned to my stool and examined the face that stared at me from the back of the mirrored bar: wrinkles around blue eyes, dark hair flecked with gray, soft flesh encircling my neck. I reached for the beer.

The silence was pounding, and Tim must have felt that something needed to be said. "Oyster was the nicest damn guy in the world. They'd better find this son of a bitch and cut off his fuckin' balls."

"Yeah, Oyster deserves at least that." But I'd been a lawyer long enough to know that there probably wouldn't be any righteous ending like Tim was demanding, even assuming that lopping off somebody's nuts as payback for cutting off a guy's head would be fair. Despite all the blather we'd told Karen, odds were that Oyster would be just one more unsolved murder.

I didn't want to be there when the press barged in; I needed to go home to Cathy. She'd be nervous as hell about the possibility that a serial killer might be on the prowl again. And I needed some time to think. It wasn't just a nagging guilt that my blabbing to a magazine had somehow sparked Oyster's demise. A dark fragment of my past still hounded me. Oyster had known nothing about what had happened, but I could never forget.

2

Cathy held up the front page of *The Plain Dealer*. A blurry photo of Oyster stared back at me. "You were right about his eyes. They do look odd."

In my faded gray sweats, I sat across the round kitchen table from her and inhaled the steam rising from my mug of coffee, black and strong. We'd watched the news reports the night before and had known that the story would be splashed all over the front page of the morning paper. I'd had a few too many after we put our daughter, Molly, to bed, and that meant for one rugged Monday. Even my eyeballs ached.

Cathy, her dark hair catching the morning light that filtered through the window, reached over an arrangement of artificial flowers to hand me the paper. "They may not have mentioned you on the news last night, but . . . "

The newspaper article more than mentioned me. The reporter found it an odd twist that I had been at the Tam, the *son of the detective who was relieved from duty due to his failure to apprehend the Butcher*. I stared at Oyster's face for a moment. The caption, of course, used his real name, but *Wilbur Frederickson* seemed foreign to me. I folded the paper and dropped it on the table.

"Just so you know, it's all in there, about your dad."

"I'll finish it later." Everybody I ran into was going to haul up the past, fix me with their sympathetic stares, and speak in hushed tones.

"Says that Oyster was a widower, two grown children. Another daughter predeceased him."

I took a sip of coffee. Oyster's late daughter was not a subject I wanted to dwell on. "I didn't know much about his family."

"You weren't that close, then?"

"Like I said last night, I'd shoot the breeze with him at the bar. A good guy, but . . ." I shifted on the padded chair and pulled the foil top from a container of strawberry yogurt that Cathy had set out. I didn't really enjoy fermented milk, but that and the occasional jog helped keep the weight down. "Do you think Molly will be okay with this?"

Cathy didn't answer right away but tugged on the sleeve of her faded blue robe. Then she said, "You just went over the magazine story with her, so I think so."

"I never should have talked to that damn rag."

"You'd have been in the article anyway."

She was right about that. I remembered hiding in the library stacks to avoid the callous playground barbs. *Hey, Coleman, is that your old man? Detective Fuck-Up?* I took a swig of coffee and cringed at the thought that some jerk kid would try the same crap with Molly, even though it would be about a dead grandfather whom she had never even met.

"We'll need to keep an eye on her, John. If there's a problem at school, you know Little Miss Stoic's not going to tell us."

"I'll talk to her when she comes down." We had adopted Molly after she'd bounced around the foster care network for all of her four years. The day we'd brought her home, she'd warily eyed the pink floral wallpaper in her bedroom, the toys and dolls from Walmart, then asked matter-of-factly how long she could stay before they came to take her away.

Cathy ran a hand along her forearm, where the sleeve of her robe ended. She reached up and rubbed her earlobe, which I'd seen her do hundreds of times. She was anxious. "I didn't bring this up with Molly, but . . . what if it's happening again?"

"Let the cops do their job before you start to worry, Cathy."

"Back then, my mom wouldn't even let us walk to school alone. You remember."

"Better than anyone. I'm just sayin' we should find out the facts before you jump to any conclusions." I reached for the remote. "Let's see what the talking heads have to say."

"I don't want you getting upset either, John."

"I'm gonna hear about this all day as it is, so we might as well find out what everyone is being told." I'd have to read the whole damn *PD* story as well.

The news came on and cut to a recorded clip of the Lakewood chief of police, a rangy guy with a bushy mustache and unblinking eyes that bored into the camera. The media was peppering him with questions about the Torso Murderer and the Butcher. It only took a minute before the chief began blinking and pulled out a hanky to wipe beads of perspiration from his forehead.

"He's not looking too happy."

"Can't blame him. There's been one murder, and the press is already dredging up crap that happened a long time ago."

I topped off my coffee and watched as Vanessa Edwards, a gorgeous black reporter, posed a question. I'd spoken with her once, years ago, when she had been covering a lawsuit over an estate, and I had represented a minor beneficiary. She asked the chief if there was any possibility that the Butcher had resurfaced.

Cathy concentrated on the screen, her brow furrowed.

The chief scoffed at the notion and surmised that a copycat killer, perhaps inspired by the recent magazine article, was much more likely. He noted the prevalence of security cameras, improved police procedure, and better forensic labs. Then he confidently predicted that they would find Oyster's killer.

"I remember my dad saying the same thing about the Butcher."

At least until the day he'd been taken off the case. Then he became accustomed to the refuge of his tattered beige easy chair and the comfort of Four Roses whiskey.

"Morning." Molly bounded down the steps and into the kitchen, clad in her favorite jeans and a loose-fitting yellow top with a demure neckline—my wife's strict upbringing would influence the attire of at least one more generation. Petite Molly, with her reddish-brown hair and pale skin, bore a remarkably close resemblance to Cathy.

"Morning, pretty girl." Too pretty, as a matter of fact. To my dismay, she was developing curves that hadn't been there a month ago.

She breezed past the table, sliding on her socks across a white tile floor that needed replacing, and popped open the door to the side-by-side Kenmore.

"Listen, honey. Mom said you read about this murder. Well, I was there when they found him."

She turned with a plastic orange juice container in hand, her eyes wide. "Jeez . . ."

"Yeah, it was terrible. And my name's in the paper this morning. They wrote about me, my dad, and all those old murders we told you about. You might have some knuckleheads saying something."

"No one said much after the magazine. They know I'll stick up for myself."

Molly, a natural athlete, was probably the best step dancer in her age group at the Irish American Club, and she was definitely the cutest in her poodle socks and ghillies. But we knew that she only danced to please us. Her real passion was sports, and she proudly toted around a bright-pink skateboard—a color, I expected, that she chose to send a message to the boys when she blew by them.

"Don't go looking for trouble, Molly. And I'm dropping you off at school today."

"Oh, Mom!"

"Watch your tone. It's just until they catch this guy, that's all." Cathy walked to the sink and rinsed her mug.

"I've got plans later. Skateboarding." She had mastered every half-pipe and mini-ramp—I made an effort to learn the lingo—at Lake-wood Park.

Cathy turned to me. "I've got a committee meeting after school."

I shrugged and looked at my little girl as she brushed strands of silky hair away from her face and munched on an apple. "I'll pick you up, out front near the bike racks. We can hit the park, then head home for dinner."

Molly said nothing, obviously copping an attitude about her mother driving her to school.

"Good. That's settled." Cathy tousled my hair as she passed by, toward the stairs. "I need to get dressed."

Molly watched her head up the steps and then set the half-eaten apple on the table. "I'm glad you came home when you did. Mom was scared."

I nodded slightly. "She worries, you know."

"Oh, believe me, I know." Grinning, she reached for the apple and took a nibble.

I stood, kissed her on the forehead, and trotted up the frayed chestnut-colored stair runner. When I entered our tight bedroom, Cathy was shimmying into a gray skirt. She hadn't donned her blouse yet; she stood there in a white bra. I'd first seen her in panties and a bra nearly thirty years ago, after our engagement, months after we'd met at a St. Patrick's Day party.

In the wall mirror mounted above the dresser, she watched me approach across the brown pile carpet. Even though I couldn't read her face, I took her by the shoulders and nuzzled the delicate skin on her neck. "I wish there were time . . . "

"Maybe this weekend, okay?"

I nodded, but no part of me wanted to wait until the weekend to have sex. Oyster's death made me burn to take Cathy right on the carpet, to feel alive and breathing and coming.

She turned and rested her hand on my cheek. "Don't get mad at me for asking, but are you going to be all right?"

"I can deal with it."

"You drank too much last night." She dropped her hand but continued to face me.

"After Molly was in bed. The thing with Oyster . . ."

"I get it, but you were pretty bombed."

"Christ, Cathy, if you'd seen that body, you'd understand."

"You still drink too much sometimes."

"Curse of the Irish." I smiled broadly.

"I'm serious."

"C'mon. You know I've cut back. I catch a game at the Tam a couple times a week. Maybe a few after work, a nightcap when she's in bed."

"I'm not looking for a fight, John. I just worry. First the magazine article, now you find a dead man. It's just . . . it's been a long time since you've had to see a therapist."

"You don't need to worry, Cathy."

She sighed and shut her eyes for a moment, and then said, "You'll tell me, won't you, if you're having problems?"

"Cathy . . . I promise." I wasn't looking for a fight either; I knew that her heart was in the right place. I gently squeezed her shoulder.

"Sometimes you're impossible."

"What about sexy, handsome . . ."

"Not even close, not last night." She picked up a pearly blouse from the dresser and slipped it on. "What about a session with Father McGraw next Sunday?"

I stopped dead, halfway to the bathroom. "Really, Cathy? I'm fine. We all are."

"You just found the body yesterday, John. Shouldn't we get ahead of the game, especially for Molly? I just want her to understand what you went through and how to deal with any problems at school."

"I think it's premature."

"You know he saved our marriage."

"But this is different." The leaden counseling sessions with our priest had helped us, no question, but dragging Molly into the equation just didn't seem necessary. "Can we talk about this later?"

Cathy nodded, tight-lipped, and I headed toward the bathroom. She called good-bye to me as I lathered in the shower, letting my skin grow soft beneath the spray of hot water. I finally emerged, toweled off, and walked directly to my oaken bureau. The envelope would be there, tucked beneath the folded woolen sweaters. I crouched, naked, and slid open the bottom drawer.

I'd shown the letter to the police after it had arrived, all those years ago. They had kept the original but given me a copy. I'd let Cathy see it after we were married, and she had wrapped me in her arms while I wept. Sometimes, nearly always beyond drunk, I'd pull the worn paper out and examine every marking, right down to the stains caused by my tears. That hadn't happened for years now, which was fine by me.

The paper unfolded, but it would not lie flat against the carpet. The stiff creases resisted, as though the writing did not wish to be read. On the original, cutout letters had been fastidiously glued to white stationery.

Dear John Coleman:

I am so sorry about your father. He was such fun. So earnest, so intense, so desperate. The ridicule when he failed to stop me, the public outcry and scorn. Then losing his position, how embarrassing! So difficult for you to have a laughingstock for a father.

And the papers said that you found him! I can imagine the mess, and you, just a high school boy. He counts as one of mine, you know. I killed him as surely as if I'd taken his liver, his lungs, and his heart.

I'll be watching you, young man.

Bold black capital letters spelled THE BUTCHER.

I had come home after football practice. My mother had been at her Altar and Rosary Society meeting, and our modest bungalow had been quiet. I went to use the bathroom, and he was slouched against the tile wall near the toilet, the bone-white porcelain spattered with red. Blood and brains were everywhere, and part of me cried aloud for the man I remembered, wishing that he were playing a macabre costume game with ketchup and cottage cheese. But another voice, deep within me, mouthed a prayer of thanks that the beast he'd become was dead forever.

On the morning of his funeral, I'd stolen into my parents' bedroom, taken his thick leather belt, and flung that stinging memory in the trash.

3

On my drive into the office, along the Shoreway, Lake Erie was as calm as the proverbial millpond, and the few skyscrapers that framed Cleveland's skyline were awash in the glow of morning sunlight. Recreational boaters dotted the blue water as they puttered away from Edgewater Marina, and in the distance, a freighter lazed northwest to Detroit. The lake wasn't always so tranquil, of course; fifteen-foot waves would hurl against the meandering shore whenever a gale swept in from Canada. On those days, sailors huddled in port, and adventurous surfers, sheathed in black wetsuits, defied the churning green-gray swell.

My office was in the Singer Building, a once prestigious location but now just a site where even small-timers like me could afford the rent. Marilyn, my perky, divorced, forty-five-year-old secretary—or "assistant," as the PC folks would say—was ensconced behind her cherry veneer reception desk when I arrived.

She was evidently between boyfriends because, once again, she had altered the color of her eye shadow, and her jet black hair was sleeked back in a new style. I shut the door behind me. "New 'do. Looking good."

"Just once, I'm waiting for you to tell me I look like shit." Marilyn had worked with me for ten years or, as she would say, a decade too long.

"So you'd walk out? Who'd convince pissed-off clients that I'm a saint? Or tell opposing counsel they can kiss my ass?"

"Yeah, yeah." She crossed her arms and leaned onto her desk. Marilyn was thin and bony, but her stare had the intensity of the nun who'd caught some buddies and me passing around a *Playboy* magazine in eighth grade. "I saw the news. You okay with all this?"

We kept a coffee pot in a narrow alcove across from her desk; I poured a cup. "It'll pass. But if the press wants to talk, I have no comment. I'm done with those bastards."

"Can't blame you. And you've already had some calls. I sent you an email." Marilyn fiddled with a long earring, copper and silver strands that shimmered in the light.

"Go ahead, beat me up for not checking the cell. I figured anything could wait until I got here. Something urgent?"

"No, but one sounds like new business, handling an estate."

"Worried about getting paid?" Big-firm lawyers can bank steady checks from corporate clients. Not me—a little estate work here, a little business stuff there, whatever I can get in the door.

"Never. I know where you live."

"Don't be smart. It's too early."

"By the way, the bloodshot eye thing? Nice."

I flashed a mock grin and walked into my utilitarian office. The faux oak paneling looked tired, the requisite degrees needed reframing, and the worn office furniture nearly screamed that it had once been marked-down inventory at a discount place on Euclid Avenue. No plaques commemorated my leadership in civic organizations; no photographs bore witness to my connections with celebrities or politicians.

The phone message was from a Jennifer Browning. The name was unfamiliar, but I sipped my coffee and dialed the number. Odds were that she knew a cop or was related to one. Because of my dad's old cronies, a lot of my clients were cops or retired cops and faithfully made referrals.

"Ms. Browning?" I said, in response to a sultry hello. "John Coleman, returning your call."

"Thanks for getting back to me." Her lyrical tone was enchanting. "I called about my father, Wilbur Frederickson."

"Oyster?"

"Yes, but I never liked that name."

If my parents had saddled me with a name like Wilbur, I would rather have been called Oyster, but I wasn't about to tell her that. "Sorry. A great guy—everybody liked him."

"I can't believe it." Jennifer was clearly struggling not to cry. "He left a will. Your business card was on his desk, your name in the paper, so I figured . . . "

"I'd be glad to help." I appreciated that she'd refrained from mentioning anything that the paper had said about my father. My calendar was virtually clear, although I didn't mention that to Jennifer as we arranged the meeting.

"I have a brother," she suddenly said. "He won't need to be there, will he?"

"No. Is there something I should know?"

"It's just . . . he's a drug addict; we're not on speaking terms."

"I'm sorry, Jennifer. That must be difficult. He'll need to sign some papers, but we can discuss that when we meet." I wasn't happy with the news. Dealing with family conflict only made my job more challenging. "My advice? Change the locks on your parents' home."

"Got it. Thank you."

"I'll watch the paper, but would you let me know when the service is? I'd like to attend." Now that I'd been retained, showing up at the funeral was basically mandatory.

"That's nice. Thank you. I'll look forward to meeting you."

We rang off. Oyster's murder was going to net me a fee, and that seemed wrong. I'd at least make sure to toast his memory with a top-shelf Irish whiskey and do a damn fine job for his heirs. I owed Oyster a good turn and, truth be told, I hoped like hell that Jennifer in the flesh wouldn't remind me of her sister, Martha, Oyster's late daughter.

Our affair had taken place in my pre-Molly days, during a rough patch, when Cathy and I had barely been speaking, let alone touching. Martha's hand had brushed mine when we'd reached for the same bowl of corn chips, beneath a multihued piñata and strands of white, red, and green bunting, during happy hour at a popular Mexican spot in Bay Village. An orange sweater clung to her, and her hazel eyes sparkled. With a toss of her blonde hair, she said that my smile was cute. We were soon at her apartment, shedding our clothes, for the happiest hour of all.

Because she'd kept her ex's last name, I hadn't known that she was Oyster's daughter, not at first. Once I figured out the connection, my cheating with Martha seemed even more problematic. Every time we were together, I knew that it was wrong—on many levels. The guilt kept mounting, until I finally summoned the courage to end our trysts. Sadly, by then, Martha had confused lust with love. The image of her, quivering beneath a tightly drawn blue sheet as streaks of mascara trailed down her cheeks, was searing. *I'll make it easy. Just get the fuck out.*

I agreed to counseling with Father McGraw—although my affair was something that I'd never confessed. Cathy and I smoothed over our simmering issues and then adopted Molly, the glue that bound us together. And Martha? She'd been buried years ago, a young cancer victim, but shaking that vision of the pain I'd inflicted on her was impossible. And that shameful memory was exactly what I deserved.

Then, out of the blue, her sister. And a junkie brother. A slaughtered father. My gut told me that handling this estate was going to be anything but routine.

4

"So, what's up?" I asked as Bernie slid into the pine booth. He wore an outfit nearly identical to his attire at the Tam—maybe he'd changed the shirt. His call just before noon, suggesting lunch, was timely. My hangover was finally drifting away, and I was ready for something to eat.

He eyed the Miller Café's floral wallpaper and kitschy knick-knacks as if he'd never seen the joint before. "You doin' okay?"

I didn't need any more hand-wringing, not even from Bernie. "I told you—"

"I'm not talkin' about Oyster and all of that. You and Cathy, how's that going?"

I hated it when he dredged up the situation between me and Cathy. Our wives were close, working together on church potlucks or parish fund-raisers and related Good Samaritan missions. When Cathy and I started having some serious issues, Mrs. Salvatore yackety-yacked to her hubby about whatever Cathy told her, and ever since, Bernie felt some sort of obligation to follow up. "Everything's fine."

"She's only worried about you, John. Called the wife, said you got toasted last night."

"Well, she's right. I'm . . . under the circumstances, I'm not gonna apologize."

"Think that's what I'm asking? I just don't wanna see all that bullshit from your past resurface and you start backsliding."

Bernie knew too much, heard too much. He'd once pulled me aside, back in the day, and said there was some lewd gossip circulating about my drinking and running around. I'd confessed to some boozy, hazy nights, but claimed that I was keeping it zipped. Even Bernie did not know the truth. "Hey, I've been a damn Boy Scout."

"Any interesting merit badges?"

"You are a dickhead."

We laughed as the waitress, a bony redhead with a long tattoo of oriental characters on her arm, scampered over to take our order. She had a cute face, and I couldn't resist asking her what the tat meant.

She shrugged. "I was hanging out with my Chinese boyfriend in New York. Him and the tattoo guy told me it meant *flying red lady*, which I thought was kind of cool." She looked down at her notepad. "After the dirtball dumped me, he said it means *dumb bitch* in Mandarin."

Straightening her arm, she gave us the whole canvas. "But it looks awesome, don't you think?"

I nodded, but wondered why people would permanently disfigure their bodies like that. I hoped that Molly would never fall for a piece of shit like the Chinese boyfriend.

We both ordered sandwiches and coffee, and she pranced away, quickly returning with two steaming mugs.

Bernie took a loud slurp. "Anybody giving you shit about your father?"

"No. There's been some calls, but I think it's just to dig for gossip. Haven't bothered to return them." Back in high school, after Dad killed himself, the bullies had been all over my ass. Bernie, being one of the few Italian kids in our school, had learned at an early age to respond to slurs of *wop* and *dago* with his fists. He'd stepped in to help me out with the worst assholes.

"Good. I talked to Jennifer Browning a bit ago, a few follow-up questions about Oyster. She said you'll be representing her."

I lowered my cup to the table. "You make it sound like that's not a good thing."

"The rumor, back in the day, was about you and the sister who died . . . "

"Martha." I eyed a framed black-and-white of downtown Cleveland on the wall, taken fifty years ago, when dark plumes of smoke from bustling steel factories jousted with billowing clouds.

"Well?"

"Nothing to talk about."

"Sorry if I hit a sore spot." He smirked and raised his eyebrows. "Umm. Well, I do miss living vicariously. To quote President Ford, 'We've all got a little lust in our hearts.'"

"That was Carter."

"I forgot—you're an authority on lust, ever since you nailed Ellen O'Donnell junior year. Can't forget her in a cheerleading uniform."

"Oh, yeah, Ample Ellen." She'd let me go so far as dry-humping her in the back of her old man's station wagon, and I'd blown my wad in about twenty seconds. I let Bernie and the other guys think that we'd screwed. "So, about Jennifer. Is there something I'm supposed to know?"

He grinned and took another swig. "Nothing about her, but her brother, Frank, is a real piece of work."

"Jennifer told me he has issues." The thought occurred to me that, although Martha had often spoken of her sister, I didn't recall any mention of a brother.

"In spades. We want to talk to him. He might know more about where the old man hung out, besides the Tam, or if somebody was pissed at him. Trouble is, can't find the bastard."

"Maybe he's too strung out to pick up a phone." For several years after my father died, the docs loaded me up with meds—multihued mood stabilizers, antidepressants. Some days and nights, when I took the wrong dose or an incorrect combination, summoning the will to make a simple phone call was impossible.

"I'm worried the kid might be makin' a run for it, Johnny. He's in some deep shit."

"You don't . . . His own father?"

"No, I don't make him for that, at least not yet. I don't think he has it in him, for one thing. Frank Frederickson is basically a fucked-up punk. When the rich white kids in Bay Village or Westlake wanted a toot, they'd head out in Daddy's BMW to see Frank. Some undercover cop, wired like a fucking Radio Shack, nailed his ass. But Frank kept his mouth shut, took the fall for a couple of guys higher up the supply chain."

"Honor among thieves, eh?" The tattooed lady returned, slid a tuna sandwich in front of me and a grilled salami and cheese for Bernie. "So, how'd he do in prison?"

"I'm told he was popular. Anyway, he met some guys inside who were hooked up in Detroit. Frank told them he could score mucho coke down here for them, open up another supply. When he got out, they came calling." Bernie chomped into his sandwich and then wiped a string of gooey cheese from his chin. "Long story short, Frank took big bucks from the Detroiters and got double-crossed by the supplier. That honor thing was a one-way street. They took the money from Frank, but he got nothin'. Except, of course, some very pissed-off guys from Detroit."

All of this was interesting, but nothing I needed to know to handle an estate. The way it sounded, Frank was back to being a player, probably trading coke to the foxy girls in exchange for a blow job. "And you're telling me this because . . ."

"This Detroit gang's a branch of a Mexican one, with ties all the way to their base, south of the border. They're called the Andar Feo. Means Walking Ugly."

"What are they—deformed?" My grin was not returned.

"If you fuck with them, they rarely kill you. They round up all the women in your family—grandmothers, mothers, aunts, daughters, cousins—they don't give a shit."

My stomach tightened, and I left the tuna sandwich on the cut-rate china plate. The waitress popped over with a thermal carafe and refilled our mugs.

Bernie leaned back in the booth and went on. "They rape 'em first, Johnny, and it doesn't matter how old or young they are. Sometimes it lasts for days. The son of a bitch they're pissed at, they keep him tied to a chair and make him watch the whole damn thing. Then, when they've had their fun, they mutilate 'em. Noses, ears, whatever the hell they want. Even if they kill the guy, they let the women live, to send a message, let people know who *not* to screw with. That's the name, right there, the Walking Ugly."

"Jesus. You warned the sister, right?" My thoughts flashed to Cathy but then centered on Molly. She was just a kid. I wanted her there, next to me in the booth, my arm around her.

"Nah, figured I'd wait until they were coming at her with a hacksaw." He gulped his coffee again. "She seemed to take it in stride, has it pretty together, for what just happened."

"You're not thinking they did Oyster, though?"

"Not their style, but we won't rule anything out." He took another bite and waved Ms. Tattoo over for some more coffee. "Am I right? You haven't met Jennifer yet?"

"No, but I'll see her at the funeral." I nudged the plate away, the sandwich untouched.

"I'll have someone there early, for a word with Frank. We'll cut him slack the day he's buryin' his father, but he's gotta promise to come in and talk. I don't wanna get rough, but he's still on parole, and if he blows us off . . ."

"If I have the chance, I'll say something."

"Here." He pulled a photo from his jacket. "Have one of his mug shots, on me."

Frank's face was drawn. His stringy, dark hair blended with a wispy goatee and mustache. An ornate tattoo, geometrical shapes of green and red and black, trailed along his neck.

"Just because you're wondering, Jennifer got the better end of the gene pool," Bernie said. "She must be midforties, but she's still a looker. Who knows? Maybe she'll remind you of the sister. Think you can keep this strictly lawyer-client?"

He grinned, so I figured it wasn't a warning and smiled back. This was the side of Bernie that I liked. Maybe I'd have a bite of that sandwich after all. "Professional all the way. Boy Scout, remember?"

"I'm sure. Actually, it'd better be. You keep your focus on Cathy."

Damn, but he could not resist Lecture Mode. I was relieved when his phone rang, and he wrestled for it in his jacket pocket. He listened, closed his eyes, and said, "On my way."

He slipped the phone in his pocket and clambered out of the booth. "They just found another body."

5

I focused on Bernie's Chevy as he pulled off the Shoreway to Lake Road, heading west. Our destination surprised me: Wagar Beach in Rocky River, a tony section of town where McMansions with circular drives, brick paver walks, and manicured hedges perched on the lakefront. Not the kind of place where I got to hang out as a kid, and not the kind of place accustomed to serving as a dumping ground for a murder victim.

As I pulled to the curb, Bernie was already running along the brick road, toward the stone stairs leading to the sheltered beach. A stone archway marked the entrance, and I lingered there with the gathering crowd. Technically, Bernie was out of his jurisdiction, since Rocky River has its own police force, but they'd work together on a murder. Dead bodies have a way of getting people to cooperate.

At least fifteen minutes elapsed before Bernie reappeared. He ducked under the sagging police tape and motioned me away from the throng. "To answer your question, it isn't Frank. No tats."

"And?" A serial killer was out there, no doubt, if this victim was carved up in a manner similar to Oyster. I shuddered, remembering my dad's pallid expression whenever another mutilated body cropped up in an abandoned parking lot or scum-filled ditch.

"Fucking mess. Head's gone, like your buddy Oyster, but this guy's also missing his hands." He shook his head and then spat out a wad of phlegm.

My eye caught some preppy teenagers decked out in skimpy bathing suits, towels draped over their shoulders. Some were hugging, and a couple of the girls were crying. "Kids find him?"

"The flies caught their attention. Skipped school for an afternoon and stumbled across the body."

They'd had quite a day at the beach, all right. "Any clothes, a wallet, like with Oyster?"

"Nothin'. Gonna be hell to ID." Bernie looked away, then back at me. "Maybe you shouldn't have come out here, shouldn't be near this shit."

"That was a long time ago, Bernie. You're worrying for nothing."

He looked over my shoulder. "Damn, the vultures are descending."

I turned to watch as a local news van barreled down Avalon Drive. I could imagine the special alerts and lurid headlines, all stemming from a quiet neighborhood accustomed to—and quite content with—staying out of the news.

"Gotta go," Bernie said, ducking back under the tape.

I had nearly reached my car when the first news van pulled to the curb. The door slid open, and out bounded Vanessa Edwards, elegant in a coffee-colored suit that beautifully matched her skin tone. Our eyes locked.

"Hey! You're . . . "

"John Coleman." The fact that she hadn't remembered my name sent my ego tumbling.

"That's right, the lawyer. I just read about you in the paper. Are you tied to this victim, too?"

"A bystander, Vanessa. That's it." I got into the car, fast. No one was going to interview me again.

"C'mon, just a few questions." She knocked on my window, then smiled and said loudly, "I'll find out—you know that. Expect a call!"

As she ran toward the cordoned area, I decided to phone Jennifer.

Hearing about this new murder on the news, on the heels of what had happened to her dad, would be jarring. It sure as hell had jarred me. Of course, I'd call Cathy, to reassure her and keep her calm. After school, we'd both talk to Molly and make sure she was okay.

Marilyn would have promptly opened a file for the estate. As expected, Jennifer's contact info scrolled up on my cell. I punched the button, pulled away from the curb, and soon had her on the line. She listened intently to the afternoon's morbid story.

"That's just terrible. Another family has to go through this."

She seemed so sensitive. It was disturbing to imagine her in the grasp of the Andar Feo. "I have to tell you, on the way over here, I was worried that it might have been Frank. Bernie Salvatore said he told you about that gang."

"That's Frank's problem." Suddenly she didn't sound so sensitive.

"To be honest, I'm more worried about you. If these guys go after . . . well, you are his sister."

"They'll have a hard time finding me; I have a different last name. Frank doesn't even have my address or phone number—that's the only way to handle an addict. Dad was the only one who'd still talk to him, God knows why."

"Just the same, do you have somewhere you can stay for a while? A friend?" I braked at the intersection with Detroit, waiting for the light to change.

"He's not a part of my life, and I won't move because he's in trouble. I'm not going anywhere, Mr. Coleman."

"Please, call me John." The light flicked green, and I pulled through, past a family-owned grocery and the glass façade of a swank wine bar. "Just think about it, okay?"

"I'm touched that you're worried, John. You take care." She hung up.

I'm touched that you're worried, John. I looked forward to meeting her in person—even if the first time would be at a funeral home. Her sexy voice alone intrigued me. I rested the phone on the console and gripped the wheel with both damp hands. What the hell was going through my mind, daydreaming about another woman? Maybe agreeing to represent Jennifer had been a mistake.

A deep breath helped to calm me. Oyster's death had brought an ugly past alive. Just as I'd been assuring everyone, though, there was nothing wrong. My main task for the day was to pick Molly up after school and hope that she wouldn't be too disappointed when she learned that we wouldn't be visiting the skateboard park. We would head straight home for a quiet, uneventful spaghetti dinner. Cathy would have polished and set the oaken table. We would talk of things other than serial killers. She would remind me of her upcoming birthday dinner, with her sister and brother-in-law. Her parents would stare down at us from faded color photographs arranged in thin wooden frames on the checkered blue-and-white wallpaper. There were photos of my mom, too, with her tight-lipped smile.

One photo of my father, handsome in a blue uniform, hung on the wall. Whenever Cathy said grace, my eyes would wander to that particular picture, and I would recall the games of catch, walleye fishing on the lake, our hikes through the Metroparks. We'd wander the trails there most Saturday mornings, just my dad and me. Afterward, he'd take me to Pete's Hotdogs on Lorain, and we'd gorge on dogs stuffed into steamed buns and topped with local Stadium mustard and greasy fried onions. Those were the memories I'd try to focus on.

But I could never, ever block out the rest.

THE MEMORIAL SERVICE FOR OYSTER WAS HELD AT A funeral home on Center Ridge Road. The ceremony, a blissfully brief Methodist affair, was so much simpler than our elaborate Catholic rituals. I waited until Jennifer had thanked the minister for his comments, and then I crossed toward the front of the small chapel to introduce myself. Bernie's assessment had been dead on. She was a younger, even prettier version of Martha: short blonde hair, hazel eyes, and creamy skin.

"Thanks for coming," she said, taking my hand. "I suppose you'd like to meet Frank."

I followed her gaze toward the floral arrangements displayed near the casket, where Frank had strolled as soon as the ceremony had concluded. He was staring at a lily of the valley, probably wondering if he could smoke it. "Yeah, I should."

"Do you mind introducing yourself? I'm . . . I'm so done with him."

"I understand."

"Well . . . " She looked away, as though she were considering whether to say anything more. With a sigh, she continued, her eyes misting over. "He's wearing Dad's retirement watch. He must have gone to the house before the locks were changed."

I didn't believe a word of what I was about to say, but an attempt at smoothing things over seemed like the right approach. "Maybe your dad gave it to him, Jennifer. I can say something to him, if you want."

She shook her head, her face locked in a tight grimace. "Dad would have known he'd pawn it. But let it go for now, John. I don't want him blowing up here." Her lyrical tone had been replaced by one of steel.

Jennifer turned to thank the remaining mourners, and I crossed the room to Frank. His handshake was limp, and his eyes seemed unnaturally bright. I would not have been surprised to learn he was high at his own father's funeral.

After introducing myself and explaining my role in handling the estate, I gave him my card. "Any questions, call me."

He stuck out his chin, bristling with his stubbly goatee. "How long will this take?"

Greedy bastard. "I'll handle everything the best I can, but it will take months to move through court. I'll need your address, phone number."

"I'm kinda between places." He nodded in the direction of Jennifer. "She has my number."

"The cops say you're a hard man to reach." I felt obligated to Bernie to raise the issue.

"Yeah, one of them stopped by earlier." His bright eyes darted around the room, as though a hit squad might burst in. "There're people after me, you know. I took a risk just being here."

"I heard that, but you're safe with the cops. They only want to see if you can help."

"Sure." He paused, glancing about. "I saw her staring at it, the watch. He gave it to me."

"Okay." I was relieved that he'd brought it up. "But natural for her to wonder about it, that's all."

"Fuck her." He stepped closer to me, his face lit by anger. "Whatever she says, me and the old man stayed close through all the bullshit."

"I hear you, Frank. No reason to get upset." I kept my voice as calm as possible. The last thing I needed would be for Jennifer to think that I'd sparked a confrontation.

"She'll try to fuck me over, you know." He clenched his teeth and nodded.

I stepped back and raised my hands. "I don't know that, Frank. Your father's will determines—"

"I don't care about no will. She will try to fuck me over." He enunciated the last words carefully, slowly, as though I were confused.

"The process is run through the court, Frank. You really don't need to worry." Great. I'd been hired only days ago and was already stepping into a mess.

"I'll be in touch, Mr. Lawyer." He took a few steps back, chuckling. "You have no idea what she's capable of."

He stuck my card in his pants pocket and turned toward the casket. I retreated in the direction of the parlor. Jennifer was chatting with some folks, so I just waved good-bye. There was no sense in further upsetting her. Bringing up her brother's cryptic comments could wait until we met in my office. I did think about telling her what he had said about the watch, but there was no way that she was going to believe him.

I stopped near the doorway by an arrangement of photos of Oyster and others on a white poster board. One showed him with Martha, smiling broadly and seated across from her at a picnic table. I looked away.

Frank was resting a hand on the cherrywood surface of the coffin, his head bowed in prayer.

6

"It was kind of you, coming to the funeral." Jennifer scanned the simple furnishings in my office and nestled into an upholstered chair.

"The ceremony was nice." Her pink dress hugged her figure nicely and accented her blonde hair. When I'd come out to greet Jennifer in the lobby, Marilyn had raised her eyebrows and shot me a wry look.

Jennifer pointed to a photo of Cathy and Molly on my desk. "Your family?"

"Yeah, our bundle of thirteen-year-old energy. Last year's Christmas show at the Palace."

"Thought I recognized the lobby, all that marble. Your daughter's the image of your wife."

I rolled my chair forward and rested my arms on the desk. "We hear that, but she's adopted."

"Could have fooled me. Great pic." Jennifer shifted her focus to the window behind me, with its view of the brick wall of the office building across the street. She shut her eyes. "Every time I looked at that closed casket, it reminded me of what happened to Dad."

I felt for her, wondering what an undertaker does when there aren't even enough parts to reassemble a corpse. "They'll trip up this creep. Maybe some clue will tie the Rocky River murder to your father's."

She shot me a skeptical look. "Everyone's talking about those serial killers from years back. The police never found a thing."

"They need time, that's all. Lab work, pathology, all of it."

I recalled the same discussion with my family, just a couple of days ago. Cathy, her earlobe scarlet from anxious rubbing, had embraced our daughter the minute we'd walked through the door. The conversation during our spaghetti dinner had been tense.

"I don't know." Jennifer crossed her legs, adjusting her snug pink dress, and her eyes misted over. "My late husband—Robert—was killed in Tijuana. A hit and run, some pickup truck. They never found who did that, either. It's not the same, of course, but . . . "

At the funeral home, I'd noticed the absence of a wedding ring and assumed, since she had a different last name than Oyster, that she was divorced. "Jesus, I'm sorry."

"We lived in San Diego then. He worked for a little import/export business and everything was great. The day he was . . . hit, we'd taken the train into Mexico like we'd done twenty times before. Just for fun." She took a tissue from her purse. "I'm sorry. It's just . . . losing my father, being at the funeral home, brought everything back."

"I understand." Better than she'd ever know; never hearing the Butcher's name again would be just fine with me. Time for a change of topic. "Your brother said some odd things when we met."

"No surprise. Did he tell you how terrible I am?"

I chuckled, despite myself. "Matter of fact, he did. He thinks you'll try to cheat him."

"*Me* cheat *him*?" She leaned forward.

"He brought up the watch, by the way. Claims that your dad gave it to him, that they were close."

Jennifer gasped, then laughed. "I'm surprised he didn't try selling you Super Bowl tickets for the Browns."

I grinned as I sat back in my chair and rested my hands in my lap. "He said something else, too, something strange, about knowing what you are capable of."

Jennifer scrunched her face, as though she found the assertion distasteful. "It really does sound like he's delusional. Can something be done so he doesn't waste his inheritance on drugs?"

"Let me see the will." She handed the document to me, and I quickly reviewed it. "With your mother and Martha gone, everything's split between you and Frank. Your dad didn't set up a trust. You could ask a court to appoint a guardian, but the judge would have to find Frank incompetent. And, sorry to say, being a drug addict isn't the same thing."

"My dad worked his whole life, and now my brother will blow half of everything." Jennifer looked away, and her eyes caught my framed law degree, awarded by Cleveland-Marshall, on the paneled wall. "If only Martha were here. We were so close . . . she'd help me get through this, for sure."

"Pancreatic cancer, right? I remember how upset your dad was." I tried not to think about sloppy Chivas kisses, the slip of a bra clasp. The way that Jennifer had behaved at the funeral, her very presence now in my office, confirmed the fact that the secret of my indiscretion was safely entombed with her sister.

She nodded. "Her, we all loved. Now I'm stuck dealing with a brother I haven't spoken to in years."

Oyster had seldom talked about his children—all our bullshitting over all those beers, and we'd barely scratched the surface. I scanned the rest of the will. "Your mom was designated as executor, so I'll petition the probate court to name you. Your brother could ask to be named, but there's no chance he'd be approved."

"As long as he gets his money, I don't think he'll care." Jennifer's eyes flashed, just like her sister's. "And I think it's a lot."

She handed me a folder, and I looked at the top statement, a mutual fund investment summary that showed an account balance of over $427,000. I studied the statement in disbelief. Never in my wildest imaginings would I have thought that Oyster had squirreled away that kind of dough.

"And look at the next. Does it say what I think it says?"

Yeah, holy shit, it did. A whole life insurance policy with a face amount of two million dollars. This would be the largest estate to ever cross my desk. I couldn't help but mentally ballpark my fee. "You and your brother are the remaining beneficiaries."

"Dad should have removed him. Wanna bet on how long it'll be before he runs through every last dime?" She toyed with a silver arrow pendant that dangled between her breasts.

"I have to ask . . . your dad was such a down-to-earth guy. A policy like this isn't cheap . . ."

"He inherited his parents' farm and sold it for a bundle—that shopping plaza in Westlake? Enough to put me through college, and Dad always said we'd be okay if anything happened to him. But I had no idea—two million in insurance?"

Jesus, all the drinks I'd shared with Oyster, and he could have bought the bar ten times over. I figured he always thought that I was the big shot, the attorney-at-law. I thumbed through a deed to the house, automobile title, a checking account statement. My father had left my late mother a pittance, and the nursing home leeches had sucked away everything, except for some cheap personal trinkets and costume jewelry: the sum total of my lofty inheritance.

"He drove used cars. Mom made some of her own clothes."

"This is . . . significant, Jennifer. Do you have a financial advisor?"

She crossed her hands over a knee. "I'm careful with money."

"Then I'll go through all of this, prepare an accounting, and let you know when we need to meet. I'll need to run some paperwork by your brother, too. He told me he'd give me a call, but just in case . . . he also said you have his number . . . ?"

She pulled it up on her cell, and I jotted it on a notepad. "If I reach him, I'll try to get him to call Salvatore, too."

"Good luck. Just make sure to tell me whatever wild stories he comes up with. I could use a good laugh now and again."

She stood up and shook my hand, then I walked her to my office door. When she smiled, I remembered her sister smiling the same way, her ruby lips just slightly parted. A little bit of my conscience crawled from its dark lair to remind me about Cathy, but despite my best efforts, I lingered a good long while on Jennifer's perfect ass as she strolled through the lobby. When Marilyn caught me looking and raised her dark eyebrows, it was my turn to shoot her a look.

Once the door closed behind Jennifer, Marilyn said, "So, what's her story?"

"Sad, actually. Widowed, and now this."

"She seems kind of . . . I don't know, detached." Marilyn turned her head to make sure I noticed her earrings, which consisted of multiple strands of gold. Fake, I assumed, since her paycheck bore my signature.

"Well, look what she's going through. Nice earrings, by the way."

"Thanks. And, by the way, I didn't know you were so into fashion."

I waited.

"I saw you checking her out when she left. Must have been admiring the dress."

"Smart ass. Why don't you order some sandwiches and take out an ad in the bar journal for a new secretary."

"Sure. Let's see . . . hostile work environment, substandard pay, fetch lunch . . . anything I'm leaving out?"

"Handsome Irish boss?"

"You getting a partner?"

I smirked, grateful that Marilyn was around to keep things light, and went back to my desk. Jennifer had started me thinking about the killings again, the oddity of so many similarly brutal murders sprawling three distinct periods. There was nothing pressing on my agenda, so I resumed my perusal of the Internet and the electronic fount of information on serial killers. I was all too familiar with the

Butcher's reign, so I directed my focus to the earlier murders, the Torso Murderer.

His first victim, a female, had never been identified. She had been dubbed the Lady of the Lake when some pieces of her dismembered body had been found scattered along the Lake Erie shore. The identity of the second victim, christened the Tattooed Man because of the six distinctive tattoos etched into his skin, also remained a mystery.

I clicked on three or four sites before stumbling across one that was a compilation of all of the articles printed about the murders by the now-defunct *Cleveland Press*. A particular photo caused me to sit up straight: Jack Corrigan, one of the guys on the force who'd taken me under his wing after all the bullshit with my father. He was much younger in the picture, but there was no mistaking that chiseled face. I devoured every word of the accompanying story.

My instinct was to call him, but Jack wasn't the type to chitchat over the telephone and patiently entertain my litany of questions. I leaned back in my chair, basked in the bright sunlight streaming through the window, and wanted a cold belt of whiskey to untangle my mind.

I read the article again, wishing that the actual newspaper was spread in front of me so I could smell the crinkled paper and examine the faded ink. One thing I knew for sure. I needed to sit Jack Corrigan down, face-to-face, and find out about the dark night in a Cleveland lumberyard when he had slugged it out with the Torso Murderer.

A fistfight with one of the deadliest killers in history, and Jack had lived to tell the tale—but never mentioned a word. What the hell?

1

"You want rocks?" Jack handed me a Pabst and shoved a chipped plate, covered with bread crumbs, to a corner of his laminated kitchen table, its dull green surface riddled with cracks. The aroma of burnt toast lingered.

I looked up at him and studied the shock of white hair that clung to his skull, the deep lines in his face. "Nah, I'm good."

"That's my boyo." He settled a bottle of Kessler's and two shot glasses on the table. "You been hangin' out downtown with the East Siders; maybe you're used to a frosted mug?"

The side of town somebody lives on—that says it all. The East Coast ends, and the Midwest begins where the muddy Cuyahoga River splits Cleveland in half. Jack chuckled at his little joke and slid onto the wooden side chair across from me. On the wall behind him, pictures of his extended family were tacked haphazardly, and a shiny gold cross crowded a washed-out photo of his late wife.

"Hell, I hear you're an honorary one of 'em now. Box seats at the orchestra, joined the art museum?" I grinned, and his face lit up for a moment.

"They can stick all that bullshit up my ass." He filled our shot glasses and tilted his toward a map of County Mayo, hanging above the table in a plain white frame. Like most Clevelanders of Irish descent, Jack's ancestors had fled Mayo during the potato famine of the 1840s.

"*Slainte.*"

We drained the Kessler's in a gulp. The whiskey, harsh for my taste, was Jack's liquor of choice. No question, he was West Side Irish to the core. The grimy Ford Fiesta in the drive, the frayed tennis shoes, and no pretense about wanting to get sauced up.

"So, you doin' okay, Jack?"

"Still on the right side of the grass, like you give a shit. Haven't heard from you in a fuckin' year."

"This is the thanks I get for making a social call? You too old and decrepit to pick up a phone?"

"Fuck you." He refilled our shot glasses. "Your little girl. Molly, right? Still playin' sports?"

"Best point guard in the league last year."

"That little shit? Good for her. We'll see how she does in high school, goin' up against those spades on the East Side. Bastards can jump over a car."

Jack's views on race were set in stone, and I didn't expect him to start waving a pennant at the parade on Martin Luther King Day. I steered the conversation. "You know that guy who was killed at the Tam? Friend of mine."

"I read all about it in the paper. I ain't blind yet."

"He was a good guy. Had these eyes . . . we called him Oyster."

"Oyster? That's a goofy fuckin' name."

"See, his eyes—"

"What's it matter now? Poor bastard's dead. You sure you wanna talk about this?"

"Can't pretend it didn't happen."

"I'm not saying that." Jack's gaze drifted across his narrow kitchen, over the scuffed, checkered green-and-white linoleum, the cluttered countertop, and the percolator that he'd probably picked up at a yard sale when I was in middle school. "Last I knew, you were doin' great. I just don't want to see you get all worked up."

"Been doing great for a long while, Jack. Years. In fact, I'm going to handle the estate." I knew he meant well. Before my old man's long, downhill slide, they'd been buddies.

"The estate? You'll be ass-deep in this stuff every day. The murder investigation, the press . . . let someone else take this one."

"It's a nice fee." His concern was touching. After the funeral, Jack had spent plenty of Sundays with me, shivering in the frigid blasts whirling from Lake Erie, while we cheered on the Browns at the old Municipal Stadium. The rank odor wafting from the urinals in the men's rooms was an indelible memory. "I've been doin' some research, Jack, trying to make sense of it. Reading up on the old Torso murders."

"You can't figure this crap out." Jack nodded and sipped his beer. "Let it go."

"I found a story in the *Press*, 1950."

His eyes widened. "That . . . ? Fuck, you do know they decided it wasn't him?"

"Yeah, but the story—"

"Oh, for . . . look, a call came in late one night that somebody was inside a factory yard, industrial area downtown. Me and my partner cruise down there and split up so he can check the front gate and me, the back. I get to the gate and it's open. I walk in, my piece and light in hand, and *bam*, somethin' bangs into my skull." Jack shook his head. "As close to knocked out as I ever been. I hit the gravel; the light and the gun went flyin'. I pop up quick and see this guy making for the gate."

"You went after him?" I already knew the answer.

"Keep in mind, he's twenty feet away, which means whatever he whacked me with, he lobbed it at me, which takes some doin'. I yell for my partner and take off. I see right away this guy's big, real fuckin' big."

"How, compared to you?"

"Must have been six-six, and more bulk, not fat. I catch up, and we go at it. He got in some good ones, but what with the army, the Academy, I knew what I was doin'.'"

I pictured them shuffling in the dirt and sawdust, trading punches, grunting.

"But wouldn't you fuckin' know it, I step in a pothole and twist my knee. Go down faster than a hooker. My partner's yellin' now, but he's not halfway across the yard, and I watch the big son of a bitch sprint into the street and disappear around the bend."

"Christ, did you . . . ?"

Jack hoisted his beer between us, as though it were some kind of stop signal. "I told you I'd tell the story. You gonna let me?"

I nodded.

"We search the yard and find a body, no head. Plus, the guy's balls were hacked off."

"Well, it had to be Torso. How could anyone think otherwise?"

"You'll have to ask the coroner back then. Prick said the job wasn't as neat as Mr. Torso would've done and some other bullshit. He argued it had been years since we'd had any other murder that might have been his. There was that one article in the paper about my fight, and that was all."

I clutched my mug. "Jesus, Jack. What the hell did he look like?"

"Too dark to be sure. All I locked on was his eyes, when we were goin' at it. Kindly, like a favorite uncle, even though he was tryin' to take me out. I did work with a sketch guy, and they ran with it, but nobody ever turned up."

"You and the Torso Murderer. My God. You shoulda told me."

He drained his beer and shrugged. "Bullshit. The higher-ups said it wasn't him, so all I fought was some guy who got away. No sense talkin' about it now."

I wanted to buoy him up, to dispel the aura of resignation that seemed to surround him. My God, if only his knee hadn't buckled. I looked at him, at those eyes that had seen things mine never would, never wanted to see, and he glanced away. Was he keeping something from me?

"Christ, you're not thinkin' there's some connection?" I drained half a shot.

"Can't say, but I'm curious if the new vics were dismembered like the vics of Torso and the Butcher. The boys downtown once described it as surgical skill. No one was just hacked apart, ever."

"I remember. My dad said you looked at vets and docs, anybody with training."

"Somethin' else, too." Jack hunched forward. "We'll see what the coroner says about all this, whether the neck muscles are retracted."

"Which means . . . ?"

"Which means, Johnny, that they were still alive, maybe conscious, when the decapitation began. That's how it was, every time, for both those killers."

I pictured Oyster's face, those blubbery eyes gaping in disbelief as he realized what was happening to him.

He paused, eyeing the Kessler's. "When the Butcher came around, we considered it—whether Torso was back again. So many similarities . . . they both had to be strong as fuck, the way they carted bodies around. Torso even carried 'em *up* the hills in Kingsbury Run."

"But it can't be Torso now, he'd be—"

"Hey, I'm old, not stupid. I can do the math. Prick would be older than me and wearin' Depends. But the Butcher, if he was in his twenties for the first go 'round, he'd only be in his sixties now. And when I was in my sixties, I could still kick some ass."

"Yeah, I heard stories." His gnarled hands and misshapen knuckles spoke volumes.

"And leavin' your friend's wallet on him, the Butcher did that sometimes. The so-called expert back then, some knobhead who never worked a beat, said the killer was sendin' a message. Guys like Oyster, regular Joes, will worry it might happen to them."

"But a copycat would know all this stuff, Jack. The Butcher vanished decades ago."

"Yeah? These whack jobs disappearing, then coming back, isn't uncommon at all. The Grim Sleeper out in California, or remember the BTK killer?"

"Bind, torture, kill, right? Oklahoma?"

"Kansas, and off the radar for fifteen years before starting up again after some rag ran an article—"

"Oh, Christ . . ." Just like *Cleveland Magazine.*

"Hey, I wasn't suggesting anything. You didn't write it." Jack took a deep sip of whiskey and dug a fingernail into a crack on the tabletop.

"Fucking reporters. I shoulda known better. I was a freshman when that article came out in the old *Cleveland Press*, about how Torso screwed up Eliot Ness, and the Butcher ruined my dad."

"You know your dad was a solid cop. Some of that shit they said . . ."

"They fuck Ness over, too?"

"Probably not as bad." Jack shrugged. "His days with the Untouchables were behind him, for sure. He did some good here, but the Torso thing ate at him. Divorced, drinking, hit and run. He was a mess."

"You worked with him?"

"Before my time. I joined up after comin' back from overseas. Peter Merylo was the lead dick then."

"Remember the title, front page? "Twins of Futility." My mother was crying, and I never saw my dad look . . . just beaten. Jesus."

"Don't start relivin' all of that, Johnny." Jack finished his shot and poured another. He filled my glass to the brim and rested his arms on the table. "You haven't dug out that letter from the Butcher, have you?"

"I'm fine, okay?"

Jack made a face. "Torso would do that too, you know. Write to people, the press, just to brag or mess with Ness. His last card was to Merylo, early fifties, couple of weeks after we found a guy minus his head and cock in a lumberyard." He caught my blank look and then continued. "He wrote that he'd enjoyed playing the game and was adjusting to his new life in Southern California. Signed by—get this—a friend."

His gaze shifted to the white plaster ceiling. No doubt he remembered all of the letters the Butcher had authored two decades later for an eager media. *Hapless* was one word the killer had used to describe my father. I'd had to look it up.

Suddenly, Jack hunched forward and shuddered, no doubt about it. There had to be something that he was hiding from me.

I pivoted the beer can and waited a beat. "C'mon, what is it, Jack?"

"Nothin' more to say. How come you're buggin' me, anyway? You obviously know how to use the Internet, Mr. Legal Beagle. Or read the fuckin' *Plain Dealer*."

"Why, when I can pick the brain of a walkin' history book? Besides, I miss ya."

"Well, next time, we're going to a bar. You're suckin' down way too much of my goddamn booze." He said it with a mellow smile.

I raised my glass. "Whiskey, invented by God so the Irish wouldn't rule the world."

Jack chuckled, even though he'd probably heard that line about a million times. "Why don't we go to one of your fancy private clubs downtown? Or don't you think I'd fit in with those dipshits wearin' three-piece suits?"

"Nah, I'll come your way." No fancy private club had ever invited me to join. I was a member of the West Side Irish American Club, but that involved no more than filling out an application and submitting a check.

He drained his shot glass and eyed me. "I'm sorry about your friend, but don't let it get to you, okay?"

"Like I said, Jack, I'm fine. I'll keep a lookout, that's all."

Jack reached over to the telephone stand against the wall, a stack of magazines and a directory piled on the shelf. He opened a narrow drawer and lifted out a gleaming handgun, a well-maintained .45.

"I'm not sayin' there's anything to worry about, but if you don't have a permit, think about getting one. You got a wife and kid to protect, you know."

A firearm was something I wasn't sure about, but I was sure of the fear that shimmered in his eyes. Oyster's death had evoked memories we all wanted to bury, and that scared even a flinty old bastard like Jack Corrigan. Only slightly against my better judgment, I let the last of the booze burn down my throat before saying good-bye.

I lingered in Jack's driveway, watching a woman in a dark burka shuffle along the sidewalk across the street. Gone were the days when it seemed like everyone in Lakewood would flock to St. Margaret Mary's and troop past the Stations of the Cross during Lent. I'd never forget the smell of greasy perch, pats of melted butter on baked potatoes, and the boisterous chatter that echoed from the ceiling of the church hall.

Would that all memories were as pleasant.

8

The following Thursday, I knocked off early and strolled to the brick-paved East Fourth, a pedestrian street lined with vintage buildings that had been converted into upscale restaurants and condos. Contemporary taverns touted mixologists, not bartenders. My favorite haunt was the patio at Cena, a trendy restaurant that attracted a disproportionate number of attractive young men and women in designer clothes. The young, professional eye-candy parade.

I needed the distraction and some time alone. My unease didn't stem just from Oyster's murder or the revelation about Jack and the Torso Murderer or even the gutted body at Wagar Beach. Despite my best efforts, I also had to wrestle with the feelings that Jennifer had revitalized. Memories of Martha. Memories of bedroom acrobatics cloaked in lies and deceit.

The waitress, a cute, young Oriental poured into a clingy striped dress and wearing a floral perfume, curtly took my order for a whiskey. She seemed on edge, even wary. I scanned the street; the usual foot traffic was considerably diminished. Even the coveted tables reserved for outdoor dining, many shielded from the sun by monogrammed umbrellas hawking a brand of alcohol, lacked the usual turnout. I knew, from experience, the visceral fear that a serial killer could cast over an entire community.

I was anticipating the soft bite of that first amber-colored drink, when Marilyn rang my cell.

"John, you're not going to like this."

My chest tightened. "I'm betting you're right."

"We got the check and final statement from Oyster's mutual fund. Two hundred thousand dollars was withdrawn, just two days before he died."

The waitress placed my drink in front of me. I mouthed for her to run a tab and took a slug of booze. "Get me Bernie Salvatore's number, and send him that statement."

There was a slight sigh, and I realized that his number was probably on my phone, but Marilyn could tell this wasn't the time to remind me. I called Bernie, told him what we'd learned, and promised that he'd be receiving a fax. Certain that Frank had pulled something, I had another drink and waited for Bernie to call back. My phone rang before I'd drained a quarter of the whiskey.

"The mutual fund guy told me that Oyster was a regular little saver, same deposit every month for over twenty years," Bernie said. "They'll scan me the docs about the withdrawal."

"Look, I know there may be things you need to keep under wraps, but to the extent that you can keep me posted . . ."

"I'll do what I can. You tell Jennifer yet?"

"Not yet, but I will." I could only imagine her reaction. "Talked to the brother at the funeral. Weird guy, and no love lost with his sister. He says she'll screw him, that she's capable of anything."

"Yeah, paroled drug addicts are traditionally good judges of character."

I chuckled. "He claims that he and Oyster were close."

"Unfortunately, the math's starting to add up. Two hundred Gs gone, the old man killed, and Frank missing."

"Maybe Oyster gave him the money. I mean, Frank was his only son. He said he'd be in touch. I'll urge him to call you."

"Good, because until he talks to me, what can I do?" He was silent for a moment, and I wondered if we'd disconnected. Then he said, "The coroner finished with the Rocky River guy. Says that a different blade, a saw tooth, was used on him, compared to Oyster."

"Different killers?"

"Just different knives. Makes it harder for us to trace. Coroner is convinced it's the same killer. Both corpses were, to use his words, skillfully dismembered."

I decided to follow up on what Jack had told me. "On the old cases, the vics were alive when—"

"I wish it weren't, John, but it's the same now. Both Oyster and the guy in Rocky River. They likely knew what was being done to 'em."

After ending the call, I imagined what it would be like to be alert when somebody started chopping into my neck. Each killer, over all these years, used the same brutal modus operandi. The thought sent a shudder through me. I took another sip of whiskey and stared at the phone. Calling Jennifer to tell her the inheritance might be light by six figures wasn't going to make my day. Or hers.

As soon as we'd exchanged pleasantries, I broke the news.

Her breath escaped in a rush: "Damn it!"

"Listen, the police are investigating—"

"There's something I need to tell you."

"Okay, shoot." Another surprise was all that I needed.

"No, not on the phone. Can we meet later? I'm off at five thirty."

I hesitated for a second. But Jennifer was a client, requesting a meeting. The fact that I found her attractive and reminiscent of someone else was beside the point. "Do you know Dino's?"

"The Italian place in Brecksville, right? I've heard it's nice."

"You'll like it. Six?"

"See you then. And John? Thank you."

I tossed the cell from one hand to the other before calling Cathy to tell her about my change of plans. She wasn't exactly pleased.

"The daughter of the dead guy? It can't wait until Monday?"

"What do you want me to do, Cathy? Tell her I'm the one lawyer who won't work nights?"

"Yeah, I do. It's scary out there."

"C'mon, I won't be late. And we'll go out this weekend."

"That's big of you. Carl and Alison, remember? Happy birthday to me."

Shit—the birthday plans with her sister and brother-in-law had completely slipped my mind. "Honey, c'mon. I'm sorry. It's just that there's a helluva lot on my plate. These killings . . . "

"May be a good reason to come home." She was rubbing her ear- lobe raw, no doubt. "Don't worry; your wife and daughter will be fine."

"Cathy . . . "

"I'm not going to argue, John."

She hung up. I nursed another drink to drown the guilt that my wife had doled out, then I headed to Dino's, an old-school joint with subdued lighting and a sleek black leather bar. I'd suggested the restaurant because it was far from my usual hangouts, so no one I knew would spot me with a beautiful blonde. *No, really, she's a client!* A padded chair at the serpentine bar was soft and welcoming. I'd taken two sips of whiskey when Jennifer floated through the door. Her tight red dress, cut nice and low, turned some heads. A string of gleaming pearls and black high-heel shoes made me forget about business, but I struggled to focus on Cathy and Molly and Father McGraw.

"You look great." The words escaped me, like an eager kid lung- ing for his first kiss. What the hell was I thinking?

She smiled demurely, and we followed the maître d' to a snug booth with a white tablecloth and red votive. She ordered a vodka tonic, and we focused on the leather-bound menus. A silver-haired waiter clad in a tuxedo brought her cocktail and took our orders. Jennifer had decided on the veal piccata, while I requested the cavatelli and a bottle of Chianti to share. After he gathered the menus and turned away, I resolved to keep things professional. "You wanted to talk, Jennifer . . . ?"

She sipped her drink. "I spoke with Dad a couple of weeks before he died, and he hinted that Frank was up to his usual tricks. I think he knew about his problem with that gang from Detroit."

"Anything specific?"

"Told me not to worry. He knew I'd just get upset."

"What makes you think he knew about the Andar Feo?"

"Because he said it was going to take money to keep Frank out of trouble. I went over all of this with the police, not thinking it had anything to do with what had happened to Dad. But when you told me about that withdrawal, the dots started to connect, and I thought you should know about our talk."

"Salvatore's frustrated because your brother won't call. I haven't heard from him since the funeral."

"I wonder if he does know something about what happened to Dad. If not, why won't he just go to the police?" The decorous waiter appeared with our wine, and while he poured, Jennifer leaned back in the booth. She looked away and tilted her head, reminding me of a fragile porcelain doll. "It's hard to think he had anything to do with it, but . . . do I even know him anymore? Martha and I begged Dad to just shut him out, but he couldn't bring himself to do it."

"Frank will reach out, eventually. Not to be crass, but he knows there's an estate involved here." I tried to imagine what it would be like to have a drug addict for a brother. "I'm sorry for, you know, the way he is."

We sipped the wine and made small talk until the waiter bustled to the table and delivered our steaming plates with a flourish. Jennifer smiled and applauded lightly. As the aromas of the lemon sauce on the piccata and the rich tomatoes that smothered my cavatelli filled the air, I tried to remember when a meal had smelled so delicious.

Jennifer sliced into her delicate veal. "Detective Salvatore said you guys go way back."

"Freshmen year, high school, the Green Wave football team." I didn't tell her that making second-string was a struggle. Before my dad had plummeted off the deep end, he'd patiently taught me the tackling drills he'd learned as a three-year varsity starter. We'd square off in our ragged backyard, my cleats tearing up the spotty grass. *Ram your shoulder in there, wrap those arms, drive, drive, drive!*

"Looks like you're still in good shape." Her face reddened and her gaze shifted from me to her plate.

"Thanks." I managed to sound flip about it, but her comment made my evening. "I jog when I can." No need to tell her that my last run had been more than three weeks back, maybe a mile along the perimeter of Lakewood Park.

"Green Wave, that's Holy Name. German school, right?" Jennifer grinned and cut another piece of veal.

"Ha! First sip of green beer at twelve and marched in ten straight St. Pat's parades."

"Our little band of Methodists always waved Irish flags. Dad said it was the Cleveland thing to do."

"Everybody's honorary Irish on March 17th."

"Thanks for including us." Her eyes twinkled as she dabbed at her mouth with the white cloth napkin. "Tell me you never dyed your hair."

"Emerald as the isle itself. Even sported a green boa one year."

"Interesting visual."

"And that was before I'd started drinking."

She laughed and arranged her napkin on the table. "Funny how Cleveland gets a bad rap, but nobody who grows up here wants to leave. Nothing else seemed right, except coming home, after Robert died. I'm glad I did, because it gave me the chance to get really close to Mom and my sister."

The tone of the conversation had taken a right turn—talking about Martha was not on my agenda. I nodded and took a gulp of wine. "I never asked you what you do."

"I manage that office supply store in Strongsville, Business One. I do some tutoring, too, ESL. You know—English as a second language? I learned Spanish in college, and it's everywhere in San Diego. *Habla algo?*"

"If you're asking whether I can speak it, I know *por favor* and *cerveza.*"

"*Eso es un principio,*" she said, shooting me a smile, her hazel eyes mesmerizing. "That's a beginning. You'll learn."

I pictured her, all prim and proper at the head of a classroom, the subject of every boy's fantasy. We continued to chat until the waiter cleared our plates. Jennifer obviously could have told me about Frank over the phone, but I wasn't complaining. I asked if she'd like a postprandial, hoping that my pronunciation was correct, and we ordered Amarettos. When I finally stole a furtive glance at my watch, it was after ten. Cathy would have my ass.

Ironically, Jennifer touched my hand, her fingers soft and warm. "Please let your wife know how much I appreciate your staying late."

I paid the check, and we strolled into the parking lot.

Only a sliver of the moon was shining, but the sky was luminous, teeming with glistening white stars. I escorted Jennifer to her late-model Caprice. Suddenly, she stood on her tiptoes, gently placed one hand behind my head, and brushed her lips against mine. The kiss wasn't passionate, but it was suggestive and sensual enough to banish all thoughts of Cathy. I wanted to succumb to Jennifer, slip that red dress over her head, strip everything off her until she wore only the pearls and the heels.

"*Necesito tu fuerza,* John. That means, I need your strength." She pulled away and got into her car. As she drove from the lot, my eyes remained locked on the glowing red taillights of her car until they vanished. I stood still, alone on the pavement, before shuffling to my Buick. What the hell had just happened? There was no doubt that I needed to block out the kiss and go home to my wife and daughter, but the enticing vision of Jennifer Browning seduced me for the entire drive.

The kitchen light was on, as usual, when I walked in from the garage. Before heading upstairs, I checked every lock. Cathy was awake and propped against the pillows in our double bed. She reached for the remote and muted the TV on the dresser.

"A little late, don't you think?"

"She's stressed out. Her father's been killed, now her brother's disappeared, and there's a problem with the estate."

Her eyes raked me from head to foot, but I didn't flinch. I was embarrassed that my old habit of checking the rearview mirror for signs of lipstick had automatically kicked in.

Cathy pointedly looked at the illuminated numbers on her night-stand clock. "It took you until almost eleven to talk about that?"

I held up the palm of my hand and shoved aside the recent memory of a soft and unexpected kiss. "Sorry. I'm tired. Dinner ran late. We can talk about it tomorrow, if you want."

"Nice birthday conversation."

I bit my tongue, stripped off the tie, and hung my jacket in the closet. "I'm making a drink. Want anything?"

"Why don't you come to bed?"

"Just a short one." I slipped out of my shoes and walked softly toward the stairs, so as not to wake Molly. Cathy must have turned the volume back on; indistinct voices followed me downstairs.

I had just poured my whiskey, and it wasn't a short one, when Cathy burst into the kitchen, her robe billowing. Her face was drawn.

"Turn on Channel Five."

I hit the remote, and Vanessa Edwards appeared on the screen. A banner that proclaimed *Breaking News* scrolled along the bottom. " . . . just released by the police. It's been authenticated. The recent killings are, indeed, the work of the Butcher."

I nearly dropped my glass. Cathy was at my side, holding my arm.

Edwards continued as the screen flashed a photo of a letter. I recognized the block-cut characters, similar to those on the photocopy buried in my dresser drawer, as the newscaster read each word aloud:

Miss me?

It has been too long. I've forgotten how much fun it is to frolic in Cleveland. And so easy! Really—a history of imbecilic cops. Your bumbling, mustachioed chief mocking the fact that I could be back after all this time. He is as clueless as the hapless Coleman all those years ago.

Yes, I've returned. Let's play the game!

THE BUTCHER

Edwards rambled on, but I didn't need to hear anymore. Hapless. That fucking word again. My dad nestled against the bathroom wall, the streaks of crimson. I was shaking, but my hand was steady as I gulped the booze.

"Forget the drink, John," Cathy said. "Just come to bed."

I nodded and followed her upstairs. But I clutched the whiskey in my hand.

9

"Should we pull her out of school?" Cathy stood near the bathroom, shifting her weight from one foot to the other. She had closed our bedroom door to prevent Molly from overhearing our conversation.

Sleep had eluded me all night, replaced by ghoulish scenes from my boyhood: photos of dead bodies and frustrated cops, my mother cowering to avoid the harsh slap of my old man's hand. Memories that smothered even a delicious parking lot kiss. I bunched the pillow under my head. "The Butcher won't attack a school. That's not his style."

"But they found that girl, back then, on a playground fence . . . " It was barely six thirty in the morning, and her fingers already seemed glued to her earlobe.

"That happened at night, Cathy. School was out. Believe me, there's safety in numbers. Calm down."

"No more soccer, though, no running off to the park. She's out too late then. I want her and that damn skateboard home."

"Cathy, school's just started up. She needs to meet the other kids and get to know the team."

"Her safety's more important." She paused for a moment and

then plunged ahead. "I think we should send her away. Remember my cousin in Chicago?"

"You're overreacting. Is every family in Cleveland gonna send their kids away?"

"Not every kid has the last name of Coleman."

"You're being . . . "

"Cautious? I remember that letter, the creepy one in your drawer. And now that magazine story. What if—"

"Hold on, okay?" I sat up quickly, and the sheet fell to my waist. "We just need to be careful. We'll pick her up, maybe set up a car pool with other parents."

Her jaw tightened, but she seemed to mull over my words. "I'm not sure it's enough."

"Think about it. We can talk more later."

"Will you consider what I said, though, about sending her away? We should discuss that, too."

"Cathy, the Butcher already screwed up my life. I will not let that happen to my daughter."

"Will you talk to her? About coming home, watching for strangers, keeping her cell on?"

We'd debated whether it made sense for a kid just entering her teens to have a cell, but Cathy had argued in favor of one, in case of emergencies. Apparently she'd been right. "Of course. And I can drop her off, pick her up, if you want."

"I'll take her, but your picking her up would be great."

"No problem." I sat up and swung my legs over the side of the bed. My head was still foggy, and a slight headache hummed away. Cathy untied her robe as she headed into the bathroom, and water soon cascaded from the shower nozzle.

I turned on the early news. The Butcher was everywhere. There was a montage of photos from the old crime scenes juxtaposed against the new ones; I recognized the dazed crowd at Wagar Beach. The alliterative effect of "The Butcher's Back" seemed irresistible to every geek with a microphone.

The flow of water ended, and Cathy, wrapped again in her blue robe and holding a towel, soon stood in the bathroom doorway. "Can you take the day off, hon? I know you didn't sleep, and . . . "

She knew that I'd be worthless at the office, a day spent fielding—or dodging—calls about my father from well-meaning acquaintances, the simply curious, or the prying press. *How are you holding up? It must be tough, reliving it. He was a good man, you know, before . . .*

I stood up, relishing the prospect of hot water lapping over my clammy skin, and headed for the bathroom. "Not a bad idea. I'll call Marilyn."

Cathy stepped in front of me. "I'm worried about you, John. Should you go talk to somebody again? I mean, just as a precaution."

"Cathy, it's been a long time."

"But now the Butcher . . . that changes things." She bit her lip. "If Molly ever saw you, the way you'd sometimes . . . "

I gripped her shoulders. "I won't let that happen. That's a promise."

"Please, just tell me if there's anything you want to talk about." Her hand rested on my chest, against my beating heart.

I kissed her forehead before stepping past her, toward the bathroom. Shedding my underwear, I stepped into the shower and leaned against the wall, beneath the nozzle. The hot spray burned into the top of my head and washed over my back. Had I been colder than usual toward Cathy? Was it because of my guilt about Jennifer's parking lot kiss?

I couldn't fault Cathy for being worried about me or having her own personal fear. Hell, the entire city would be in an uproar by now, the Internet atwitter with rumors and innuendo. Every family would hunker down and worry about naive kids crossing a deserted playground. No one would slip a debit card into an ATM without a cautious look around. Everyone who used a parking lot at any mall in Northeast Ohio would be wary of their surroundings.

But someone, somewhere, would make a mistake.

I toweled off, threw on a pair of jeans and a polo shirt, and headed down to the kitchen. Shaving could wait for a day.

Molly and Cathy were seated next to each other at the table, and Cathy nodded at the cup of steaming java she'd poured for me.

"I already told Mom," Molly said. "You guys don't have to worry about me."

"It's not that." I sat and welcomed the aroma of hot coffee. "We know you won't do anything stupid, honey, but you just need to be extra, extra careful. That's all we ask."

"Make sure you charge your cell," Cathy said. "Stick with your friends."

"Can I ask a question?" Molly looked at me. "Are you okay?"

"Just tired, that's all."

"That's not what I meant. You told me about the Butcher and your dad. I read the magazine, and now the papers."

"You don't need to worry about me either, Molly." Her concern made me melt, and I knew in my heart that it had not been prompted by anything that Cathy had said to her. "Go on, you two; I'll see you tonight."

Cathy kissed my cheek and Molly hugged me, clinging tight for longer than usual.

As Cathy backed out of the drive, I stood in the front door and waved good-bye, relishing the smile Molly flashed from the passenger seat, her energetic wave. She was more worried about me than she was afraid of the furtive Butcher. But she hadn't lived it. Not like Cathy, and most assuredly, not like me.

"No problem. I can take care of things here," Marilyn said when I phoned from the kitchen to tell her about my change of plans. "I'll call if something comes up."

"Thanks. Have a good weekend, but watch yourself." An uncomfortable vision of Marilyn's severed head, her long, colorful earrings scattering the light, flashed through my mind.

"Don't worry. Flirting with a knife salesman is absolutely out of the question. Unless he's really, really cute."

"I should know better than to try and give you advice." I opened the refrigerator door and grabbed a yogurt. "See you Monday."

"Something to look forward to."

"I'll miss you, too. Seriously, though, be careful."

"I'll take that as an admission that you find me irreplaceable."

Marilyn put up a brave front, but I could sense that she was fearful, like anyone should be. She lived alone in a condominium in Bay Village, with no one to hold when there was an unexpected squeak of a floorboard in the dead of night.

We ended our call, and I grabbed a teaspoon from the drawer and stirred the blueberry sauce from the bottom of the container. The large red hands of the clock ticked away. The urge to stomp back upstairs, sprawl on the floor, and reread the message from the Butcher was nearly irresistible. Then my cell buzzed.

I sank into a chair and set my yogurt on the table. The number looked mildly familiar. Frank Frederickson's, maybe? Sure enough, when I answered, he said, "Miss me, lawyer man?"

"Thanks for calling, Frank. We really should talk."

"Yeah. How's my inheritance coming along?" I heard him take a long draw and figured that whatever he was inhaling had a fifty-fifty chance of being legal.

"Still working on the estate. Takes time. I'm doing the best—"

"I don't have time. I need my fucking money."

I sat up straight. "It's a court matter, Frank. I can't rush it."

"Did she tell you to stall?"

"Hell, no. C'mon. I know about the Andar Feo. Why won't you meet with the cops? Maybe they can help. I'll go with you, if you want."

"They won't believe a fucking word I say."

"Have you thought about what they do to women? They cut them up, their faces. Have you thought about your sister?"

"I could only hope." He laughed.

I nearly blurted out that he was a prick, but pulled back. I had to keep him on the line. "The cops just want to talk about what happened to your father."

"This isn't about the money I got from the old man, and I don't know a damn thing about what happened to him, you got that?"

"Then tell them that."

He inhaled, held it for at least a ten count, and then exhaled. "You trust her, don't you? Still think that she won't try to fuck me over?"

"No one's trying to fuck anyone over, Frank."

"You need to keep your eyes open. I should tell you some things about sweet little Jennifer."

I was speechless for a moment, not sure that I wanted to know. "So talk."

"Yeah, I thought that might get your attention." He chuckled. "Saint Jennifer teaching you Spanish yet, talking about those poor Mexican immigrants she cares so much about?"

"What do you mean, Frank?"

"You may be a lawyer, but you sound pretty fucking clueless."

I didn't react but said evenly, "That makes two of us, doesn't it? Talking to the cops can only help. If the Andar Feo find you—"

"You just don't get it. It's not them I'm afraid of."

"Jesus, Frank, tell me what's going on."

"I'll think about it, lawyer man. Maybe I'll talk to you, since you're in charge of the money. I'm sure as fuck not talking to anyone else." He paused and smoked something once again. "But I'm not sure I can trust you, not sure I can take the risk."

He hung up.

I hit callback immediately, but he didn't pick up. I'd have to call Jennifer and Bernie, and talk to both of them about Frank's cryptic statements. And the return of the Butcher. I decided to phone Jennifer first.

She recognized my voice, and I couldn't help but feel flattered. "Before you say anything, John, I need to apologize for, you know, what happened after dinner . . . "

"No apology needed." The kiss, wrong though it might have been, was a memory to savor. "You're under a lot of pressure, and we'd had a few drinks."

"Yeah, but I know you're married. I don't know what came over me. *Un poco loco.*"

"No—and those words I understand." I cleared my throat. "I wanted to tell you that Frank just called and, well, I thought we should talk about the Butcher, too. I couldn't sleep."

"Neither could I. Every time I closed my eyes, I saw my dad and thought of what was done to him. Oh . . . " She choked back tears. "I'm sorry."

"Maybe this isn't the best time." And I wasn't sure that I could help her. I wanted to crawl into bed and pull the covers to my chin. "We can talk about Frank later."

"No, I want to hear." She sniffled.

I gave her the recap of my conversation with her brother, and then said, "Obviously, I'll call Bernie Salvatore. He'll want to know that Frank apparently has the missing money. The other stuff . . . "

"I told you, John, he's delusional." Jennifer sighed. "I think he makes things up, fantasizes, sees what he wants to see, hears what he wants to hear."

"Yeah." She was right, no doubt, but I was nonetheless curious to hear every word that might rattle out of Frank's mouth. "About your dad, if you ever want to talk, I'm here."

"I appreciate that, you know." There was a sound, as though she were gently blowing her nose. "Your calling like this means a lot to me; it really does."

"I'm glad. I—"

"Let's talk again soon, please." She was softly crying. "Please. I need that right now."

She disconnected. The call to Bernie could wait a bit. I needed a moment, just for me. My eyes roved over the refrigerator, the stove, the cluttered countertop, then out the small window over the sink. Just what the hell was happening?

10

We met Alison and Carl for dinner at Pier W, a stylish seafood restaurant in Lakewood that showcased an elaborate two-story fish tank teeming with darting, multicolored species. A burnished metal bar was flanked by shelves stocked with assorted liquors and topped by an array of cognac, featuring a crystal bottle of Louis XIII. The glass-walled dining room was kissed by the sunset over Lake Erie, and clouds blazed with impossibly crisp shades of red and yellow and orange, reflected in the midnight blue water.

What stood out, though, on a Saturday night, were the empty bar stools and vacant tables covered in ghostly white tablecloths. Pier W never had vacancies on a weekend night. Even Cathy had considered canceling the corner table that she'd reserved for her birthday celebration, but I'd talked her out of it. The Butcher would not dictate any aspect of my life.

"So this newbie from the 'burbs—two days on the job and looks to be about sixteen—doesn't know that the Croats and Serbs and them run all the consonants together." The dim restaurant lighting cast a soft glow on Carl's chubby face. "She thinks it's misspelled and changes the name!"

As Carl chuckled about his enthralling adventures working as a clerk at the Lakewood Municipal Court, Alison adjusted her bright-red shawl. "Boy, honey, that story's nearly as funny as it was when you told it last time."

"Well, fuck, I just won't say anything." Carl had started on his second gin martini, with three olives. He couldn't handle gin. If he didn't slow down, he was going to lapse into one of his churlish moods.

"Just kidding, dear." Alison draped an arm over his rounded shoulders. "If it weren't for you, we'd have to listen to John all night."

She looked at me, and I wasn't sure if her lips curled into a smile or a sneer. She was dead on, though. Carl couldn't tell a decent story to save his ass, but I knew what they were doing, all of them: tiptoeing around the subject of the Butcher. Cathy had probably called Alison before dinner, reminding her to rein in Carl and avoid the topic. *I don't want John dwelling on that.*

Although I kept up a front, the truth was that the Butcher's return had begun to gnaw at me like a sick, catchy jingle. Every night, sleep was fitful and sporadic. My imagination sprang from doorknobs slowly turning to window locks twisting open. Four or five times a night, I padded down the hallway to check on Molly.

"Here's to Cathy." I raised my glass.

"And to all of us, getting together." Cathy clinked her glass against Alison's. They could have been twins. Cathy was only three years older, but didn't look it. The women tended to dress alike, typically a conservative blouse paired with a matching skirt. When they giggled, they'd even hunch their shoulders exactly the same way.

"It's been too long," Alison said, and she sounded sincere, although we both knew that the comment wasn't intended for me. From the day we met, it was apparent that Alison thought her sister could have done better. I'd come to accept that she was probably right.

"Absolutely," I said. "We really have to do this more often."

Alison mimicked my broad smile, and I handed Cathy her gift. The copper necklace was attractive, affordable, and even gift wrapped—by the clerk. "Happy birthday, baby."

Cathy rested her hand on the nape of my neck and drew me to

her for a perfunctory thank-you kiss. As I slipped my arm around her, saw her comely face framed against the descending sun, it was easy to understand why I'd fallen in love with her all those years ago. She withdrew her hand and excused herself to go to the ladies' room. Alison, of course, tagged along.

Being stuck with Carl would be either awkward or excruciatingly dull. Maybe both. I took an ample belt of scotch as he straightened the lapels of his bargain-basement sport coat and leaned across the table.

"Just so you know, Cathy wonders if you're runnin' around on her."

His comment threw me back a little, even though Cathy's resentment of my late evening dinner with Jennifer had been clear. God knows, despite whatever had happened in the distant past, I was now toeing the line—except for one little kiss in a parking lot. I looked away from Carl and out the window. "Well, she's wrong."

"Just sayin'."

If Carl thought that he had suddenly become my confidante, he was nuts. "How's work?"

He hesitated a moment, as if he wanted to pursue the topic of my running around, then said, "They hired some office consultant—a real prick, but what're ya gonna do? He wants to change this, change that, so we change. Why make waves?"

I only nodded, trying to imagine what it would be like to be stuck in a bureaucracy, following orders, keeping my head down, just getting by.

Carl rolled his shoulders and made a face, then stared into his gin like a shaman probing for signs. "The Butcher comin' back . . . she's worried about how you're handling that. We all are."

"I'll be okay, Carl." I couldn't blame him for raising the topic, even if Cathy had placed it off limits. He wasn't alone. Ever since the news, Cathy had asked me, too often, if we should talk about my father or the worn letter in my dresser drawer. Jack had called, and I'd assured him that all was well. Bernie and I had talked for some time, too, when I'd phoned to tell him about my odd conversation with Frank.

"Not sayin' you won't. It's just . . . you could put it all behind you, before. Now, we're reliving it."

"My old man's dead. I've been dealing with that for years. Like I said, there's no problem." I turned the conversation to the Indians and kept up the prattle until Alison and Cathy returned.

"I gave Molly a quick call," Cathy said, sliding onto her seat. "She's having fun but says she would have been fine at home."

We'd let Molly stay alone a few times after she turned thirteen, but with the recent killings, Cathy would have none of that. Molly had bristled when we'd suggested having someone come over. *A babysitter? Really?* But she'd solved the problem by offering to overnight at a friend's. I was just grateful that Cathy had not pursued the notion of sending Molly to live with her relatives in Chicago.

"Kids. At thirteen, they're invincible." Carl, my brother-in-law-turned-philosopher, raised a knowing eyebrow.

Alison gave me a tight smile. "We should probably order."

I could only speculate about the exchange between Cathy and her sister in the ladies' room. Just as I was about to say something else, try to be nice, there was an outburst in the bar. Someone cursed loudly. My first thought was that either the Indians had given up a homer or somebody had started a fight. But some guy yelled, "Not again," and right away, I knew exactly what had happened. I hustled over to the television affixed to the gleaming steel wall.

Shaker Heights this time, on the East Side. Once the wealthiest community in the nation, it still harbored some sprawling mansions where they'd make guys like me enter through the back door.

A steely Vanessa Edwards stared into the camera. An unidentified woman walking her dog had found the body—"dismembered," Vanessa breathed into the microphone—in an obscure clearing in a park. I imagined a leisurely evening stroll interrupted by good old Fido, breaking ahead to wedge his snout into some guy's chest cavity.

Carl shook his head as I returned to the table, and Alison covered her face with her hands. Cathy simply stared at me, eyes wide. They'd all guessed what had happened, and three massacres were enough to jolt anyone.

I didn't sit down.

"It seems like I should be there." Whether for me or my family or for Jennifer, it didn't much matter.

"What?" Cathy covered her mouth with her fingers for just a moment and then clasped her hands as if in prayer. "Why?"

I turned to Carl and Alison. "Will you take her home, stay with her until I get back?"

Carl sat up straight and raised his palms, as if to calm me down. "You can't be serious."

"It's my damn birthday." Cathy's tone was strident.

"I need to be there and see for myself."

"I've been afraid of this, John," she said flatly. "You're not being rational."

"Sit down, finish your drink," Alison said.

"Don't tell me what to do." I knew that she was relishing the moment, hoping that I'd storm out. She could have one of her *I told you so* moments with my wife.

"Everybody, just settle down." Carl lowered his hands, then raised them again. "Let's talk about it, John."

The keys were right on the table, and I resisted the urge to snatch them and bolt. Cathy followed my gaze and slowly shook her head. She said, "You can call Bernie and find out everything."

I nodded and ran a hand through my hair. She was right, and I knew it. They could never understand how I felt, though. None of their fathers had shoved a gun into his mouth, none of them had received a threatening letter that had scarred them for life. I dropped into my chair. "Yeah. I'll call him in the morning. Find out what the hell happened."

Cathy reached over and caressed my upper back with the palm of her hand. Carl picked up his menu and spread it open. "I'm thinking of the lobster pappardelle."

I nodded, not hungry at all. Outside, the sun had nearly disappeared, and the sky was fading to black.

THE SILENCE WAS STIFLING ON THE WAY HOME. I WASN'T sure if Cathy was angry or just confused. When we walked into the kitchen from the garage, she dropped her purse on the table and turned to me.

"Can we talk for a while, John?" She rested her hands on her hips.

"Sure. Want a drink?"

"Do you have to . . . ?"

"Just a short one." I hadn't had much at dinner and wanted one now, just to take the edge off.

"Whatever." She pivoted toward the living room, her gray skirt flapping against her calves.

I poured a whiskey and followed. For a moment, I paused on the edge of the oval carpet atop the hardwood floor. I watched Cathy perch on the edge of the couch, near the seldom-used brick fireplace. A silver crucifix hung above the mantel.

"I don't want an argument, John." She stared at the glass-topped coffee table that displayed a few ceramic figurines and a copy of the Holy Bible. "It's just that, tonight . . . you scared me a little."

I leaned into the wall. "I just felt like it was something I had to do. But I didn't. You were right. I'll call Bernie tomorrow."

"That's not all that I'm talking about. I think maybe you need to see somebody again. Father McGraw, or a counselor."

"I'm not going to run to some counselor just because the Butcher's back." Great. Now I sounded like the damn papers.

"I'm not asking you to do it because of the Butcher, John. I want you to do it for Molly and me." She edged back on the sofa and crossed her arms. "It's the little things. What happened tonight . . . your staying out late with that Browning woman . . . you just don't seem to be yourself."

I didn't tell Cathy about my call to Jennifer, after I'd heard from Frank. I crossed the room and dropped into the recliner on the other side of the coffee table. "I've said it before, Cathy. I'm okay."

She uncrossed her arms and leaned forward, elbows on her knees. "Things have been pretty good between us for a long time. I just don't want to see that changing."

I took a sip of whiskey and placed the glass on the table. "I'll give it some thought, Cathy."

"Your favorite way of saying *no*." She sagged back into the sofa. "For Molly, John?"

She was playing the daughter card, knowing that I'd do anything for my girl. "I promise to think about it, okay?"

Shaking her head, she stood up, a look of resignation—or disappointment?—on her face. "You make it so hard sometimes."

She stepped past the coffee table and drifted to the staircase. After staring at me for a long moment, she gripped the rail and seemed to haul herself up the steps. I checked the locks again and then walked into the kitchen to refill my tumbler with ice and whiskey.

Cathy was overreacting.

I could handle whatever came my way.

11

"I swear to God, Bernie. I nearly left her birthday dinner to drive to Shaker." We were in the break room in the basement of the Lakewood Police Department. When I called, Bernie told me that he was jammed, so I promised to just swing by and take five minutes of his time.

"Cathy's birthday, and you nearly bailed? What the hell were you thinking?" Bernie sat across the Formica tabletop from me, his paw wrapped around a chipped mug of plain black coffee. "Soon as you found Oyster, I told you not to get wrapped up in this shit."

"Hey, I stayed with her, all right? I just need to know what happened this time."

Bernie squirmed in his orange plastic molded chair. The slump of his shoulders seemed more pronounced than ever, his jacket more rumpled. "Not much to tell you that wasn't on the news. Same pattern. This one was a black guy. Headless, with his hands cut off."

"Jesus, three in a row."

"No ID. A lot like Rocky River."

"Has the coroner told you anything more about him, or Oyster?"

He hesitated, tilting his cup until the coffee bubbled against the rim. "He said half the docs on his staff couldn't do such delicate work—his words—of separating meat from bone."

"Great. Jennifer will love hearing that about her father."

"The forearms of the Rocky River guy were cut away at the elbows—very precisely, according to the doc. I already told you that the knife was different than the one used with Oyster, right?"

I nodded. Delicate. Skillful. Precise. "All men, so far. It was never like that before. There were always some female vics, too."

"Brilliant insight. I told you I've got stuff to do, you know."

"Don't bust my balls. The guy last night was killed near the Shaker line. That's through Kingsbury Run, where Torso dumped—"

"John, I know that." Bernie edged forward and rested his elbows on the table. "Leave all of this to us. We know what we're doin'."

"I understand, Bernie." I leaned forward too. "It's just that . . . Cathy is wigged out. Even talked about sending Molly to relatives in Chicago. You know about the letter, how the Butcher said he'd be watching. What if he is? My wife, my kid?"

"You're overreacting."

I leaned back, the plastic seat bending. "Just keep me in the loop, that's all I ask. Remember Jack Corrigan?"

He grinned. "How can anyone forget him?"

"We spent some time together, going over all the old cases, and I've read everything I can find on the Internet. Maybe there's something I can offer, fill in some blanks."

"We have experts on this. They're forming a task force. I'm meeting with one of them soon." Bernie pointedly looked at his watch. "Heard from Frank again? We've got nothin'."

He didn't need to spell out that the conversation was about over. "Not since that last call. I just don't know what to make of him. Mistrusts Jennifer, that's for sure. He makes it sound like he's afraid of her."

"What's your take on her?" He drained his mug.

"Normal, as far as I can tell." Except, maybe, for kissing an older, married man on the lips in the parking lot at Dino's. "Convinced that her brother's delusional."

Bernie gave me an appraising look and then glanced at his watch again. "I'm supposed to meet with Detective Coufalik now. Wendy Coufalik. A no-nonsense type, trained in this serial killer crap. She'll interface with the FBI. Let me see if she'll talk to you."

"Really?" Damn, Bernie was listening to me after all.

"Tell her everything Frank said. Maybe she'll think of something I haven't. Worth a shot." He stood up and shoved the chair snugly against the table. "Give me a minute."

Ten minutes later, I was trotting up the steps to a conference room on the first floor, where he introduced me to Wendy Coufalik. She was stout, like a weightlifter, and premature wrinkles lined her forehead. Bernie sat next to her while I slid onto the metal chair across the table. Utilitarian brown carpet covered the conference room floor, and photos of public officials hung on nicked white walls.

"So, you a Cleveland native?" I said, just to break the ice.

"Slavic Village." Her voice was low and firm. She reached across the rectangular conference table, over a pen and pad, to give me a firm handshake. Her roots told me plenty. Slavic Village had transformed over the years from a tough Eastern European immigrant neighborhood in the shadow of the steel mills to a volatile mix of mostly unemployed blacks and whites.

"I've been to the Red Chimney restaurant over there. It's—"

"So, how long did you know Wilbur Frederickson?" She'd hung a blue blazer over the back of her chair, and a white button-down shirt hung loosely on her, the top button undone.

Coufalik wasn't exactly making me feel all warm and fuzzy. "I already told them all the background info. I thought—"

"I know what you thought. Bernie told me why you wanted to talk. But if we're doing this, we're doing it my way. From the beginning. Got it?"

I shrugged, taken aback by her sledgehammer approach. "I knew him for years, just a casual relationship. I'd see him at the Tam O'Shanter, the bar we hung out in. He was a good guy."

"Did you socialize with him, other than at the bar?"

"No. I don't think I ever saw him outside the Tam."

"Did he talk of beefs he had with anybody?" She tapped her pen on the table. Bernie saw me looking at a coffeemaker next to a stack of Styrofoam cups and gave me a nod.

"Never. He wasn't that kind of guy. People liked him."

"Anything about his son?"

I got up and poured a cup. "Everything I know, Bernie told me. I don't even recall Oyster mentioning him."

"And it wasn't money problems. Bernie told me he had a pot."

"More than anyone could have imagined." I sat back down. The coffee was thin and tasted bitter, which I should have anticipated, because Bernie wasn't drinking any.

Coufalik looked at him, then down at the table, apparently considering where to go next. She made a note, and I tried to read it, upside down, but she cupped her hand over the pad. She looked up and asked, "Who knew he was loaded?"

"I really don't know, but probably no one. He sure never let on."

"What about regulars at the bar?"

"There were a couple of other guys, but we all went by first names. Tim and Karen, they're the owners, might know."

Coufalik nodded and made another note. "Why did the daughter call you about the estate?"

"She said he had my card, which was probably in case he got stopped by one of your guys after a few too many."

I chuckled, but Coufalik didn't react. "What's she say about her brother?"

I hesitated; the question put me in an awkward position. "Look, she's a client, and I can't divulge any conversations subject to the attorney–client privilege."

Coufalik looked at me and rapped her pen on the table.

"Let's just say she's said nothing inconsistent with what Bernie told me about Frank, or what I understand Jennifer has said to Bernie, okay?" I wasn't sure if my statement violated the attorney–client privilege, but I'd live with it, because having Coufalik pissed off at me wasn't high on my list.

She trained her keen eyes on me. "I understand you've talked to Frank Frederickson. Tell me exactly what he said."

"Sure." I focused on my brief conversations with the elusive Frank. "First time was at his father's funeral. He wanted to know how long it would take to settle the estate, but he said something odd about Jennifer. That he knew what she was capable of, whatever that means."

"Any idea?"

I shook my head and glanced at Bernie, who was eyeing my Styrofoam cup. Probably against his better judgment, he rose to get himself some. "The second time was a phone call. He's convinced that she'll cheat him out of the money and that I need to open my eyes. He also said he knows nothing about Oyster's death and that the money he got from him was legit."

"Is that what he said?"

I struggled to recall Frank's exact words. "Not exactly, no. I think it was that all of this has nothing to do with the money he got from the old man."

"Different ways to read that." Coufalik drilled her eyes into me. "That all?"

"When I brought up the Andar Feo, he said it wasn't them that he was afraid of. He said that I was clueless about his sister, that he could tell me things about her. No specifics."

"You tried calling him, I suppose?"

"Same number that Bernie has. Frank never picks up."

Coufalik kept her eyes locked on mine. "So what about her, this Jennifer Browning?"

I almost told her that she was going down the wrong path, but instead, just answered her question. "Seems totally aboveboard to me. After all, Frank's pretty screwed up, right?"

"I didn't ask about Frank. Did she ever ask you to cheat him, give her some advantage?"

I considered raising the attorney–client privilege issue again, but what I had to say could only help Jennifer. Screw it. "As a matter of fact, no. She's even worried that he'll blow his inheritance; she asked me about a guardian."

Coufalik edged her pad out of the way and leaned on the table. "Why is Frank only calling you?"

"Because I'm handling the estate, right? He wants his money."

"Well, let us know immediately if you hear from him again."

"Of course. And remember, I want to meet with him too, and go over some financial issues. Makes my job a lot easier. We're on the same page here."

She nodded and folded her notepad. "Thanks for stopping by."

She stood and slung the jacket over her shoulder. As she turned to leave, I couldn't help but notice her firm butt and guessed that she was probably a regular on the treadmill. She must have sensed me looking, because she pivoted in my direction.

"Really?" Her eyes drilled into me again. Shaking her head, she walked out, and the door whacked shut behind her.

Bernie twisted the Styrofoam cup in his hands. His face was flushed. "Nice. Smooth, John."

"Jesus, Bernie, I didn't . . . I came down here with the best intentions and feel like I got the bum's rush."

"She's not the patient sort. Now, you'll let this thing go?"

Right then, it became as clear as the Rock & Roll Hall of Fame's glass pyramid. Bernie had spoken to Coufalik of my history, of his opinion that I should walk away from anything to do with the Butcher before I crashed and burned. *Do me a solid; I've known the guy forever. Sit down with him, ride him hard, and maybe he'll put this to bed.*

I didn't call him on it directly, but said, "You just want me to fade into the sunset, right, Bernie?"

"Actually, that is right." He looked across at me, with those same eyes I'd seen for more than four decades. "Your only role in this is as the attorney for the estate, Johnny, nothing more. Just keep me in the loop, if you get a call from Frank."

I shifted my gaze to the black-and-white photographs on the wall. "So now I'm like an answering service for the Lakewood Police."

Bernie spread his arms. "Hey . . . "

"Don't worry." I waved him off. "And I think he'll call. He's eager for his share, no doubt."

Bernie folded his hands on the table. "Of course, we both know that you might not hear from him anymore. He could have decided that the rest of his inheritance isn't worth the risk of drawing the attention of the Andar Feo. He could've just disappeared. Or, he could be in a position where he can't make a call, if you get my drift."

"Yeah, I've thought of that. Poor bastard."

Bernie leaned forward, cradled the cup in his hands, and rested on his elbows. "Remember that time, freshman year, you got all fucked up, pissed at your old man again, and climbed that trestle out in Bay Village? You were screamin' at the top of your lungs that you were the King of the Fucking World, acting like a damn lunatic, and . . . you're kind of on edge now."

"Bernie, c'mon . . . "

"This is a friend talkin' here. None of us become kings, right? We wind up with mortgages and marriages and jobs we'd like to shove. And findin' Oyster . . . that kind of thing can throw you for a loop. I think you should see a priest, a counselor, whatever you have to do."

"Okay, Bernie." I wondered if Cathy had called him and had a little chat.

"I'm gonna tell you something now that the public won't know, something about the killing in Shaker Heights. I want you to understand that you're in way over your pay grade."

I leaned forward.

"It wasn't just his head that was cut off, Johnny. Butcher did somethin' new with this one. Sliced his dick up like a banana, left the pieces in his gut." He abruptly stood and grabbed his jacket. "Now, you focus on Cathy and Molly and walk away from this shit. Got it?"

I took a swig of the tepid coffee and nodded.

12

As I pulled out of the lot, I called Marilyn and arranged to take the rest of the day off. Waiting on Frank was eating at me—I couldn't imagine even a lowlife like him being used for carving practice by the Andar Feo. And I had no idea what to make of his guarded comments about his sister. Instead of sitting around and waiting for his call, I decided to take the initiative. Maybe Jennifer had forgotten something, some detail of his life, that might help us figure out a clue to finding him.

Or perhaps there were other reasons that I wanted to talk with her. The previous day, following our tense discussion after her birthday dinner, Cathy and I had exchanged few words. More than once, my mind had drifted to a recollection of Jennifer's tender kiss. As I began dialing her number, my thoughts were once again of her sensual embrace, her lips. My finger wavered over the last digit, but I completed the call.

I immediately thought better of it and nearly hung up, but she was suddenly on the line.

"It's good to hear from you, John." Hearing her voice was like tasting maple syrup. "And I'm doing better. Talking to you helped."

"Good, I'm glad we talked too." I turned toward Clifton Boulevard to avoid the annoying series of traffic signals on Detroit Road. I'd thought about our call, our kiss too much. "Look, I just saw Bernie Salvatore, and he asked about Frank again. They've run into a dead end. I think it's time to get proactive and quit waiting on Frank."

"What do you mean? He's—"

"I'm going to try to find him."

There was a sharp intake of breath. "This is a matter for the cops, John. You already told me that."

"Yup, but like I said, they're getting nowhere."

"I don't know . . . "

"And it makes handling the estate easier, too. If I can get him to buy into your decisions about what to liquidate, what to distribute . . . "

"I'm not worried about that, John. No matter what, I'll be fair."

"I know that. Still, the way he is, who knows what he might try to claim later?"

She sighed. "But searching for him? It just sounds risky."

"I'm only talking about asking around, that's all." I turned right at an intersection marked by a landmark restaurant built to resemble a lighthouse and headed east to reconnect with Detroit. "We know where he last lived; I'll start with the neighbors. Someone might know him and have some idea where he'd hang out."

"Haven't the police already done that?"

"Sure, but the type of people he'd know don't enjoy talking to cops, let alone giving them tips. My angle will be different, a little Irish charm. If nothing else, when he hears that I'm looking, he might decide to call."

There was a pause on her end, and then she said, "Maybe I should go with you."

I expected that if Frank knew Jennifer was on his tail, he would vanish. "You know what he said about you. If he hears that you're searching—"

"Let's not make his imaginings our problem, John."

I wanted to avoid an argument, so I shifted my approach. "I expect, despite everything, that you're worried about your brother. But it's not safe. I'm headed through Gordon Square now, and it gets pretty rough from here on."

"Don't misunderstand; I'm not worried about him at all." There was steel beneath the timbre of her voice. "But I don't believe for a second that Dad gave him that money legitimately, and I want the truth."

"Not a good idea." I passed a few popular restaurants near the revived Capitol Theatre, but I knew that the stretch of gritty blocks ahead hadn't exactly jumped on the urban renewal bandwagon. "Someone who looks like you, going into the places where your brother probably hung out . . . "

"Flattery will get you everywhere, John, but c'mon. Where should I meet you?" Her tone was beguiling.

She had chutzpah, for sure. "Let's compromise. There's a diner near Frank's old hood, Ed's Eggs on Detroit. The food's nothing special, but the crowd's not bad, and the parking lot's lit. Drinks on me."

"All right, Senor Hero, we'll do it your way."

"Can't stay late. My wife's upset about this Butcher scare and . . . my kid—I want to be there to tuck her in."

"Of course. You just be careful out there."

There was a genuine concern in her voice that touched me, not to mention the fact that I melted at the hero bullshit and had to admit that I wanted to see her, at least for a while. We arranged a time to meet at Ed's Eggs, and I slowed to turn onto West Forty-Second, the location of Frank's last known apartment.

I dodged a few potholes on the rugged street and found a place to park. My Buick contrasted with the beaters lining the curb. The houses were an arm's length apart, mostly duplexes that cried out for coats of paint and a rehab crew.

I soon wearied of flashing my photo of Frank at unreceptive residents. Just when I was about to call it a day, though, some ape-man, backed up by a slightly more hairy pit bull, let on that he'd seen my elusive quarry at a bar called the Alley.

I knew of the roughhouse joint, but only because the crime

reporters for the *PD* often mentioned the name. The ape-man gave me curt directions, and I soon found myself pulling to the curb in front of a yellowed concrete building with a single darkened window. Scrawled white lettering on a faded red sign, bolted onto a black door, announced that I'd found the right place.

Inside, the ambiance was equally charming. A timeworn wooden bar along one wall hosted a scruffy collection of patrons, mostly clad in leather and jeans. Long hair and unkempt beards seemed to be the fashion code. Four top tables were sparsely occupied, and a couple of tattered dartboards hung on cheap paneling. The decor consisted of posters featuring gorgeous chicks, draped in revealing strips of leather and splayed across gleaming motorcycles.

The bartender was a sweaty, fat guy with a pockmarked face and a black ponytail. He eyed me up and down as I moseyed to the bar. "Need something?"

"Budweiser, thanks. Draft." My eye caught a couple of scraggly dudes in black leather vests playing pool with two waifish girls, both parading garishly colored hair and bare midriffs.

He ambled over and drew the beer, unconcerned about a generous amount of foam. A golden earring in the shape of an Iron Cross dangled from one ear. Marilyn had much better taste. "Buck twenty-five."

At least the price was right. "I'm looking for somebody—"

"You a cop?"

"No, a lawyer."

"Ohhh, sorry, *coun-se-lor*." He raised his eyebrows and mugged for the creepy barflies, who laughed. Every set of eyes seemed to bore into me.

"The guy's name is Frank Frederickson. I'm told he hung out here."

He shook his head. "Doesn't ring a bell."

"Thin guy, little mustache, some tats. Here's a pic."

He barely glanced at the photo and rolled his eyes at the other barstool guys. "Like I said, nope."

"Hey, I hate botherin' you, man, but this is important."

"We get all sorts of important shit in here."

I turned to his audience. "C'mon, any of you know who I'm talkin' about?"

The bartender raised a hand. "Nobody comes down here to get no third degree. Take a fuckin' hike."

"Thanks for nothing." I shoved away from the bar.

I'd taken about two steps when somebody grabbed me by the shoulder and spun me around. I was face-to-face with a big son of a bitch wearing a white muscle shirt and a chain knotted around his waist for a makeshift belt. One pumped-up bicep sported a tattoo of a red skull with yellow flames shooting from the eye sockets. I guessed he was the bouncer when he leaned over me and said, "Like he told you, get the fuck out." His breath smelled like he'd been eating cigarettes.

All conversation had died. Other patrons watched us now, enjoying the intimidation of a middle-aged white dude. A Hispanic guy at a table in the far corner stared over his shoulder, and the back of his denim jacket read Andar Feo. Jesus Christ, someone had told them about the Alley too. I had to call Bernie.

"Hey, be cool. I'm leaving."

Hearing the tremor in my voice, the bastard sneered. The steps toward the exit seemed to take forever as every hard eye burned into my back. Once outside, though, I stopped dead. Two more Hispanic guys, clad in Andar Feo jackets, stood near the curb. Strolling away as nonchalantly as possible, I pulled out my cell and scrolled to Salvatore's contact info.

He picked up, thank God, on the second ring. "Bernie, it's John. I'm at the Alley Bar—"

"The Alley? Are you fuckin' kidding me?"

A hand gruffly landed on my shoulder and spun me around again. The bouncer's fist drove into my nose and knocked me backward, into the hard ground. The cell went flying. I pressed a hand against my face and felt the smear of blood.

"Just a reminder not to come back."

I stood up. The guy had a couple of inches and a lot of muscle on me. All I had on him was a lot of hard-lived years and the occasional jog. Despite Jack's coaching, fighting was not my strong suit. The bouncer leered, daring me to try something. Maybe it was the Butcher, maybe the tension at home, maybe everyone asking if I was *okay*, but I clenched my fists. He smiled and motioned me forward. He seemed surprised when I threw a right hand at his chin, but he blocked the punch and hit me once, twice, in the gut. My butt was planted on the grass again, the wind knocked out of me.

The bouncer loomed, his tattoo visible in the streetlight, and then hauled off and kicked me in the ribs. When the Andar Feo guys chuckled and strolled over, the bouncer said, "Guy's a lawyer."

The Mexicans exchanged a glance that seemed to say *well, that explains everything.* I prayed that the three of them didn't gang up on me and that neither of the Andar Feo guys felt like honing his carving skills. My ribs were on fire, but I sat up and bluffed, "The cops know I'm here."

They laughed like hell, as though I wasn't worth their time, and strolled back into the bar. I crawled around to find my cell and catch my breath. Bernie had disconnected but had tried calling, twice. Rolling to my knees, I stood up and pressed the callback.

"Talk to me, John."

"Some fucker coldcocked me."

"What the hell were you doin' at the goddamn Alley?"

I pressed my hanky against my nose. "A guy gave me a lead on Frank—"

"You didn't call me? You fuckin' promised."

"I wanted to check it out."

"That worked real well."

"Bernie, Jesus. The Andar Feo were here, three of 'em. That's why I called."

"Wow. Why don't you see if you can buy them a beer, ask if they'll wait around to chat with some cops?"

"Bernie . . . "

"You get another damn tip, you call me. Maybe now you'll figure out you should be home with Cathy, not runnin' around, getting into street fights."

"I'm only tryin' to help. I'm the one Frank's talking to, nobody else."

"So that means you should play detective. The Alley? What the hell." He took his time spitting out each word. "Thought you had your ass kicked enough in high school. Get the fuck home!"

"I hear you, Bernie." Home, sure, but not right away. I'd promised Jennifer that we'd meet at Ed's Eggs, but that was nothing my old friend needed to know.

The nosebleed seemed to have stopped, although a few drops had trickled onto my beige shirt. My nose and ribs throbbed. But the beating would be worth it if only Frank would surface. I had to stare into his shifty eyes, probe every word he said, and determine for myself if Jennifer was telling me the truth.

13

"Jesus," Jennifer said as I took the seat across from her. The bright lights of Ed's Eggs seemed to illuminate my swollen nose and the drops of blood on my shirt. It seemed as though customers at every table and the Formica-topped breakfast bar craned their necks in my direction. "What happened?"

"Some asshole jumped me outside a bar where Frank might have been."

"Looks like he didn't buy your Irish charm."

"I know I look a mess, but I didn't want to stand you up." A waitress who looked like she could have played for the Browns lumbered toward the table and gave me a long look. We ordered drinks but declined her proffer of discolored plastic menus. Although Ed's had a reputation of catering to people who were sloshed enough to eat hubcaps, the food wasn't really that bad. I just wasn't hungry.

Jennifer scrutinized my face. "Should I take you to the ER?"

"No, it's okay. Not the first time I've been punched." Truth be told, my last fight was in ninth grade. After that, luckily, everyone understood that Bernie was my protector. "All I learned about Frank was where he used to drink. But the Andar Feo, they were there."

"You called the cops?"

"Yeah, but that gang's not hanging around to chitchat, and if they did, what would they say?" The fact that the Andar Feo had been nearby was chilling. I pictured Jennifer with no lips, only a stark grimace of skeletal teeth.

She reached over and gripped my hand. "At least you tried."

Her touch was warm and tender. How could someone so sensitive be the ghoul that Frank claimed to fear? The waitress returned with our drinks, and I took a sip of the whiskey, which reduced the throbbing in my head by a degree. Jennifer pulled out her own photo of Frank; he looked just as homely in her pic as he did in mine.

"Ever see this guy?"

"I think so." The waitress scrunched her face together, the fat forming thick crests under her eyes as her jowls rose. "He might hang with Mary sometimes."

"Could we see her? He's my brother; it's important."

She shrugged as she turned away. "Okay. Soon as she's back from her break."

"Christ, I should've started here." I raised my eyebrows. "Might have saved me a nose."

Moments later, a lean girl pushed through a set of double doors from the kitchen. The waitress waved and pointed at us. "These people wanna talk to you."

Cautious, Mary approached. She was pleasant looking, if not exactly pretty, with thick shadow, the color of spinach, rimming her eyes. Jennifer explained who we were and handed her the headshot of Frank.

Mary's green-ringed baby browns widened just a hair, and she studiously examined the photo for a long while. Then she grimaced and said, "Sorry, can't place him."

"Look, I'm his sister, and I need to talk to him." She tipped her head in my direction. "He's our lawyer."

Mary eyed me. "When I got divorced, the lawyer came out of it better than me."

Great. Some sleazebag with a briefcase had made it less likely that she'd trust me. "Sure you don't recognize him?"

"I'd like to help, but . . . "

"Believe me, we're here for his own good." I handed her my card and drained the whiskey. "Office and cell. If you see Frank, have him call me, okay?"

She twisted my card gingerly between her thumb and forefinger, as if she were trying to avoid the taint of lawyer. "Okay. If I see him, I mean."

Before we left, I went to the bathroom and rinsed my nostrils of dried blood. Goddamn but my face felt raw, and the splashing water stung. The mirror prodded me to suck in my gut and tuck in the bloody shirt. When I returned, we made our way to the parking lot.

"She's lying," Jennifer said. "She knows where he is."

"My guess is that she knows a way to reach Frank, maybe even where he is. The ball's in his court then."

"Just like it's been."

We reached her car, and she turned to face me. I didn't want the evening to end, particularly not on a discussion of Frank and the Andar Feo. "If things were different, I'd take you someplace else, someplace nice for a nightcap . . . "

She smiled, stepped forward, and rested her hand on my arm. "Maybe another time?"

I pictured Martha, and Cathy. Molly dropping her skateboard at the door to give me a hug. But Jennifer looked so damn pretty, and the desire for another kiss, like that night at Dino's, was intense. I wanted to embrace her, to toss aside every conversation with Father McGraw, and screw her in the cramped front seat of my Buick. She faced me, her lips mere inches from mine. I glanced up, past the lights in the parking lot and into the darkness and glimmering stars so far above, but no words came to me.

She broke the electric silence. "I think I'd better go." As she opened the car door, I stepped back and was left to wonder whether I would have crossed the line. Again. I had vowed that my affair with Martha would be the last, but that promise had almost teetered in the parking lot of Ed's Eggs. Oddly, her sister seemed to be some indecipherable link to Jennifer, but that was not all that bound us. There was also the Butcher and what he'd done to her father. To my father. And Frank, in a way, was a link all his own. Frank—and the secrets he harbored.

I turned toward my car. It was time to go home to my wife and daughter.

When I came in from the garage, I hesitated in the kitchen before walking into the living room. Cathy gasped at the sight of my bloated nose. She clicked off the television and sprang from the sofa. "Jesus, John . . . what the hell happened?"

"I was asking around about Frank Frederickson, and some ass-hole bouncer belted me." My guilt about the parking lot interlude spiked with every quick step that she took toward me. I wanted to be away from the Bible and the crucifix and her. "Let me shower."

"It's nearly ten. You didn't answer your cell." Her hands cradled my face as she examined my nose.

I pulled out my phone. "Must have powered this damn thing off. Pretty out of it after the guy sucker-punched me."

"John . . . " She dropped her hands and stepped back, her eyes narrowing. "Boozing? I can smell it."

"Just stopped for one, to clear my head."

"You could have had a drink here. You left us alone."

"Let it go, Cathy. I just got beat up—"

"What if you have a concussion? Let's get to the ER."

"No. Not even a headache. Let me clean up."

"Don't be stubborn, not now." She reached out, as if to take me by the arm.

I stepped back. "Jesus, knock it off!"

She jerked as though I'd slapped her. Nodding toward the stairs, she hissed, "Keep your voice down, damn it." She returned to the sofa and curled her legs beneath her.

"I'm sorry." I took a breath to calm myself and ran a hand across my forehead. "We can talk once I've washed up."

"Listen to yourself. Think about what happened to you tonight. A fight?"

"I just wanna clean up and go to bed."

"Some reporters called, too, wanting to know what you thought about all these killings. I told them that you had no comment, like you said." Her hands tightened into fists in her lap. "I wanted to scream at them to leave you alone."

"They'll stop pestering me once they understand that my lips are sealed."

"Vanessa Edwards, the pretty black one, said that she knows you."

"She covered a case of mine once." Even Vanessa would have to back off, eventually.

Molly's feet padded down the steps. I wanted to bolt. I sure as hell didn't want her to see me in a blood-spotted beige shirt, spinning half-truths to her mother, but there was nowhere to hide. She stood on the bottom step, her mouth agape.

"Daddy . . . " Her dark eyes fixed on my face and welled with tears, a rare show of emotion. And to think that, less than an hour ago, I'd been ready to screw a woman who was not her mother.

"A bad man attacked me, honey. I fought back, like I told you to, but he was younger, bigger."

"Are you okay?"

"I'm fine. Go on back to bed. Daddy's going to shower."

She didn't move, but glanced at Cathy and back to me. "Why did you yell at Mom?"

I swallowed. "It's my fault. I shouldn't have stayed out. With the Butcher out there, I should have been home, with you and your mom."

"We talked about him at school today." She stepped onto the hardwood floor and padded to Cathy. "The other kids said I must know more than anybody, because of my grandfather."

Cathy wrapped her arms around her. "You know, until they catch him, we just want to make sure that you're safe. Remember my cousin Kate from Chicago and her husband, Peter?"

"Sure."

I took a step toward them. "What are you doing?" I asked her, my voice low, warning.

She ignored me. "You liked them when they visited. They said you could stay with them, just until this is over."

"Damn it, Cathy!" I wanted to snatch the perfectly poised figurines from the coffee table and smash every one. "We talked about—"

"Watch your mouth," she snapped.

Molly said, "I'm not going anywhere."

Cathy's voice softened. "Listen to me, honey. It will just be for a while. Dad's business is keeping him out late, and he can't always be here to take care of us."

"Wait a minute," I said. "That's—"

Molly, the child of foster care, unfamiliar places, and lonely nights, held up a small hand to silence me. "I'm not doing it."

"Why don't you go up and let your dad and me talk?" Cathy said. "We can—"

"Mom, I'm not going anywhere. And I won't stay inside all day, either. You said that you trusted me." She was talking to both of us now. "You said to be careful, but never afraid. I'm not going to be stupid, and I'm going to be me. Just like you said."

Cathy and I didn't utter a word. We had just been put in place by our thirteen-year-old daughter.

"And, Dad, you should learn to duck." Molly pulled out of her mother's arms and trotted up the steps.

Cathy gave me a long look. "Don't you dare be upset with me. You won't go to a counselor, and now you're going out and getting beat up, your daughter sees you . . . "

"I can't believe you brought that up. I told you how I felt."

Her chin jutted defiantly. "One of us has to make the right decision. Molly comes first."

"Oh, for . . . of course she does." I sat on the other end of the sofa. "Cathy, I had no way of knowing that somebody was going to take a swing at me. This won't happen again."

"I want to trust you, John." She stood and walked around the coffee table, away from me, toward the stairs. "But you're just not being yourself."

"I'll be here, Cathy." I leaned forward and spread my hands.

She didn't pause as she went upstairs. "We can talk more tomorrow."

I poured a nice, stiff drink in the kitchen and returned to the living room, in the shadow of the cross above the mantel, to watch the news. Bernie was pissed at me, I'd gotten my ass kicked, my daughter had seen my mess of a face, my wife wanted to send Molly to Chicago, and the Butcher was on the loose.

Then there was Jennifer.

14

"So many different smells!" Molly wrinkled her nose as the competing aromas drifted toward us: pungent raw meat, freshly baked breads, the fishy smell of perch and walleye. We'd traipsed down the bustling Twenty-Fifth Street and passed through a set of weathered green doors into the century-old West Side Market.

"It was just like this when I was a kid, sweetie." I'd had a direct talk with Cathy following our exchange in the living room and insisted that I could—and would—spend more time with Molly. Late nights out were also off the agenda, although Cathy had seemed to sense my hesitancy to make that promise. But I had made it, and I'd meant every word, because Molly had to come first.

We navigated through aisles jammed with hectic shoppers inspecting stalls brimming with headcheese and kielbasa, rice hurka and blood sausage. A little bonding time with my daughter, followed by a steak dinner with my family on a Saturday night. Although Cathy and I remained testy, we had agreed to do our best to make our home as normal as possible, for Molly's sake.

Havlicek's Meats was my favorite purveyor of slabs of beef in the market, maybe because my old man used to take me there when I was a kid and he was a bigshot cop. Havlicek's was a bit of a local leg-end, as the oldest—and probably the best—meat stand in the market. Even though Oyster and I might have argued over who was the best Browns running back or the greatest Indians team, we'd always agreed that no one topped Havlicek's.

The grandson of the founder was toiling away behind the counter as we approached. He had always been a stocky, stern-looking man, but his crewcut was now pure white.

"Hey, Mr. Havlicek. John Coleman."

"Well, well, look who drove in from the suburbs." He grinned, wiped his palms on a grimy apron, and reached across the counter to shake hands. "It's been months. Get tired of goin' to Heinen's?"

"Guilty as charged." I raised my arms in mock surrender. "Remember my little girl, Molly?"

He beamed in recognition and spread his Popeye-like arms wide. "How could I forget such a pretty young lady? You've grown!"

Blushing, Molly leaned into me.

"Remember what I told you about my stall?"

Molly giggled. "I forget."

"Our beef is so tender, you wonder how the cows walked."

Now Molly full-out laughed. "I remember! I didn't get it at first."

Havlicek gave her a wink and then turned to me. "I've been thinking about you, your old man."

"I know, hard to believe it's the Butcher, after all these years."

"Yeah . . . I just wish they called him something else." Havlicek shrugged, and even Molly smiled at his gallows humor.

"You knew Oyster Frederickson, right? He used to come here too."

"Sure, the guy with the eyes. Nice guy. Helluva thing."

"I was there . . . " I noticed Molly looking up at me. It was time to change the subject, and I ran my hand through her hair. "You should ask Mr. Havlicek about the time he stole that ball . . . "

Molly gave me a blank look, and I said, "Just pulling your leg, honey. He has the same name as a famous basketball player, before your time."

"I was in Boston once, when he was still playin'. You wouldn't believe the restaurant reservations I got." Havlicek nodded to a few people who had lined up behind me and asked, "So, what can I do you for today? Rib eyes look great."

I nodded, and he stooped to reach into the stand. As he wrapped the meat and slid the parcel of white butcher paper into a plastic bag, my attention drifted to a dark-haired woman in the rear of the stall, methodically slicing through cuts of meat. I wondered how long she'd had this job to make it appear so effortless, almost graceful. My mind flashed to Oyster, what had happened to him. I turned my gaze from the knife and paid Havlicek.

As Molly and I worked our way through the crowd, I glanced at my watch. I was meeting Jack Corrigan for lunch, but there was still plenty of time to kill. "You want a pop, Molly, or chocolate milk?"

She raised her eyebrows and smiled broadly, so we strolled into the snug café nestled in a corner of the market. Brick columns supported an arched ceiling covered in turquoise tile, creating a light, airy feel. We snared the one open booth, and I sat facing my daughter, bracing for the conversation that I knew we needed.

A harried waitress with frizzy blonde hair took our order. Once she left, I groped for the right words. Molly made it easy, asking, "Is this where we're going to talk about the fight you and Mom had?"

I did smile, despite myself. "It wasn't really a fight. Just . . . you know."

"Just an argument? Sounded like a fight to me, but what do I know? I'm just a kid."

"You're a smart-aleck kid, is what you are." I grinned. "Call it what you want; we made up. I'm just sorry you heard us."

"Did Mom really think I'd go to Chicago?"

"She's just worried is all." The waitress set our drinks down, and I drew the coffee mug toward me. "That's what moms do."

"I'm not going, no matter what." Her jawline was rigid.

"I know that, and really, so does your mom. I think she was just upset with me."

Molly took a sip of her sugar-and-caffeine-free pop. "She hates it when you're late. And now that the killer is back, she's afraid."

"The Butcher isn't coming after any of us, honey. Your mom—"

"You don't understand. She's afraid for you." Molly stirred her pop with the straw.

I felt myself tense. "Did she say that?"

"No, but I can tell." She took another sip, looked around the room, then back at me. "Mom says that, when you got punched a couple of nights ago, you were in a terrible neighborhood."

"Yeah, I was." I forced a grin. "Even dads make mistakes."

"She says you were lucky, that it could have been worse. Killed, even." Her eyes were moist.

I wanted to toss the table aside and draw her to me for a hug. But I knew that Molly would not appreciate the gesture—at least, not in public. Instead, I said, "Don't worry. I promised your mom that nothing like that would happen again."

I surreptitiously glanced at the clock mounted on the wall, but Molly noticed. So much for my stealthy moves.

"Are you going to be late?" she asked.

"No, no. I can cancel if you want." I hoped she could tell that I was being sincere. Raising a teenage daughter is not for the faint of heart.

"Uh-uh. Tell Mr. Corrigan I said hello." Molly slurped the last of her drink through the straw. "I remember him, that time he came to the house. He has a mean face, but he's nice."

"What did I tell you?"

She nudged the glass to the center of the table and sighed. "I know. Never judge a book by its cover."

I DROPPED MOLLY AT THE HOUSE AND HEADED STRAIGHT for the Tam, arriving just ten minutes late. Jack Corrigan was three-quarters of the way down the polished bar, with a mug of beer and a shot glass in front of him.

"I thought you said noon." The big bastard looked perfectly at home. His leathery mitt nearly swallowed his mug.

"I figured you wouldn't mind waiting, as long as it was some-where you could get a drink." Jack had called the day before to arrange for lunch, which made me curious. I'd suggested the Tam, figuring it was time for me to slide back onto my usual stool. Jack said he'd been there before, which was no surprise.

Despite the time that had passed since my altercation at the Alley, my nose was still puffy.

Of course, Jack noticed right away. "So what happened to the schnoz?"

There was no way to put a positive spin on the story, because Jack wasn't a guy who would have gone down with one punch. I slid onto a stool and waved to Karen. "Out lookin' for my client's brother and ran into some trouble."

"How many were there?"

He asked it deadpan, but I knew he was baiting me and would sniff out a lie in about a second. "Guy was as big as a goddamn truck and half my age. Half my age and he does this, the prick."

"So you're out doin' a cop's job and get beat up by a kid. Helluva game plan you got, Ace."

Karen saved me by setting my usual beer on the bar. Her blue eyes sparkled as always, and she looked vibrant in an emerald green sweater. I hadn't seen her since Oyster's funeral. "Doin' okay?"

"Still hard to believe it was the Butcher," she said. "Right in our alley. I try not to think about it, but he's all over the papers, the TV."

"Press called me, but I'm not talking. They twist everything."

"What do you expect? You ever confuse any of those faggots with Walter Cronkite?" Jack asked. "They'll leave you alone after awhile. Too many other dickheads want to be in the spotlight, throw in their two cents. I mean, not that you're a dickhead . . ."

I grinned, but my gaze wandered toward the back door, leading out into that alley.

Karen broke my train of thought when she slid a couple of menus on the bar and told us to let her know if we wanted to order anything. The Tam served classic bar food, which would be fine with Jack. No Cuban sandwiches, no fish tacos, nothing trendy or foreign for him to bitch about. Of course, he still might start in about the rock and roll bands. A poster on the wall behind him, a psychedelic rendering of long hair and hazy smoke, touted an appearance by Grand Funk Railroad at the old Agora Ballroom, near Cleveland State.

"So, why the call?"

Jack folded his arms on the bar. "I sat down with Bernie Salvatore and Dickless Tracy about the killings. Apparently, I'm the only cop still around who worked on both Torso and the Butcher."

"You guys used to have, like, class reunions?" At least I got a smirk out of him. "That Coufalik's a piece of work."

"Built like a brick shithouse, and twice as hard. She don't much like you."

"We got off to a bad start."

Jack sighed and pushed away from the bar, stretching his back. "Bernie thinks you're getting carried away with these murders. She thinks you're, well . . . *strange* was the word."

So this was what our meeting was about. Not to catch up and shoot the shit, not to banter about the murders, but to talk about what a problem I was. "Bernie worries too much. His wife's close to mine, they talk, you know how it is."

"He says you nearly left Cathy's birthday dinner to get to that crime scene in Shaker?"

Bernie must have had a helluva conversation with Jack. "So? I didn't go."

"Yeah, but then you did go lookin' for the brother."

"Look, I wanna talk with him, too, about the estate. I was only trying to help." I sipped the cold beer. "I thought that was what they wanted."

"Oh, they ask you to try and track him down in some shithole neighborhood?" He glanced at my nose. "That's workin' out well for you."

"Lookin' back on it, I made a mistake, all right?"

Jack raised his eyebrows, then picked up the menu, but dropped it back on the bar after a couple of seconds. "He said you're representing the daughter, a hot blonde. You workin' some angle to get into her panties?"

His question threw me off. "Hell no, I'm only trying to look out for this girl. Bernie tell you about the Andar Feo?"

"You know how many families of victims I worked with, fathers who wanted to take things into their own hands? If Blondie's in trouble, you can't save her, Johnny." Jack finished his shot. "You gonna eat?"

We ordered cheeseburgers, and Karen didn't ask how we wanted them cooked, because the Tam wasn't that kind of place. She did offer us grilled onions; we both accepted and ordered more beers.

Karen put in our order and leaned against the bar back. "Your cop buddies tell you anything that's not in the papers?"

"Talk to Jack. He worked all the old cases, Torso and the Butcher."

Her eyes lit up like she was a high school girl about to play spin the bottle with the star quarterback. "I didn't know that."

Jack waved a hand dismissively. "Ancient history. I don't know anything about what's goin' on that ain't already in the news."

"Well, do you think they have some suspects by now, who the Butcher might be? I mean, three murders . . . " Karen sounded anxious, and I couldn't blame her. She had just planned to empty a wastebasket when she'd stumbled across Oyster stuffed in her Dumpster.

"Don't know," Jack said. "And if I did, I couldn't tell you."

Karen was undeterred. "Look, I'm not criticizing the cops; I'm really not. But the Torso Murderer and the Butcher got away with it. And now he's back . . . "

Jack answered her patiently. "Most murders are between people who know each other, and there's a reason, like sex or money. But serial killers murder strangers. Look at any of 'em—Boston Strangler,

Ted Bundy, that Sowell guy right here in Cleveland a couple years back. Tough cases to solve."

"But they caught those guys."

Karen was throwing down a gauntlet, and I wondered how Jack would react. But he took a sip of Pabst and remained calm. "They got a lucky break in every one of those, plain and simple. Christ, we thought we had that with Torso too, but . . . hell, you don't wanna hear this shit."

"Actually, I do." Karen's eyes were bright, intense.

"We called him the chicken guy." Jack was the classic old-timer who delighted in regaling a pretty woman half his age. "Now, the whole thing seems kinda funny."

I'd read all of this on the web, but Karen didn't know what the hell he was talking about. "The chicken guy?"

"Investigation was going full-bore, the city was damn near on lockdown, and a hooker comes to us. I'll never forget—her name was Sheila. She says some truck driver, a regular customer, would pay her to strip to her panties and bra, but he never wanted to touch her or anything. Looking at Sheila, I understood that—no mistakin' her for one of those Victoria Secret numbers."

Karen chuckled, and I joined in. Jack was on a roll. She said, "Why do you call him the chicken guy?"

"Guy would have a chicken with him, a live one, and tie it to the leg of a table or chair." Jack hesitated. "Not sure this part is . . . somethin' I should be saying in front of a lady."

"Don't worry. Workin' in a bar, I've heard it all."

"Well, he'd . . . touch himself, you see, and when he was about . . . done, would have her cut off the head of the chicken. Told her he liked the blood, the way it squirted."

Karen pushed herself up from the bar. "No way."

"There," I said. "Something you haven't heard before."

"We called the trucker in, and he showed up like it was nothing. Good-lookin' Joe, too. Usually, pervs will make all sorts of excuses, but this guy comes right out and says he likes watching chickens bleed out. No law's bein' broke, he says, so what's the problem? We check his logbook, and he's got a perfect alibi—wasn't in town during any of the killings."

"What about for animal cruelty?" Karen asked, her blue eyes flashing at Jack.

"Right, for a fuckin' chicken. Then along came another guy, one we all liked for it, a big son of a bitch named Frank Sweeney, a doc."

I'd read about him. "There was a mayor or something back then with that name, right?"

"A congressman, and the doctor was his cousin."

"That's right, but you couldn't make it stick."

"Are you tellin' her the story, or me?" Jack gestured for another shot, which Karen promptly poured. She left the bottle on the bar, like she wasn't going anywhere. "There was a lot that pointed to the guy. He'd know, of course, how to dissect a body, and he looked strong enough to lug around a vic, dead or alive. Plus, he was a drunk and a switch-hitter."

"Sounds like some slasher flick character." Karen leaned on the bar, hanging on Jack's every word.

"The perfect suspect, but the lie box was shaky, and he was in hospitals gettin' treated for the booze at the same time some of the vics were killed. Fucker eventually committed himself."

A young Mexican kid emerged from the kitchen and slid two hamburgers in front of us. The smell of grease and meat wafted into my nostrils, and I was suddenly ravenous.

Jack swallowed a quick bite and continued. "Remember the old Third District, the Roaring Third? Hookers, blind pigs, gambling, whatever. Old-timers told me that Ness once had them search the entire district, house by house. Got zip."

"Ness had them pretend they were conducting fire safety inspections," I said to Karen. "Believe it's the largest warrantless search in history."

"Well, Mr. Attorney, you have to understand how desperate Ness and Merylo were. Every lead was tracked down. Merylo even went to some shitburg near Pittsburgh, after they found three headless bodies in a boxcar at the rail yard. And one odd thing I never forgot, the imprint of a woman's high heel shoe in the blood."

"Creepy." Karen straightened up. "Burgers okay?"

Jack gave her a thumbs-up sign. "There was other shit too, but none of it panned out."

"So what about the Butcher?" Karen asked.

"Nothing—despite the damn fine job Johnny's father did runnin' the show. Only thing we got was the usual wackos coming in to confess. That happens all the time in these kinda cases."

"You're not exactly filling me with confidence that they'll catch the guy this time." Karen nodded at my beer mug, and I gave her a high sign. I declined the offer of a shot.

Jack quietly sipped his drink. "All I can tell you is everyone with a badge is doin' the best he—*they*—can."

Karen leaned on the bar. "But why would the Butcher stop for so long, then come back?"

"Jack told me that's not uncommon with serial killers." I looked at him for validation.

He swallowed the last bite of burger and shoved his plate across the bar. "Ask me, anybody who thinks they can figure out killers like these is wasting time."

A comment I believe he aimed in my direction.

"Not very reassuring," Karen said.

"Gun sales are off the charts." Jack jabbed a thick finger at Karen. "You should think about getting a permit."

"I am. You guys all set? I've gotta work on inventory." Gently, she patted the back of Jack's hand. "If I offended you in any way, I apologize. I know the cops are out there . . . "

He looked surprised that she'd touched him, but smiled. "Honey, I'm too old and too mean to offend."

She walked away, and I caught Jack checking out the sway of her jeans. Not bad, having some steam left in his eighties. "Thanks for having lunch. You could have just called me."

"Don't go all mushy. I've been wipin' your ass for too many years, and it's a hard habit to break." Jack picked up the tab from the bar. "This is on me. Go on home, tell the wife and kid I said hello."

I was reminded of the days when he would treat me to a hot dog or a pop at a Cavs game or the county fair. "Thanks, Jack. But watch yourself. I think Karen's interested."

He chortled. "Get the fuck outta here."

Smiling, I brushed past him, but he spun the stool around and grabbed my arm. His grip was firm and strong. He scrutinized my face, as though he were appraising me. Then he said, his tone measured, "Don't take on your father's problems, Johnny."

I nodded and, when he finally relaxed his hold and looked away, headed for the door.

15

"So you enjoyed the park yesterday, with your dad?" Cathy swallowed a bite of her toast and cast a glance in my direction.

"I was burning it. Did I tell you about the Ollie I pulled? My kickflips?" Molly gulped some orange juice.

Cathy shook her head. "You'll have to remind me someday what that all means."

"I'm not sure that Mom really wants to know." All weekend, Cathy and I had put up a façade for our daughter, but were otherwise observing a mutual silent treatment. Getting out of the house with Molly had been the highlight of my Sunday.

Molly raised her hands. "One fall, Dad, the whole time. One."

Cathy grimaced, and I said, "I wasn't going to mention that."

"C'mon, knowing how to fall is half the fun." Molly drained the last of her juice.

Cathy arched an eyebrow. "Well, fun yourself upstairs, and don't forget to brush—"

"I know the drill, Mom." As Molly bounded out of the kitchen and toward the stairs, Cathy looked at me and said to her, "You can tell me all about your tricks tonight, when Dad's home for dinner."

"Okay, I'll explain them, againnnnn . . . "

As soon as Molly's footsteps faded, I said, "'When Dad's home for dinner'?"

"Why? Is that a problem?" Cathy picked up her dishes and headed for the sink.

"You don't need to talk like that in front of Molly."

She turned and shrugged, then leaned back on the countertop. "Talk like what? All I said was—"

"I told you I'd knock off the late nights. You don't need to remind me." I shoved my mug, splashing some coffee on the table.

Cathy marched past me. "Fine. See you tonight."

I waited a beat. "Maybe I'll be late."

I didn't turn around but sensed her stop at the base of the stairs. Before storming up the steps, she hissed, "Don't be an ass."

I grabbed my worn briefcase and bolted for the garage. An accident on the Shoreway slowed traffic to a crawl, which did nothing to lighten my mood. Largely for Molly, I had committed to certain changes, but I'd be damned if I would wear a leash.

When I entered the office, my mood lightened at the sight of Marilyn. From each of her earlobes sprang a cascade of black and red braided wire, with a sliver of turquoise and bold golden feathers at each end. I shifted my briefcase from one hand to the other. "The Pocahontas look?"

"You should see my headdress and tomahawk." She arched both eyebrows.

"Ever think you might be scaring guys away?"

"Let the cowards run. I'm waiting for a warrior, John."

I chuckled and strolled past her, toward my office, but turned in the doorway. "You'll let me know when you find him?"

"Don't worry. I'll fax in my resignation from his private jet on our way to Paris." She shook a finger at me and winked.

Marilyn's moment of levity warmed me, and I settled in at my desk to plow through what should have been a day like any other.

And then, just when I'd begun to shuffle through the weekend mail, my cell buzzed, and Jennifer's name flashed on the caller ID.

She purred hello, then asked, "You feeling okay?"

There was genuine concern in her voice, and I could not block the memory of the parking lot at Ed's Eggs, when all I'd wanted to do was kiss her. "Pretty much back to normal, except for a nose that's still a couple of sizes too big."

"A good look, I'm sure!" She laughed, but then her serious tone surfaced. "I spent the weekend organizing all of Dad's paperwork. Took me hours."

"Find any accounts we don't know about?"

"I don't think so, but some of this stuff I just don't understand. Could you take a look?"

Oyster was probably the sort who would squirrel away every form and slip of paperwork, not knowing when it might be needed. "Sure. Can you drop it by the office?"

She exhaled. "There's a lot, John. Boxes. I don't know what your schedule is like, but I can leave work early if you could swing by . . . "

I lowered the phone and pressed it against my neck, ran my free hand through my hair. My eyes rested on the framed photo of Cathy and Molly. I heard Cathy's words, about being home for dinner. Just before she'd chided me not to be an ass.

She must have sensed my hesitation, because she cleared her throat and said, "Everything's organized, best I could, on my dining room table. C'mon, John; I'm not going to bite."

A bite wasn't exactly my worry. I considered asking Marilyn to come along, but was a chaperone really necessary? Christ, I was being too guarded. It wouldn't be the first time that I'd visited someone's home to help sort through a raft of confusing documents. My meeting with Jennifer was simple, mundane business.

I just had to forget a certain whiff of perfume, a suggestive embrace, and the stubborn recollection of a parking lot kiss.

"John, you still there?"

I raised the phone to my lips. "No, I understand. I just can't stay late."

"Of course. Your family." She clucked her tongue. "Can you make it by five? Need directions?"

"Trusty GPS. See you then." Five o'clock would give me time to sift through the paperwork for an hour or so and still be home in time for dinner. I could leave a message on Cathy's cell that I'd be running a little late—or maybe I wouldn't leave a message. Showing up later than she expected might set the proper boundary, even if she called me an ass all night.

There was nothing unusual about leaving the office early, so Marilyn didn't bat an eye when I prepared for a late afternoon exit. As the elevator descended, I focused on my promise to Bernie, that my relationship with Jennifer would remain strictly professional. By the time I reached the garage and headed toward my Buick, my nerves were tingling. I slid onto the driver's seat and cradled the keychain in my hand, reminding myself that I wasn't going on a date. The afternoon would be spent doing nothing more than reviewing a box full of a dead man's papers. I slid the key into the ignition, and the engine purred to life.

Jennifer lived in Parma, a bedroom community that had taken baby steps toward becoming more cosmopolitan. Her apartment complex was off the main road and partially concealed behind an unattractive strip mall. I pulled into a guest slot in the parking lot at the rear of her building. There was a directory near the door, sheltered beneath a beige awning. Jennifer soon buzzed me in. She was waiting at her doorway when I got there, and she greeted me with a sly smile. I followed her inside, conscious of her tight jeans and bright yellow blouse.

A couple of abstract paintings popped against sleek white walls, and a contemporary white leather couch and matching chairs bordered a sinuous glass coffee table. Colorful pillows added some sizzle to the plain furniture, all artfully positioned over wall-to-wall beige carpeting. A large plasma screen and sleek sound system faced the couch. The room opened onto a pleasant, compact patio, lined with greenery.

"Great job decorating, Jennifer. The place looks fantastic."

"Thank you." She reached for my nose but didn't touch it. "Not that bad. Still sore?"

"I'll tough it out, somehow."

"Okay, Mr. Hero." She laughed and gestured expansively toward her dining alcove. Neatly arranged stacks of paper covered the wooden table. "Let's see how your special powers handle all of this."

Relieved that we had so quickly progressed to business, I followed her into the dining room.

She quickly explained how the documents were organized, then said, "So that's about it. I'll let you get to it." She switched on a stereo, housed in a glass and aluminum unit mounted on the wall behind us. "Let me get you a glass of wine. I picked up some Chianti."

"Sure." Chianti—the wine we had enjoyed during our dinner at Dino's. Her choice of music was calm and mellow. Under other circumstances, I might have interpreted it as romantic, but I wasn't going to allow my thoughts to run in that direction.

As Jennifer headed for the kitchen, I noticed several photos, framed in black lacquered wood, arranged on a small desk near the dining table. One was of Martha and Jennifer, the resemblance striking, and another was of a good-looking guy with light brown hair and intense, dark eyes. The late husband, Robert, I assumed. He'd probably thought he had life by the ass, until his unfortunate encounter with a truck. There was a small framed photo of a younger Frank, taken on a sunshiny day in San Diego, with its distinctive skyline and the graceful Coronado Bridge spanning the bay. Jennifer's arm was draped over his shoulder. Apparently they'd been friendly at some point in their adult lives.

Jennifer appeared at my side and handed me a glass of wine. "Thanks for coming over and taking a look at this."

"That's okay; it shouldn't take long." Very aware that she didn't move away from me, I pulled out a chair, set my glass on the table, and began with the row of documents to my right. Jennifer hovered, offering the occasional comment between sips of wine.

All of ten minutes had elapsed before it was clear that the paperwork, although voluminous, was inconsequential. There were a few old title insurance policies and copies of deeds, but the bulk of the documents were mutual fund statements and routine insurance company forms. Years of meticulously maintained, and substantially worthless, sheaves of paper. Had she seriously been unable to come to that conclusion on her own?

I thumbed through the last set, a compilation of savings account statements, and looked up at Jennifer. "Sorry, nothing new here."

"Well, at least now I know. Thanks." She took hold of my forearm, drew me up. "Let's make a cheese tray and visit for a while."

I stood, facing her, and she handed me my wine glass. "I really should get going."

"I'm not going to have you drive all the way out here and spend just fifteen minutes. Let me be a proper hostess."

She turned and went into the kitchen. I followed. She opened her refrigerator door, then bent over to gather some provisions.

Any of my lingering thoughts of bank statements and insurance policies quickly evaporated. The jeans hugged every one of her delicious curves. I knew that I needed to set down the glass of wine and say good-bye and walk out the door. But I stood, frozen in place, as she straightened, cradling some wrapped cheeses in one hand and a roll of white butcher paper in the other.

"Here." She handed the roll to me. "Be a dear and slice some of that, would you? Summer sausage. Oh, and grab an apple, too."

I followed her gaze toward the sink and a large chef's knife atop a wooden cutting board. A bowl of fruit, apples and oranges, was nearby. As I unwrapped the thick sausage and made the first cut, Jennifer sidled up next to me and peeled away the thin plastic that encased Gouda, goat milk, and a thick cheddar cheese.

"Am I doing better than Ed's Eggs?" She looked up at me and grinned.

I shrugged. "Have a Formica table somewhere?"

She playfully slapped my arm. While she arranged the cheeses and some crackers on a silver platter, I added several slices of sausage. The sharp knife made quick work of the apple; I arranged the sections along the edge of the tray.

"Not bad," Jennifer said as she gathered a few spreading knives and napkins. "If Ed ever needs a sous chef . . . "

I followed, tray in hand, as she flashed that smile again and strolled out of the kitchen. I sank into one of the padded leather chairs. Jennifer nestled into the couch, near my chair, and our knees were inches apart. She seemed to become more beautiful with every moment that passed.

"I'm glad you stayed, John." She spread some of the soft Gouda on a cracker. "I've wanted to ask: what did you mean the other night? You said, 'If things were different . . . '"

I took a sip of wine and examined the bright lines in one of the abstracts on the wall. She could be direct, for sure. "I . . . I don't know what to say, Jennifer. When I'm with you . . . but, Jesus, I have a wife and kid. I shouldn't even be here."

"But you are." Jennifer leaned forward, took the glass from my hand, and stood. She stretched languorously along the leather armrest on my chair, tilted her alluring face toward mine, and our lips met, our tongues caressed. Her mouth moved against me firmly, forcibly, and I longed for her, to taste her and feel her and plunge inside her. I lifted my arms to embrace her, but she broke away with a throaty chuckle and stood before me. Her breasts were taut against the yellow blouse.

I felt glued to the chair, and not just because of a raging hard-on. There was no turning back, and I was prepared to break every promise to Cathy and Father McGraw. The ethical prohibition against sleeping with a client lost all meaning, and the fact that Bernie Salvatore would detest me mattered nothing. Jennifer wanted me. She wasn't telling me how to live my life, wasn't calling me an ass.

She took my hand and led me to the bedroom. A cream-colored bedroom set was barely illuminated by the dim glow of an accent lamp. We kissed with the hungry abandon of teenagers. She undid the buttons on my shirt one by one, pausing only to nibble at my lips, my throat, my chest. Soon, I was naked and erect and had managed to slip off her blouse and jeans. Her taut skin was warm to the touch and impossibly smooth. A whiff of perfume was floral, enticing.

She stopped me from unhooking the clasp of her bra and guided me onto the comforter. She posed, in pink lace panties and bra, and allowed me to take in her voluptuous body. When she at last unclasped her bra, the straps dangled on her shoulders until she shimmied, and the garment dropped to the floor. She haltingly lowered her tight panties and unveiled a Brazilian bikini wax, the first I'd ever seen in person. The Pope himself would have forgiven me had he seen what stood at the foot of the bed.

With an undulating feline crawl, she drifted across the comforter and up my body, her breasts brushing my stomach, my chest, until her lips reached mine. She cradled my face in her palms and whispered into my ear, her breath hot and guttural. "I've wanted you, John. Wanted you from the moment I saw you."

She took a foil packet from a nightstand drawer and playfully rolled a condom down my cock. Soon, she was straddling me, her erect nipples brushing against my eager lips. Her back arched as she rocked to a rhythm of her own. Her breathing quickened and, when she at last cried out and collapsed on top of me, her fingers entwined in my hair, I came with her. My body shuddered until I felt completely drained. We clung to each other as our breathing slowed.

As Jennifer rolled onto her back, next to me, my eyes drifted to a picture in a gold frame on the dresser: Martha. Hell, it was like she'd been watching us.

"Wow." Jennifer leaned across my chest and flicked her tongue against my lips. "Freshen up; I'll be right back."

Jennifer likely expected another go-round, but twice in one night was a distant memory. I sat up, gathered myself, and went into the bathroom. I flicked on the lights, which bordered the mirror above the sink. The disappointing results from my half-hearted effort at jogging were on full display. I sucked in my gut. Then I washed, killed the light, and crawled back into bed as Jennifer came down the hall.

Still wearing nothing more than a big smile, she paused in the doorway, holding a can of whipped cream in one hand and a jar of strawberry jam in the other, her breasts poised between them. "I'm not a very good hostess. Would you like dessert?"

Getting hard again was definitely not going to be a problem.

We took turns making each other come, and I knew that whipped cream would never taste the same. After I burst the second time, she drew herself up, draped a leg across my thighs, and rested her head on my shoulder. I licked a trace of strawberry jam from her cheek. We barely said anything.

When I finally stole a glance at the clock on the nightstand, it was well past dinnertime. Hell, I wouldn't arrive home until after ten o'clock. If I'd wanted to send a message to Cathy, I'd sent a damn strong one. I closed my eyes for a moment, trying not to think about her. Or my little girl.

I rolled out of bed. "Time to go . . . sorry."

She eyed me as I went into the bathroom, my legs unsteady. "We never touched the cheese tray."

"Somehow, I forgot all about it." I washed and then gathered my clothes. I needed to leave.

Jennifer watched as I dressed. Her neck was still flushed and her nipples erect. "*Eres muy guapo*. Know what that means?"

My mind wrapped around the words as I finished buttoning my shirt and slipped on the slacks. "All I know is *muy*."

"It means you're very handsome."

I hadn't heard the word in a while, other than when Cathy said it to reassure me as my hairline receded and the wrinkles on my forehead became more pronounced. "Thank you."

"You okay, John?" She sat up and draped her arms over her knees. "This was special. We both know that."

The only words I could manage were, "Yes, it was wonderful."

I watched as the light seemed to wash from her eyes. She was silent for a moment, then said, "So where do we go from here?"

I took a breath and fastened my belt buckle. "I'll call you tomorrow; we can talk."

She lay back against the pillows. "That sounds like you're already thinking of a way to let me down easy."

"No. I mean, I need some time. It's . . . it's complicated."

"It doesn't have to be, John. Don't make it sound like a movie." She sat up quickly, her blonde tresses falling forward. "If you were happy in your marriage, you wouldn't be here."

"And there's my daughter, Molly, to think about." I rested my hands on my hips. "Now, I feel guilty even saying her name."

"Sounds like you should have thought a little more before we jumped into bed." She looked away from me.

"Jennifer, I'm sorry. You're amazing, but . . . " Suddenly, thinking about my marriage, about Molly, felt like lead in the pit of my gut. "I will call, and we can talk this through. I do think you'll need to get another lawyer, though."

She laughed and faced me again. "I'm happy with you."

I raised my hands. "It's not—"

"Are you worried about the ethical problem, John? That *having sex with a client* thing?" She shrugged and smiled.

Either, ethically, what we'd done didn't bother her, or she was conveying a subtle threat. I just couldn't tell.

"Don't worry. Our little secret." She lay back again, her cheeks flaring, and drew the comforter up to her chin. "And do think about it, about us. Make sure to lock the door behind you."

I didn't want to end the evening with her upset. "Jennifer . . . "

She reached over and switched off the light. In the dark, her voice drifted to me. "I'll look forward to your call."

I shuffled down the hallway and scanned the table full of documents, the untouched cheese tray, the chair where I'd let it begin. By the time I reached the Buick, my thoughts were a jumble. Draping my arms over the steering wheel, I leaned forward to rest my forehead on the back of my hands. If Cathy hadn't pissed me off, I might never have driven to Parma. I pictured Jennifer, on display in her pink underwear, and knew that no man could have resisted her. I'd been caught up in a bad combination of circumstances.

I leaned back and stared at the roof of the car. Then I bit my lip and launched forward, my fist pounding the steering wheel. Blaming anyone but me was just dishonest. I had committed adultery again. From the moment I'd agreed to meet at Jennifer's apartment, I'd known what might happen. I sat in the muted light of the parking lot for at least another ten minutes before starting the car. I shifted into gear and drove below the speed limit all the way to the highway.

The garage door seemed to rumble particularly loudly, as if to signal my late arrival. As usual, Cathy had left the kitchen light on. Even though I'd washed at Jennifer's, I used the bathroom next to the living room to scrub myself again. I checked for any trace of jam, then examined my cheeks and earlobes for any hint of whipped cream.

I tread quietly upstairs. The light on the nightstand was on. She was in bed, lying on her side, the covers drawn about her waist, and her back to me. She seemed asleep, thankfully. I undressed quietly before slipping between the sheets.

"Good time?" She kept her back to me.

"I wish."

She rolled over and sat up. "Chasing the Butcher around town?"

"I'm sorry, Cathy. Lost track of time, then stopped for a drink." Every word sounded lame.

"You missed dinner, wanting to make a point. Screw you."

Knowing where I'd been, instead of being home, with my daughter, made me squirm. "I should have called, but it was already late . . . "

"Do you really think I'm stupid?" She wrenched her face toward mine. Tears glimmered on her cheeks. She kept her voice low, like the hiss of a snake, to keep from disturbing Molly. "You're running around and lying to me."

I rose up on my elbows. I didn't recall when I'd seen her so angry, so hurt. "Don't . . . "

"If it's over, John, it's over," she said without regret, only resignation. "I can't keep doing this, please. I'm done."

She turned away and switched out the light. Her muffled sobs meant that further conversation was shut down for the night, which was fine by me. I lay there, thinking of our years together, the things we'd done. And then my thoughts drifted to Jennifer Browning and her dimly lit bedroom.

Soon, those thoughts caromed to Molly. I got out of bed to head for the bathroom, but my legs seemed to falter. Cathy was livid, and I'd hurt Molly by not being there when she wanted her dad. And Jennifer? I had no idea how to handle her or her promise to keep "our little secret." If she felt wronged and filed a grievance with the bar association, my career and marriage would unravel slowly, painfully, and publicly. Jesus, what if Frank wasn't a total nutcase and his warnings about Jennifer had some substance?

Downstairs, in my kitchen cabinet, whiskey beckoned. And sleeping on the couch, in the solitude of the living room, seemed like the right thing to do.

16

"Looks like nothing important," Marilyn said, sliding a couple of letters onto my desk.

I barely acknowledged her. Sleep had been a few hours of a whiskey-induced stupor. A graphic vision of Jennifer's Brazilian wax still hovered in front of me like a hologram. My eyes fluttered to my desk and the photo of Cathy and Molly.

"Thanks," I murmured.

Marilyn placed her arms akimbo, long turquoise earrings framing her face. "So, what's going on? You look like you're lost in space."

"Still thinking about getting beat up by that punk." Actually, the experience with Jennifer had been far more profound. I'd been beaten up before, but I'd only had sex like that once.

"Well, you can hardly tell. I mean, you look almost human."

"Only because I went down with the first punch."

"Lucky you."

I forced a laugh, and Marilyn walked back to her desk. Physically, I wasn't in bad shape, although my ribs remained bruised and painful. But, try as I might, I couldn't forget the image of Jennifer Browning's lithe, naked body. I tried to pretend that our evening together had not happened, that I hadn't actually driven to her apartment. I'd been called to court. I'd had a flat. I'd suffered a heart attack. But I couldn't escape the vision of her pink panties or the taste of whipped cream. Nor, despite my responsibilities to Cathy and Molly, could I deny the lure of Jennifer's delicate application of strawberry jam.

That morning, when Cathy had commenced her morning routine in the kitchen, I'd retreated upstairs and lingered in bed until the garage door had squeaked open. I knew that she would be on her way to drop Molly at school, then she'd take off to work. She would need time to calm down, and I needed to corral my rambling thoughts. If I failed to reassure Cathy, my marriage would be in real jeopardy. As would be my relationship with Molly. Yet Jennifer expected a call.

The telephone rang. I heard Marilyn's chipper greeting, then she quickly buzzed my extension.

"It's Frank Frederickson." Her words came in a flurry.

My hand shot for the phone. "Hello, Frank. Glad you called."

"I've got it figured out." His words were rushed.

"I'm listening. Frank?" Just talking to the guy made my office seem uncomfortably warm.

"How we'll play this. I want witness protection."

I looked out my window, at the tan brick building across the street. "For what?"

"You'll see."

"I'm not your lawyer, okay? And I've never handled this sort of thing. I can—"

"They'll wanna hear what I have to say." He coughed, then caught his breath and inhaled something.

The edge in his voice was making me nervous. "I'll get you a lawyer, or you can just tell the cops."

"No. I'm not going anywhere, not talking to anybody else."

And I had thought this would be a simple estate case, a great fee. "I'm not the one you should be talking to, Frank, not about this. Now, the estate—"

"We'll talk about everything. You need to hear me out and help me work a deal. I need you to figure out how to get me my inheritance." He inhaled again, and I half expected the scent of marijuana to waft through my phone. "I'm still not sure I can trust you, lawyer man, but we need to talk before it's too late."

"Jesus, you're confusing me. Too late for what?"

He laughed—a smoker's laugh: I heard the phlegm gurgle in his chest. "Too late for me, for the love of God. She'll stop at nothing."

I paused, listening to him breathe. "Listen to me, okay? You—"

"No, you listen to me. Watch for a text from me, later, with an address and a time. Tonight. Just you—nobody else. I can see the street, easy. Anyone else shows up, I will not be here."

I rested the phone on my cheek and stared at the photo of Cathy and Molly.

"Make a decision, lawyer man. I talk to you, or I talk to nobody."

What had I gotten myself wrapped up in? "Whatever you tell me, I'll take it to the cops, see what can be done. Understood?"

"That's why we're talking."

"C'mon, Frank. Give me some idea. What the hell is going on?"

He was silent for so long, I thought he'd hung up. Then he said, "Let's just say that the hit-and-run with her husband? The import/export business? Bullshit."

All I heard was his raspy breathing over the line, and then he hung up. Sweat was making the receiver slippery in my hand, and my temples throbbed. I stared at the phone, as though summoning Frank to call again. What the fuck was he claiming was bullshit? Jennifer's story about her husband's death had sounded legitimate. She had teared up, for Christ's sake.

I thought about phoning Bernie, but immediately dismissed the idea. What the hell was I going to tell him? If Frank did text me about where to meet, Bernie might want to take over, and Frank would run or clam up. I'd rather face an ass-kicking by Bernie than lose Frank.

Deciding what to do about Jennifer was more difficult. I had not expected that our first conversation after making love would be about her brother. But if I met with him without telling her that he'd called, she'd be livid and might march down to the Bar Association with details of our tryst. Besides, I was curious about what she would say when I mentioned Frank's oblique comments about the hit-and-run and the import/export business.

I dialed her cell, and she picked up on the second ring. "So you did call, like you promised."

"Yes, but this isn't about us, Jennifer. I heard from Frank again."

"Oh, God. What did he say this time?" She sounded exasperated, but I sensed that she was also curious.

"He wants to talk, to me, one-on-one."

"Seriously?" She clucked her tongue. "If you're meeting him, I'm going with you."

"Hold on. He was adamant, Jennifer. Not you, and no cops. Besides, do you think he'd talk if you're there?"

She didn't respond immediately, then she said, "You have a point, but Jesus, John, you didn't get an address, a phone number?"

"The call was over before I had the chance. He babbled for a while, kind of out of it, and said he'd text me later. Let's hope he does."

"Damn it." She paused, and then asked, "Did he spin any tales this time?"

I measured my words. "He claims that the hit-and-run in Tijuana, the import/export business, were bullshit."

"Total nonsense, John. He's so screwed up."

Her response came as no surprise, but I was now acutely aware that I had not heard Frank's version of the story. "He wants witness protection. I told him I know nothing about that, but he insists on talking to me."

"He's insane." She was emphatic.

I wanted her to be right. I wanted to be able to trust her. "If he follows up, I'll meet with him and call you right away."

She sighed. "And we do need to talk about us."

"I know." And part of *us* meant my Bar Association issue. "Whatever happens between you and me, I wish you'd reconsider having me as your lawyer. That makes this really complicated. I can make you a list, if you want."

"I don't want, John. We've had this discussion. I like you as my lawyer." When she continued, her tone was suggestive. "In fact, there's a lot about you that I like."

I swallowed, wishing that the picture of Cathy and Molly weren't on my desk. Cathy was beyond angry, Jennifer was beckoning, and my moral compass was wavering. "Soon, I promise. I'm still wrapping my head around everything—"

"Don't overprocess it, John. What do you want, what would make you happy? Think about it."

She hung up. I would have preferred that our conversation had been in person, over a drink or a cup of coffee, so that I could have read her expression. I wasn't sure what had just happened. But it was clear that I would have to trust her regarding my ethical concerns—and more. There was nothing to prevent her from contacting Cathy and suggesting that the two of them meet for a nice, long lunch.

Concentrating on work was difficult; a drink would have been nice, but the distinct possibility of a text from Frank meant that there would be no leaving my desk. I filled Marilyn in on my conversation with him and buried myself in some bullshit paperwork. Lunch rolled around, and Marilyn picked up some tolerable sandwiches from a dingy café downstairs.

"You sure you're okay?" She set my corned beef, in greasy deli wrap, on the desk.

Marilyn was such a decent person, and she actually gave a damn about me, so I felt a pang of guilt. If she knew the truth about a certain blonde, she wouldn't be so kindly disposed. "This thing with Frank . . . "

"Maybe he'll actually get back to you."

I knew that I'd be worthless the rest of the day, my mind ricocheting between Frank and Jennifer and Cathy. "Why don't you knock off for the afternoon? No sense in both of us staring at the phone."

"I'm pretty good at it. Remember, I'm single."

"Well, go shimmy past a construction site, see what happens."

"Thanks for the dating advice." She grinned. "I'm outta here, but call me if you forget how to turn off your computer."

The door clicked shut behind her. I was glad to be alone in the quiet of my office. I shuffled some papers around, drank some coffee, took a piss, popped antacids, and watched the clock. Repeat. And, during every long minute, I was totally preoccupied with the mess of my personal life. What the hell should I do? As five o'clock rolled around, I was about to abandon hope that Frank would text. I needed to retreat to Cena for a stiff drink.

Then the cell phone buzzed. A concise message read *2nite, 6, 103 Findley, 2nd flr.*

Frank, Frank, Frank. If he'd been in front of me, I might have planted one on his bristly cheek. Google Maps located the address—a side street in the old Tremont neighborhood. Even at rush hour, I'd have no trouble making it on time, but I still hustled down to the garage.

Soon, I was tooling past abandoned storefronts and mom-and-pop shops that budding entrepreneurs had transformed into glam restaurants and popular nightclubs. Contemporary housing projects had sprouted in the midst of faded neighborhoods. But Tremont's tough underbelly was still evident in the wandering homeless and abandoned cars, the stray dogs. I wasn't surprised to find that Frank was hidden somewhere beneath the long shadows cast by the spires of orthodox churches erected decades ago.

When I reached the address he'd given me, I paused outside to take in a decrepit double that was surely the neighborhood eyesore in a block of boarded-up houses and trash-strewn yards. A dirt path, bordered by crabgrass, led to a teetering porch. Dark curtains covered every window.

I rang the buzzer for the upper level and, hearing no ring, rapped loudly on the dry wooden door. Nothing. I double-checked the address and glanced at my watch. Definitely on time. On impulse, I tried the knob. The door was unlocked; it swung open with a firm shove. A dark staircase led to the upper apartment. I called Frank's name.

There was no answering voice, no sudden footstep.

Maybe he was just asleep. I called out again, but only a distant horn broke the silence. My breathing became shallow. There was a glimmer of light upstairs, perhaps a low-wattage lamp or a tendril of sunlight defying the protective curtains. I pulled out my cell and used its muted light to guide me up the bare steps. Turning back just didn't seem right.

My footsteps seemed unnaturally loud as I creaked up the stairs. The stairway, bordered by peeling wallpaper, opened up into what appeared to be a living room. A large easy chair, a milk crate that served as a table, and a small television with tin foil balled on the end of the antenna seemed to be the only furnishings. A burned-out candle rested on the milk crate, illuminated by a ray of light that penetrated a narrow gap in the thick curtains. As my eyes adjusted to the gloom, I realized there was a guy sitting in the chair. The high, curved back hid him, but an arm dangled over the side, a strip of elastic tube knotted around the bicep. Frank had been shooting up and nodded off.

"Frank?" I asked, moving toward him. Then he was there, right in front of me, and I wanted to avert my gaze but couldn't. His empty eyes stared back at me, his throat parted by a deep and jagged gash. My shoes slid in the slick blood that pooled at the base of the chair as I tried to back away. A cluster of black flies had already found him and frenzied about, just as they had in his father's raw torso. I pivoted and staggered down the dark stairs to the yard.

Frank sure as fuck wasn't going to be talking to anybody.

17

I was in a daze when the crime scene investigators took my fingerprints, in addition to imprints and photos of my shoes. But the fog
quickly lifted when Bernie stormed from that house of death and
hustled across the weed-choked yard. His eyes blazed. "You fucked up."

"Bernie, it—"

"Shut up!" His face shook and a clenched fist jabbed the air with
each word. "I talked to you about this, about calling me."

I took a step back. "There wasn't a choice; he told me he wouldn't
talk to you. Christ, Bernie, I called as soon as I found him."

"Yeah? Well, he's dead."

"He said he wanted to meet and tell me shit about Jennifer, then
he hung up. He texted later, with an address, but it was only an hour
ago." Stifling hot air drifted in from Lake Erie, and curious neighbors
ringed the cordon of yellow police tape. There were a lot of ratty
T-shirts and hoodies on display.

"You had a fucking hour. Do you call me? No, you drive here with
your thumb up your ass. You knew that gang was looking for him."

"Well, they found him. I mean, it had to be them, right?"

"No, I think it was a couple nuns from Saint Joe's, decided to go cut some guy's throat for fun." He looked back at the house, at the blue uniforms milling about. "My guess is that the Andar Feo got their dough from the dear departed. Maybe they're out looking for your girlfriend now."

His comment hit pay dirt. Damn. He'd kick my ass if he found out the truth. But what he said scared the shit out of me. "He didn't have her address, not even her phone. He couldn't have told them if he wanted to."

"Relax. It's not their MO. They cut up the girl to send a message to the guy, remember?" He pointed back at the house, and I relived the silent sight of Frank, the iron scent of his blood. "They already gave him a fuckin' message."

"What do I do now, Bernie?" Christ, it seemed like we were back in high school again.

"Well, you already trotted through the blood pool. I'd call that enough for one night. Go home to Cathy."

"Someone needs to tell Jennifer."

"A car's already there, John. Let the cops handle it; they're pros. Unless there's something you're not telling me."

"Jesus, Bernie, no. It's just that . . . her father, now her brother. She is my client, and I was the one who found Frank. Seems like she should hear something from me."

"If you feel compelled to call her, do that from your car." He ran a hand over his face and, when he spoke again, was calmer. "You know, while you're driving home to see your wife and kid."

"Yeah," I muttered, not yet ready to face Cathy. I still had no idea what to say to her. Or maybe I was afraid of the cutting words she might cast at me.

"So walk through it again, your conversation with Frank."

I shrugged, trying to recall every word. "He said he wanted immunity, that their import/export business and the hit-and-run that killed Jennifer's husband was all bullshit."

"So you called her and not me after Frank hung up. What the

fuck is wrong with you?" He cocked an eyebrow at me. "How well do you know her?"

It struck me that I wasn't so sure anymore. All I really knew about her was that she was awesome in bed. God, did I wish there had been the opportunity to talk with Frank. "Well, hell, Bernie, I'd pick her over her brother. Who would you believe?"

He scrunched his face, as though the answer wasn't clear to him, then turned and looked back at the mottled house. "The fact that they killed him here might help. Maybe they got sloppy. We'll find somethin'."

"Will you let me know everything you turn up, Bernie?"

He looked at me in disbelief. "Why, so you can fuck it up? This is a police investigation and, last I knew, you don't have a uniform. We've had this talk."

"I just mean anything I can pass along to Jennifer. Maybe you'll find the money . . . "

"Odds of that are zero to shit. And we'll call her directly, whenever we need to." He looked away, back at Frank's apartment again. "What you saw up there, Johnny . . . I think it's a good night for you to get some sleep. Just go the fuck home."

"We've had this talk, too. I'm okay." I remembered slipping in blood before, long ago, trying to adjust my dad's position. His head being so near the toilet didn't seem right.

Bernie grimaced and took a beat. "I'll need to see you tomorrow about what happened here. There'll be a lot of pissed-off people when they find out you didn't call me, particularly since you made a mosh pit of the crime scene. I'll try to keep a lid on it."

Over his shoulder, I saw Wendy Coufalik duck under the yellow tape and burst toward us. My sphincter tightened.

"So you knew two of the vics now and were first on the scene here. Coincidence?"

Her face was inches from mine, her breath the odor of stale coffee.

"Jesus, I explained everything to Bernie."

"I'll fill you in," he said. "I like the Mexican gang for this one. I'll be surprised if this kid's death is related to his old man's."

She ignored him and snapped at me. "You played Lone Ranger on this? Sounds like obstruction of an investigation to me."

"I was just trying to help." That hadn't quite worked.

Bernie stepped in, thank God, and said to Coufalik, "Let him go; I'll fill you in."

She looked at him for a long moment and then turned to me. "I may want to talk to you directly. I assume you don't have any travel plans."

Her implication was unsettling. "I'm not going anywhere. I—"

"Get the fuck outta here." Bernie's eyes drilled into me. "Home. Straight home."

I understood that Bernie didn't want me attempting to justify anything to Coufalik, so I turned toward my car. I caught my breath when Vanessa Edwards seemed to step out of nowhere, a cameraman behind her. "Mr. Coleman, you were present when the Butcher's first victim was found, and we've been informed that you just discovered the body of his son. Are the murders related? Any comment?"

I couldn't believe this was happening. I nearly turned around, preferring to have Coufalik chew me a new one. But I raised my hands at Vanessa and walked on, shaking my head, wanting only to escape in my Buick.

"Hey, just doing my job. You're not clamming up on me, are you?"

"C'mon, Vanessa, no comment. Ask the cops for a statement." I plowed onward.

"Wait a minute, John. Off the record." She lowered the microphone, waved the cameraman away, and stuck to my shoulder. She was damn good at quick-stepping in high heels. "What the hell's going on? I've seen you at three crime scenes now—what's your tie-in?"

The last thing I needed was the press crawling up my ass, scrounging for details. But pissing off Vanessa Edwards would not be a good idea, so I gave her an answer that seemed like a plausible reason why an interview was out of bounds. "Look, I can't make any comment because a police investigation is ongoing."

She looked skeptical. "I'm just asking about you. You were at the Lakewood scene, Rocky River—"

"Vanessa, look, that's really all I can say." My Buick was now just a few feet away.

"C'mon, what the hell's this all about?"

I opened the car door and settled inside, wishing I knew the answer. I gave Vanessa a wave and started the engine. I'd only driven a couple of miles, debating whether to go home or to a bar, when my cell rang. I fished it out of the cup holder. It looked like I wouldn't need to call Jennifer; she was calling me.

There was no greeting. "You need to come over, John. There's something you have to see."

I knew one thing: nothing good would come of visiting Jennifer at her apartment again, even on the night of her brother's murder. "Jennifer, I'm really sorry about your brother, but this may not be the best time—"

"This isn't about us, John." There was a sharp intake of breath. "It's about your wife and daughter."

18

Jennifer hung up before I said another word. A round-trip to Parma would stall my return home, and Cathy would be primed to explode. I couldn't very well call her and tell her about Frank's death, because then she'd know that there was no reason *not* to come home. I'd have to come up with yet one more creative excuse, and Jennifer would need to understand that my visit had to be brief.

Something had surely rattled her about Cathy and Molly, on the very night of her brother's murder, and I wondered what the hell was waiting for me in her apartment. There had been enough surprises for one day. Powering off the cell in case Cathy decided to phone, I dismissed the notion that she might have contacted Jennifer and confronted her, point blank, about us, because Cathy would not have known how to contact her.

When Jennifer opened the door to her unit, I noticed that her face was drained of color. Despite their estrangement, the reality of Frank's brutal death had to come as a shock. I dropped my keys on a recessed shelf in an alcove near the door and awkwardly extended my arms for a hug that I would keep as nonsexual as possible. She stepped into my embrace, and my fingers brushed her satiny hair. She was wearing flannel pajamas, buttoned at the neck. I tried blocking out the thought that she still managed to look sexy as hell.

We slowly separated, and she took a deep breath. "The cops said that he did text you?"

"Yeah, late in the day. No message, except where and when to meet."

"Jesus, John, if you'd gotten there any sooner, you might have walked in on it."

"I hadn't really thought about that." I imagined Cathy and Molly, on the sofa in our living room, listening to the cops explain that my throat had been slashed in some Tremont hovel. "I'm really sorry, Jennifer, but I can't stay. You said—"

"I checked the mail after the police left." I followed her into the dining room, and she pointed to a large white envelope and a stack of photos on the table.

The top photograph was of Frank. My eyes drifted to his thin neck, and I recalled the dark rivulets of blood. Beneath his photo was a candid shot of Jennifer, taken outside of a Heinen's grocery. The next photo was of Mary, in the parking lot at Ed's Eggs. The print looked like it had been taken with a telephoto lens, because Mary seemed completely unaware that she was being photographed. I glanced back at the photos of Jennifer and Frank—these, too, seemed to be surveillance photographs.

The next photo, however, stopped me cold: a shot of Marilyn, passing through the lobby of the Singer Building, carrying her usual handbag and sporting a pair of vibrant earrings. I stared for a minute, trying to understand why someone would send Jennifer a photo of my secretary. Like the others, Marilyn appeared not to have known that she was the focus of a viewfinder.

The following photo was of me, seated on the patio at Cena on a sunny day. I turned to Jennifer. "What the fuck?" Someone had taken the shot from near the intersection with Prospect Avenue. There was a cocktail in front of me, and I was staring at the action on the street.

The last photo, though, turned me numb. Cathy and Molly. In Cathy's Chevy, at the end of our driveway. Based on the angle, it appeared that someone sitting in a parked car along the street had taken the shot. I swallowed hard.

"That's your wife, daughter . . . "

I felt oddly sorry for Jennifer—the flannel-pajama-clad beauty I'd made love to, smacked with the reality of my marriage on the day of her brother's death. "Yes. Cathy, Molly, in our driveway."

"I recognized them from the picture in your office. Cathy looks older here."

"That one was taken a long time ago. She still looks good." The words caught in my throat.

Jennifer's lips tightened. "I'm not saying she doesn't."

I picked up the envelope. Jennifer's address was handwritten, and there was no return. "Any idea . . . ?"

She shook her head. "John, I'm scared."

I felt detached, paralyzed. Cathy—cowering behind the living room curtains, locking up, double-checking, terrified the Butcher was out there. And my Molly. Had my actions somehow put them in danger?

I stepped away from Jennifer. "This is bullshit. I'm calling Salvatore."

"What's it mean, John?"

"No fucking idea. Looks like someone's trying to scare us, scare you."

"But why . . . your wife and daughter?"

I shook my head, powered up the cell, and dialed Bernie. He answered on the second ring, and that was the last good thing about the conversation.

"Where the hell are you?"

"Jennifer's. Look, I know what you said . . . " My voice hushed, I headed into the living room and told him about the photos.

"You are a complete moron."

"You can kick my ass later, but these fuckin' photos—her, me, Frank, Cathy, for Christ's sake. *Cathy*. Bernie, there's a picture of her and Molly."

He didn't say anything for a few seconds. "Glad you're so concerned about your family. Bring me all this shit tomorrow. Let me guess, you fingered the photos and the envelope."

"Jesus, Bernie, so did Jennifer. It's not like—"

"You're a regular Sherlock Holmes. Bring it to me and, right now, zip up your pants and get the fuck outta there."

I lowered my voice still further, barely whispering. "It ain't like that, Bernie. Jesus, her brother just got murdered, now these frickin' photos . . ."

"I can't fucking hear you. Look, asshole, you're puttin' yourself in a situation. If it blows apart, don't come crying to me."

He hung up, and I returned to Jennifer's side, flicking my cell off again because I just could not handle a call from Cathy. "He wants me to bring these to him in the morning."

"God, I need a drink. Could you pour some wine?"

Nodding, I walked into the kitchen. The mini wooden rack on the kitchen counter was bare, so I swung open the refrigerator door in case she had a half-empty bottle. Nothing. I called to her, "Outta luck, Jen."

She strolled into the kitchen and leaned against the counter. Her lower lip trembled a bit. "Would you mind running out . . . ?"

"I really need to get home, Jennifer. I'm sorry." I was already going to be way late—if that even mattered at this point.

"It's just up at the corner; a three-minute stroll. Please? I know you can't stay."

She looked so vulnerable. There was no way that Cathy hadn't locked every door and window. She and Molly would be safe until I got home. Despite knowing that Cathy would be beyond the boiling point, I nodded. "Let's hope the convenience store has a decent bottle."

She brightened, her eyes finally showing some light. "You're very kind, John. I'm just so spaced out . . ."

"Don't worry about it."

She laid a perfectly manicured hand on my arm. "I should probably eat something, too. After the police left, I wasn't hungry, but now . . ."

"How's a turkey sandwich sound? Homemade—by Subway."

"Perfect. Take my keys. The apartment's on the silver ring. And be careful, John."

I locked the door behind me and walked outside. Despite the balmy night, I felt chilled and sick with fear. Maybe it was the fact that I'd just been skating in Frank's goddamn blood, maybe it was the photos, but I was jumpy as all hell. There was still a serial killer out there, and I sure as shit didn't want somebody blindsiding me while I was running a damn errand. *Did you hear about John Coleman? Yeah, they found him with his nuts sliced off, stuffed right inside a turkey hoagie from Subway.* I felt like a punk-ass for letting myself wonder if maybe I should have driven all of about three hundred yards.

The convenience store had a fifteen-dollar bottle of red that I fig-ured wouldn't taste like rotgut. I felt like screaming at the girl behind the Subway next door to just slap some turkey inside a loaf of bread and stop reciting optional condiments. When the bagged sandwich was finally in hand, I clutched the wine bottle by the neck to swing it like a club if some maniac attacked me and tried to cut off my dick and my head. About halfway back to the apartment, somebody slammed a car door and startled me. It was nothing, just some guy going into the CVS.

When I entered Jennifer's apartment, she was sitting at her dining table, now clear of her father's papers. She had set out two plates, wine glasses, and a corkscrew.

I set the sandwich and the wine on the table. "I really should go."

"Five minutes, John, that's all. I have some questions. You proba-bly haven't eaten either. Half a sandwich."

"Five minutes." My eyes drifted to the small desk and the photos of Martha, Oyster, Frank, and the late hubby. My skin crawled; Jen-nifer now seemed to have an austere shrine to dead relatives. And I'd found two of them and screwed one. I opened the wine and filled both of our glasses.

"This makes me the sole beneficiary on Dad's insurance, right?"

For someone whose brother had just been murdered, Jennifer seemed incredibly detached. Certain people can appear as though they never sweat. She looked like an animated statue, chiseled from ice.

I sat across from her and took a sip of wine. There were so many cryptic depths to her, and I was just muddling about on the surface. What was the face of the real Jennifer Browning? "I'll send Frank's death certificate to the insurance company as soon as I can."

She nodded and turned the wineglass with her delicate fingers, staring at the burgundy reflection on the table. "I suppose it will take awhile?"

"It will. A claim this size, they'll check everything out."

She took a bite of her sandwich and nodded. After she swallowed, she set the sandwich on the table and leaned back in her chair. "I understand your decision. I saw the concern on your face when you looked at those photos. You love her."

I couldn't shake the photo of Cathy innocently backing her Chevy out of the driveway, Molly strapped into the passenger seat. "We've been married a long time. I just don't want to hurt them. My daughter . . . she had a rough time of it. Foster care and all of that. I don't know that she could handle it if our marriage fell apart."

"It's okay to say that you love her." Jennifer took a sip of wine. She had already steeled herself for this moment, I realized. There were no tears, just resignation. "Somehow, I thought we'd be more than a one-night stand."

"We can still be—"

"Friends?" She laughed. "Go home to your family, John. Take care of them." She shoved the sandwich away from her and pulled the wine glass close, near the edge of the table. "We're okay. Really, we are."

The way that she mouthed those words struck me as odd, but I chalked the feeling up to the blood I'd waded in and the disconcerting photos I couldn't explain. I had clearly been given a cue to say good night. I grabbed the photos and envelope but stopped at the door. Curse me, but despite every word, gazing at her made me remember being wrapped in her sheets.

"Tonight probably wasn't the best time for us to talk," I said.

Jennifer shrugged. "Don't prolong anything, John. That will just make it more difficult for me."

"It's not just my family. I don't want to hurt you, either." I remembered Martha's hysteria the night I'd ended our relationship. So maybe Jennifer was right: the sooner, the better, for all of us. If only I could stop thinking of her naked on top of me, the way she had moaned, the way she had tasted.

"And you don't have to worry; I won't hurt you." She nodded her head once, twice. "You trust me, don't you?"

I wasn't clear whether she was discussing my emotions or the leverage she had over me. But there was only one answer, in spite of every lingering doubt. "Of course."

"Glad that's not an issue." She picked up the sandwich but paused before taking a bite. "Make sure the door locks behind you. Good night."

I retrieved my keys from the shelf, walked into the hallway, and down to the parking lot. An evening breeze chilled my neck. With a glance over my shoulder, I turned on the cell. It was half past midnight, and Cathy had called. Twice, in fact. I prayed that nothing had happened to my family while I'd been eating a turkey hoagie and sipping wine with Jennifer.

Cathy answered on the first ring. "You son of a bitch."

"I'm sorry. Oyster's son was killed tonight." I reached the Buick, clambered inside, and locked the doors.

"I know. It's been on the news for hours. Where the hell have you been?"

"Cathy . . . " It seemed as though words were fighting not to come out of my gaping mouth.

Telling her then about the photographs would have been a mistake. There was no explanation, and she'd spend the night awake, worrying.

"Never mind," she said. "I don't need your lies. There's a monster out there, and you act like nothing's going on. Getting into fights, staying out all fucking night, and you don't even think to let me know you're okay?"

"Just wait—"

"I'm not done! Stay out! Wherever you are, I don't care. But don't you dare come home."

I started to lie, to tell her I'd gotten drunk after finding Frank, but she stampeded over me.

"The doors are locked, and I'm going to bed. Molly's asleep. Don't you think the Butcher kills these people at night, in the dark? How do you know you're not being followed now, running around like you do?"

My eyes pivoted to the rearview mirror and out the car windows. She had no idea how close to the truth she was—the photo of me, the one of her and Molly in the Chevy. "Cathy, I'm sober, and I'll come straight home. We can talk, promise."

"It's too late. I don't want you here."

"Don't do this, Cathy. I'll sleep on the couch again, if you want." She didn't understand how much I suddenly wanted to be there, with her and Molly.

"If you're with someone, just stay with her. If you're alone, get a room. I'm sure you know where you can rent one by the hour."

"You're out of line, Cathy."

"Me? That's a laugh." I expected that both of her earlobes were bright red, but there was no tremor in her voice. "Molly cried herself to sleep tonight, worried about you. Wonders what the hell you were doing in Tremont with a dead man."

"Just let me come home. I'll explain."

"You have no idea how much I wanted you here. I wanted you to check the locks, watch over our daughter."

"Give me the chance."

"I . . . " Her voice broke. "I don't need you tonight."

"But Molly—"

"She's finally sleeping. Give her that."

She wasn't going to change her mind. I scanned the dark silhouettes of parked vehicles once again and broke the silence. "I'll go to the office, sleep on the couch. But call me if you need anything, anything at all."

"I don't care where you go, John. And what I needed was to have you here to say good night to Molly."

"You made your point." She'd be safe tonight, no different from the nights when I'd been there, or when I hadn't. "Let's talk tomorrow, after you've calmed down."

"I'm perfectly calm, damn it. But you're right, we'll talk, because I will not keep doing this."

"When you come home from school, I'll be there. We can sit in the living room. Molly will be at practice."

"Perfect. I'll make a fucking casserole, and we can light a candle." She sniffled, and I gnawed at my lower lip. Why did I think it made any difference where we sat?

"Don't do anything stupid tonight, John. And if you were with somebody else, make sure you find the spine to tell me that tomorrow."

19

There was a sudden rap on the office door. My eyes popped open.

"Coffee's on!"

I'd left a note for Marilyn, in case she came in before I awoke, which was exactly what had happened. A vision of Frank roared at me; I sprang up on the lumpy couch. Finding one body like that was enough, but a father *and* a son? To say that sleep had been fitful would be an understatement. I dressed, thankful that I'd hung the shirt so it didn't look like I'd worn it for multiple days—maybe just two. A hot shower would have been a dream, let alone fresh underwear.

I walked stiffly to the coffee alcove. As Marilyn handed me a cup of steaming java, she eyed the shirt and the stubble on my face. "Just so you know, you look like hell. This about the Frederickson boy? The news said you found him."

Thinking of Frank without envisioning that bloody gash in his throat was impossible, but for Marilyn to assume that I'd wound up on the office couch because of my hellish night was a relief. "Yeah. Pretty flipped out and drank way too much to drive. Seeing Oyster, then Frank. Damn."

"And two murders, like we're cursed." She toyed with a white feather in her earring. "That poor girl . . . "

"Girl? What do you mean?"

She looked up at me, surprised. "You haven't . . . "

"What?"

"I heard on the news, on the way in. There was another killing, the body dumped right downtown." Marilyn crossed her arms as if she were hugging herself.

I brushed past her desk toward the dinky old television set in my office. Grabbing the remote, I punched buttons to hone in on a station airing a report on the killing. The newscaster was a young guy of Greek descent who emphasized every sensational word: the *torso* of a *dismembered* white *female* had been found in an *alley* connected to a valet parking lot, one used by patrons of the popular East Fourth Street *entertainment district*. The police were *withholding* further information, pending notification of *next of kin*.

"Doesn't seem possible." Marilyn had trailed behind me. Her beige dress seemed appropriately somber. "There're hundreds of people on Fourth any night of the week."

"The body had to have been dumped after the bars closed." East Fourth, where I'd sat at Cena, oblivious to the fact that someone was snapping my picture. Pictures. Cathy and Molly, Jennifer. There was no way that Cathy would have left the house last night, no matter how angry she was with me, not with our daughter in bed. But Jennifer? Christ, could she have been so upset when I left that she'd gone out?

"Excuse me, Marilyn, I need to make a call." I put a hand on her back and guided her toward the door. She looked perplexed, but that wasn't my concern. There was no way I could allow her to overhear my conversation with a certain blonde.

Jennifer didn't pick up her landline or cell, so I left a message asking her to call me right away. Sinking into the chair, I cupped my hands over my face. Whether driven by concern or guilt, I needed to know that Jennifer was okay and not lying naked and cut up in a damn alley. Bernie Salvatore would know all of the grisly details, but he'd be all over my ass about my late-night visit to her apartment.

The safe bet was Jack Corrigan. He'd make a call to somebody still on the force and tell me what he found out, no bullshit about it. He answered on the second ring. "Yeah?"

"Jack, John Coleman. I need a favor."

"Rough go last night. Saw about Frank Frederickson on the news."

"But there's been another murder, some girl off East Fourth."

"I know. Watchin' it on the TV now."

"Can you make a call, find out if it's Jennifer Browning?"

"Why the hell would you think that?"

"She wasn't acting like herself, after finding out about her brother." There was no need to tell Jack anything more.

"How do you know that?"

Fuck. "I saw her."

"So you are gettin' some ass."

"C'mon, Jack, don't bust my balls. It's a lot more involved than you think. I'll fill you in later."

"Can't wait to hear." He took a sip of what I assumed was coffee. "Don't piss on yourself. I'll get back to you."

He hung up, and I wallowed into the leather of my chair. I was sweating into my already gamy shorts, and the tepid coffee roiled in my stomach. I considered calling Jennifer at work, although I thought it highly unlikely that she would have gone into work under the circumstances. I was about to try calling her again when my cell buzzed. Jennifer. I lay my head back and answered.

"I didn't expect to hear from you, John. Sorry I didn't pick up; I was in the shower."

"Did you see the news? They found a dead woman, a white woman."

"I know, but what . . . "

"I thought, maybe, that you'd gone out." Suddenly, my call didn't seem to make any sense. "Sorry, I was . . . worried. I mean, your brother, those photos."

A few seconds slipped away, and I felt like a fool, but she said, "Thanks for caring, John. Last night was tough. For a lot of reasons."

There was an empty silence between us until, finally, I said, "I just had to know that you were all right."

"Getting the wine for me, that was nice. I'm sorry I made you late again, but those pictures . . . "

"Cathy's upset."

"That's my fault. I'm sorry." She sounded genuinely sympathetic.

"No, no . . . We've been having some problems." I leaned forward, elbows on my desk. Jesus, what the hell was I thinking, saying that? Was I going to use Jennifer as my marriage counselor? "Look, I've gotta go. I'm just glad you're okay."

"And I'm glad you called, John." There was that honeyed voice again. "Remember what I said, about making yourself happy. If you ever want to talk, or anything, you know how to reach me."

She rang off. I sat for a long minute, as confused as ever, knowing that she was apparently leaving a door open. But what had Frank wanted to confide in me about his enigmatic sister? I knew that I shouldn't even be wondering, because my attention should have been riveted on my upcoming living room chat with Cathy. And what that would mean for me and Molly.

When I called Jack to tell him that Jennifer was okay, his phone line was busy. He was probably on the line with an old crony. Jack didn't own a cell—*damn people can hunt you down wherever you are*—so connecting with him took me a couple of tries.

"She's okay, Jack. Just talked to her."

"Yeah, they told me it ain't your girl, but there might be somethin' quirky about the murder."

We've got slashed-up bodies littered across town, missing heads and arms and legs and dicks, and he's calling this killing *quirky*? "What the hell's that mean, Jack?"

"Don't know for sure. The guy I talked to is gonna run down some rumors and get back to me. I'll call you when I know."

Fuck. It wasn't yet ten o'clock, and I already needed a drink. Jack was always good for an early tipple. Plus, I could swing by the Lakewood Police Department and drop off the photos for Salvatore. "What about lunch? We can talk then."

"People keep seein' us hanging out, they're gonna start rumors. But it's on me this time."

"You don't—"

"Hey, I ain't no charity case. Plus, I wanna find out how good this broad is in the sack."

He hung up.

With Cathy at work, I'd have plenty of time to sneak in— into my own home—and clean up before meeting Jack. On the way out, I decided to tell Marilyn about the photos. She was hunched over her desk, earrings dangling along her cheeks, while she made notes on the pages of a brief that I'd asked her to proofread. She raised her head as I approached.

"Where you off to, sport?"

"Shouldn't that be Mr. Sport?" I grinned, wishing that I could keep the mood light. "Look, I need to tell you something, but I want you to know right up front that it's nothing to get upset about."

"Okay, I'm upset." She leaned back in her chair and rested her hands on the desktop. "You finally going to tell me what's been happening?"

"I don't know, Marilyn." I leaned into the file cabinet next to her desk. "This is probably nothing, but Jennifer Browning received some pictures in the mail. Shots of her, her brother, and me. Cathy and Molly. And one of you."

Marilyn's face flushed pink. "You gotta be shitting me."

"I know, it's weird, right?" I stepped away from the file cabinet. "They're in my car. I'm dropping them off with Bernie Salvatore now."

"Jesus, John." She cast a glance toward the door, the feather in her earring fluttering.

"Notify building security, tell them what happened so they'll keep an eye out."

"I though you said there was nothing to worry about."

I raised my hands. "Just being cautious. If you want some time off . . . "

"So I can sit home by myself and watch for strange photographers? I'm better off in the building, all these people around. With these killings, the security guys act like this is the White House." She looked at me pointedly. "Is there something else, besides these murders? Something with you? You haven't been yourself since you got involved in this mess."

"Relax, Marilyn. I'll call you after lunch." I already felt like taking the rest of the day off.

"I've known you for a long time—"

I headed for the door. "Trust me. Everything's under control."

After dropping the photos off with the Lakewood Police, I would join Jack for a lunch. Then I would probably take the rest of the afternoon off to steel myself for the parlay with Cathy. We would sit as husband and wife in our tidy living room, lock eyes across the figurines and the Bible, and I had no idea what was going to happen.

20

"She was a copycat killing."

"The Gates Mills girl?"

We were at the Parkview Cafe, a longtime hideaway with decent food and generous pours, tucked away at the end of a residential street in a decaying blue-collar neighborhood.

"Who the hell you think I'm talkin' about, Queen Elizabeth?" Jack took a swig.

"I mean, I don't get it. Now somebody's copying the Butcher?"

"No, the Butcher is copying the Torso Murderer. My guy told me that the Butcher did the Gates Mills girl just the way Torso murdered a woman back in nineteen fuckin' thirty-seven."

"How'd they ID her?" I leaned into the red bumper that fronted the long wooden bar.

"Left her purse, right where her head should have been. The Butcher wanted us to know who she was, just like with Oyster. Robbery wasn't the motive; her credit cards and cash weren't touched."

The bartender, a young, perky girl with stringy blonde hair and breasts barely contained by her V-neck, gestured toward Jack's shot glass, and he nodded. Determined to stick with beer, I asked for a bottle, letting my gaze wander over the profusion of faded sports memorabilia and dated photos of local celebrities that lined the varnished pine walls. We perused our menus, then fixed on the TV above the bar when the noon news came on. The lead story was about the two murders in one night, Frank and the Fourth Street girl.

The screen caught the bartender's attention, and then she shook her head. "This is gonna kill us. Dinner business is already shot. Why can't they catch the son of a bitch?"

"Don't give up yet, honey," Jack said, flipping through the menu. "The way he's piling up bodies, he just might make a mistake."

"As long as it's not me."

"C'mon," I said, "You've got the frickin' Fraternal Order of Police right down the street."

"Still, I'm careful. I used to close all by myself. Now my brother comes in to watch my back."

I ordered pierogis, Jack a ham and cheese with fries. The bartender was like everybody else in town, fixated by the uncertainty of it all. A guy from a bar in Lakewood, a beach in Rocky River, a park in Shaker, and now a girl from Gates Mills. There was no pattern, not by sex or age or race or anything. If the Butcher wanted to terrorize a community, chalk that one up for him.

The bartender plunked the beers on the bar, and I drew my mug toward me. "Maybe it was coincidence. I mean, they cut up Oyster, too, and the others. Maybe this time, what was done just happened to match the old case."

"Shoulda let you eat your lunch first, because it isn't pretty." Jack took another sip of whiskey and stared into the mirror behind the bar. "No coincidence, Johnny. He left a telltale sign, matching exactly what the Torso Killer did. Her asshole was stretched out, and a man's pants pocket was stuffed in her rectum. Not somethin' you see every day, or want to."

Jack and I didn't say anything for a while, just glancing at the TV. The bartender approached, carrying our food, and slid the whitish plates onto the bar. I decided to join Jack in a shot.

"But why do that, copy a murder from so long ago?" I couldn't get the raw image out of my mind.

"Who knows? Go ask Salvatore's girlfriend, the so-called expert. I told you, it's impossible to figure these freaks out." Jack swallowed a bite of his sandwich. "I'll tell you something else, somethin' not made public back then, but one of the Butcher's kills from the '70s was a copycat too."

"Whaddya mean?"

"What I mean is the Butcher hacked somebody up then, too, just the way the Torso Murderer did years ago. It was the only murder where Torso carved out the guts but left the heart. That's exactly what the Butcher did, more than three decades later. Then, last night, another one."

"Some kind of tribute?"

"Who knows?"

Above the bar, near the TV, hung a framed copy of the *PD* from 1948, proclaiming the Cleveland Indians' victory over the Boston Braves in the World Series. Before my time—hell, my generation was more accustomed to serial killers than championships. "Any leads with the Gates Mills kid?"

"They got jack shit. Nothing links the vics. A different type of knife was used every time. The bodies were cut up different, dumped in different spots, and each vic was a different type of person. They haven't even identified the bodies from Rocky River or Shaker. Unless the Butcher slips up, he could just disappear again."

"So what you told the bartender, about him making a mistake, you think that's bullshit."

"I said that to make her feel better. This Butcher's too damn careful. Look, if we can't catch the son of a bitch, maybe the best thing is if he does like before: stops. Killed five in a row, *bing, bing, bing*, then vanished."

"So that leaves one more murder to go, best case. Not exactly a good ending for whoever victim number five happens to be."

Jack gave me a piercing stare. "Still worried about Blondie?"

"C'mon, Jack. Her and every woman I care about." I knew that he would ask about Cathy, so I decided to just put it on the table. "Cathy tossed my ass out last night."

Jack tilted back in his chair, exposing the white grizzle flecking the underside of his jaw. "This is supposed to be the part where I let out a big sigh. 'The difficulty in life is the choice.'"

"I don't know . . . "

He chortled and looked at me in disbelief. "For Christ's sake, they stop teaching literature? Only one of the great Irish novelists, George Moore. One of ours, and you don't know him?"

"So you were an English major—studied by candlelight, right?" I fixed on a faded color photo behind the bar of the Kardiac Kids, the Browns' legends from 1980. Guys who had played their guts out and earned Cleveland some respect, three decades ago.

"Funny, Johnny Boy, but those words are as wise as they come."

"And what lesson is it I'm supposed to learn from the words of the eminent Mr. Moore?"

He shrugged. "How're you gonna watch out for both of 'em? 'Less you can be two places at once. The difficult choice, dumbass."

I cut a cheese pierogi in half, let it sit. "I don't know what you're talkin' about, Jack. Cathy and me—"

"You gonna bullshit me? I goddamn helped raise you, and you're gonna bullshit me?"

"Jack . . . "

"I can't live your life. I know what the right choice is, but I can't make it for you."

Whenever he'd given me advice, the words tended to sink in. My reflection in the mirror, a man in the fourth quarter of life, stared back at me. "I'm talking with Cathy, okay? I wanna keep things together."

"You sounded off base this morning, when you called," he said. "Worried about the hot piece you've been sniffin' after."

"Of course I was worried. She—"

"Meanwhile, the missus is layin' up in your marital bed, freezing her ass off because her man walked out."

"Hey, she threw me out."

He laughed out loud, like he'd just heard the funniest damn joke ever. "Yeah, right. This was all her fault."

I gulped down the rest of my shot.

Jack tapped his big knotty finger against the bar. "Clear to me you didn't listen. I warned you not to get sucked into this thing. Warned you clear as hell, and now you're not thinkin' straight."

"You're just wrong, Jack."

He eyed me as if I had failed in not finding the strength to stay away from the entire mess.

I eyed him right back. "And Jennifer . . . that's—"

"—the one you've been fucking."

"I'm not answering that."

"Wasn't a question."

"Last night—yesterday, sometime—she received some photos in the mail. It's crazy, I know, but they're like surveillance photos of her and . . . me, Cathy, and Molly."

"Somebody tailin' you?"

"I don't know what to think. Jennifer's scared. Seeing those pics rattled the hell out of her. Me too. I mean, even my secretary's in there."

"What about Cathy?"

"Give me a break, Jack. I told you that she tossed me out. Those photos aren't the kind of thing you talk about over the phone."

He sneered, his eyes hard. "Maybe you should have got your ass in your car and gone to see her."

"Damn it, I am going to see her. Just what the hell do you make of it?"

Jack squinted and mulled over my question. "Hard to tell. Usu- ally, when pictures are sent to somebody, it's to scare 'em or shut 'em up. You know, when parents are supposed to testify against some mobbed-up prick, they get a photo of their little Joan skipping home from school. In your case, Molly."

"I can't see that here."

"I don't know. Can't believe it has anything to do with your old man. Maybe it has something to do with you runnin' around on your wife."

"Damn it, it's not like that."

"Fifty-eight years, Johnny. Fifty-eight years, me and the missus. Look, I was no saint comin' up. There were plenty of holster humpers around, and the only good time in life is a strange piece of ass, right? Well, you gotta accept that marriage is a tradeoff. You're drawing in on sixty, right?"

"Sooner than I wished."

"You better take stock. You got a wife and a kid, a home. You really gonna toss that aside for fresh pussy you just met? If it doesn't work out, what's your plan? Run back to Cathy with your dick in hand?"

"It's not that simple. She's really pissed. I think she might tell me that she wants out."

"You think? How can you not know?" He mumbled something and looked away, then turned back to me. "If you're right, you better get on your knees and beg forgiveness, dumb ass, 'cause you don't know what you have. You should see yourself whenever you talk about your little girl."

"Jack—"

"Never mind, that's all I got to say. You ignore my advice anyway." He snagged a fry drizzled in ketchup and popped it into his mouth. "I suppose you never got a permit, either?"

"I'm still giving that some thought." I had never considered owning a gun, much less carrying one, but maybe he was right.

"You do that. You need to give thought to a whole lot of shit." He stood, in his long-sleeved brown shirt and faded jeans, and faced me. "I'll see you around."

Jack lumbered past the scattered tables, the stand-up piano, and the shuffleboard game. Customers glanced at him, obviously impressed by his size and his don't-fuck-with-me demeanor.

His broad shoulders nearly filled the doorway as he shoved the screen wide open and was gone.

21

The fact that I'd managed to piss off Jack, on top of everything else, was hard to believe. I went back to the office and puttered around for most of the afternoon, but then told Marilyn that I was knocking off. I needed a drink and time to gather my thoughts. The Great Lakes Brewing Company, a local microbrew on a brick side street not far from the market, had been one of my haunts back in the day. I still popped in on occasion and, after my discussion with Jack, it seemed like a perfect day for a visit.

When I shoved open the bar's heavy wooden door, the place was uncharacteristically like a tomb. I would be the only patron, which was fine by me. I wondered if there were any statistics about a region's business decline per serial killing. A grungy bartender sported long dark hair and a thick, silvery necklace. I didn't recognize the name of the band scrawled on his orange T-shirt. I ordered a Dortmunder Gold.

He drew a perfect pour and slid the pint in front of me. "You've got the Eliot Ness stool."

"I remember the story." Someone had tried to assassinate Ness while he was seated at the polished oaken bar. His feet had rested, just like mine, on the shiny brass foot rail.

"They say those nicks are from the bullets." He pointed to three chips in the paneled wall. I'd been at the bar often enough to know that the cause of the marks was uncertain, but the assassination angle made for a great story.

"Let me have a shot with this, will ya?" I could kill the afternoon by nursing a couple of drinks at Great Lakes and go home early in the evening when Cathy would be back from work.

The television above the bar announced a special report, delivered by the same Greek kid I'd seen before, Mr. Breathless. He was giving an update on the last Butcher killing, because the cops had released a photo and identified the victim: Barbara Nichols. Her face, her dead, pretty face, filled the screen.

"Wow. What a fox," the bartender said. She was—no, had been—a blonde. Her hair trickled over her shoulders and framed a comely face with a toothpaste-commercial smile.

"Can you imagine telling the parents?" I thought of the nearby market and all of that dead meat. For some reason, I visualized Barbara Nichols stuffed in a glass-fronted stall, her head gone and a swatch of cloth stuck up her ass. There was nothing remotely erotic about the image. A shiver ran along my spine; I reached past the beer for a healthy dose of whiskey.

"Creeps me out just thinkin' about it. And another one, that guy with his throat cut."

I nodded, deciding not to tell him that the man who had discovered Frank was sitting in front of him. Draining the shot glass, I motioned for another. Eliot Ness had been just as confused about the Torso Murderer as I was about the Butcher.

"Somethin' to eat? Twenty percent off everything."

"Maybe later." The guy had an odd sense of timing, thinking that anyone would have an appetite after hearing about Barbara Nichols. I'd checked in earlier with Marilyn, who'd confirmed that my schedule was clear. She'd asked again if everything was okay; I'd lied again and told her it was. Okay? People were dying around me, and I was riddled with confusion about the situation with Cathy and Jennifer. Above all else, there was the specter of Molly. *The difficulty in life is the choice.*

Jack had reinforced my inclination to bring the relationship with Jennifer to a firm and abrupt end. Cathy had been there for me, by my side through the meds and the shrinks. And Molly was paramount. When I'd slinked past Molly's bedroom to head downstairs after that fateful interlude with Jennifer, I hadn't even been able to bring myself to look in on her.

I needed to dredge up my balls for the one-on-one with Cathy. The simple fact was that I had no explanation for the late nights. Maybe the best I could hope for was to beg forgiveness and ask her to let us just move on. Promising to recommit to our sessions with Father McGraw would be essential. But every succinct little speech that came to mind sounded trite. And if Cathy said that she'd had enough and ordered me to pack a bag, get the hell out, I wasn't even sure where I'd spend the night. The bartender set the fresh round in front of me, and I sipped the whiskey, recalling Jennifer's comfy leather furniture. One glimpse of her pink underwear that night, and my mind had drilled in on one thing and one thing only. I had failed to even consider the ramifications— such as endangering my relationship with Molly.

If Cathy tossed me in the street, I'd have to, at the very least, drop to my knees and implore her to temper any explanation to our daughter. We could explain to Molly that I needed some time alone, that I was going through a difficult period . . . any rationale that avoided words or phrases such as *abandoned, ran out, threw our marriage away*—all of which, of course, would be perfectly appropriate.

The temptation to rationalize my adultery was immense. Jennifer had lunged for me, her tongue eager, her fingers exploring, her mouth enveloping the strawberry jam coating my erection. And her last statement to me, about knowing where to find her if I wanted to talk. *Or anything.* I shook my head and finished the shot.

"One more, okay?" I said to the barman. "Whiskey: more sincere than a woman's kiss, right?"

He gave me a long look. "You sure about that shot?"

Sometimes the old days seemed attractive, before the PC folks took over and getting hammered became some kind of crime. Now some punk in a T-shirt was determining my alcohol intake. I sat there for a couple of minutes, debating whether to argue with him. He studiously ignored me and polished the far end of the bar. Maybe the booze I'd washed down with Jack at the Parkview had stuck with me and I was coming across as more hammered than I thought.

I was about to give the guy some lip when the TV caught my attention. They were broadcasting another piece on Barbara Nichols, the screen filled with her winsome visage. Somebody had lost a daughter. I shut my eyes and thought of Molly's pretty, innocent face. If she was torn from my life, I could not carry on. Even the prospect of no longer living under the same roof was painful. I shoved away the half-empty mug of beer.

"Hey," I said, to catch the bartender's attention. I glanced at my watch. I was already going to be late, and I sure as hell had better not show up smashed. "Just a cup of coffee, black. And a large ice water."

He shrugged. "You got it."

There was a multipaned window at the end of the bar. Twilight had descended over the city like a morbid warning, prompting people everywhere to get their kids inside and secure the doors. I thought of Cathy and Molly and how I should have been with them every single night when they were sitting home behind the double locks. I vaguely wondered whether a telephone discussion with Cathy might be the better choice. Just my voice and hers, talking in the shadows. Later, I could call Jack and offer to buy him a couple of drinks, smooth things over. Maybe I could even phone Jennifer and work toward an understanding. All the scattered little pieces of my life could be arranged in one long night.

I sipped the hot coffee and then rubbed my face with my hands. Who was I kidding? There would be no tidy ending. Cathy deserved to stare into my eyes and tell me exactly what she wanted. Let her scream, let her cry, let her roll her hand into a fist and strike me. I was mired in a quicksand mess of my own making. I had forfeited any right to object. After finishing the coffee and draining the water in a few long gulps, I paid the tab.

Outside, I paused under a streetlight, styled after an old gas lamp, to turn my cell back on. No calls. Cathy would be waiting now, watching the clock. I focused on my drunken march along the brick sidewalk, toward the parking lot. The bartender had been right; I'd had enough. The attendant had departed for the day, and only a few cars remained. Except for a couple of stoner kids carousing on the corner, the streets were barren.

I was halfway to my Buick when I heard a faint voice, a soft cry. "Help me."

It sounded, definitely, like a woman's voice. The plea came from a narrow alley that led all the way from the parking lot to the next street. I stared at the dark opening, hoping that my imagination had been in overdrive. Hearing nothing more, I turned back toward the car. Then, unmistakably, there was the voice again. I looked around and tentatively stepped toward the alley. Not twenty feet down the corridor, a figure was huddled against the brick wall.

She looked up as I approached, her features obscure in the dim light. "They're gone. Took my purse."

"Sorry." The alley reeked as if half the city's wino population urinated back there. "Are you hurt?"

She shook her head. I helped her up and offered to call the police. As she smiled, a sliver of light caught her face and she looked vaguely familiar. With a glance over my shoulder, she said, "For Daddy."

There was a sudden movement behind me. Something hard smacked against my head, and my legs buckled. Tiny dots of lights twinkled as the dark stones of the alley floor rushed toward me.

22

"Come now, wake up. That's a good boy."

The cooing voice drifted to me as the sharp odor of ammonia bit into my nostrils. My head jerked as my brain throbbed to consciousness. Cold steel bit into my wrists, and I grasped that I was hanging by my arms, suspended from the ceiling. Tape was plastered across my mouth, securing a wad of mildewed cloth as a gag.

"Remember me?"

I willed my eyes open. The woman before me appeared to be in her late sixties. Her shiny hair was dyed raven-black, and her lips were coated with bright red lipstick. I suddenly recognized her as the woman who worked at Havlicek's.

She gripped my face and peered up at me as though she were conducting an inspection. As if reading my mind, she said, "You now know who I really am, of course."

My throat was parched, and I was about to piss myself. The Butcher. I remembered the black guy with no dick, Barbara Nichols, and what'd been done to her ass. Oyster and some unknown corpse on a beach, all carved apart.

She released her hold on me and stepped away. "I know, you're thinking how ironic that I really am a butcher. Isn't life humorous?" She plucked a stray thread from her red cocktail dress. "The work is enjoyable, even if Mr. Havlicek is a dullard."

I had been stripped, and my feet were fixed in manacles, connected by an iron bar bolted into the floor. My eyes darted, wild, taking in the cramped room. An old white refrigerator was shoved against the concrete wall near me. A filthy window casing, the panes covered in ragged black curtains, was set high in the opposite wall. A long wooden workbench was positioned beneath the window, and an array of tools littered the worktop—knives, saws, and a meat cleaver.

"I'm so glad you've recovered. Sometimes he hits with such force that the game is already over." She turned and barked up the staircase, "Billy!"

The staircase was separated from the room by a stark wooden wall, and heavy footfalls pounded down the steps. A huge man, at least six foot four, lurched into view. His muscles bulged beneath a skintight black T-shirt, and his bald head shone in the basement lights.

"Please, meet my little brother." The Butcher rested a hand against my cheek. "Please understand that he's not being rude, Mr. Coleman. Billy doesn't talk; he just assists me."

A monster, and his name was Billy, like a kid? He shuffled a few steps toward me and fixed his dead-fish eyes on mine. He said not a word.

"There is a delicious symmetry here, don't you think? The games I played with your father, and now you are here, in my home, to play some other games." She crossed her arms. "Tell me, after he shot himself, did you have to clean up the mess?"

I wanted to kill her. I wanted to break my shackles, grab a knife from the workbench, and drive the blade into her chest.

A smile tugged at the Butcher's red lips. "Sounds are muffled here, Mr. Coleman, but please don't cry out. We're just going to have a pleasant little chat. Billy?"

He handed her a pair of latex surgical gloves.

"These days, one can't be too careful," she remarked as she slipped them on.

She ripped the tape from my mouth and removed the cloth, damp with my saliva. Billy, having donned his own pair of gloves, took the rag from her. His thick knuckles were visible through the stretched white latex.

"Please, let me go." My voice was a whisper. "I have a wife, a daughter."

The Butcher chuckled. "I'm well aware of that, Mr. Coleman. I've watched you, intermittently, over the years. They're both quite pretty."

"Please." The thought that she'd seen Cathy and my little girl was unbearable. Tears filled my eyes. I prayed to God that the sacrifice of my life would ensure that she'd never follow my family again.

"Really, begging? That is so unseemly. I'm sure that your wife and child will miss you terribly. You can take comfort in that."

The finality of her words made me shut my eyes for a moment. I didn't want to wind up in a deserted alley with my dick cut off and a rag stuffed up my ass. Molly couldn't grow up plagued by nightmares of a butchered father. And Cathy—in the back of my mind, I realized that she was the one I thought of, not Jennifer—should be nestled on the living room sofa with me, holding hands.

I wanted the chance to make it right.

"You're not making this very interesting, Mr. Coleman. Should we just replace the gag and continue on?"

I knew that she was toying with me as part of her sick game but had no idea what to say to a woman who'd abducted me, trussed me naked, and hung me from a ceiling. "No, I . . . I . . . "

"Come now, please, don't bore me. You remember my letter, of course?" She reached forward to massage my nipples with the latex gloves.

"I was just a kid."

"Haunted you, didn't it? I'm an expert in psychology, you see. Nightmares, Mr. Coleman. I know exactly how to cause them."

She could never know how well she'd succeeded. My tantrums, the dreams. Wetting my bed in high school, for God's sake.

She pinched my cheeks. "I needed to make certain that you'd remember me and wonder if I was *watching* you. The day your father cheated me, I decided that you would be my final victim. How delicious."

"Cheated you? You drove him . . . "

"To blow his brains out? Are those the words you were groping for? Or should I say, for which you were groping?"

I remembered the mop, the sponge, the smear of red and white. "You bitch."

Her eyes grew wide, and she stepped back, motioning to Billy. He swayed toward me and punched me in the stomach. The bouncer at the Alley wouldn't have stood a chance against him. I sagged against the chain that suspended me from the ceiling and, as the wind rushed from me, I nearly vomited.

"Profanity is prohibited in my house," the Butcher said.

My stomach cramped, my guts felt ruptured. Air came in quick gasps.

She sauntered toward me and rested a solicitous hand against my cheek. "Are you all right?"

I struggled to catch my breath. She wanted me conscious and alert for whatever she had in store. Billy hovered nearby, his fists clenched.

"I so enjoyed breaking your father, Mr. Coleman—delicious— but he took the coward's way out."

A vivid image of that gory bathroom replayed in my mind. "He was no coward."

"But I valued our jousting, and he ended it too soon, don't you see? That was cheating. The police nearly did apprehend us; your father made far more progress than he ever knew."

"You called him hapless."

She pursed those red lips. "Because of him, we had to collect our trophies elsewhere, enjoyable out-of-town jaunts. Playing was easy— hitchhikers, runaways. Nobody misses the dregs."

I wondered how many devastated families she had left in her squalid wake, parents and spouses and shattered children who would never forget that someone they loved had been dismembered and left to rot. *Trophies?*

"We enjoyed our trips, Mr. Coleman, but my intention never wavered. Returning and once more outwitting the press and those idiots in blue. A triumphant reiteration of our Cleveland game—ending with you."

Jack's line about figuring these sick fucks out, came back to me. There would be no reconciliation with Cathy. Molly would grow up without a father. The Butcher was insane, and I was going to die.

Strutting away from me, her heels clacking against the floor, she popped open the refrigerator. The door swung toward me so I was unable to see inside. "Say *hello* to your friend."

She extended her arm, her fingers knotted in the hair of Oyster's severed head. Those curious eyes were now opaque, not really eyes anymore, but desiccated lumps of soft flesh. His skin was pallid, and the neck tissue, where they'd knifed through, was a dark grayish hue.

"We peel away the flesh after awhile and preserve the skulls." She sounded like a proud collector of rare artifacts. "Oyster's eyes are so unique, don't you think? A special treat for my brother."

Billy's head bobbed, and he rocked back and forth on his heels, his blank gaze fixed on Oyster's bulbous eyes. Bile rose in my throat, and a sob escaped me. She returned Oyster's head, like leftover pasta, to the refrigerator and approached me, her bright lips leading the way.

"We knew each other from Havlicek's, so choosing when and how to take him was an exceptionally facile way to resume our Cleveland fun. Not that you were much more of a challenge."

I envisioned her, skulking in the dark, waiting for me to close the tab at Great Lakes and fall for her simple ruse. Setting me up so that Billy boy could slam something into my skull.

"I chose Oyster, of course, because you knew him. Did his death unsettle you, Mr. Coleman?" She chuckled.

I lifted my head. "Did you kill his son, too?"

"Not my style. Amateurish."

"Photos, of me and my family. Oyster's daughter. You took those."

She scrunched her face dismissively. "No idea what you're talking about, although that sounds like quite clever fun." She reached toward Billy, and he dropped the gag in her hand, as though they were a practiced surgical team. "You've made our conversation tedious."

"Wait, please." I knew that once the gag was in, she'd want to play with her toys on the workbench.

"We'll chat some more later." She rested the palm of her free hand against the last part of my anatomy I wanted her touching. "There will come a time when you snap, when you'll babble and drool and weep. But I'll take every possible measure to preserve your lucidity as long as humanly possible."

A chill ran through me as she cradled the most precious part of me in her palm. Her hand moved to my chest. My heart was pounding, and I imagined her grabbing it, squeezing the beating organ, my blood running through her fingers.

She nodded to her brother. "Let's play."

I clenched my mouth shut, but Billy grabbed my jaw and squeezed, forcing my gnashing teeth apart. He held my head in place, while the Butcher inserted the grimy rag and applied thick strips of tape. She smiled and then marched over to the workbench, the heels of her shoes striking the concrete floor. *Click, clack, click, clack.* Her back was to me, but I heard her rummaging, metal striking metal, while Billy ran his index finger up and down my arm. He glared at me, and I shuddered. The Butcher turned, holding a long-handled bolt cutter.

"Which little piggy, Billy?"

He made a sound, like a cough, and crouched down. His stubby finger tapped against the little toe on my left foot.

The Butcher smiled, and minute cracks appeared in her lipstick. "A good choice."

She scrunched her face and fixed her piercing eyes on me. Billy stood, watching. The room was as silent as snowfall. My feet were totally immobilized. I tugged against the restraints, swiveled my waist a few inches, as the Butcher gripped the bolt cutter with both hands. She opened the handles, snapped them shut, once, twice, three times. "Billy oils all the working parts."

The Butcher lowered the cutter, and I curled the toes of my foot as tightly as possible. She chuckled. "That never works."

She fit the scissor-like blades around my little toe. Waiting, she forced me to sense the cold weight of the blades, feel their sharpness. My skin parted as she rocked the instrument back and forth. Her florid lips pursed, she cracked the handles together, and my foot was drenched from the blood.

I screamed into the gag, and it filled every crevice in my mouth. Tears burned in my eyes. A madwoman in a red dress and her lunatic brother were prepared to hack me to bits.

The Butcher stepped away and surveyed her handiwork, handing the dripping bolt cutter to Billy. "That's how I was taught to do it, Mr. Coleman, by our father."

She smiled warmly at Billy. "He looks so much like his daddy."

23

"There, there." The Butcher's voice was soothing. She stroked my hair, and my skin quivered at her touch. I was repulsed by her grotesque red lips. "Sometimes, when we traveled, we'd meet Daddy and enjoy the game together. You know to whom I'm referring, don't you?"

The stub of my toe throbbed, blood pooled beneath my foot, and my balls shriveled. The children of the Torso Murderer, taught by him, belonging to him. A son and a daughter, raised in the family business of slaughter. *For Daddy*.

She studied my face and smiled. "You're not as stupid as I thought."

My God, had he kidnapped the Butcher and Billy, did he have a lover—or had he snatched an innocent woman and forced her to bear his children?

"Daddy never wanted to leave Cleveland. He loved the Indians, the Browns." She shook her head, breaking the reverie, and her tone dropped an octave. "But then someone saw his face. We had to move."

Jack Corrigan, the night of the fight in the lumberyard.

"We played the game all our lives. For a long while, I was what we referred to as *bait*. As a child, a little girl lost. Later, a pretty young thing in an alley. Then . . . well, like tonight. People are so predictable, especially men."

She cackled, and my skin crawled. "I'm going to remove another piece of you, Mr. Coleman."

There would be no escape for me, no quick and merciful death— only the same protracted torture that had been meted out to Oyster and Barbara Nichols and all of the other poor bastards. *Heavenly Father, please let me live to see my little girl grow up. I'll turn my life around, I swear.* But that hellish basement bore no trace of anything holy.

The Butcher extended a hand toward Billy, and he obediently handed her the bolt cutter. "Symmetry, remember?" She leaned forward until her face was inches from mine. Her bright lips clenched in a grimace and her tone dropped to a low, even whisper. She reached down and placed her hand against me again. "So what do I do about this, since you only have one?"

She straightened and turned, patting her hair with one hand and clutching the bolt cutter with the other. Shaking her head, she paced deliberately around me, pausing to lightly stroke my back with her fingers. Jennifer had last touched me like that, but the Butcher's touch was unnerving. And my memory of the night with Jennifer, of the games we'd played, seemed surreal. Far more vivid were images of Cathy and Molly, of an outing to the zoo, of my daughter pedaling her bike. Or just the two of them, with me, at our breakfast table.

The Butcher halted in front of me and patted her hair again. Working the blades around my toe, she turned to her brother and grinned. Billy was expressionless as she snapped the bolt cutter shut.

I quivered violently, that disgusting bolt of cloth wedged into my mouth, again muffling my screams. The Butcher reached down and picked up the bloody digit. Waggling my toe in the dank air between us, she then held it under my nose, forcing me to inhale my own pungent, bloody scent.

They would cut and chop and saw pieces of me, until only a raving shell of a man remained.

"What should we play with next, Mr. Coleman? More toes? Fingers? Maybe thin slices from your buttocks?"

The Butcher drew the toe away from my sickened nostrils. The joy of the game made her eyes gleam.

"Did you know that the ancient Chinese were capable of making twenty thousand precision slices before a man would die? You could apparently watch his heart beat through a thin membrane of tissue. After all these years, I'm still not that proficient, but we all need aspirations."

My thoughts focused on Cathy and Molly, forcing my mind to another place and willing the nightmare to end. But I knew the pain, whether twenty cuts or twenty thousand, would snatch me back to reality and the sound of my own muffled cries.

She dropped my toe; it plopped onto the floor. "Maybe I should maximize the pieces, like I did with the penis from the Shaker Heights trophy. Allow me to consider that."

I prayed that Cathy would be okay, even find someone else, and that Molly would grow up strong and tough. And without nightmares. Even Jennifer was included in my prayer; I hoped that she would understand why my thoughts were of them, not of her. There was a memory of her sister, Martha, of how she'd been hurt. But none of my sins, not even lumped all together in the crumbled paper bag of my life, justified a death like the one I was going to suffer.

"What about those nipples, Mr. Coleman? Quite symmetrical. Or testicles?" She tapped a finger against her chin. "Daddy always said to be patient and wait for inspiration." She sidled up to her brother. "What do you think, Billy? What next?"

He trudged forward and stared into my eyes before pressing a pudgy index finger into my nose.

"An interesting choice. He usually likes the head intact, and we really can't maintain symmetry with a nose, can we?" The Butcher strolled to her workbench and spoke to me over her shoulder. "Daddy was so pleased that we continued our craft, as he phrased it, in Cleveland.

And he was so proud of our success. Of course, your father knew all about that, our first time around. You can ask him." She turned to me. "Oh, wait—no, you can't!"

Despite the cuts, despite my naked vulnerability, I surged toward her, and the manacles bit into my wrists.

She just smiled, amused, and held up a fillet knife. "Daddy has considered returning to Cleveland for one more game. He so enjoys my stories about the Coleman family."

I reacted as though Billy had struck me again.

"Why, you look surprised, Mr. Coleman. Delicious. Let me assure you, our daddy is very much alive."

24

"This will bleed a bit, Mr. Coleman. You'll want to keep your head down to prevent the blood from trickling into your throat. I'll cauterize everything in due time, to help you enjoy the game for as long as possible. I have a very precise butane torch."

Billy stepped behind me and applied a vise-like grip to my head, locking it in place. He'd had practice, no doubt. I peered down and watched his sister scrutinize my nose. She ran the blade along my right nostril.

"This will be more painful than when I removed your toes, Mr. Coleman."

She squeezed my nostrils together and shoved my nose left, then right.

"So many options. I can grasp your nose with a pair of pliers and cut from the top down. Or I can make a deep, vertical incision and slice away each half. Hmm . . . hmm."

I was fixated on her every movement. I prayed again, asking forgiveness for my sins and the comfort of death. For Cathy and Molly to live long, safe lives. And for the Butcher and Billy to die in the most excruciating manner that God could contemplate.

She changed her grip on the knife and steadied the blade, poised for an incision.

The doorbell rang.

The sound was muted and indistinct. The door at the top of the steps was obviously thick enough to muffle noise, but the faint ringing seemed to me like the resounding peal of a church bell.

The Butcher froze, and Billy's vise-like grip tightened on my skull. Even if I didn't deserve saving, I renewed my prayers and promised absolute faith, fidelity, and total devotion to Cathy and Molly.

Neither of them moved. As the silence lengthened, I watched the Butcher visibly relax. She looked at me, cocked her head to one side, and opened her mouth to say something. Then came a persistent knocking, dull thud after thud, and again, the stifled *ding, ding, ding* of the bell.

As the ringing faded, I pictured my final chance for salvation giving up, turning, and walking away. The Butcher smiled, and the last trace of hope squirmed out of me—until the ringing resumed, seconds later, followed by another round of banging on the door.

This someone wasn't leaving. The Butcher scowled and rested the fillet knife on the floor, between my feet. She returned to the workbench, picked up a wicked-looking cleaver, and waved her brother toward the wooden wall adjacent to the staircase. He released his grip on me and trod away, those massive arms dangling at his sides. As he positioned himself by the wall, she handed him the weapon and patted his shoulder.

"Stay here." The Butcher spoke as though she were giving a command to a pet. Smiling through the garish lipstick, she turned to me. "Be right back!"

The measure of cheer in her voice was disquieting. I listened to her *clack, clack, clack* up the stairs. Billy's face twisted into a harrowing, moronic grin.

I surmised that there was a landing at the top of the steps, probably an entrance from a driveway. Although no aspect of my life warranted divine intervention, I begged for whoever was at the top of the steps to do something, anything to release me from the meat hook. Billy flattened against the wall and examined me, his gaze wandering from my face to the raw stubs on my feet.

The voices above were indistinct and barely audible. Oddly, it struck me that I didn't even know what time of day it was. I discerned a man's voice, then a woman's—not the Butcher's. There was a sudden crack, as though the door had been flung open and banged against a wall. Shouts and curses filled the stairway, and heavy footfalls thudded down the steps. Bernie Salvatore emerged at the bottom of the stairs, his Glock gripped firmly in both hands. Wendy Coufalik rushed after him. She held her weapon in one hand and clutched the handcuffed Butcher by the scruff of her neck.

"John!" Bernie gasped. "What the—"

I jerked my head violently toward Billy. The cleaver, backed by every ounce of Billy's mass, was already arcing toward Bernie. Catching my gesture at the last possible moment, Bernie dove to the floor and spun onto his back. Curling forward, he trained his handgun on Billy. The sharp blade of the cleaver bit into the wall, but Billy yanked it free in one motion.

Coufalik roughly shoved the Butcher to her knees and, training her handgun on Billy, radioed for backup.

"Drop it!" Bernie rose to a knee and then stood. "On the floor! Now!"

Billy looked wildly about the room. He was grunting, his mouth agape. This was not some dark alley, some unsuspecting victim.

The Butcher crawled to the refrigerator and huddled against the wall. Coufalik holstered her radio and joined Bernie in ordering Billy to drop the weapon, their commands blending into one strident torrent.

I twisted to see the Butcher, and her steely eyes were focused on her brother. I wanted to scream at her to tell him to surrender, to drop the cleaver and lie on the floor. But she shrieked, "Kill them for Daddy!"

Billy straightened to his full height. With a guttural roar, he brandished the cleaver above his head and stormed forward. Bernie fired once into the giant's chest, the harsh shot reverberating against the thick walls, and Billy staggered backward. Amazingly, he didn't fall but regained his balance and stood, weaving, never losing his grip on the cleaver.

The silence in the room was broken only by the cackle of the radio and a gurgling sound from Billy's chest as blood and air seeped from the wound. My ears rang, and the sharp stench of cordite burned into my nostrils. Billy's uncomprehending eyes settled on the Butcher.

She nodded and mouthed the words, "For Daddy."

He lurched forward, hefting the cleaver and grunting with each dogged step. Bernie and Coufalik fired in unison, one shot striking Billy dead center in the chest and the other zipping into his forehead. His entire body shuddered, and he dropped the cleaver, the blade clattering against the concrete slab. Despite the deafening gunshots, I heard his head crack on the harsh floor when his immense body collapsed.

"Thank you for that, although I must say that your initial shot displayed rather shoddy marksmanship." The Butcher's words were distinct, even though my ears seemed to be swathed in cotton. "Given his mental state, I expect that he would have avoided prison, but I am well aware of the misery he would have endured in a state institution."

"Then you know what the fuck you can look forward to," Coufalik snapped.

Bernie checked Billy's pulse and radioed for a meat wagon.

"As they say, profanity is the effort of a weak mind to express itself." The Butcher chuckled, fucking *chuckled*. "My, my, I think we'll have some enjoyable interrogation sessions."

Coufalik ignored her and, stepping to me, stooped to pick up my severed toes. She spoke over her shoulder to Bernie. "I'll find some ice upstairs and get the kit from the car."

"Medics will be here soon." Bernie holstered his radio and said to me, "Let's get you the fuck outta here."

I dangled from the manacles as he tore at a strip of tape from my mouth. Nothing would be sweeter than a breath of fresh air, and I was eager to spit out the goddamn chunk of stinking cloth. I wanted to be with Cathy, to cradle my wife and whisper to her every staunch promise made while dangling from the wooden beam in that basement of nightmares. I was going to live.

Once Bernie worked the gag free, I couldn't stop from crying. "Jesus, Bernie, Jesus, Jesus, Jesus . . . "

He cradled my face in his gruff hands. "You're safe. It's okay now. Safe."

But the Butcher chuckled again. "You'll never be safe, Mr. Coleman."

"Shut the fuck up." Bernie jammed a pointed finger in her direction, then took long strides to the workbench and rummaged through the clutter to find the keys to my metallic cuffs.

Coufalik hustled back downstairs and immediately went to work bandaging the stubs of what had been my toes. I was conscious of my nakedness but didn't care. That she'd once been pissed at me for looking at her ass struck me as ironic.

When Bernie released my arms, I collapsed against the cold wall, the concrete abrading the skin on my back. He handed the keys to Coufalik, and she loosened the biting clasps around my ankles. They helped me shuffle a few steps forward, away from my blood, and lowered me to the floor. I was a body's length from the Butcher.

"She said their father was the Torso Murderer."

Coufalik looked skeptical, like I was bullshitting her, despite my condition.

Bernie's jaw dropped. "No way."

"He's telling the truth, you know," the Butcher said calmly.

"And he's still alive."

"Now you are delusional, Mr. Coleman. Probably the loss of blood. My father's been dead for years."

"Bullshit," I snapped, glaring at her. "I heard you." I lowered my gaze to my ruined feet. The blood seeping from my toes had mostly congealed, but there were thin red trails on the concrete. "And that . . . that fridge, they kept Oyster's head in there." I gestured in its general direction, my eyes lowered. They'd find me damn credible when they popped open the Frigidaire.

Bernie nodded to Coufalik and snapped on a pair of gloves. They reminded me of the ones worn by the Butcher and Billy, and a shudder went through me. Bernie strode to the refrigerator and swung the door open. From my position, I still couldn't see inside, thank God. He stood there for several long beats before closing the door carefully, maybe reverently. "Sweet Jesus Christ, it's full of skulls."

The Butcher giggled, or maybe that was my imagination.

Then a wave of blue uniforms washed down the steps, radios crackling and guns drawn. I felt light, nearly buoyant, and I began to weep uncontrollably, unashamed. I'd see Cathy again, make it right, and we'd cuddle on the sofa in the living room. Molly would wrap her arms around me, the aroma of familiar shampoo in her hair.

Someone tossed me a blanket. I draped the cloth over my shoulders and sat there, weeping, naked in my blood.

25

"I got here as soon as I could, John." Cathy's eyes were red-rimmed, and she looked exhausted.

A sedative given to me by the ambulance drivers had knocked me out for a while. I came to in the recovery room, groggy but aware of my surroundings. The logos on the tidy white uniforms told me that I'd been admitted to a hospital with an excellent reputation for patching up people who have unfortunate encounters with guns or knives. My feet had been swaddled.

Cathy walked to my bed and took my extended hand. She wore an outfit that was perfect for an elementary school teacher—a brown dress drawn at the waist with a white belt—and had never looked so beautiful to me.

"The surgeon said that they couldn't reattach your toes. Too mangled and contaminated from the floor."

"Where's Molly?" I wanted them both. Life would go on without toes.

"With Alison. I just wasn't sure how you'd be, whether she should see you . . . "

She'd made the right call. When the police told her that they'd found me naked in the Butcher's basement, hanging from the ceiling, she had to wonder about my state of mind. "Yeah, but . . . soon. Is she okay?"

Cathy released my hand, put her purse on the nightstand, and dropped into an orange plastic chair near me. "What happened is all over the news. Even Molly's a little freaked out. She said to tell you that she loves you."

I shut my eyes to block out the oddly disquieting room—all white and barren and sterile. "I want us to be together."

When she looked at me, her eyes welled with tears. "Will you get help, John?"

"Cathy—"

"Let me finish. In a way, I'm not surprised about this." Her fingers reached for an earlobe. "How you've been acting . . . I warned you that there'd be trouble."

I settled into the stiff mattress, the firm pillow. Under the sheets, I felt for my dick, just to make sure. "What happened to me down there . . . every thought was about you and Molly, that you'd be lost to me, forever. I prayed for the chance to make it right, Cathy. Please, give me that."

"John . . . "

"This won't be like before, I promise. The psychiatrist, the drinking, I'll handle everything."

"Whatever happens between us, if you want Molly as part of your life, you need to quit."

I was letting those words sink in when a young black woman in a crisp white uniform came through the door and interrupted our conversation. She strode to the bedside, checked a couple of monitors, and asked brusquely, "How you feeling?"

"Under the circumstances, great." I didn't tell her that the prospect that my wife wouldn't take me back was worse than the vision of bolt cutters and red lips. Maybe a meeting with Father McGraw would help. Then, I could solemnly relate the promises made while hanging from that fucking rafter, every word. Let Cathy see me, hear me, touch my hand when I swore on everything that was holy never to hurt her again.

"There's some other folks who want to talk to you." Her white blouse swirled as she turned toward the door.

"But I'm with my wife." I pictured a cadre of reporters streaming in, led by Vanessa Edwards, peppering me with questions about my father's suicide and which parts of me the Butcher had lopped off in her medieval cellar. "I'm not giving any interviews."

"It's the police," she said over her shoulder.

She walked out, swinging the door wide for Bernie Salvatore and Wendy Coufalik. I wasn't sure how to react when they marched in. He seemed glum, but she looked oddly perky. Whatever. I owed them my life and was grateful—even to the tough broad from Slavic Village.

Cathy walked over and wrapped her arms around Bernie. "They told me what happened. Is this . . . ?"

"Detective Coufalik, Cathy Coleman." Bernie introduced them, and they shook hands while Cathy murmured her thanks.

"What you did . . . what to say . . . " My mouth suddenly felt very dry, and I sipped water from a Styrofoam cup on the table.

Coufalik shrugged. "Doing our job."

"How the hell did you find me?" I thought back to the workbench, the knives and the saws and the bolt cutter, and I trembled.

Bernie shrugged. "Some kids called in a 911 and said they'd seen a guy dragged into a van. It was dark, so none of them could be sure of the make or color."

I recalled the rowdy kids who had been outside of Great Lakes, just before I'd been lured into that dark alley.

"The van was parked out of the light, and they gave us a shit description of you and the guy doin' the dragging. Big and bald was the best they could do. Sound familiar?" Bernie shifted his weight, turning his head in Cathy's direction. "Nothing on the driver, but it must have been the Butcher."

"This gives me the chills," Cathy said. She went back to the hospital chair and sat, her fingers gripping a reddish earlobe.

Bernie refocused on me. "The kids froze at first, but one of them had the presence of mind to grab his cell and snap a picture of the plate when the van pulled away. The angle was bad, so we only got a blurry partial, but it was something to work with."

"They said that technology is better these days, that it would trip the Butcher up this time," Cathy said, reminding me of our conversation in the kitchen when the nightmare had just begun. "I bet they weren't thinking of a cell phone."

"Your car was one of the few in the nearby lot. They called Cathy, and she was already worried that you hadn't come home." Bernie stared up, as though to examine the white tile ceiling. I knew that he was thinking of another night when I hadn't come home, despite his admonition.

"I was waiting for you, John, in the living room. Then they called . . . " Cathy began sobbing, her shoulders shaking, and I reached for her and took her hand.

"If only . . . God, I nearly lost everything." Tears welled, even though I was embarrassed to cry in front of Coufalik again. "Sorry . . . "

"Forget it," Bernie said, the same way he had back when I'd screwed up a play for the Green Wave. *Gotta move forward.* "When I heard that it might be you, I put us on the case. Took awhile, 'cause we only had the partial plate."

"But how'd you figure it was the Butcher?" I slipped my hand from Cathy's and wiped my eyes.

"We didn't. If we'd known that, we would have shown up with a SWAT team. Other vans matched the partial, too. Captain put three cars on this, but a lady her age wasn't high on the list of possibles. Her's was the third we checked." Bernie shrugged. "When she answers the door, all prim and proper, I figure it's a dead end. She says she rarely drives and wasn't out at all yesterday. I was ready to pack it in."

"But her being all dressed up, at home, before noon, struck me as weird," Coufalik said. "I'm checking out her shoes, and there's this streak of fresh blood. She's not bleeding, so I ask her what happened, and she got shifty."

Bernie nodded. "Something wasn't right. With the partial, the blood, you missing, we weren't waiting for a warrant."

"You're damn lucky she was wearing light-colored shoes. If she'd had on black ones, we probably wouldn't be talking now."

"So who is she?" Cathy said.

"Mary Smith. The brother was William." Coufalik raised her eyebrows.

"We'll comb the records," Bernie said. "But if that's their real identities, I'll eat dirt."

"What about the Torso Murderer . . . their father?" I would never forget the pride that shone in her eyes when she made that claim.

"We'll tear that house apart to see if we can find anything on him." Bernie didn't sound at all convinced that they would.

"She said that my dad . . . he nearly figured them out." My eyes were teary again, at the memory of my unshaven father with a bottle of Four Roses.

"No surprise, huh? We all know he was a solid cop." He glanced out the window, and I followed his gaze but didn't see what caught his attention. "Cathy, can you give us a moment with John?"

Cathy hesitated, seemingly confused by his request. So was I. "You can talk in front of her, Bernie."

He shifted his feet. "We'd like to talk to you, alone."

"It's okay," Cathy said. She stood, picked up her purse, and gave me a weak smile. "I'll be right outside."

The door latched shut, and Bernie shoved his hands in his pockets. "Ahh, fuck . . . you're a shit, but I'm still sorry about this, John."

Coufalik nodded, like that was her cue. "There's a warrant for you, Mr. Coleman. You're under arrest for the murder of Frank Frederickson. You have the right to remain . . . "

"What?" My voice echoed from the floor, the ceiling, and the white block walls. "Bernie . . . ?"

Coufalik ignored me and kept icily reciting my rights. She finished and smirked. "So, how'd it go down?"

I was never the smartest goddamn lawyer in the world but knew enough to shut the hell up when reminded of the right to remain silent. "I'm calling an attorney."

"You sure?" Now Coufalik sounded sympathetic, like she'd suddenly become my friend. "The prosecutor might go lighter if you work with us, save us all a lot of trouble."

"I said I want a lawyer."

"Have it your way." With a nod to Bernie, she turned toward the door. "There'll be a guard outside until the docs clear you, then a police escort to jail."

"This is bullshit, Bernie. You know me. What the hell am I going to tell Cathy?"

"I can't help you with that, John." He locked eyes with me for a moment, and I thought that he was going to say something else, but he turned and followed Coufalik.

I was sure he was tempted to ladle out guilt like shit porridge about Jennifer Browning and was grateful that he didn't. If only I'd followed his admonition to go home to Cathy, I might not have wound up in a hospital bed, missing toes and under arrest. I turned my face to the window and listened to the footsteps of Coufalik and my old high school buddy until the door closed behind them.

How the hell would Cathy react when she learned of my arrest, for murder no less? All the prayers and promises made while hanging naked from a chain might have been for nothing. And Jennifer? I'd contemplated a gentle, mature parting of the ways. *Oh, by the way, that unpleasantness involving your brother? Don't let that come between us.*

The blinds were wide open; I gazed at the concrete bridges that soared over the nearby zoo in the valley below. We'd taken Molly there several times and traipsed through the rain forest exhibit, where she'd made faces at the baby orangutans. Even though the sky was bright and blue, my world was saturated with red, all that blood. Mine,

Oyster's, Frank's. The clouds were the wrong shapes—knives and axes and cleavers.

My thoughts were suddenly flooded by visions of clanging doors and steel cages, and I wanted to believe that there was no way Jennifer had anything to do with my predicament.

26

"I knew you were in trouble when I saw the cop in the hallway." Cathy's voice was emotionless. She had turned the chair away from the bedside and sat facing me. "But murder . . . what the hell happened, John?"

Telling her about the warrant had been difficult enough, but the fact that I had no answers left me unbalanced. "For the life of me, I don't know. They don't have to explain the grounds for an arrest."

"I can call Bernie."

"No. You'll put him in a box. The prosecutor's office is running the show. I'll get a lawyer, a copy of the police report." A public record, which the media would have their grimy hands on soon enough. "You'd better get to Molly. This will be all over the news."

"Jesus." She stood and crossed her arms. "You'll let me know when you find out?"

"I will, absolutely." I knew that she had to be told about the photos sent to Jennifer. The timing and place were all wrong, but she had to know. "Cathy, someone mailed Jennifer Browning, Oyster's daughter, some photos. Of her, of me. And you and Molly, in the driveway."

"What . . . why the hell didn't you tell me?" Her arms fell to her sides and she took a step toward me. "Why would somebody do that?"

"Bernie knows about this, and Jack Corrigan does too. Nobody can figure it out. I was going to tell you, but . . . "

She moved her head slowly, from side to side. "Why, John, why?"

I shut my eyes, opened them, and stared at the white ceiling. "Just keep an eye out, okay?"

"What did you get us into? There's Molly to think of, for the love of God."

"Tell her I love her and that I didn't do this." I took a deep breath. "I'll call you after I've talked to the lawyer."

"I don't know how to explain this to her." She snatched her purse from the roll-a-way table near the foot of the bed. She was shaking and her lips trembled.

"And I love you too, Cathy."

The words were barely out of my mouth, and she was gone. I felt worse than if the Butcher had dissected every joint with her wicked fillet knife. I rubbed clammy hands over my face and forced myself to concentrate on the one issue within my control: finding a lawyer. And that ball had to start rolling immediately. My cell was certainly logged into an evidence bag somewhere, so I picked up the tan phone by the bed and called the office. As expected, Marilyn answered on the second ring.

"It's me."

"John! Where are you?"

"The fricking hospital." I didn't know where to begin, how to answer the questions she'd have.

"Are you okay? The news said—"

"I won't be jogging for a while, let's put it that way. But . . . I don't even know what to say . . . I've been arrested for murder, Frank Frederickson."

"What . . . you?"

"I didn't do it."

"I never thought that."

Her loyalty meant more than anything did at that moment. I wiped a tear from my cheek. "Can you get me the number for Arlene Johnson?"

"I've seen her in the papers. The black woman, right?"

"Remember that electrician I wrote a will for? The guy who later got caught up in the school bid rigging mess?"

"The *PD* had a field day."

"He wanted a top criminal defense lawyer, and Johnson was one name I gave him. She got the guy off, the only one of all those contractors to walk. Impressed me, since the son of a bitch was guilty as hell."

"Will she know—"

"She should remember me. We talked at least once, so I could give her background on the client."

Marilyn promised to arrange a time for a conference. She was probably surprised by my choice of counsel. I didn't know many minorities of any kind, and there certainly weren't any in my circle of friends. But the color of someone's skin doesn't matter—especially if you think the person can save your ass.

Arlene Johnson's assistant called me about twenty minutes later to arrange for a late afternoon meeting. Someone brought me a tray of food, and I shoved carrots and spaghetti around with my fork, all the while praying that Arlene could resolve my problems.

Precisely on time, she made her entrance, wearing a yellow-and-black plaid knee-length skirt, matching jacket, and a white blouse with a collar. A substantial gold necklace, matched by a pair of earrings, gleamed. Her face was strong, with high cheekbones and intense, dark eyes.

"You get the charges dropped yet?" I said.

Arlene didn't return my grin but pursed her lips and sat in the plastic chair wedged between the bed and the wall. She lowered her black leather briefcase to the floor; her measured demeanor made me squirm.

"It's been awhile, Johnny." Her tone was crisp and confident, her diction precise. She glanced at the foot of the bed. "Sounds like you had a rough time."

"Cut two toes clean off. Bolt cutter."

"I squirm just thinking about it. Are you sure about talking now?"

"Yeah. I need some good news."

"Wish that I had some."

"C'mon, what can they have?"

"Plenty." She pulled a yellow legal pad and a copy of the police report from her briefcase. "The complainant is your former client, Jennifer Browning."

I had spent the morning trying to convince myself that Jennifer wasn't the one, couldn't be. I remembered being with her, touching, laughing, coming.

Arlene looked at me and hesitated. "You okay? We can do this tomorrow."

I shook my head and motioned for her to continue. Another day, another week, another life wasn't going to help.

"She says you were searching for her brother and found him, dead. Next thing she knows, you show up at her apartment to comfort her." She tossed her shoulder-length hair and looked at me expectantly.

"Well, she called me."

"And you went?"

"If I could take that back . . . " I imagined Cathy, waiting for me to come home, her gaze wandering over the crucifix above the mantle and the arrangement of the ceramic figurines.

"It gets better. She claims you'd already seduced her. Says she trusted you completely and that you promised to leave your wife. Before I go any further, answer a simple question: Did you sleep with her?"

There wasn't anything simple about it. A yellow streak rose from my spine and told me to deny the tryst, but Jennifer could probably prove it. My fingerprints would be all over her apartment. Maybe she'd saved her bedding, à la Monica Lewinsky and her blue dress, and they'd find my DNA. If Arlene found out that I'd lied about the sex, my credibility would be as absent as my little toes, and she'd dump me in a minute. "Look, my wife and I were having some issues—"

"I'll decide how to spin it. It's a yes-or-no question. Give me the answer."

I raised my eyes to meet hers. "Yes."

"Just in case you weren't thinking about it at the time, a lot of jurors don't like cheats—hope you're not offended by the term—especially guys who've been cheating on their wives. What's her name, and did she know?"

"Cathy, and—oh, fuck, no."

"Sorry. It's all in the report and all over the news. They didn't skimp on the juicy details, either."

"Cathy and me, I was going to try to work this out."

"I don't know what to tell you. The best you can do is to call her later. You've got a Go-Directly-to-Jail card. When you leave today, it'll be with the police, and you won't be going home."

"What about bail?" I wanted to see Cathy, in our home, and confess face-to-face. Let her slap me, pull out a fucking bolt cutter of her own and have at it, I didn't care.

"It's standard procedure to spend one night in the can before you can see a judge and set bond. There's nothing I can do about that."

I lay back and worked my head into the pillow, shut my eyes. The prospect of a shift in a cell block with guys who could eat me for lunch was frightening. I hadn't even been able to defend myself against an asshole bouncer.

"There won't be anything easy about what you'll be going through." I heard Arlene flip back to her notes. "Browning says she started to think about the timing of everything, how you'd discouraged her from going to the meeting with Frank. She got suspicious and called Bernie Salvatore, whom she's already met, and told him what was going on between you."

I fixed my eyes on the drop ceiling. Bernie had probably slammed his fist into a desk when Jennifer had confirmed his suspicions that we were fooling around, despite my denial. No wonder he'd told me I was a shit when they'd arrested me.

"Because he knows you, Salvatore had a Detective Coufalik take over. She obtains a warrant to search the vehicle, tells the judge they're worried about foul play."

"But a murder rap? Gimme a break. Jennifer's brother turns up dead, money's gone, they find my car in a parking lot—they've got nothing." I could only imagine Coufalik's zeal as she tore apart my car.

"Sorry, but there's more." She leaned forward and studied my face. "They found money in your trunk. Thirty-five grand, give or take. And her father's retirement watch, which Jennifer says he'd given to his son."

Seconds passed while I processed what she'd told me. "Somebody put that stuff there, Arlene, I'm telling you. This is bullshit, no way. And what happened to the rest of the money Frank had?"

Arlene shrugged. "They figure you stashed it somewhere."

"Yeah, right. Check my fucking mattress. And why the hell pop a murder charge because they found some money in my trunk? Hell, even if they claim I took the cash, they got nothing—"

"That's not all, Johnny. They found something else with the money and the watch, down in the wheel well."

"Yeah?"

"Yeah." She looked at me. "In the streets, they'd call it a big-ass knife. One covered with Frank Frederickson's blood and your fingerprints. Can you explain that away?"

I went limp. What the fuck?

27

"Arlene, I didn't do this. Someone's setting me up, somehow—Jennifer had—"

"You have a lot to explain, and we'll do it later, at my office. No interruptions, nobody walking in on us 'by mistake.'" She nodded toward the door, her golden necklace dangling. "I'm told they're getting your discharge papers ready; the cops want to get the hell out of here."

"Look, I've handled some misdemeanor crap, but a felony's above my pay grade. So I spend a night in the can, then the arraignment's tomorrow?"

"You'll be charged with murder in muny court, then bound over to common pleas for trial."

"What about bond?"

"I'll try to make you look like a saint and keep the number low. If things go our way, the judge will set something between five hundred thousand to a million." Arlene was, no doubt, used to shell-shocked looks on clients' faces—she didn't even pause. "Whatever the number, you'll probably need twenty percent cash as bail. Something else you'll need to bring up with your wife, since I assume your assets are joint."

"Jesus, what if she says no?"

"We'll cross that bridge then, John. You'd better think about how to handle the conversation."

"This will be tough, Arlene." I evaluated the equity in the house and a couple of modest mutual-fund accounts. "You know I'm just a solo guy, made sixty-five grand last year. With Cathy's salary, we do okay, but . . . "

"If you can't make it, we'll talk to a bondsman. But there's a fee, and they'll make you post security for the full amount. Cathy will have to sign off on that, too. Either way, unless you want to sit in a cell through trial, you'll need her help."

"Picked a good time to piss her off, didn't I?" My gaze drifted to the window again as I thought of the zoo and those rugged steel cages.

"And there's me too, Johnny. I don't come cheap, you know that."

I shut my eyes. "How much we talkin'?"

"All I can do is ballpark, you know that. If it goes all the way to trial, you're probably looking at a hundred grand for my fee, easy. And I recommend you hire a private investigator, too. If you're telling me that what the prosecutor has is all bullshit, we need to prove it."

"Let's hope it doesn't go that far." A trial would wipe me out.

"Look, if you want to check around, see if somebody will take the case for less, I'll understand."

"No, I want you. This is my life on the line here, Arlene."

"The money situation is what it is. If you walk, you can rebuild. I need you focused on your case, understand?" She leaned forward, elbows on her knees, the golden necklace swinging toward me.

I swallowed hard and looked at her. "I couldn't leave my wife, Arlene. The night I was with Jennifer . . . it didn't feel right."

Suddenly, right in front of her, my voice grew thick and husky. I lifted a shaky hand to shield my eyes and started bawling, weak sounds squeaking from my throat, and couldn't stop. Arlene said nothing. I wallowed in the shame of it all—the Butcher, Jennifer, my treatment of Cathy. Gradually, my breathing slowed. Arlene unexpectedly put a hand on my arm, and I bolted upright. "Jesus, what . . . "

"You sure you're okay?" She narrowed her eyes.

I took a tissue from the nightstand to wipe my eyes, my gaze darting from the floor to the ceiling to the wall, anything to avoid looking at her. The pathetic voice that wiggled out was me as a boy, begging the old man to leave my mother alone. "Sorry, I don't know what happened."

"It's all right; you've been through hell," Arlene said softly. "But I'm going to suggest a couple of professionals, people I know. They can help."

I wormed my head into the pillow. "I expect you've read my history, like everyone else in town. But people don't know about the shrinks I used to see, the meds they prescribed. It's been awhile."

"That's totally understandable. You should think about calling one of them now."

"Arlene, it's not like—"

"Think about it. I need you at the top of your game for this ride, Johnny."

I nodded. "Okay, promise."

"All right." She leaned back in her chair. "I assume you haven't been in the can before?"

"No, believe it or not, even after some wild nights in college."

"Here's what to expect. The cops who take you from here to there will try to rattle you, make you say something stupid. They'll be creative, like asking whether you killed Frank because he wouldn't give you a hand job, stuff like that. You say nothing—got it? Keep your mouth shut."

"That I can do." Even contemplating the experience was intimidating.

"You'll enter the jail complex through the lower level of the Justice Center garage. That's good, because there won't be any press around."

I pictured the media swarming, hoping for footage of a stumbling accused murderer. I gestured to my crutches, leaning against the closet. "Will they use a wheelchair, or can I keep these?"

"You'll keep them, and those crutches will get you a private cell. They keep a few available for head cases or, in your situation, the worry that someone might try to use a crutch as a weapon."

"Nice place."

"You'll be fingerprinted, then strip-searched to find out if you're trying to smuggle anything in."

I grimaced. "Like a bottle of booze?"

"You'd be surprised. It'll be a visual inspection only, but I'm told that time passes slowly when someone wearing latex gloves is staring at your asshole. Stay cool."

I thought of the Butcher and Billy, touching me. "Maybe after hanging naked from a basement rafter, this will be a piece of cake."

"You've got the right attitude." She crossed her legs and adjusted her skirt. "They'll inventory your belongings and issue a jail uniform. Now, when they escort you to your cell, the other inmates will ride your white self. The aisle is wide, to make sure that no one can assault a guard, so you won't be touched. Just face forward, don't respond, and get into your cell."

"I'll be locked in all night, right? I mean, no one . . . "

"You'll be safe and sound, and I'll see you in the morning."

I stared out the window again and remembered joking around with Bernie about Frank's popularity in the joint. "Is it true what they say, about prison? That the wolves in there . . . you know, are they going to knock out my teeth to make sure I give good blow jobs?"

Arlene uncrossed her legs and shifted in the plastic chair. "We're going to work together to make sure that prison isn't in your future, John."

"But, worst case."

"Believe me, if you're headed for prison, we'll have a whole other conversation."

"Doesn't sound like they'll serve soda bread on holidays."

"That's a safe bet." She glanced at a handsome silver watch. "I'd better be going. Any more questions?"

"No . . . but, Arlene, I want you to be certain of one thing. I swear to Jesus fucking Christ I didn't do this."

"I believe you." She returned the notepad to her black briefcase. "The problem is, Jesus Christ isn't hearing the case. It's twelve slobs in a jury box, Johnny. Twelve slobs in the box."

28

Arlene's yellow-and-black plaid skirt disappeared as she closed the door behind her. I swung my legs over the side of the bed, my toes throbbing at the sudden rush of blood, and steeled myself for an exchange with Cathy. To guard against the possibility of a dropped call, I phoned the house line. Of course, there was no chance that she would want anything to do with me after learning about Jennifer, but making bail was a priority. Even more critical was preserving some relationship with Molly.

I should have anticipated that Alison would be with her. She answered on the second ring, which I usually thought was a good thing, but not if it meant conversing with a pissed-off sister-in-law.

"It's me. I've gotta talk to Cathy."

A moment of dead air, then, "What the hell's wrong with you?"

"Look—"

"What the fuck? She was all torn up about what the Butcher did to you, then she finds out you've been screwing around."

"Alison, I need—"

"And a murder charge, you son of a bitch? All over the fucking TV. Quite a father figure."

I waited a beat to see if she'd start up again. "Let me talk to her, Alison."

"No way. She's resting."

"They're taking me to jail. I just need to say some things."

"So, tell me. I'll let her know."

I nearly drove my fist into the metal bed frame. I found myself shouting, "God damn it, Alison! She's my *wife*. Put her on the *fucking* phone!"

"Oh, yeah? Fuck *you!*"

Alison was, no doubt, prepared to jam the receiver into the cradle. I bit my lower lip. When the wave of emotion receded, my tone was measured. "Please, just a minute with her. My wife needs to hear me, to listen. Please."

There was silence, then a muffled sound; she must have cupped her hand over the mouthpiece. After a long pause, Cathy came on the line and said, "I'm filing for divorce."

Every syllable stung, even though the words came as no surprise. The only response that choked out of me was, "I understand."

"I just want it over, John, to be away from you." She spoke in a rush, like she'd practiced what to say and now felt compelled to follow the script. Alison and Carl had probably rehearsed it with her.

I gripped the bed railing. "None of this is your fault."

"I know that."

Maybe the best thing for everyone would be for me to just vault out of the fucking window. I twisted the receiver in my hand, wanting to crack the solid plastic against my teeth, but there were words she needed to hear. "And you need to know it was a mistake." *I really didn't want to have sex with Jennifer, but there was strawberry jam and whipped cream . . .*

"I should have left you a long time ago." Without doubt, she had dredged up a residue of emotion from deep within, recalled my prior denials from my days of running around with Martha, and concluded that I had lied to her more than once. "Did you love her, John?"

There was a weakness in the pit of my gut, just as when the Butcher had *click-clacked* toward me with that swaying bolt cutter. "Cathy, I . . . it was one time."

She started laughing—I couldn't believe it—laughing real loud and then gasping, again and again, like she was hyperventilating. "I'm moving in with Alison."

"No. I'll find somewhere—"

"Fuck you! I'm only here now to get our things. Kids are already driving by, taking pictures on their phones. And someone sent your girlfriend one of Molly and me in our own driveway! I will *not* stay here! This is your fucking house. Fucking, fucking, fucking . . . "

The noise that burst into my ear could only have been from Cathy striking the receiver against the wall, again and again. She was screaming *cheater* and *liar*, and there was the sound of glass breaking and then Alison saying, "Don't call her again."

"Alison, whatever you're thinking, she has to help with bail. I—"

"Ask your girlfriend."

"Don't do this to me."

"It's not her problem, John, it's yours."

"You're pissed off now, okay? But . . . I can't stay in one of those places. They do things in there to guys like me. Please."

"Serves you right."

"They've got gangs in there. Black gangs, Mexicans, Puerto Ricans, whatever. And punks like me. I'm begging you here. I want to see my little girl again."

My voice cracked, and Alison ended the call without saying another word. I was still staring at the tan phone, the push-button pad, when one of the cops stuck his head in the doorway.

"Let's go. We're cuttin' you too much slack already."

"Okay," I replied, embarrassed that he'd seen the tears in my eyes, and hobbled over to the crutches. Because of the bandages, I'd wear the hospital slippers instead of my shoes. My slacks and shirt from the night that the Butcher had abducted me were on hangers.

Not a button was torn, and the zipper was intact. She had meticulously stripped me naked. Bile rose in my throat at the thought of that demented bitch neatly folding my slacks, slipping off my underwear. I stared at the clothes for a while before summoning the resolve to dress and then pulled on the shirt. First thing, every bit of the defiled clothing would be doused with gasoline and torched.

If only what I'd done to a wife and daughter who loved me could be so easily burned away.

29

When the municipal judge rose from the beech wood bench, Arlene and I stood respectfully at the defense table. The judge had accepted the argument that I wasn't a flight risk but set bond at a cool million dollars. She'd also ordered me to surrender my passport, which was a bit of overkill because I didn't have one.

"Just be thankful the County Bond Commissioner didn't recommend something higher." Arlene organized the papers spread on the worn table and filed them in her briefcase. "By the way, you look natty in orange."

"Thanks." Stepping into the nearly fluorescent jumpsuit had felt like stripping away a layer of dignity. "So what's the next step?"

"I've already lined up that bondsman I told you about, Jeff Huggins." She slid the briefcase strap over her shoulder.

"I've seen some of his ads."

"He's doing a lien search now and will try to rush this through as a favor to me." We headed across the brown carpet and past the jury box to the single door through which the incarcerated were escorted. That would include me, unless and until I could arrange bail.

"But if Cathy won't sign, what the hell good is Huggins?" I'd told

Arlene earlier about the fiasco of a telephone call that had taken place with my wife.

She turned to face me in the subdued lighting of the courthouse. "I'm an optimist, John. If I can convince Cathy to help, you come straight to my office as soon as Huggins posts bond. Take a cab; the press won't wait around all day."

"But if she tells you to pound salt?"

"We'll have to go to Plan B."

"Which is?"

"I'll let you know when I figure that out."

Even if Cathy agreed to help, the process was going to drain everything that we had spent a lifetime accumulating. I followed Arlene through the corridor and to the jail elevator. An escort cop who trailed behind slouched in a corner and ignored us. "I couldn't believe all the press in court."

"They always roll out when a lawyer's in the hot seat. Besides, you survived the Butcher; you're a celebrity now." Arlene smiled wryly. "They'll set up a pooled feed for the trial."

"I forgot that they could be right in the courtroom." Which only confirmed my small-time-player status—I had never handled a case of enough interest to attract a news crew.

"Mandatory, per our Supreme Court. All a judge can do is control the number of cameras and where they're placed." The elevator opened and Arlene sidled out, headed for the St. Clair exit. "Wish me good luck with your wife."

The sullen cop deposited me in a holding cell, but I was eventually escorted to a close, windowless room to meet with Huggins. His huge ass balanced on a folding chair, he crooked a thick finger to summon me to a small conference table, then shoved some papers in my direction. There were sweat stains under the armpits of his wrinkled white shirt, and he smelled like a stale gym. "Look them over. The top one sets the amount of the bond."

I didn't even look at the documents; I was already weary of the administrative bullshit of the system and being treated like a number. "My name's John Coleman, by the way."

He raised his thick eyebrows, poised like caterpillars on his pudgy face. "I know. Johnson explain the process?"

"She did. I'm a lawyer too—"

"Not to me. I'm bonding you out of jail, for a fee. That's our relationship." He picked at something on his shirt, likely a fleck of last week's meatball sub. "There's also a mortgage, and the assignment of your life insurance policy. I'll fill in the numbers later."

Huggins absolutely didn't give a shit whether I was guilty or innocent, whether I lived or died or skulked away to Brazil. The guy had probably seen everything, heard every excuse imaginable, and now cared only about his money and his security. I inked the signature lines and slapped the docs in front of him. "Anything else?"

"Nope. Johnson said to get these to her, and she'll let me know if your wife signs off. That'll do it." He assembled the papers, shoved the packet into a battered black briefcase, and rumbled out without so much as a good-bye or a good luck. I was returned to the barren holding cell.

An eternity later, a cop rolled back the barred door. That meant one thing: Cathy had agreed to sign the bond documents. Soon wearing my own clothes and feverishly working the crutches, I left the towering cream-colored Justice Center behind me and hailed a cab to Arlene's modern office building on Superior Avenue.

A swarm of tailored suits, briefcases, and shiny shoes coursed through the vaulted atrium, beneath a pyramidal ceiling of maroon and onyx tile. A guard at the security desk handed over an ID badge and directed me to a bank of mirrored elevators. When I stepped into Arlene's mahogany-paneled office, her attractive receptionist, a middle-aged black woman, warmly welcomed me. Accused rapists, thieves, and murderers file in, and she needs to smile and promise that Ms. Johnson will be right with them. Would you like some coffee? How about a sharper knife, for next time? Cream? A false passport?

When I was escorted into her office, Arlene reached across an ebony granite desktop to greet me with a handshake. Her yellow blouse provided a dash of color beneath her muted brown suit. "Cathy came down and signed the papers, but she doesn't want any misunderstandings. Your marriage is over."

"What changed her mind?" I sank into one of two white leather chairs and leaned my crutches against the other. Vivid abstract paintings on the beige painted walls reminded me of Jennifer's apartment. Great.

"First, I reminded her that what happened between the two of you has nothing to do with the trial. Your adultery is an issue for the domestic relations court."

"Thank God for small favors." I gave a half-smile, which probably resembled Oyster's grimace when they'd hauled his skull from the Frigidaire.

"Second, and she brought this up before I did, she doesn't want the father of her daughter to be making license plates for the state. She put Molly first, John."

"No surprise there." Through Arlene's window, Lake Erie sparkled in the sunlight, and I remembered an anniversary dinner with Cathy, on a cruise ship. We had motored past the hulking Browns Stadium and watched the setting sun reflect on the gleaming Rock and Roll Hall of Fame.

"By the way, her sister would lock you away forever. Quite a mouth, for a good Catholic girl. Getting past her took some doing. You owe me."

"You have no idea. But now that I'm out, we're done with Huggins? By the way, he's not exactly a warm and fuzzy kind of guy."

"Find me a bail bondsman who is. And we should be done with him, but Mark Flanagan has your case."

"Flanagan? Shit."

"Know him?"

"Just by reputation. The Flanagan clan was too lace curtain to hang out with the Colemans." Some viewed the chief assistant prosecutor as a pit viper, others as an aggressive public vigilante, but no one ever claimed that he was less than stellar in a courtroom. He could more than hold his own, even against Arlene Johnson.

"He told me he's asking for a higher bond at your arraignment."

"Should I be worried?"

"Not particularly. Flanagan tries this stunt in every high-profile case. He rarely succeeds, but it plays well to the law-and-order types." Arlene sat back in her chair. "And he pulled something else before you were processed out. We can deal with this, so take it in stride. He filed a motion for a temporary restraining order, freezing your accounts. Business and personal."

I took a breath. "No way."

"His office submitted an affidavit, claiming they need time to determine whether you've scammed any other client accounts, and they want to prevent a transfer of any funds converted from the estate of Wilbur Frederickson . . . "

My eye drifted to framed photographs of her with the mayor, two ex-governors, and President Obama arranged on a credenza behind her.

"John?"

"Yeah. Sorry."

She scanned my face, appraising me. "You're going to have to be on top of your game to help me and get through this."

"I am. Just give me some time, okay? The last few days . . . "

"I told you that you should call a professional, John. Anyone who'd gone through what you did sure as hell would. Will you?"

"I can get through this, Arlene. I'm just tired and . . . all this stuff at once." No more shrinks, no more pill boxes. "What did the judge say?"

She kept her eyes fixed on me. "She conducted a hearing by phone and essentially granted his motion. But she released enough to allow for bail, something to live on during the proceedings, and costs of trial, including me."

"I suppose I should feel good about that." Everything was happening so goddamn fast.

"John, face facts. Flanagan's got a hard-on about this one. My guess: he'll capitalize on the publicity and run for judge next election."

"I'll vote for him if he loses my case."

"Since you're wondering, we've been opposite each other before. I think our win–loss record is tied." She picked up a folder and flicked it open. "You'll want to see these. Flanagan sent them over this morning. He didn't have to do this until the first pretrial but obviously doesn't feel the need to hold anything back."

She removed some photos from the folder. A couple of pictures were of my car, a few more of money in plastic bags, tagged for identification. I examined two close-ups of the "weapon"—a heavy chef's knife, clearly visible through the plastic.

"Well?" she asked, idly toying with her opal necklace.

I nodded, not quite believing what was in front of me. "I used that knife in Jennifer Browning's kitchen to cut some meat, an apple."

"Start at the beginning, John. Let's go." She pulled a notepad in front of her and hunched forward, a silver Mont Blanc in hand.

I walked Arlene through a chronology of my dalliance with Jennifer. From our first meeting in my office, the kiss in Dino's parking lot, the rendezvous at her apartment, the mysterious and disconcerting photographs. I detailed my visit to the Alley, my thrashing by the bouncer, the odd phone call with Frank before his murder.

About the only thing I didn't describe was the initial chill of the whipped cream on my naked balls.

30

"So you're thinking that she killed her own brother, took the money, and planted the knife and some of the cash in your car?"

"You want motivation? How about she's the sole heir for over two mil."

Arlene raised her eyebrows. "There's plenty of folks in my family that I dislike, but I'm not shopping for knives, no matter how much cash might be involved."

"But they had no communication, for years."

"So he couldn't have said anything that would upset her enough to kill him."

I stared out the window, fixing for a moment on the gauzy contrails traced in the sky. "Maybe the Andar Feo—even Bernie Salvatore thought of them after I found Frank."

"Then how'd the money wind up in your trunk? Was the gang making a charitable donation?"

"She sent me out for a bottle of wine and a damn sandwich, from Subway. Think about it. She had plenty of time to plant the evidence in my trunk." Christ, I should have listened to Bernie Salvatore when he told me to go home that night.

"Would that have mattered?" Arlene tapped her pen against a paperweight on her desk, a swirl of color encased in glass. "Fact is, John, if she'd called you the next day, you'd have run to her like a puppy. No surprise. You're not the first man to shut down his brain for sex—hand job, blow job, straight fuck. You guys will risk anything."

Her choice of words surprised me, but I expected that she was capable of handling a conversation with any rung of society, from gangbangers to the chairs of corporate boards. "It wasn't like that, Arlene. We were together one time."

"You think that helps?"

"I made a mistake, Arlene. She was just so *gorgeous* to me. That sounds . . . "

Arlene rolled her eyes. "Wow. I can see my opening statement now. Ladies and gentlemen of the jury, it's forgivable if my client found her gorgeous. What do you think, John? How does *glamorous* sound? Or should I go gutter and just say *tight pussy*?"

"But . . . she led me on, Arlene. She kissed me first. Then, at her apartment, she initiated the whole thing."

She leaned back and folded her arms. "You're serious? Where's this going—that you were date-raped?"

"You made your point, thanks."

"Think about it. I need the jury to believe she used you like a puppet. Because, the problem is, you had the motive, the opportunity, and the means. Having issues with your wife—your words—makes a man think about money a lot."

"No, no . . . " The way that Arlene was assessing my conduct was disturbing. "I wanted to save the marriage. I've got a kid, a daughter."

"So you want me to sell you as the repentant family man?" Arlene rested her pen on the desk. "You're not giving me a lot here, John."

"I'm telling you, Jennifer planned this. Talk about motive. She did it, or somebody helped her. She had plenty of time; I called her hours before leaving for Frank's."

"But you said she claimed she didn't know where he was. The

coroner puts the time of death within an hour or two before you found Frank. You said his text, with the address, was sent about an hour before you went to his house?"

"Yeah." I leaned forward. Finally, a ray of hope. "Jesus, I wouldn't have had time to kill him."

Arlene shook her head. "Maybe, maybe not. They can argue you got there early, whacked him, cleaned yourself up somewhere, stashed the knife and the dough, then went back and called the cops. They'll say you contaminated the crime scene on purpose when you played slip-slide in the blood."

"But I had to drive to Tremont. It was rush hour. I mean—"

"Look, just playing devil's advocate here, but if I'm Flanagan, I'd suggest that Frank might have given you his address when he first called. There's a few hours' window on TOD, you went there midafternoon, killed him, and sent yourself the text later from Frank's phone."

"But he didn't give me the address when he called."

Arlene pursed her lips, shook her head. "Think, John. Too bad he didn't text you then. How can I prove he didn't tell you the address?"

"Because it's the truth. Jennifer knows that; I told her."

"Are you kidding me?" Arlene looked at me as though my face had sprouted a third eye. "If she set you up, you think she won't deny it? And if she didn't know where Frank was, how could she kill him?"

"Jesus, I don't know." I raised my hands. "Maybe she found the address somehow, had time enough to kill him, then go back home."

"Yep. And, if you had the address, there was plenty of time for you to kill him, pretend to find him dead later, then call the cops. Anyone see you that afternoon?"

I closed my eyes and held them shut for a long second. "I sent my secretary home for the day."

"Great. The jury won't find anything suspicious in that."

"But . . . hey, whoever killed him could have texted me from his phone, lured me in."

Arlene nodded and rolled the opal on her necklace between her fingers. "And you helpfully walked right into it."

"But there'd be fingerprints on the phone!"

"Not if they held it in something, like a glove or handkerchief, and used a pen or pencil on the keypad. Which, by the way, is probably just what Flanagan will suggest you might have done."

"C'mon . . . what about the photos?"

"What about them, Johnny?" Arlene's tone verged on condescending. She was exasperated, I could tell. "All I can say about them now is that it looks like somebody was trying to scare her—the same girl you're accusing of being a cold-blooded murderess."

"Christ! But it had to be her."

Arlene turned her chair toward the window and seemed to scan the horizon. "Think carefully about what you're saying. If she killed him, why not just take the money Frank had—every lousy bill! Why stash it in your trunk? Everyone would have thought the Andar Feo had boosted the cash, and she could have walked. No fuss, no muss. And if it was this dastardly Mexican gang, and not her, why'd she have to set you up?"

I swallowed hard. My lawyer was fast losing confidence in my position. "I have thought about it, Arlene. Jennifer wouldn't have wanted them to beat her to Frank. Don't forget, it looked like he had Oyster's two hundred grand. Based on what they found in my trunk, that was for real—where else could that kind of money come from?"

Arlene turned back from the window and leaned on her desk, her shoulders slumped. "I'll give you that, but Jennifer is inheriting more money than most people ever dream about. Why take the chance?"

"Because she couldn't count on the Andar Feo, don't you see? I mean, these guys aren't locals. They might have even left town—it's not like they inked a deal with Jennifer. She had no guarantees what they'd do, and she could have ended up the prime suspect. But if the finger's pointing in my direction, she's scot free. Frank's case is closed with no suspicions about her, no questions—ever."

Arlene's eyes burned into mine, and then she picked up her pen and made a few notes. Standing, she strolled to the window and leaned into the burnished metal frame that separated the nearly floor-to-ceiling windows. "You do understand, we'll need to convince a jury that she's one devious-ass black widow. Problem is, she *is* a widow—one you just described as gorgeous—with a regular job, who helps immigrants learn English. Persuading them that Jennifer crawled out from under a rock won't be easy."

"Damn, Arlene, she had me convinced that she wanted me. That was one giant sucker punch."

"Which makes you . . . ?"

I didn't say anything. God, I wanted a drink, wanted out of there.

"John, you're not a bad-looking man, not at all. But you're older and married. You really thought that Miss Gorgeous couldn't wait for you to yank down her panties?"

I stared hard at the floor. "C'mon, you already made your point."

"The *point* is that I don't have much here to go with. Arguing it was her or a Mexican drug gang will be a tough sell."

"Maybe the Butcher. I mean, she killed Oyster . . . "

Arlene straightened and took a step toward me. "Jesus Christ! Did the Butcher plant a knife, which you just told me belonged to Jennifer, in your car? Were all of them—Jennifer, the bikers, the Butcher, and her brother—conspiring? What about the Pope? Him, too? Give me something here."

I couldn't blame her for being frustrated. My story sounded like a stretch, even to me. "I'm telling you the truth, Arlene."

She walked back to her chair and, sitting, braced her arms against the desk. "You've been in this business long enough to know that the first casualty of war—or whatever the hell we do in a courtroom—is the truth. I can't rely on the truth. I need to rely on creating reasonable doubt in the minds of the jurors."

"Arlene, if I had anything more to tell you, I would. Has anyone checked for her prints? The knife, my car keys, my trunk . . . " I felt as though I had lost control, like the night that the tattooed punk had beaten my ass. I remembered lying there, being kicked, watching the Andar Feo guys laugh. Abruptly, my memory shifted to the image of the Butcher bearing down, wielding her bolt cutter.

Arlene eased forward and crossed her arms on the desk. "We'll have it all checked out, but if she did touch anything, and she's half as calculating as you say, we both know she wore gloves. If she does have the money, the cash is most assuredly not resting in a bank account traceable to her."

"You're not exactly filling me with hope here."

"By the way, about that retirement watch—gold, by the way—they'll argue you took it off his corpse."

"Who would give a junkie a gold watch? He'd pawn it in a minute."

"Good point, but I'm betting the jury will be more concerned with how it wound up in your trunk."

"Well, hell, why didn't I steal the poor kid's socks while I was at it?"

"Johnny, get a grip." She splayed her hands on the desk and tapped her fingers on the granite for a moment. "You've done jury work. I know not much criminal, but you have tried some cases, right?"

I nodded. The thrum of the air conditioner ceased, and the sudden silence was jarring. "Some."

"I've got a lawyer who slept with his client, cheated on his wife. Who had thirty-five thousand dollars in the trunk of his car, the victim's watch, along with—get this—a nice, big knife covered with his fingerprints and the blood of the dead man. Have I left anything out?"

I looked away, out the window, at the vast expanse of Lake Erie.

"How do you think a jury will assess that evidence?" She followed my gaze over the lake. "This is difficult for you, but we have to face facts. And Fact Number One is that you present a helluva tough case. I'm a damn good lawyer, not a magician."

Some other voice was talking in the room—it couldn't have been mine—asking if I risked lethal injection.

"There's not a doubt in my mind that Flanagan will go for the death penalty." Arlene raised her eyebrows.

The sky outside was bright blue, nearly cloudless, the kind of day where I used to escape from work early, knock back a few, and ogle pretty women. "Damn it, I didn't do this."

"I'm not saying you did, but there are some procedural things you'd better understand. Flanagan will argue to the grand jury—he may be there as we speak—that they should indict you for aggravated murder with a felony murder specification. In your case, that means the murder occurred during the commission of a robbery. If the grand jury agrees that there's probable cause for that charge, you're facing the death penalty."

I knew enough to understand that no one, not even my lawyer, could appear before the grand jury to present my side of the story; it would be strictly Flanagan's show. "Do you think they'll indict?"

"In this county, the defense bar likes to say that a grand jury will indict a ham sandwich." She picked up the photographs of the knife and dropped them in front of me. "Yeah. I think they'll indict."

I wanted to toss aside the fucking crutches and bolt to the elevator. "What about a lie detector?"

"Sorry. The prosecutor offers you the lie box only at his discretion. Flanagan never offers it in capital cases."

"Can the prick make me see a shrink?"

"First, he's Mr. Flanagan to you. Make this personal, and he'll eat you for lunch. If I need to put you on the stand and he gets under your skin, it's over. And, no, he can't make you see a shrink, because we're not making your mental state an issue. We'll argue that you were set up, not that you killed someone because of your mental state."

"What about my history—the psychiatrists, the medications?

Can he find out about that and try to use it against me?" I imagined the doctors' notes splayed across Page One of the *PD*.

"HIPAA protects your health care records. Unless we bring it up—which we won't—it's off limits."

That was a relief, but what she said about taking the stand scared me. Flanagan would be merciless. "So you're thinking I might have to testify?"

"The last thing that any defense lawyer wants is to put the client on the stand. So don't sweat it, for now. A trial is like a chess game, and we can't decide every move in advance."

Chess. Yeah, Jennifer was the queen, and I was her pawn to maneuver.

Or sacrifice.

"One more thing. Hey, you still with me? We'll need an investigator, and a good one. I have some recommendations, unless you have somebody in mind."

Right away, I thought of Jack. I could hear him already. *What the fuck you got yourself into now, Johnny? Hope the pussy was worth it.* "I do know somebody. Jack Corrigan, an ex-cop who did PI work after he left the force. He's up there, but in his day, there wasn't anybody better."

The fact that Jack drank too much gave me pause, but he knew the ropes, was a tough SOB, and I trusted him. Arlene let me use one of her conference rooms, where her framed undergraduate degree from Howard University hung next to a diploma from Georgetown Law School. Jack answered right away, as if he'd been expecting my call.

"Didn't I fuckin' warn you, tell you to stay away from this shit?" he yelled.

"I know you're pissed at me, but I'm calling for help."

"Well, you sure as hell need it."

I counted to three. "I want you as our investigator, Jack. This murder thing . . . "

"Thing? Wake the fuck up. You're in some serious shit."

"That's why I'm calling you. I'll pay you, of course."

"Ahh, fuck. Like I need this." There was a long pause. "Who's your lawyer?"

"Arlene Johnson."

Another pause. "The black one?"

"That's her." I had to cut Jack some slack. In his day, there probably hadn't been a black, let alone a woman, in a position of authority—and certainly not in Lakewood.

"Look, I know some lawyers who are good with these kinda cases."

"I want her, Jack. If you tell me you can't work with her, I'll understand."

"I'll think about it, get back to you."

"Thanks."

"Don't thank me yet, I ain't said *yes*. You know, it's been all over the news, what you done."

"I know."

"Your wife and kid had to see that shit."

"I know that, Jack. This isn't the time for a lecture; it's bad enough as it is."

"I'm sure it is. George Moore? The choice? You sure as hell made the wrong one, Johnny."

The line went dead.

31

"I really thought that she might bump the bond up to two mil." The separate counsel tables were only a few feet apart, and Mark Flanagan turned to Arlene when the arraignment concluded. His brown hair was fashionably long, framing a chiseled face and unusually vivid green eyes.

"Not given the County Bond Commissioner's recommendation." Arlene's confident reply bolstered me. The judge had listened to their arguments intently. Had the court agreed with Flanagan, I'd be spending a lot of time staring at walls.

"So you're ready for our next go-round. What are we now, 6–6?" Flanagan stood, and I judged him to be just short of six feet tall and in his midthirties. He'd been a popular wrestler at St. Edwards' High School and, later, at John Carroll University. I remembered him from the sports pages, and it looked like he'd stayed in damn good shape. Since he pointedly ignored me, I remained seated, my crutches resting against a chair near the empty jury box.

"Good memory. I haven't forgotten our last dance, that felony weapons charge, when you laughed after my guy refused to cop a plea. The jury acquitted in under an hour."

Flanagan gave her his deadly Great White grin. "I remember. But that won't be an issue here; there won't be any deal offered. Just so you know."

"Just so you know, we weren't looking for one." Arlene smoothed a lapel on her charcoal suit.

Flanagan flashed his full grill once again and turned toward the cluster of cameras—his chance for a little publicity. Vanessa Edwards was there, and I recognized some of the other talking heads, too.

The grand jury had fulfilled Arlene's prediction and indicted me for murder with a felony murder spec. We waived a preliminary hearing, because the only issue would be whether probable cause existed to issue the warrant for my arrest. Arlene assured me that a bloody knife covered with my fingerprints would do the trick, and there was no sense in giving the prosecutor an easy win and the media a headline.

We headed toward a side exit, to an elevator that was off-limits to the press, and I finally breathed a sigh of relief. "Good work in there, Arlene. If she'd raised the bond . . . "

"One step in a long journey, John."

"What do you think of the judge?" For trial, my case had been assigned to Howard Seidelson, whom I'd never appeared before or even met, since he lived in one of the Jewish communities on the east side of town.

"Competent. Not especially bright, but he knows how to run a jury trial, I'll give him that."

"I guess that's something." I could have chosen a three-judge panel to decide my fate, instead of a jury. Either way, the decision had to be unanimous, and the odds of persuading one out of twelve were better than one out of three.

"Tell your man, Corrigan, that we need to know if he's on board. If he's waffling, we need to get somebody else. Talk to him and call me, okay?"

After promising to follow up, I took a cab home, my crutches balanced on my thighs. The driver, a black dude wearing a faded Kent

State cap, kept glancing in the rearview mirror, like he was wondering if I was *that guy*.

The lake was angry; rollers the color of graphite surged into the jetty at Edgewater Park and burst into the air. The wind was already whipping through the trees. I was relieved that we reached my house before the coming storm hit.

I sat at the kitchen table, surveying the coffee cups and plates that needed scraping and loading into the dishwasher. A dollop of butter had melted on a plate that I'd failed to return to the refrigerator. I reached for the phone and dialed Jack.

"So you heard," he said, actually sounding a tad excited. "I just found out myself."

"Heard what? I've been in court, my arraignment."

"They found the Butcher dead in her cell this morning." He sounded almost gleeful to be the one to tell me. He sipped something. Coffee or Kessler's, most likely, or maybe both. "Suspect she had a heart attack in her sleep."

I said nothing for a long moment, reflecting on her and Billy, the bolt cutter, my muffled screams. "Are you buying it, Jack? She probably got into the infirmary somehow, took some kinda pills. She wasn't going to prison."

"So? She's dead. Does it matter?"

"Doesn't seem right that she goes out like that."

"She'll burn in eternal hell, Johnny. Gotta have faith."

"Yeah, faith." My life was on trial, and the Butcher had just drifted away. I had hoped that she'd somehow avoid the death penalty and live a long life, tormented by sadistic prison guards in a place of cold gray steel. And as much rough, nonconsensual sex with bullying inmates as a human could possibly tolerate.

"They tell me they found nothin' in the house to identify Torso. The county has birth records for a Mary and William Smith. Death certificates, too. Infants killed in a house fire in the early fifties."

"What's that mean?"

"Our friend Torso had the names and DOBs from the paper, or a tombstone, of two dead kids. Back then, that's all he would have needed to obtain IDs for his own—what should we call them? Spawn?"

"Sounds about right." I could think of a lot of labels that applied to the Butcher and Billy. "Listen, about my case, Jack. You in? The lawyer wants to know."

He hesitated. "What you did to Cathy was wrong. You had no business screwin' that Browning broad, and you weren't straight with me."

"Christ, Jack, you want me to fall on my sword, I will. I'm askin' for your help here."

"I shoulda seen all this coming when you couldn't let go of the murders."

"Damn it, Jack." I clenched the receiver. "I was right. The Butcher was watching me, my family."

He cleared his throat and it sounded like he spit something up. "I'll give you that, Johnny, but you went way over the top. Getting your ass beat at some dive, the mess with Frank . . . and Jennifer? Jesus."

I pressed my free hand into the table top. "I suppose it doesn't matter now."

"I wished you'd listened to me. That's all I'm sayin'."

"Look, if you're tellin' me to get somebody—"

"Who knows you better than me?" He took a slurp of whatever he was drinking. "Fuck it. I'm in, but it ain't about you. It's for your old man and Cathy and most of all, your little girl."

A single tear appeared in the corner of my eye. I imagined that Jack was with me in my empty house, reaching across the table and resting a hand on my shoulder. "You know I appreciate this."

"Hell, I just can't let you screw this up, too. When's your court date?"

"They haven't set it yet, but Arlene expects it will be sometime next spring."

"We'll see. Some of them judges are slower than molasses. When do you want me to start?"

"Let me call Arlene and find out. What do you charge for this kind of thing, anyway?" There was no way that Jack was doing it for the money. I sensed that he really was protecting me and looking forward to one last chance to swing into action.

"Not enough, I expect. We'll talk. Hey, turn on the TV. There's a report about the Butcher now."

I hung up and flicked on the television. A photo of the Butcher, smiling and kindly, filled the screen. Was that really the face of the woman who had driven my father to his grave, had wielded the sharp blades that sliced my toes away? *For Daddy*. I glanced at the cupboard where my liquor was stored. But knocking one back, with dark memories of that basement fresh on my mind, seemed like a mistake.

The rain began, pitter-pattering on the shingles, and thunder rumbled in the distance. I negotiated my way into the living room and, checking the mail slot by the front door, leafed through a couple of bills and a sheaf of discount ads. My hand froze for a moment on the final letter, from a law firm known for handling domestic relations matters. I tore the envelope open. The attorney, a woman I did not know, informed me that she represented Cathy Coleman, who was filing for divorce.

The second paragraph was the one that caused me to sit down on the couch and rest the letter on the coffee table. I read the paragraph a few times, focusing on the words *visitation would not be in the best interests of your child*. My temples throbbed.

I accepted that my life was shattered. The divorce was expected, my tattered career was finished, and my next job would involve peddling beef 'n cheddars at Arby's. Whatever friends I had would shun me. *You're a shit*, had been Bernie's accurate and painful words.

But I would not give up my Molly.

I didn't handle domestic relations cases but knew that even accused murderers could see their kids. Innocent until proven guilty and all that. My alleged crime was not one of sexual violence, and I had never even swatted Molly, let alone hurt her.

Cathy wouldn't answer if I called her cell, that was for sure. There really wasn't a choice but to try and haggle my way past her sister again. Not giving a damn about the crutches, I lurched to my feet and hobbled toward the kitchen phone. Instead of Alison, my brother-in-law answered the phone.

"Let me talk to her, Carl." I sat down at the barren table where my family had once shared breakfast.

"You shouldn't be calling here."

"Carl . . . "

"She doesn't want to talk to you."

There was a crack of thunder as the rain picked up, and I clenched the phone. "Put her on the fucking line."

"Screw you."

"Damn it, Carl. It's about Molly. If I have to get into my fucking car and drive over there, I will."

"I'll call the police."

His threat prompted me to laugh. "Think I give a shit? Is a trespassing charge gonna make my life any worse? This is my daughter we're talking about. Put Cathy on."

I could sense his hesitation, pictured him muffling the phone with his sweaty palm. His voice was indistinct, and then Alison's came through clearly as she admonished Cathy: "Don't be stupid!"

But Cathy came on the line. "This isn't a good idea, John. The lawyer said you might—"

"Fuck the lawyer. I won't fight you on anything, anything you want. But I will do anything to see Molly. Spend every last dime, represent myself, whatever it takes. Just don't try to keep her from me."

She was quiet, and pellets of rain hammered into the windows. "Your own lawyer should handle this. Let them talk."

"We don't need lawyers to work this out. You can supervise the visits if you want. I'll see a shrink, quit the booze, start going to Mass again. Swear to God, just let me see her."

"Interesting choice of words, John. You, swearing to God, after what you've done."

"Cathy . . . "

"Never mind." She was quiet, and I pictured her, head bowed, clutching her earlobe. "Molly's not been herself with all that's going on. I'm making her go to school, but she doesn't want to anymore. The other kids . . . "

I knew what she was going through. Did my little girl have somebody like Bernie in her life? She didn't need anyone to fight her fights, but the thought of all the hurt and anger bottled up inside Molly was maddening. "We need to talk to her, Cathy. You and me. Just the three of us, no lawyers."

"Except you?"

"C'mon, I'll be fair about this."

"I've already sat down with her and explained everything."

"She needs to hear from me that this has nothing to do with you. Every mistake was mine, and I'm sorry. And she has to understand that it's not about her. Sometimes, kids blame themselves; you know that."

Silent again, Cathy breathed into the phone. Then she said, "Let me think about it. I'll call you."

"Wait." There was one question that I needed to ask. "Was it your idea, the no visitation?"

She hesitated. "No. The lawyer suggested that we start there. I went along."

"We don't need lawyers negotiating, sending us bills. We can work this out."

"I said I'll call."

"She's my girl, Cathy. I lost my dad and grew up with Jack Corrigan and other guys who felt sorry for me. That can't happen with Molly. I have to be there for her, don't you see?"

Cathy sighed, and her voice grew husky. "What the hell were you thinking, John?"

She hung up. I cradled the phone and shuffled to the freezer, no longer preoccupied with thoughts of the Butcher or Oyster's frozen visage. I dropped some cubes into a tumbler; soon, the ice crackled beneath a healthy dose of whiskey.

Months would pass before the trial began, and I'd be damned if I would wait that long without seeing Molly. And a worse outcome loomed, too: losing the case and visiting with my daughter occasionally, if Cathy would even escort her to prison. I pictured Molly inching through a security line, prison guards roughly patting her down, a hand slipping here, there. By mistake, of course. We'd have to speak through a Plexiglas window, our voices distorted by tinny-sounding telephones. Or perhaps we'd be allowed to meet in a supervised communal area, seated at a bolted-down table, where they would let me hold her hand for a few precious minutes. She'd tell me about driving lessons and her cute boyfriend and dancing the night away at the prom.

The rain hammered against my house in unrelenting sheets.

32

Cathy still had on one of her teacher outfits, a beige skirt paired with a white blouse. Molly wore her faded jeans and a black T-shirt with the word *Extreme* scrawled in yellow lettering. She hugged me when we met at the door, but the embrace was half-hearted and brief.

We sat in the living room, exactly where my discussion with Cathy about the fragile state of our marriage was to have occurred. Cathy and Molly were on the sofa, and I settled into my easy chair on the opposite side of the coffee table.

After Cathy had called and agreed to meet, my mind had been devoted to planning what to say to my daughter. Now, every word that tumbled out of my mouth sounded stilted.

"Your dad did a very bad, very stupid thing." I was conscious that my head bobbed, as though encouraging Molly to agree with me.

"I read it in the paper and talked about it with Mom." Molly parroted my nod.

All the manuals advise against discussing the sex thing when an affair causes a divorce, instead recommending the use of terms like *feelings* or *growing in different directions*. Unfortunately, that advice was not practical when my fling with Jennifer had been a headline on the front page.

"What you need to know, Molly, is that your mom is not to blame, not in any way."

She nodded her head very slowly and then said to me, "Jimmy Cannon bets that Mom's a lousy fuck since you were screwing around."

"Molly!" Cathy reddened. "That's not language we use."

"Ignore idiots like him." But I knew from my own experience that she couldn't. There was a ditty that my mom would recite to me that sticks and stones would break my bones, but words would never hurt me. Whoever coined the phrase had never heard the words that had tormented me on the playground or the ones that were likely being hurled at Molly every day. I wanted to kill Jimmy Cannon.

"And they say you must have murdered that man. They found the knife in your car." Molly's eyes were wide and questioning, waiting for me to respond.

"No, honey, I didn't do it. They've made a mistake, a terrible, terrible, mistake." The urge to hold her, stroke her hair, and tell her that everything would be okay was overwhelming.

"But how did the knife get in your car?" She hunched forward, her chin poised above the Bible on the coffee table.

"I don't know. Somebody put it there. You'll see, at trial."

Molly nodded, clearly skeptical. I would have preferred another interrogation by Arlene.

Cathy said, "Dad wants to see you while we're living apart. Maybe you can spend some weekends here, in your old room. Would you like that?"

My sweaty fingers pressed together while Molly contemplated her response. Finally, she said, "I guess that would be okay."

My eyes welled, and I wiped the tears away with the back of my hand. "Thanks, sweetie. We'll have fun, you'll see. We can go to a movie, get something to eat."

She made a face. "I think it's better if we just stay here."

My teenage daughter was reluctant to appear with me in public, anticipating the stares and whispers. "Whatever you want."

She sank back into the sofa and looked from me to Cathy. "Are you guys mad at me for anything?"

Cathy nestled Molly's tiny hand in her own. "God, no."

"Because they sent me away before, you know, when people didn't want me."

"That's . . . that's got nothing to do with this, Molly. All of this is because of me." Forgetting how vulnerable she was, inside the shell of her tomboy image, was too easy. Cathy drew her close and enveloped her in a tight hug. I had lost the privilege of striding around the table and wrapping them both in my arms.

After awhile, Cathy sat upright and boosted Molly from the sofa. "Why don't you get that stuff you wanted from your room, sweetie? Let me talk to your dad for a minute."

Molly stood and then looked down at my sandals. "What about your feet, Dad?"

"Just fine, honey. Who needs all those toes? I'll get by." The pain was lessening, and hobbling short distances without the crutches had become routine. Other than two ugly scars, which would forever remind me of a dank basement and bright red lips, I'd eventually be fine.

As Molly padded upstairs, Cathy turned to me and folded her hands in her lap. "What about us, John? Financially."

My eyes dropped and scanned the figurines on the table. "This will probably take everything we have." I looked up at her; she was nodding. "I don't know how else to say it."

"I'm not surprised. Carl's asked around about these types of cases."

"We'll have to work out a budget. Until, you know . . . " I couldn't bring myself to say it.

"The divorce." Cathy was reserved, nearly emotionless. She seemed to sit in the shadow of the cross above the fireplace.

"I'll talk to your lawyer." I cleared my throat. "My situation complicates everything."

Cathy reached out and ran a finger over the glass surface of the table. "If it weren't for Molly, I'd probably approach all of this differently."

I watched her finger meander aimlessly. "Thank you for letting me see her."

She took a deep breath and sat up straight. "And what about your work?"

"I'm not sure, really. My practice is dead." I leaned forward and rested my elbows on my thighs. The landlord was already planning, no doubt, to scrub my name from the office door. "Marilyn is transferring files. She knows I'm shutting down and is looking for something else."

"She won't have any problem, will she?"

I shook my head. "She's damn good, and I'll give her a helluva reference." If anyone valued my opinion. *He cheated on his wife and might have killed someone, but he sure knows his secretaries!*

Suddenly, Cathy's shell cracked. Her lip trembled and her eyes filled with tears. "I thought we'd retire together, be okay."

I felt my own lip quiver and cleared my throat. "I've got responsibilities yet, to you, to Molly. I'll clear my name and find something. I promise."

"Alison says we can stay as long as we want." Cathy looked away, at nothing, and wiped her tears.

I stared at the balletic figurines. "My lawyer will let me help on the case, too, legal research and that sort of thing, to keep her fee down."

"Nice of her." She took a deep breath, gathering herself. "Call me. We'll work out a schedule for Molly."

Our daughter's footsteps sounded on the stairs, and Cathy stood as Molly darted into the room, a knapsack slung over her shoulder. If she noticed Cathy's reddened eyes, she didn't say anything.

"Got everything you need, little lady?" I went to her, and we walked together to the door. Cathy passed by me and out onto the porch. Molly hugged me, resting her hands on my back for just a moment.

As Cathy backed out of the driveway, I waved. Molly returned a single flick of her hand. They looked like they did in the photograph that had unsettled me in Jennifer's apartment. I turned and stared at the cross in my living room, praying that they would be safe.

33

"Like she said, hit-and-run in Tijuana." Jack Corrigan leaned back into the white leather chair next to me and spoke to Arlene, who was seated at her desk. I stared past him and out the window, at a hazy blue sky and slate-colored lake. "The place wasn't so rough back then—although you could still get about anything you wanted, legal or not—and the California types would shoot down for a cheap weekend."

Jack had been working the streets, calling his old cohorts, but not a single helpful fact had turned up as we marked off calendar dates until trial. We'd meet periodically, the three of us, to brainstorm, listen to Jack's update, and discuss anything we needed to do in preparation for trial. Life had settled into a routine, the only bright spot being Molly's visits every other weekend. I'd even gone for a couple of semi-jogs in Lakewood Park and learned to balance with missing digits.

"What else?" Arlene asked. They looked like creatures from different worlds: Arlene so polished, so poised, in a gray business suit, and Jack in a dingy blue shirt, tucked into a pair of faded corduroys. His white T-shirt was visible through the open collar, and he'd draped his worn leather jacket, needed to ward off a brisk fall breeze, over the back of the chair. Jack had cocked an eyebrow when he'd first seen

Arlene—a regal, brown-skinned woman in a power suit—but he'd accepted that hiring her was my decision and let it rest.

"Him working for some kind of import/export business in San Diego, that checked out. Pretty common down there. But other than confirming his employment, they haven't been very helpful."

"Maybe we're wasting time and money." Arlene, taking notes, sounded testy as she rolled the Mont Blanc between her fingers. "Not a hole in her story."

"Yeah, but Frank calling John like he did, talking about the hit-and-run, the import/export . . . somethin' seemed fishy to me . . . "

I could tell Arlene was irritated that Jack had paused for effect. She stopped twirling the pen. "And?"

"I hate to say it, but we need somebody on the ground out there, someone connected in San Diego, like I am here. We can keep a leash on him, Johnny, keep the costs down."

"Is it worth it? Shit like that happens all the time in Tijuana, doesn't it?"

"Have somebody snoop around, maybe for just a day. Won't cost that much. I think we ought to know if the marriage was solid, if her husband's death was legit." Jack fiddled with the flap on the black leather case strapped to his belt, where he kept his phone. Arlene had insisted that Jack pick up a cell so we could all reach each other as needed.

"I need more than a hunch—it has to be something we can use in court," she said.

"Okay, fine. Coleman's only on trial for his life. Guess there's no need to follow my gut. I've only been doing this since before—"

"Since before my people were allowed into Lakewood?"

Jack's eyes narrowed, and he looked from her to me, nonplussed. "What's that supposed to mean?"

"Oh, 'scuse me Officer Corr-i-gan. I sho' nuff don't know what come ovah me, thinkin' I had cause to make some kinda point. Let me do a li'l Oprah head-bobble now and get on back to mah place."

I was stunned. Arlene's dialect was straight from an episode of

Amos 'n Andy. Never, ever, had she spoken that way. She stared at Jack until he averted his eyes, shifting his gaze out the window and over Lake Erie.

"Hold on, hold on." A rift on my team would be a disaster. "I'm feeling just desperate enough to hire somebody on the other side of the country to go chat up a bunch of people who don't give a shit about me." Another expense. The judge had lifted the injunction freezing my accounts, because Flanagan had found no evidence that I'd scammed any client funds, but the assets that remained were dwindling fast.

Jack looked at Arlene as if he were going to say something, but thought better than to spark a fight. Although it was cool outside, the sun was burning in through the windows, and the room was warm, despite the air conditioning. I had prayed that Jack would unearth a lucky shamrock, but it wasn't looking so good. And what bug had crawled up Arlene's ass?

"Fine," Jack said. "I'll take care of it."

"Tell the guy to get on it, because we're running out of time." She spoke in her usual corporate, I'm-in-charge voice.

I was afraid that Jack was going to reply with *yes, boss*, but he just nodded. "I did check the parking lot at her apartment, like you asked, but the only camera is on the door with the building directory, where the tenants have to buzz people in. The parking lot's not monitored. Jennifer coulda used a side door to put the shit in your trunk, easy, and let herself back in."

"Any luck with that girl from Ed's Eggs, Mary?" I wanted her questioned because, just maybe, Jennifer had gone back to the restaurant and convinced Mary to tell her where to find Frank.

"I've done my best, Johnny. No sign of her."

"Well, Christ, go back. Find out her schedule, wait for her."

"You're not getting it. I mean, she missed a shift and never came back. No one at that greasy spoon's heard from her. I've tried trackin' her down, but she's goddamn disappeared."

"Disappeared . . . ?"

Arlene said, "People on the low rung of the ladder slip through the cracks all the time, John, you know that."

Her observation only served to reinforce what the Butcher had said, about the *dregs*. "But—look, this may sound crazy . . . maybe Jennifer did something to her, killed her, too. We both thought she knew where Frank was."

They exchanged glances, and Arlene said, "I understand you're trying to figure everything out, but you can't spitball in front of a jury. Without Mary—or at least someone who can link her to Jennifer—we've got nothing."

"I'll try once more, but don't hold your breath." Jack kind of spat out the words, like he was irritated with me and tired of chasing dead ends. "I checked out the neighborhood where Frank was killed again, too. I'm turnin' nobody up who can put Jennifer near Frank's place, not that anybody's exactly lining up to talk to me. The people who work with Jennifer at Business One got no problems with her, and that place where she teaches English to the . . . Spanish, nothin' there, either."

Jack had caught himself before he used a word other than *Spanish*. And I didn't think he'd really care that the immigrants Jennifer taught were most likely not from Spain.

"And, the damn thing, John, is all these restaurant people. They saw you with Jennifer, trying to find out where Frank was. And, well . . . "

"Go on."

"You let everyone know that you were wrapped up in the killings, the Butcher stuff. That cop, Coufalik, finds it strange that you kept showing up at crime scenes. Salvatore don't wanna say nothin', you can tell—although he's pissed about you cheatin' on Cathy—but he's stuck and can't deny when and where he saw you. Coufalik said somethin' about maybe you got bit by the murder bug, like Frank was practically begging to get himself killed."

The absurdity of what Jack just said slapped me so hard that I nearly vaulted from the chair. Jack and Arlene were serious, though; apparently, they did not find Coufalik's assessment as ludicrous as I did. Arlene rapped her pen against that colorful paperweight a couple of times, *click-click.*

"And none of her prints are on your car."

"No surprise. I don't know . . . just keep doing what you're doing." Arlene uttered the words as though she had already concluded that Jack's efforts would remain futile.

"Sure. And I'll try to learn how to make a point without pissing people off."

Arlene's face tensed, but she let the remark pass. Jack hoisted himself from the leather chair and left without a good-bye. I started to rise, but Arlene waved me down. "You told me you've known Corrigan most of your life."

"We go back a long ways. He was there for me when my father passed."

"Then maybe you've heard some rumors about him. Back in the day, he had a rep for bustin' the heads of any of my people who crossed into Lakewood. Maybe not as bad a spot for us as Little Italy, but close."

Time was when blacks didn't venture into certain areas of town. Little Italy, on the East Side, had been one. Lakewood, I knew, had been another. "That kind of crap was a long time ago, Arlene."

"Doesn't excuse it, now, does it? There's nothing about it in his jacket; I just heard through the grapevine. You told me how tough he was, his fight with—possibly—the Torso Murderer, but I guess you didn't know about this side of him."

"Arlene—"

"You wanted him on the case, so he's on the case, but if I'd known about this before, we'd be using someone else." Her dark eyes flashed at me. "He's doing the job, and that's what matters. But I'll bet he probably walks out of here, meets his Irish cronies for a drink, and wonders how the hell you could have hired a nigger lawyer."

I squirmed in my chair, thinking of jokes we'd shared at the Tam; I felt like a schoolboy under her withering stare.

"So many white folks think everything's all better now—we even got us a Pres-i-dent. But I never forget that guys like Corrigan got away with what they did, and there's plenty like him still around. Every test I ever took, every speech I ever gave, there was something to prove to his kind."

I stared at the plush carpet for a moment before raising my head. "Can you still work with him?"

She folded her hands and gazed across her granite desktop, her intense dark eyes burning into me. "I'll work with the devil himself, if that's what it takes."

"The old Faustian bargain?"

"It's you who may need to sell your soul, not me. And if that time comes, Johnny, you'd better be prepared. Because right now, we don't have much else."

34

"One more, okay?" Molly said, bouncing up from the bleacher-style seat and trotting toward the skateboard run, just south of the tennis courts in Lakewood Park. I shoved my hands into the pockets of my down jacket and watched her dip and weave along the concrete. I'd eventually come to understand the various moves—fakie, boardslide, grind—but learning Latin in ninth grade had been easier, encouraged by the rap of a nun's ruler across my knuckles.

Lakewood Park had changed since I was a kid. There hadn't been any access to Lake Erie back then, except for the times in high school when my buddies and I had risked scaling the steep cliffs to challenge each other's testosterone. Years later, the county installed a terraced ramp, bordered by lime-green railings, that zig-zagged downhill to the break wall. The monkey bars and tall swings of my youth had been hauled away and replaced by colorful plastic configurations with safety railings, all positioned over rubber mats.

Even Molly, zipping along in her jeans and hoodie, wore headgear and kneepads, equipment that had never existed when I was her age. She executed some maneuver, grabbing the front of her board, then spinning and landing smoothly. Effortlessly, she rolled off the track and bounced slightly to flip the board into the air. She caught the front lip, where she had fixed her grip tape—sandpaper—to ensure better footing, and ran to me.

"Looking good, sweetie," I said.

She pulled off her helmet and ran a hand through her tousled hair. "Want me to teach you?"

"Maybe, some day."

She laughed and joined me in the seats. I wished that time would slow down.

"You see that spit of land, just past the baseball diamond? That's where runaway slaves boarded ferries to Canada. Last stop on the Underground Railroad." I pointed past the oaks, mostly denuded of leaves, as another winter was nearly upon us.

"You told me that before. Plus, we had a field trip here."

"Same thing when I was a kid."

"Really? They had buses back then?" Her eyes twinkled, which was rare. Skateboarding was the one thing that seemed to bring her true joy.

"Smart aleck. And we all carried vinyl lunchboxes."

"Wow," she deadpanned. "How retro."

"I probably spent as much time here as you do. They showed movies every Friday, when it didn't rain. That pool's where they taught me to swim." And where I'd first screwed up the courage to spark an awkward conversation with Ellen O'Donnell, irresistible in her lime green Speedo.

Lakewood had been special for Cathy and me, too. I glanced over my shoulder, at the fence that bordered the park. On the other side, a dirt road ran nearly to the edge of the shale cliff, before it twisted and circled through the undeveloped woods. Paths snaked away from the old road, through the trees, to secluded clearings near the cliff face. The stunning view of Lake Erie attracted plenty of young folks who were eager for a kiss, maybe more.

The first time I'd driven Cathy there, toting a blanket and a bottle of cheap wine, we'd necked and listened to the waves lap at the shore below. After we were married, we'd stroll through the park, and Cathy would tease me about that night. *How far did you think I'd let you get for a two-dollar bottle of Boone's Farm?*

And, sooner than I wanted to imagine, my thirteen-year-old daughter would be making that same kind of stroll.

"So what are you thinkin' about?" Molly broke my reverie.

"Nothing, really. How's school?"

She lowered her eyes, as though guarding against an onslaught of boring conversation. "If I tell you it's fine, can I go skate?"

"Be serious for a second. How's it going? Is that jerk who said bad things about Mom still hassling you?"

"Jimmy Cannon?" Molly faced forward. "Promise you won't tell?"

I didn't want to keep secrets about our daughter from Cathy, but if Molly had a problem, one of us should know. "Okay. What's up?"

"He cornered me after school and said that he saw a picture in the paper of Jennifer Browning. He thought she'd be a good fuck."

"Molly . . . "

"I'm just telling you what he said. Then he laughed and said that you'd be the one fucked in prison, by niggers and spics—those were his words." She gazed over the skateboard run and across the parking lot.

My eyes wandered in the same direction as hers. "So, what happened?"

Molly turned to me. "I punched him, right in the gut. He took a swing at me, but I ducked and hit him in the nose. He started crying like a wuss."

I wanted to cheer and give her a high five, but instead I said, "He could get you in trouble, Molly. You know what the school says about fighting."

"He didn't tell anybody, Dad, and he won't. He doesn't want the whole school to know he got beat up by a girl."

I barely suppressed a smile. "When this kind of stuff happens, will you tell me about it? Or Mom?"

"Mom worries too much."

"How's she doing?" My conversations with Cathy were few, and generally, they were focused on the logistics of Molly's visitations. Our divorce was technically not final, but only because of the difficulty in agreeing upon a financial settlement, due to my situation. Cathy, bless her, wasn't pushing, which allowed me to focus on my case.

With the toe of her tennis shoe, Molly pushed the skateboard back and forth, exposing a multihued sock.

"I'm not trying to put you in the middle, sweetie. I just want to know if she's okay."

"She tries to act like things are all right, that living with Aunt Alison and Uncle Carl is normal. But we sleep in their guest room. With the twin beds? Sometimes, I wake up at night and hear her crying."

"Just give her a hug, honey." I nearly added, give her one for me.

Molly popped the front of the skateboard up and examined the grip tape. "Is it true what Jimmy Cannon said, what will happen to you if you go to jail?"

There was no need to explain the difference between jail and prison. "Honey, I don't intend to go anywhere. I'm innocent, and I have a great lawyer."

"But some kids say you're guilty and they'll stick a needle in you to kill you."

"Ignore all of that. We're a long way from worrying about any of that stuff. The trial comes first, and the great thing about America is that I'm innocent until proven guilty. And they won't be able to prove me guilty."

My stoic little princess dropped the skateboard and, choking up, spun into my arms. "Please don't let anything happen to you, Daddy. Please."

I stroked her hair and clasped her to me. "Let it out, Molly. Believe me, I've cried plenty."

I don't know how much time slipped past before she untangled herself from me and wiped at her eyes. She stood, put her helmet on, and planted one foot on the pink skateboard. "One last run."

There were a few other kids showing their stuff, but Molly was the best. Fast and controlled and beautiful to watch. I jingled the car keys in my jacket pocket and watched my little princess circle and soar. She'd be the sole bright spot in my life while cold winter storms marked my approaching trial date. I turned toward the promontory at the cliff's edge, where escaped slaves would clamber down to a waiting ferry and cross the choppy waters of Lake Erie to the Canadian shore.

There was no ferry boat waiting for me.

35

"So, yeah, I'm okay with the jury. Not particularly the lady alternate, because she's young and might feel some bond with Jennifer, but we were out of challenges." Arlene wore a lightweight beige suit and cream-colored blouse. The last of our lake effect snow had finally melted away, and it was an unseasonably warm spring day.

She delivered her assessment as Jack and I huddled over coffee in one of her conference rooms. Arlene had engaged the prospects as if they were her neighbors, probing their backgrounds and experiences. She'd been able to bounce six of them who'd struck her the wrong way.

"Well, I gotta ask you," Jack said. "What the hell happened to a jury of his peers? I made a list: two black men, three black women, two white women, three white men, and two Puerto Ricans. Man and a woman."

"*Peers* doesn't mean that John gets jurors just like him."

"It is what it is, Jack," I said. Arlene sounded testy, and Jack seemed on the verge of pushing the wrong buttons. Three long days spent selecting a jury might account for our edginess.

"Yeah? Well, you coulda gone to the fuckin' mall and picked the first sixteen people who wandered out of Costco."

"If you're criticizing—"

"I'm not criticizing at all. I was there, saw the pool. It just doesn't seem fair."

"You did great, Arlene." I shot Jack a look. Opening statements were set for the next afternoon; the judge had a personal matter to handle in the morning.

I'd be spending another long evening cloistered in my home. Now that the trial was imminent, I was again a feature story. Based upon the cars that trickled by, my house was viewed as a freak show tent. Even my trips to the grocery store were limited, and my sporadic jogging had become a memory.

"You should know, a source called me on my way in." Arlene leaned forward and pushed a yellow legal pad aside. The burnished oak conference table reflected the golden bracelet on her wrist. "Jennifer's lawyer released a statement this morning, while we were in court. She's been paid by the insurance company."

Jennifer's tussle with the carrier, which had dragged its feet because of the "uncertain" circumstances of her brother's death, had made the papers. "Man, that just seems . . . "

"Let it go. It doesn't affect the trial," Arlene said.

"Butcher came to the end of the line; maybe Jennifer will get hers, too." Jack's phone buzzed; he stared at it for a moment, surprised, before heading for the door. "'Scuse me."

Arlene glanced at her watch. "You look beat, John. Go on home. I need to work on the opening. Get some rest tonight; the jury needs to see you fresh."

"Sorry. I'm feelin' a little lost here." Jennifer now had her money. Meanwhile, a teary-eyed Marilyn had helped me cram the detritus of my shuttered practice into mismatched boxes.

"Well, find yourself, John. You know what's at stake."

Jack, looking drawn, returned to the room. "The chief's office just called. I told them to fax it here."

"Fax what?"

"Can't believe it," Jack muttered.

"What is it?" I tried to imagine what would rattle him.

"C'mon, we can read it together." We followed him around the corner, to the alcove filled with paper and office supplies. Jack gripped the document as it hummed through the fax machine. "The handwriting's been authenticated, matches the ones sent to Detective Merylo all them years back. It was mailed to the chief, with a request to direct it to me."

We huddled around a nearby desk.

Hello, Jack Corrigan:

I read about your role in the trial of the despicable man who entrapped my daughter and son. I wanted to see them one more time, to hold them, but now they are gone. You remember me, don't you, the night we met face-to-face? You must be a boastful man, Jack. The newspaper made it sound like I was lucky to escape, to flee like a coward. We both know what really happened, don't we?

I can still see your scared Mick features, those begging eyes. Do you remember mine, the color of them? Someone must pay for what happened to my children. Perhaps we'll meet again.

Cleveland has changed so much that becoming accustomed to the city has taken some time. But I'm prepared now. My plans are complete. Let's see if the current boors in blue are more of a challenge than Eliot Ness and Peter Merylo and his pathetic bunch. That includes you, Jack Corrigan. Tell Cleveland I've come home.

Jack looked stunned. *Meet again*: the two words were clearly a threat. I wished the letter could be dismissed as a hoax. One look at Jack, however, told me that the danger was all too real.

"You can't worry about this, Jack." My words rang hollow. "It's not 1950 anymore."

"Maybe I can settle what I started sixty years ago."

Exactly the answer I'd expect from Jack, but the bravado seemed forced.

"Jesus, Jack." Arlene scanned the letter again. "You have to ask about protection, around the clock."

"I can take care of myself, 'specially against some prick older than me."

"Nothing wrong with asking for backup. I need you focused here."

"You sayin' I can't do my job?"

"C'mon, Jack, she didn't say that at all." The last thing I needed was for the two of them to go at it again. "What the hell's he mean, about what you told the papers?"

"No idea." Jack spit out the words, and his gruff face bobbed in my direction. "But it ain't just me who has somethin' to worry about. Who was it he said entrapped his son and daughter?"

"The letter wasn't directed to me, Jack."

"So you think a guy who killed a couple dozen people is that obvious?" He leaned into the door frame. "I'm not tryin' to be an alarmist, but it was *despicable* you he was talking about."

My brain was crackling like a dying fluorescent tube; I sank back against a row of shelves. I needed a drink. Arlene rested a hand on my shoulder, and there was Jack's strong face in front of mine. Something had snapped within me, deep inside. I couldn't contemplate what the Torso Murderer would do to me, to my heart and my head and my cock.

36

"You were right about the news, Jack. Headline in the *PD*: 'I've Come Home.' They try talking to you?" His Fiesta smelled like french fries from the fast-food wrappers blanketing the backseat. Thankfully, the spring weather was warm enough for me to crack the window and allow in some fresh air.

"Every fuckin' TV station, every rag, radio. Told 'em all no comment, even if I was thinking *go to hell*. If they wouldn't listen to me in 1950, they ain't hearin' from me now."

"I couldn't sleep, Jack, not a damn wink. Kept checking the locks, watchin' the yard . . . " My intestines rumbled, upset from the booze I had swilled down the night before. The late start for the trial was a godsend, because some extra shut-eye and a long shower helped me pull my act together.

"Maybe now you'll get a CCW permit, like I told you."

The price I'd pay for accepting Jack's offer to drive me back and forth to court would apparently be a daily lecture. "Would they even issue one, when I'm on trial for murder?"

"Why not? You haven't been convicted of a damn thing."

"With my luck, the bastard would grab the gun and shoot me."

Truth was, firearms made me uneasy. My father had never whipped out his service revolver, but my mother and I had been well aware that, during the darkest of his rages, a gun had been in our house.

"Not a bad way to go, all things considerin'."

"I'm serious, Jack."

"Like they say, chill. You're in court all day, behind locked doors all night. Gettin' clubbed in an alley won't happen again." He gazed through the windshield at a sun-drenched Lake Erie, at last free of the winter ice floes. "You should, A, get a gun and, B, concentrate on your case."

"On trial for murder and a serial killer on my ass."

"Be grateful you live an interesting life." He pulled off the Shoreway, past the gritty façades of turn-of-the-century office buildings and warehouses, and headed down Lakeside Avenue to the multileveled concrete garage nearest the courthouse.

Judge Seidelson had allowed us to continue using the side entrance to the courtroom to avoid the press. As Jack shuffled into the gallery, Arlene stood at the defense table to greet me. She wore a black business suit over a demure white blouse and, as usual, a cheap ballpoint rested atop her notepad, in place of her Mont Blanc. She eyed my conservative dress—blue jacket, gray slacks, a muted red tie. "Very presentable, Counselor."

"Just following your fashion advice." Even before jury selection began, Arlene had admonished me not to wear anything showy or expensive—not that I owned that type of wardrobe, anyway.

She caught me glancing at the pooled media feed and jammed spectator section. "All here for the openings, John. Your case has everything. Lawyer on trial for murder, the knockout blonde and her dead brother. Oh, and a serial killer. I can't wait to watch CNN."

Arlene was clearly trying to keep things light, but her effort was lost on me. Flanagan arranged his papers at the table nearest the jury box and gave me a passing glance. I resumed scanning the room and did a double-take: Cathy was huddled against the far wall in the gallery. She gave me a half-hearted smile, one that meant the world to me, and I managed one of my own in return.

"Christ," I murmured. "Cathy came."

"Don't read too much into it. We spoke briefly when she arrived. She believes you, but she wants to hear the evidence herself." Arlene sat down and then caught my gaze after I surveyed the rest of the gallery. "Don't worry, she's not here. Jennifer's a witness, so she can't sit in court and listen to other testimony. You won't see your friend until they call her to the stand."

Judge Seidelson took the bench, dispensed with some preliminary matters for the benefit of the jurors, and moved quickly to opening statements. Flanagan was in his element, smiling a bright greeting and delving into the heart of the case. He flashed a blown-up photograph of Frank Frederickson, taken back when wearing a corduroy suit and a yellow tie was fashionable, before he ended up as a dopehead with a scarlet gash engraved in his throat.

"Frank Frederickson. You will hear, during the course of this trial, that Frank had a troubled life." Flanagan held the photo aloft as he sauntered to the center of the courtroom, allowing the jury to imagine a living, breathing Frank. "But he had a life! One wrongfully taken from him by this defendant, this man, John Coleman, attorney at law!"

His face was a mask of indignation, and he made my name sound like something to be scraped from the bottom of a shoe.

"But why, you ask, would he do it? Let's talk about the defendant's infidelity, how he needed the money to pursue an innocent younger woman."

The jury followed Flanagan's every measured gesture, every subtle change of expression, and every cast of those blazing green eyes. He was a master storyteller, only periodically glancing at a yellow notepad that seemed like a baton when he raised his arms for effect. Even his spin on my interlude with the Butcher was clever.

"No one wants to imagine being indebted to a serial killer, but the Butcher did all of us a huge favor. Imagine, if she had not captured the defendant, he might have gotten away with his brutal act. He could have claimed that this mysterious Mexican gang took the money. Maybe even that Jennifer had it. But when the police searched his car, searched his trunk, searched his wheel well, the defendant had nowhere to run."

He recited the forensic evidence against me, bit by damning bit. The matching prints, my cell records, my footprints in the blood. He finished with a flourish by again waving the photograph of Frank before the jury. He began in a whisper and gradually raised his voice, building to a dramatic finale. "So Frank Frederickson is no longer with us. A young man, prime of life, gone with the stroke of a knife. And why? Because of an adulterous murderer who acted on his base wants of *lust* and *greed*!"

His eyes spit contempt, and Flanagan locked them on me as he milked the last few words. He strode back to his table, the victorious wrestler anticipating another medal.

Arlene rose immediately to break his spell. "Yes, Frank is gone." She picked up the photo of him and then placed it back on the table almost reverently, as though putting the poor young man to rest. "But he isn't gone because John Coleman killed him. If John were on trial for adultery or poor judgment or for the emotional pain he caused his wife and daughter, he'd be guilty. But he's on trial for murder, and we'll show you that he's being blamed for something he didn't do. He made himself an easy target; that doesn't make him a killer.

"Take a good look at my client. What, exactly, was Jennifer Browning's attraction to John, an older, married man?" Arlene didn't copy Flanagan's theatrics; there was no yellow notepad in her hand. She was the college professor, yet her manner of speech was genuine. "Let me be clear about her simple goal: she wanted to find someone she could manipulate."

She paused and stared at me, letting the jury take me in for what I was: a middle-aged ass who had looked for some thrills on the side. But a murderer?

"Yes, John Coleman made a mistake, one that destroyed his

marriage. But that doesn't make him a killer. John was born here, went to Holy Name High School, right here in Cleveland. College and law school, too, at Cleveland State and Cleveland-Marshall. Built his career here."

Arlene continued to personalize me, letting the jury know that, despite my colossal screw-up, I was a regular guy who'd built a business and had no criminal past. I was grateful that there was no public record of my drinking binges or my affair with Martha. She segued into undermining the prosecution's case.

"Jennifer Browning had no relationship with her brother Frank. And her motive for wanting him out of the way? What about being sole heir of her father's estate, which would gain her more than a million dollars? And Jennifer was not the only one who had a reason for wanting Frank dead. You'll hear evidence that the Andar Feo, the drug gang that my worthy opponent claims to be a nonissue, was particularly violent. They wanted Frank dead because of his involvement in a botched drug deal. This case has quite a cast of characters, but one thing will stand out. There is more than one potential killer of Frank Frederickson, and John Coleman isn't on the list."

She attacked the state's forensic evidence as well, including the fact that my prints were plastered all over the murder weapon.

"And that fingerprint evidence that Mr. Flanagan emphasized? We'll show you that there are serious questions about what those prints mean. The state can't just prove that Mr. Coleman's prints are on the knife. They must prove that he used the knife to kill Frank Frederickson."

She wove it all together, and the jury was locked on her, just as they'd been on Flanagan. She ended by standing in front of the jury box, her hands pressed together as though she were praying, and she moved them in unison for emphasis. "There is a lot that you will and should dislike about John, what he's done to his wife and to his daughter and to his profession, but there is no proof beyond a reasonable doubt that he was the killer of Frank Frederickson. When you've heard all of the evidence, ladies and gentlemen, there is but one conclusion: John Coleman is not guilty."

With a firm nod to the jury, Arlene concluded her opening comments. The clock read quarter to five, so Seidelson adjourned for the
day. The jury filed out, none of them looking at me, and the judge
called counsel to the bench. Sitting alone at the table, I realized that
Arlene had been wrong about Jennifer not being in the courtroom. I
sensed her hot voice, somehow inside my mind, laughing at me.

Arlene returned to our table and stuffed a stack of manila folders
into her leather briefcase. "The judge wanted to know what to expect
tomorrow. Flanagan's starting with the deputy coroner, then on to
those cops, Salvatore and Coufalik. Then—you okay?"

Bernie Salvatore testifying against me was still difficult to digest,
even though I'd anticipated facing him for months. My heart told me
that there was no way he would relish taking the stand, but Coufalik
would be gunning for me. "You did a real good job. Your opening."

"There's a lot more work to do, John."

"They say most jurors make up their minds during opening
statements."

"That's what a lot of so-called experts claim. Truth is, you can't
be sure of a damn thing until they read the verdict." She snapped her
briefcase shut. "Let's go. The real work starts tomorrow."

When Jack dropped me off, I grabbed a beer and dropped into a
chair at the kitchen table. For some reason, a film of dust on the fake
flowers in the ceramic bowl caught my attention. I loosened my tie,
too drained to hoist myself upstairs and change, and turned on the
news. There was a brief clip of Flanagan and Arlene delivering their
opening statements and a close-up shot of a sullen and squinty-eyed
me. My fifteen minutes of fame, as an admitted immoral cheat, one
who might be headed for the needle.

I started thinking about Coufalik, how she'd been the one to
supervise the scene when they'd searched my car. Bernie hadn't been
there. What if she'd done something with the evidence just to screw me,

still angry about the day she had warned me not to stare at her ass? The angry scowl on her face was unforgettable. But would she have really set me up on a murder rap, just because she thought I was a jerk? Maybe my suspicions were idiotic, a desperation shot, but there was a way to find out—and what the hell was there to lose? I took a swig, turned down the volume on the TV, and called my brother-in-law.

Of course, Alison answered.

"It's John."

"She's tired. Sitting in that courtroom, hearing how you cheated on her all over again."

"I'm not calling for Cathy. I need to talk to Carl."

She was silent for a moment, as though debating whether to grill me about why I wanted to talk to her husband, but then Carl came on the line.

"If you're asking for money, the answer's *no*." I could sense Alison standing behind him, monitoring his every word. "Cathy told me it's tight, but we're helpin' out with her and Molly as it is. We—"

"It's not that, Carl. There's something you can do for me. Check the file on my case." My gaze drifted to the refrigerator, and I imagined every shelf lined with skulls.

"John . . ."

"Just to see if they're holding anything back, or if they fudged something. That's all I'm askin'."

"No." He didn't hesitate. I pictured him looking at Alison, her approving nod as he stood up to me.

"Carl, this isn't the serial killer bullshit we talked about before. This is me. My life on the fuckin' line. I'm just asking you to look."

The son of a bitch hung up.

I stared at the phone for a moment before shoving away from the table and slamming the receiver into the cradle. The ceramic bowl and spray of artificial flowers rocked back and forth. Just when my vocabulary of curse words had been exhausted, the phone rang. What the hell?

"I'll take a look." Carl was terse. "That's all. Got it?"

"That's all I ask. Jesus, thanks."

"Don't thank me. Cathy wants this done, so I'm doing it. You were a prick to her, what you did, but she doesn't think you killed the guy."

"Let me talk to her, Carl."

"No."

"Ask her, okay? Let her decide."

"Jesus, you've got some nerve."

There was a long silence until Cathy, sweet Cathy, whispered into the phone. "You think the cops did something wrong? Bernie wouldn't—"

"Not him, no. But . . . it doesn't make sense." Hot tears suddenly welled up. "I didn't do it, but they've got all this stuff. My fingerprints, for God's sake, my fingerprints on the knife . . . maybe Carl . . . "

"You need to keep it together, John. You have a good lawyer."

"I know, but . . . damn it, there's so much, coming from all directions . . . "

"What do you want from me?" Cathy sounded like she was crying too. "I have my hands full with Molly."

I paused, surprised. "But she seemed okay . . . " And then it hit me: of course, Molly wouldn't want to burden me with her problems, not on top of what was already happening in my life.

"She's getting into fights, and she swore at one of the teachers. They'll probably suspend her."

"I'll talk to her." I was responsible for all of the tumbling dominoes. "When she's here this weekend, we can sort through it."

"I'm not sure that's a good idea anymore."

Her words took a moment to sink in. "But . . . we had a deal."

"I know what we said, John, but it's just not working. You're back in the news, every day. She shouldn't be around you until the trial is over."

I leaned into the wall. If Cathy were still with me, the flowers would have been dusted, every plate cleaned, the floor mopped. "Not now, don't do this to me."

"You're being selfish." There was no rancor in her tone, just a simple statement of fact. "You need to think about Molly."

"Of course, but . . . " My little girl fighting, swearing, running off. God, the playground must have become a nightmare. "What if I come over to Alison's sometime, just for a while?"

"Can't you give me this, please? You may be on trial, but this is hell for all of us. The kids stare at me like . . . some kind of guilt by association. I can't even go to Heinen's without seeing the whispers, the pointing."

"Cathy, if there were any way to change things . . . " I leaned into the wall and sank to the floor. "Thanks for coming today."

"I'm not there to play the good wife, John. I'm there for me, to watch everyone take the stand and swear on a Bible to tell the truth. I want to believe you."

"I told you the truth."

"Not about Jennifer Browning." She was definitely crying now. "And now the Torso Murderer's come back. Everything seems so upside down."

"I go to bed every night, afraid."

"Everyone does."

"But for me—"

"Please. I just can't do this." Her words were ragged as she choked back tears. "Good-bye."

The phone clicked off. They were everywhere, my Cathy and my Molly: in the faded coffee pot, the scarred surface of the countertop, the stark face of the clock as the red hands relentlessly ticked away the remaining minutes of my existence. I fetched a bottle and a glass and woke up on the cold kitchen tile at two a.m. A smart, cautious man would have checked the locks again, but I didn't care.

Didn't care at all.

37

"So he definitely did not die from a drug overdose." Jerome Becker, the Deputy Cuyahoga County Medical Examiner—still called *coroner* by most—was a straitlaced sort of guy, about fifty, who nevertheless looked like a prep boy in his starched white shirt and plain blue tie.

Flanagan's direct examination was succinct, and he established the chain of custody for the knife found in my trunk. "And did you identify the blood that was found on the blade?"

"I did. It was Frank Frederickson's."

Flanagan flashed an enlarged photograph of Frank, as found at the Tremont house, on a video screen. Christ, a groundhog would have understood that the poor bastard's throat had been slit. I resisted the temptation to turn and witness Cathy's reaction. She had cast a curt nod in my direction upon entering the courtroom that morning.

"The knife is absolutely consistent with the injury inflicted on the decedent." Becker was an earnest sort who nodded to emphasize his conclusions.

Flanagan kept the photo on display, letting the jury wonder what kind of a monster I was to have committed such a gruesome crime.

And each juror would question, too, whether sweet little Jennifer could have been responsible in any way for *that* happening to her own brother.

" . . . and the killer could have avoided the blood spatter by slitting Mr. Frederickson's throat from behind."

Flanagan asked him some wrap-up questions, then returned to his table.

As Arlene rose for cross-examination, I tempered my expectations. A real-life cross is seldom like what you see in the movies or on television. Witnesses rarely break down on the stand, and good lawyers know the exact questions they want to ask. A fundamental rule of cross—one obeyed even by wannabes, like me—is that you never ask a question unless you already know the answer.

Arlene blew up a picture of the knife and addressed Coroner Becker. "Sir, you recall telling Mr. Flanagan that this knife is *consistent with* the type of wound made to Mr. Frederickson's neck?"

"I do."

"Would you explain to the jury what you mean by *consistent with?*"

"Sure." Becker faced the jury box. Experienced expert witnesses know to make eye contact with the jury from time to time. "It means that the knife in question could definitely have caused the injury to Mr. Frederickson."

"But you would agree that comparing a knife to a wound is not like matching a bullet to a gun?" Arlene stood at the podium in the center of the room, which compelled Becker to focus his attention in her direction and away from the jury.

"Absolutely. All you can say about a knife, based on the dimensions and size, is that it could have caused a wound. Similar knives, or other instruments, would create a similar-looking wound."

"So you would agree that another knife could have been used to kill Frank Frederickson?"

I knew where she was going and was anxious to see how this line of questioning would play out.

Becker glanced smugly at the jury. "No, Counselor, I won't agree with that. You're forgetting my earlier testimony. We found the decedent's blood on the blade of this knife. There is no question it was the murder weapon."

"Sir, with all due respect, I did listen to your earlier testimony. But you weren't in the room when Frank Frederickson was killed, were you?"

"Of course not."

"Isn't it possible the killer could have dipped the knife that you examined in Frank's blood to frame my client?"

Flanagan jumped to his feet. "Your Honor, this is absurd speculation—"

Judge Seidelson banged his gavel. "There will be no speaking objections in my courtroom. Counsel, approach the bench."

Seidelson conducted a quick sidebar conference, out of earshot of the jury, and overruled the objection. But Flanagan's attempt at what is known as a speaking objection was clever. By stating the basis for the objection in front of the jury—*absurd speculation*—he undermined Arlene's question, even if the judge did not rule in his favor. The attorneys returned to their places as if they were actors in a play, and Arlene repeated her question to Becker.

He smiled benignly. "I guess anything's possible."

Arlene knew that she'd scored a few points, which is typically the best result possible on cross, and ended her examination. The jury might think that Becker's concession was minor, but they'd have to consider the possibility. Anything to create that sliver of reasonable doubt. Even so, I could hear Jennifer again, jeering: *Is that all you got?*

They called Bernie Salvatore to the stand, and he shuffled past our table on the way. He looked like his usual self, except that he'd donned a plain blue tie, which ended about four inches north of his naval. Flanagan asked him some preliminary questions to establish his background and training and then launched into a line of questions directly about my case.

"In fact, you played football with the defendant in high school?" Flanagan glanced at the jurors. They'd understand that even an old teammate was testifying against me.

"Correct. Holy Name." Bernie never once looked over at me. He had to know, in the depth of his soul, that murder wasn't included in the litany of my sins.

In response to Flanagan's questioning, Bernie confirmed that I'd called him after finding Frank Frederickson and that Frank's finger-prints were the only ones on the cell phone. His hand smoothed the unfamiliar tie, and he shifted the knot.

"And did you discuss with the defendant the money that had been in Mr. Frederickson's possession?" In his natty black-and-white pinstripe, Flanagan seemed burnished with authority.

"Yes, and I told him to tell his client, Jennifer Browning, that we'd be unlikely to recover it."

"Did the defendant tell you that he had all or any of the money?"

Bernie shook his head and looked at me for the first time. "No."

Flanagan walked away from the podium and tapped his fingertips together, near his chest. "Had you encountered the defendant at other crime scenes, prior to Mr. Frederickson's death?"

Arlene objected. She had anticipated that Flanagan would argue that my visits to the Butcher's dumping grounds were relevant to the issue of premeditation. Like, maybe I was visiting the crime scenes to pick up some pointers about killing. Seidelson apparently agreed with Flanagan's position, because he instructed Bernie to answer the question.

"Yeah, he was there when the first victim, Frank's father, was found in Lakewood, and he followed me to the crime scene of the second victim. We'd been having lunch."

"And did he contact you regarding the third victim?"

"He did."

"How long after the body was found?"

"The next morning. He wanted to meet, so we did."

"Did he tell you what he'd considered doing when he found out about that killing?"

"Yes." Bernie ran a finger under his collar and grimaced, as if the tie were choking him. "He told me he'd thought of driving to the crime scene when he heard about it."

"And where was he when he heard about it?"

"At his wife's birthday dinner, a restaurant on the West Side."

"And where did the murder occur?"

"Shaker Heights."

Flanagan paused and glanced over at the jury, as if to telegraph that only a nut job would consider leaving his wife's birthday dinner to drive across town and pop up at a crime scene. He had made it sound as though I was traipsing to crime scenes and begging to talk with the police.

Then, before Flanagan could ask another question, Bernie smoothed his tie and continued. "To be complete, John's dad was in charge of the original Butcher investigation. He committed suicide, and the Butcher wrote to John, saying that she would be watching him. And we all know that, later, the Butcher did kidnap him."

For just a moment, I could tell, Flanagan lost his poise. Bernie had spoken in a sympathetic tone and twice referred to me by my first name, humanizing me before the jury, and making it look like I wasn't a head case after all. My bet was that he had determined not to follow Flanagan's script.

Flanagan quickly recovered. "What else did you discuss that morning?"

"He had some questions about the killings."

"What sort of questions?"

"What had happened to the guy, what the coroner had found out about the victim in Rocky River, whether there were similarities, that sort of thing."

"Did you respond?"

"Yeah, I told him to leave it alone, that it was police business."

"Did he make a request of you that night?"

"He asked to meet with Detective Wendy Coufalik. She has a background in serial killings and was assigned to the task force handling the investigation."

"Very well. We'll ask Detective Coufalik about that meeting."

Arlene rose, passing Flanagan as she approached the podium, and the contrast between them—white and black, man and woman—couldn't have been starker. There wasn't much that Arlene could accomplish with Bernie on cross, but I was convinced that he wouldn't sell me out. My breathing slowed as Arlene asked one question in particular.

"Tell me, Detective, you testified that you've known John Coleman since high school. Did he have a reputation for violence?" Arlene had explained to me that a defendant's reputation for violence is relevant in a murder case, and I'd trusted Bernie to tell the truth.

Flanagan objected, likely surprised that we'd asked the question of a witness for the prosecution. Seidelson let him answer.

My old Green Wave teammate looked at me and held my gaze. "No. Not at all."

We adjourned for the day. Bernie had stuck by me, no waffling, and the courtroom felt a tad less oppressive for one day. Even though I saw Cathy hurry out without a backward glance, by the time we reached Jack's car, I was smiling, which had become a nearly forgotten trait.

"Salvatore did you a solid in there," Jack said as we drove. "I bet he surprised the fuck out of Flanagan, and then he answered Arlene just the way you wanted."

"Yeah, I needed that. After that call with Cathy last night . . . "

"Like I said this morning, if you're serious about talking with her, your only chance is to go through Father McGraw. Her sister's not doin' you any favors."

"She never liked me, not from day one."

"Good judge of character." His mouth was somewhere between a sneer and a smile, but he made me laugh.

"Christ, I remember when she lit into me about something once, can't even remember what, but for a Catholic-school girl, she was damn creative. 'Numbnut prick,' 'shitlicking cocksucker'—think about that—and she ended with 'fucking flying fucked fucker.'"

Jack was chuckling, and I was whooping. The levity of the moment took hold, and we spit out every curse word we knew, each one funnier than the last, until we were hysterical. Jack wiped tears from his eyes just to see the road. I raised mine to the heavens and thanked God for allowing a man who'd been tortured, who'd lost his wife, who was on trial for murder, and who had a serial killer on his ass to laugh like that. For a few brief miles along the Shoreway, with the pink rays of the descending sun reflecting in a placid Lake Erie, I relished a moment of solace.

38

My memory of that momentary euphoria faded the next morning, when they called Wendy Coufalik to the stand. She stepped past our table and shot me a look that would have melted lead. Flanagan asked her about the crime scene that she'd supervised, in the parking lot near Great Lakes, where they found my car. She testified that she had been suspicious of my interest in the crime scenes and that I had been the one to find Frank's body. Her testimony was pretty dull-ass routine until they got to my meeting with her and Bernie at the Lakewood Police station.

"And did he have any new information about Wilbur Frederickson?"

"Not a thing." She looked from me to the jury. "Mr. Coleman clearly had some problems."

Arlene objected, and Judge Seidelson ordered the jury to disregard the remark. My mental state was not at issue, but Flanagan's cagey trick had worked. He'd no doubt coached Coufalik on what to say, and the thought that an experienced police officer felt I was off-kilter would linger in the back of the jurors' minds.

Flanagan asked a few closing questions before Arlene rose and smoothed the front of her tailored jacket. "To follow up on Mr.

Flanagan's last few questions, you are a police officer, not a psychologist, correct?"

"I already testified about my work as a police officer and never claimed to be anything else." Coufalik was brusque. I glanced over at Flanagan and sensed he was uneasy about her tone.

"Fine." Arlene was unfazed. "So, are you a psychologist?"

"I think I just answered that." Reality hit me: Coufalik resented being questioned by an African-American. She couldn't escape the little girl who had grown up in Slavic Village, treading on racial tension and ethnic slurs.

"I'd like a yes-or-no answer." Arlene would not allow Coufalik to control the examination.

"I've given you my answer."

Judge Seidelson stepped in. "Detective, it's not an argument. You can answer that question: *yes* or *no.*"

For a minute, I thought that Coufalik was going to say something to him, but she turned back to Arlene. "No."

"Let me turn to the crime scene at Frank's apartment. You saw Mr. Coleman there that night, didn't you?"

"I sure did, and now we know why he was there."

"Again, can you answer my question with a *yes* or *no*?"

Coufalik hesitated, but I knew that she wouldn't want to provoke Judge Seidelson a second time. "Yes."

"And you were well aware that he had been looking for Frank for some time, right?"

"Define what you mean by *some time*." Coufalik was sitting ramrod straight.

Arlene remained unperturbed. "I'll rephrase. In fact, when you met with him at the Lakewood police headquarters, as you described on direct, you talked with him about looking for Frank Frederickson, correct?"

"I believe so." Coufalik was fighting that yes-or-no thing.

"To be precise, you encouraged him to find Mr. Frederickson, didn't you?"

"We thought he could help."

"Yet you testified earlier, in response to Mr. Flanagan, about your suspicion," Arlene said, making air quotes to further undermine Coufalik's words, "at seeing him at another crime scene. Why would you be suspicious upon finding him at Frank Frederickson's?"

Coufalik shifted in the witness stand, and I expected that she was raging with the desire to simply have at it with Arlene in a parking lot. She paused for a moment. "It just struck me as too coincidental."

Arlene smiled. Coincidences don't mean a lot, not when the prosecutor has to prove you guilty beyond a reasonable doubt. "Coincidental. Hmm . . . well, let me ask you just a couple of questions about your meeting with Mr. Coleman at the Lakewood Police headquarters. Did you make a statement to him as you were leaving the meeting room?"

Coufalik almost sneered. "Yeah, I caught him staring at my backside. I looked at him, like, *really?*"

I wished that Cathy wasn't in the room to hear this line of questioning, but I understood where Arlene was headed.

"You don't much like Mr. Coleman, do you?"

"This case has nothing to do with whether I like him or not."

"Can we agree you didn't like it when you felt he was looking at your backside?"

I glanced over at the jury, and a couple of them were grinning.

"Would you?" Coufalik looked smug, like she'd scored a point. She said it in a way that inferred that Arlene might enjoy a glance, that any black woman would naturally appreciate someone staring at her booty.

Arlene's diction remained precise and her demeanor unaffected. I pictured them in a gravel schoolyard, circling, ringed by a group of other kids urging them to get it on. She said, "Detective, we all know it's your testimony we're interested in now, and you didn't like it, did you?"

"No, Counselor, I didn't." She sounded snarky as hell.

"Thank you, Detective. I have no further questions." Arlene, I'd bet, would be the one to finish a schoolyard brawl.

Flanagan didn't ask her any questions on redirect, which told me that he just wanted her off the stand. It wasn't so much what she had said, but the way she had said it. And the back-and-forth about her backside was important. The testimony wouldn't hurt me, because I was already a cheating pig in the eyes of the jury. But Arlene had established that the detective who was in charge of the crime scene didn't much care for me and maybe even held a grudge.

Following an afternoon lunch break, Flanagan qualified his fingerprint expert, Kenneth Wilson, without objection from us. Wilson was articulate and polished, leading the jury through a discussion of ridge characteristics and points and latent prints.

He pointed to a large blowup of a print. "Latent prints aren't visible but can be made so by chemicals or powders."

"And how are they preserved?" Flanagan was on cruise control with this guy. Wilson was a good witness, well-groomed and wearing a stylish pinstripe suit.

"By photography, or using lift tape to transfer them onto a contrasting surface."

"Was that technique used in this case?"

"Absolutely. We found fingerprints and a partial palm print on a large knife in the wheel well of the defendant's Buick."

"Were those prints compared to those of Mr. Coleman?"

Wilson nodded. "We found thirteen points of comparison that matched between the two sets of fingerprints, many more than are needed for me to give an opinion as to whether the prints are a match."

Flanagan waited a beat. "And did you form an opinion, Mr. Wilson, to a reasonable degree of scientific certainty, as to whether the prints are a match?"

"I did."

Oh, for Christ's sake, I thought, just spit it out.

"And would you give your opinion to the jury?"

"Gladly. It is my opinion that the prints left on the knife found in the trunk of Mr. Coleman's car are, indeed, his. I am so certain of my opinion that I believe it is one hundred percent correct."

Experts can only testify as to expert opinions, not expert facts, so the way Wilson had framed his statement was clever. Flanagan asked nothing further, and Arlene began her cross. She'd really done her homework on the prints, consulting an expert of her own, which necessitated one more dip into my already dwindling coffers. I could only hope the investment paid off.

She walked through some basics, even having Wilson admit that the theory underlying fingerprint analysis—that no two individuals have the same prints—could not be scientifically validated. She then referred to the blown-up photos and drew his attention to a few areas. "Sir, the prints here are indistinct. Is there terminology you use to describe those areas?"

"Yes, we typically use terms such as *smudged* or *blurred.*"

"I see. And the handle of the knife, would you agree that it is a nonporous surface?" Arlene put a photo of the knife up on the screen.

"Yes." Wilson shifted on the stand.

"What significance is a nonporous surface to a fingerprint analyst?" Arlene, in total control as always, shifted the slides so that the fingerprints were again displayed for the jury.

"Well, as I already told Mr. Flanagan, fingerprints are created when the fingers touch a surface and leave behind a trace of body oil. On porous surfaces, the oil can be absorbed, so the prints don't hold as well, which is why you won't find prints on money or articles of clothing. That's not a problem with an item like the handle of that knife. You may see some blurring; that's not uncommon at all."

"And you can't be certain what caused the blurring or smudging here, can you?"

Instead of just answering *no*, Wilson tried to get cute. "I can't be sure. Perhaps the defendant did it himself, afterward, when the knife came into contact with something before it was put in the trunk."

"But you don't know that, do you?" Cross is all about control, which is tough with a sharp witness. Arlene needed to take Wilson in a certain direction, and I sensed she was getting there.

"Of course not."

"There's no evidence that whoever used this knife tried to wipe it clean, is there?"

"No, but sometimes, in the heat of the moment, people don't think things through."

"But you don't know that either, do you? All you know is that no one tried to wipe the prints from the knife, right?"

"Correct." Wilson leaned forward, resting his elbows on his thighs, apparently accepting that Arlene had a tight hold on the reins.

"Sir, I want to ask you a hypothetical. Assume that John Coleman left his prints on this knife before the night that Frank Frederickson was killed. If the killer later used the same knife, couldn't that account for the smudging of Mr. Coleman's prints?"

Wilson fidgeted with his tie and paused, which is never a good thing in front of a jury—they'll figure the witness is groping for an answer. The jury members all stared at the photo of the knife. My prints were from the end of the handle down; the smudges were nearest the blade. What Arlene was suggesting certainly appeared plausible—particularly if whoever grasped the knife after me had a smaller hand.

"There are a lot of things that can cause—"

"Sir, my question is about one thing: could the smudging have been caused by someone else using this knife after my client left his fingerprints on it?"

"That's one possibility," Wilson said.

"And you found no other prints on the knife, did you?"

"No, only Mr. Coleman's."

"So if someone else had handled the knife after Mr. Coleman, they'd have worn gloves?"

"If you're asking hypothetically—"

"Of course."

"Hypothetically, if someone handled the knife after Mr. Coleman, they could have worn gloves."

"And you'd also agree that Mr. Coleman, an attorney with nearly three decades of legal experience, did not wear gloves when he handled the knife and made no effort to wipe his prints from the handle, correct?"

"I would agree with that."

"Have you ever enjoyed sliced sausage, maybe fruit, at your home, Mr. Wilson?"

"Yes, on many occasions, in fact."

"Have you ever worn gloves or wiped your prints from the knife afterward?"

Wilson looked at Flanagan, then back to Arlene. No one would do that if they were just preparing snacks prior to a cozy conversation with Jennifer Browning. "Of course not."

"There was some discussion in opening statements, Mr. Wilson, about a text message received by Mr. Coleman approximately one hour before he says he found Frank Frederickson dead. There were no prints other than Frank Frederickson's on his cell phone, correct?"

"That is correct."

"But someone else could have worn gloves and sent Mr. Coleman the text message, couldn't they?"

"So could your client; he could have sent the message to himself."

"So you believe that Mr. Coleman did not wear gloves when he allegedly used a knife to kill Frank Frederickson, but then remembered to put on a pair to allegedly send himself a text?"

Wilson glanced at Flanagan, as if he were waiting for a lifeline. They had to have anticipated the question, but Arlene was wielding a bludgeon here. "I couldn't possibly know what the defendant was thinking."

"Thank you, Mr. Wilson." Arlene smiled and took her seat next to mine. For the first time in several insufferable weeks, I thought maybe there was a glimmer of hope. It was nearly five o'clock, so we adjourned for the day, and Arlene told me that Jennifer Browning would be the first witness in the morning. On her way to the witness stand, she'd pass through the gallery, where Cathy would be sitting. Then she'd ease by our table, her hips undulating just feet from me. *I own you, John.* My glimmer of hope slipped away.

As Arlene gathered her papers, I pulled her aside. "Look, I'm not sure it's a good idea for Cathy to be here tomorrow. Can you give her a call? She's not talking to . . . "

I didn't need to finish the sentence.

"Not a good idea for her or for you?"

"C'mon, she's not gonna want to hear what Jennifer has to say."

"Can't imagine them in the same room together, can you?" She shoved her papers into her briefcase. "I'll talk with her, but you know it's her choice."

I nodded my thanks and checked my phone. Carl had left a message, saying that he'd call that night. Jesus, the jury now knew that Coufalik didn't view me as her bosom buddy, and if Carl uncovered anything suspicious about the search of my vehicle, the impact would be enormous. Jack dropped me at home, and I busied myself checking locks and reheating some pasta. After dinner, I essentially paced, staring at the carpet and my watch, until my brother-in-law finally phoned.

"Sorry, John. It's all in order. Nothing missing, nothing changed, everything by the book."

"You gotta be shitting me." I leaned into the door frame.

"I checked, as promised." He was silent for a five count. "Cathy's goin' through hell. And Molly? Christ."

"There's no need to remind me, Carl."

"Why don't you just plead guilty, end it?"

I stared at the worn floor and the scratched countertop. My own damn brother-in-law. "I didn't do it."

"Maybe you got all fucked up—"

"Drop it, Carl."

"Whatever you say." Another five count. "Remember, you brought this on yourself. Cathy didn't do a damn thing."

"You think I don't know that? I never meant to hurt them. You—"

"Christ, how you can say this shit, I just don't know. Don't call, don't write, and good fuckin' luck."

I stood in the glow of the kitchen light and glared at the dead black receiver.

39

"Shit. Nothin'?"

I'd just told Jack, on the way to court, that Carl had come up empty.

"Yeah, says he wonders why I just don't plead." My brother-in-law was not the cavalry, and there wasn't any silver bullet, no ferry to Canada.

"Son of a bitch." Jack snorted and then cackled. "Maybe Torso will find ya first, spare you the trial."

I looked over at him, and he was grinning at me. "Fuck, even when I can sleep, I dream about that bastard comin' through a window."

"You haven't checked into a CCW, have you?"

"It's just not my thing, Jack. You packin' now?"

He nodded toward the glove box. "In there. Can't take it into the courthouse, even with a permit."

"After everything that's happened, maybe I should strap a butcher knife to my waist, see how that plays with the jury."

Jack chuckled. "People are givin' every old guy out there the evil eye, like, *Is that bastard the Torso Murderer?* I even catch people doin' that to *me*. Hell, some lynch mob's probably gonna torch an old folks home."

"Everybody's scared, is all. I just hope the prick is bad off, like with a cane. Or scooter."

"He was strong as an ape." Jack cocked an eyebrow and reached up to scratch it. "I suppose I'm the one guy who doesn't really have to worry, even with that letter. They're watching me."

He gave a nod of his head, and I turned. A plain blue Chevy was a few hundred yards behind us, in another lane, and traveling at the same speed.

"I said no stinkin' protection, but once you've worn the uniform . . . " He sucked in some saliva and swallowed. "Picked up on 'em a little bit ago, but expect they've been following me around ever since the letter came, keepin' an eye out."

I had a fleeting wish that they'd take me under their wing, too, protect me and keep me safe, but that wasn't going to happen. As we headed up in the elevator, I imagined seeing Jennifer again; the thought was crippling. When we entered the courtroom, I noted that Cathy was already seated in the gallery. Avoiding eye contact with her, I joined Arlene at the defense table.

"We had a cordial conversation, but she wants to hear Jennifer's story herself," Arlene said, buttoning the single pearly button on her gray jacket. Judge Seidelson entered the courtroom through a door behind the bench, and we all rose at the bailiff's command. My knees wobbled. Jennifer and Cathy would soon be in the same room.

Seidelson struck his gavel, and the courtroom came to order. Flanagan called Jennifer to the stand, and I turned to watch her enter. She wore a demure green dress and that plain silver pendant, the one that had beckoned me to her cleavage so long ago. I sensed Cathy's steely gaze boring into me as she imagined Jennifer's body entwined with mine.

Jennifer settled naturally into the witness stand. *A widow, mother deceased, father murdered. ESL volunteer.* Anointing her seemed like the next rung on the ladder. Flanagan proceeded to have her testify about retaining me as her lawyer. He wasted no time drilling into the juicy bits.

"And did you ultimately become intimate with the defendant?"

Cathy's hand would be drifting toward an earlobe, and I couldn't bear to look.

Jennifer dropped her head and then turned those pretty eyes toward the jury. "I'm so embarrassed. He led me to believe that he'd leave his wife for me. He was older, but . . . so caring, so supportive, when I needed that."

"Did you believe there was a future with Mr. Coleman?"

"I certainly thought so. With my dad, and then my brother . . . I felt so alone, and he was there for me. Everything was a whirlwind, but I . . . I needed him."

"Did—"

Jennifer began to cry and sought out Cathy in the spectator benches. "I'm so sorry."

Cathy staggered to her feet. There was an audible moan as she fixed her tearful eyes on me, and I averted my gaze. The scene could not have played better for Flanagan if he had choreographed the drama. And Arlene couldn't very well object without searing the moment even more indelibly in the minds of the jurors. Everyone in that courtroom focused on Cathy, on her quivering in a blue dress, searching for a way out of the gallery. Sobbing and shaking, she stumbled over people's feet—and then Jack was there, an arm around her, guiding her to the door.

As the commotion in the courtroom quieted, Jennifer caught my eye, holding my furtive gaze for just a moment. *You're way out of your league, Johnny.*

Seidelson said to her, "Would you like a recess?"

"No, thank you." Jennifer pulled a tissue from her purse and dabbed her eyes. "I know this is important."

Flanagan, his chiseled face projecting sympathy, waited until she'd composed herself. "I know this isn't easy, Ms. Browning, but did there come a time when the defendant asked to meet at your apartment?"

"Yes. I called him and told him that I had organized all of my dad's papers. I said I'd bring them to his office, but he said it would be easier if he just came by my place. I . . . " She wiped her eyes with the tissue again. "I'm sorry. I feel so stupid now. He kissed me, told me how much he cared for me, that he was falling in love . . . "

She left no doubt: *I'd* seduced *her*. Flanagan soon moved on to my nocturnal visit to her apartment, the night of her brother's murder. She testified about calling me after receiving some disturbing photographs in the mail. Flanagan had her describe them.

"What was the defendant's response?"

"He wanted to see me, to comfort me, and insisted on coming over."

"What took place when he arrived?"

"He looked at the photos, called Detective Salvatore about them, and then . . . tried kissing me, wanting to make love the very night my brother . . . " Her face contorted in disgust, and that damn tissue dried her eyes once again.

I could sense the tension rise in Arlene. My level of deviancy had just elevated, and Jennifer's testimony was unassailable: I'd been at the apartment and had phoned Bernie. Cathy would hear about my *kissing* and *making love* on the evening news. Those words would echo in Molly's ears.

When the tissue was cradled in her lap, Flanagan reviewed Jennifer's ensuing suspicions that prompted her to call Salvatore. Then he asked, "We've heard testimony to the effect that the defendant did not have a history of violent behavior. Do you have any information to the contrary?"

Jennifer nodded. "He told me he assaulted a man when he was out looking for my brother. Words were exchanged, and John said he just blew up and punched the guy, that he'd been in fights before. He had a bloody nose and seemed proud of that."

So Bernie had been wrong about me, and I was just the type to start a brawl with an innocent bystander. Maybe the sort to cut a man's throat. Even if Jack could track down the bouncer from the

Alley to rebut Jennifer's testimony, would the prick admit that he basically beat the shit out of me?

"I want to wrap up by asking you some difficult questions, Jennifer, about the murder of your brother. Is that all right?"

She nodded demurely, her eyes doe-like.

"You've seen photographs of the knife used to kill him. Is it at all possible that the defendant could have touched that knife in your apartment?"

"No. I never, in my life, owned a knife like that."

"When did you last see your father's gold retirement watch?"

"On my brother's wrist. He treasured that gift from Dad."

"With your brother's death, are you now the sole beneficiary of your father's two-million-dollar insurance policy?"

"Yes, but I was already inheriting over a million dollars." She paused for the perfect amount of time, staring at us with those big, innocent hazel eyes. "For anyone to think . . . even with all of his troubles, I never wanted anything more than for Frank to recover. I prayed for him daily."

She started shuddering and tearing up again—God, she was good at that. Flanagan gave her a moment. "Let me ask one final question, Jennifer. Were you connected in any way with the murder of your brother?"

She turned to the jury. "Absolutely not. Despite all of his problems, I loved him and always hoped he'd come back into my life."

Her lower lip trembled. Certain people are exceptionally good at making blatant lies sound like the truth: test-a-lying instead of testifying. She was a master. I imagined Jennifer with the Butcher in her dank basement, as they each wielded bolt cutters and stepped toward me. Jennifer would snap her cutter open and position the blades around my cock and balls.

Judge Seidelson nodded to Arlene, and she walked to the podium, taking with her the notes she'd made during direct examination. She was dogged and methodical, but Jennifer wasn't shaken.

Ice. For her finale, Arlene ended with a routine we'd practiced in her office. She walked to our table and removed a large knife from her briefcase.

"Ms. Browning, if you'll indulge me, I have here a knife with the same dimensions as the murder weapon. Could I ask you to hold it, please?"

Jennifer made a face, like the very idea of touching a knife was repugnant, but gingerly took the handle from Arlene. I couldn't help but think of the O.J. Simpson trial and the *if it doesn't fit, you must acquit* line. What if our planned demonstration went awry?

"Could you move your hand closer to the blade?"

Jennifer kept the sour face but did as Arlene requested.

"And would you please extend the knife toward me, so the jury has a full view?"

As Jennifer reached forward, it was clear that she, or someone, could have gripped the knife and smudged some, but not all, of my fingerprints. I breathed a sigh of relief. Our little exercise had worked: we had successfully shown that another person could have wielded the knife after me. One more seed of doubt as to my guilt.

Flanagan conducted a brief redirect, allowing Jennifer to affirm that she hadn't and wouldn't and couldn't ever harm her brother. I thought she shot a glance at me as she stepped down from the witness stand, a wry grin playing on her lips. *We both know it wasn't enough, Johnny. Don't forget to buy a huge jar of Vaseline; you'll need it when you become some gang's favorite bitch.*

Flanagan announced that the state had no further witnesses and rested the prosecution's case. Arlene and Flanagan sparred for a bit over some routine motions, but the judge denied them and adjourned for a lunch break.

Arlene sat down, leaned into me, and whispered, "She held up, John. You'll have to testify."

No one could counter Jennifer's testimony but me: I was my only way out. In a dark corner of my mind, she was smirking, tracing that silken tongue along her upper lip. *Can't focus, John? Thinking of your swollen cock pressed between my tits?*

I could not help but stare at the witness stand, my mind locked on the upcoming confrontation with Flanagan. Perhaps a better fate would be for the Torso Murderer to find me and shove his knife in hard.

40

My throat was bone dry when the bailiff swore me in. Arlene's initial questions established my Cleveland roots and unblemished record, but she quickly pivoted to my relationship with Jennifer. Although I could deny my one-time lover's characterization of what had happened, Arlene had explained that there was no point in contesting the details of my adultery. The better strategy was to focus on the core defense: I did not kill Frank Frederickson.

"John, you've heard the opening statements, including mine. Do you deny the affair with Jennifer Browning?"

"No. I could argue about how it happened, what was said. But the bottom line is that I was unfaithful to my wife, and I am sorry for that—every minute." I searched out Cathy. She had returned to the courtroom following the lunch break, and her expression was locked in a tight grimace.

"Then let's talk about what you are on trial for: the murder of Frank Frederickson." She flashed a police photo on the screen, one taken of Frank when he'd been found dead in his chair. "Simple question. Did you do this to him?"

"No." From my perch on the witness stand, I was acutely aware of my surroundings: the courtroom full of people, the camera feed capturing my every expression, and all eyes of the jury riveted on my sweaty mug.

"Then let's back up. Tell us what brought you to his apartment that afternoon."

I detailed the facts that led to my discovery of Frank's body, and then Arlene pointed to the grisly photograph again.

"What did you do when you saw this in person?"

"I was shocked, slipped in his blood trying to get out of there. Once outside, I called the police."

"You didn't go anywhere first and try to clean your shoes?"

"No."

"Did you call me, or another lawyer, before contacting the police?"

"No."

"Why not?"

"Because I hadn't done anything wrong." If my intent was to kill Frank, the jury would have to consider why I didn't have a better plan than to stand outside of his house, my shoes covered in his blood, and wait for the cops.

"And the money that was found in the trunk of your car, did you steal that?"

"Absolutely not. And I certainly didn't put it there." The simple and direct truth. The significance of the money that the police had confiscated could not be underestimated. A guilty verdict on the theft charge alone guaranteed prison time, and the Bar Association would revoke my license to practice law.

Arlene had me describe my stroll to the convenience store to fetch Jennifer a sandwich and some wine, while my car keys were in her possession, and then she asked me about the night I'd been smacked around by the bouncer.

"I never hit him. He knocked me down, kicked me, beat me up pretty good."

"Before that night, when was the last time you were in a fight?"

"Ninth grade. Jimmy Madison. He beat me up pretty good too."

I glanced at the jury, and a few of them were chuckling. Maybe I wasn't such a rat, after all, but just an ordinary guy who had made some mistakes and was, as they say, in the wrong place at the wrong time. When Arlene wrapped up her direct, Flanagan strode to the podium and drilled me with those emerald green eyes.

"So, Mr. Coleman," he said and then paused. A full one, two, three. "Did you also have an affair with Jennifer Browning's late sister, Martha?"

I feared losing control of my bladder. The emeralds bored into me. *Rumors, back in the day, you and the sister* . . . Bernie. The son of a bitch. I thought he'd done me a solid, but my old high school buddy, my stalwart teammate, had sold me out.

Arlene objected, then she and Flanagan stormed to a sidebar with Judge Seidelson. Before he shushed them, I heard Arlene say *irrelevant* and *prejudicial*. Flanagan countered that his question not only bore on my credibility, but also to premeditation, because my plot could have been based on information Martha gave me about Frank or Oyster. But how Seidelson ruled really didn't matter, because the jury had heard the damning question and watched me hesitate like a doe in the headlights' glare.

The judge ordered me to answer. Arlene paced back to her seat, her narrowed eyes radiating betrayal. Jesus, I would have told her about Martha if I'd had any inkling that anyone knew about it. Bernie must have uncovered some proof, though, because Flanagan wouldn't have asked the question without knowing the answer. I looked at him and said, "Yes."

There was a commotion in the back of the courtroom, and Cathy stalked out, shaking off Corrigan's hand on her shoulder. Vanessa Edwards plunged after her. I had just ensured that there would be no huddling with Father McGraw to salvage our relationship. And Molly—new ammunition for the taunting bullies. My stomach heaved, and Flanagan's voice slapped me again.

"Don't you think that the fact that you had an affair with her sister was something you should have disclosed to Jennifer?"

"No, I . . ." Fuck. Arlene had instructed me to answer *yes* or *no*, or ask for clarification if the question wasn't clear. But I perfectly understood what Flanagan was asking and had no idea how to answer it with a *yes* or *no*. "Well, I never meant for that night with Jennifer to happen. Besides, her sister's gone now . . . there was no reason to bring it up."

I sounded like some raincoat-in-the-park kind of guy, flashing himself to a girl my daughter's age. One juror, a Hispanic woman in the front row, pursed her lips and shook her head. Flanagan toyed with me, tormented me, made me sit and suffer and clear my throat and hem and haw and swivel in my seat. The searing agony of the bolt cutter was nothing compared to his precise and relentless infliction of emotional distress. Arlene tried to shield me with an objection whenever she could, but reassembling my shattered credibility was beyond even her gifts.

" . . . and wouldn't the two hundred thousand dollars tide you over nicely until you were close enough to Jennifer that she'd take care of you?"

"That's not what happened."

"So we're to trust you, Mr. Coleman? Tell me, you vowed to be faithful to your wife when you married her?"

"Yes, sir."

"Did you break that vow, or did your wife agree that you could seduce Jennifer Browning?"

"It wasn't like that. My wife didn't know anything about us."

"So you broke your vow, lied to your wife?"

I was barely aware of answering his last several questions. Twice, Flanagan instructed me to repeat a mumbled response. When the pummeling was finally over, Arlene didn't launch into any redirect, because I was done. Cooked. My law school professors had taught me that no one could ever be sure of what is whirling inside the minds of a jury. Except now, there was no need to even look at them. I knew.

When the judge excused me to return to the defense table, the court-room floor seemed to sway.

Flanagan had gutted me as efficiently as the Butcher would have, as the Torso Murderer might. But the merciless man behind those glittering green eyes was the cruelest of all—he was going to let me live.

41

Arlene told Judge Seidelson that we had no further witnesses and rested our case. The judge instructed everyone that closing arguments would commence in the morning. As the jury filed out, Arlene thrust papers into her briefcase. Jack walked through the gate that separated the gallery from the courtroom proper, shrugged, and then gave me a blank look, like *what the fuck?*

"I need to talk with him, Jack," Arlene said, her voice edgy.

"I can wait, if you want, Johnny . . . "

"No, I'll catch a cab." Truth was, I didn't want to explain about Martha to Jack, either.

I followed Arlene into a vacant jury room, and she dropped into a chair. For the first time since we'd met, her eyes were dim. "So, when were you going to tell me about boffing the sister?"

I sank into a chair like a chastened schoolboy and tried to answer her question, but the words were jumbled. "No one knew . . . Salvatore, the prick, once told me he'd heard rumors, but I never, ever . . . "

"He's a cop first." Her eyes burned into me, and meeting her gaze was impossible. "Think he couldn't find proof if he wanted to? Ever take your honey to dinner somewhere? What about a motel?

Unless you fucked her in Buenos Aires, somebody sure as hell saw you together. All you guys think you're so damn clever."

"But—"

She interrupted, as though she weren't even listening to me. "Maybe Flanagan found out, doing his own investigation."

"But why would he even think about me and Martha?"

"Ever think that Jennifer might have known all along? Maybe the sisters even had a chitchat, before Martha kicked off, about the size of your dick."

"No, Arlene, fuck it, no. Her sister would come up in conversation sometimes, and Jennifer had no idea."

"Oh, right. You did such a masterful job of reading her."

"Well, should we have recalled—?"

"What? You're second-guessing my decision to rest . . . "

"No, I—"

"You recall a witness if there is surprise testimony, or the prosecutor held something back. There was no surprise here, no holding back, because *you* knew. The only one in the fucking courtroom who should have known and didn't, was me!"

"Calm down, Arlene. It was my fuck-up."

"Unbelievable." She straightened her arms against the table and dropped her head. After a moment, she sat back. "If you'd told me, Martha would have been handled during my direct. You would have still sounded like an asshole, but I could have controlled the situation."

"All I can say is that I'm sorry."

She shook her head, her lips drawn tight, and then said, "I had a stake in this too, and you made me look stupid. Every lawyer in town will wonder if my brilliant strategy was to play hide-the-ball-from-the-jury. Perhaps you never figured it out, but I worked my ass off to build *my* life. Fucking Flanagan left a land mine for me, and my own client let me step on it."

Flanagan had not raised my affair with Martha during his case-in-chief, predicting—accurately—that I'd have to take the stand.

Drawing the admission out of me on cross was much more damning. "Like I said, Arlene, I'm sorry. I don't know what else to say."

"This case came down to your word against hers. How do you like them apples?" She looked away in disgust.

"You have no idea . . . is there something I can do . . . help prep for the close?" I needed her to deliver the closing argument of a lifetime, but I'd crushed her, sucked the spirit out of her.

She tossed her hair and leaned onto the table. Accepting my apology wasn't on her agenda. "Don't worry about the close. I need to figure a way to spin the pile of shit you left me into gold for the jury. But if it goes south, you'll know one big reason why. And don't get too drunk tonight. The least you can do is be half-ass alert tomorrow."

She was up and gone. I waited several minutes, knowing that she didn't want me to accompany her in the elevator, before heading down to St. Clair and hailing a taxi. The cabbie who eventually pulled to the curb wasn't a chatty type, thank God. He examined me in the rearview mirror and seemed to recognize my face from all the press coverage, but had the decency to just drive. The radio blared hip-hop, a genre that I found grating and one likely to dominate my cell block.

The locks went unchecked that night. What the fuck did it matter? I considered just opening the front door, scattering some knives on the kitchen counter, and inviting Torso to have at it. With a stiff whiskey in hand, I crawled into bed and stared at the ceiling. Jennifer marched into my head with her teasing voice. *How could you not have known I'd be a great witness? Pretending comes naturally to me, even faking pleasure at the thrust of your tired body against mine. You made it so easy.*

I rearranged the pillow about a hundred damn times, wanting nothing more than to drown in a bucket of booze. Bernie. Fucking, fucking Bernie. Arlene's admonition to show up in the morning without a hangover was fresh on my mind, but my thoughts wandered in a different direction. Maybe the prudent course was to swallow a bottle of aspirin and wash the pills down with a fifth.

I'd been able to maintain the course because of Molly and, maybe, the slim possibility of making things right with Cathy. My wife was now out of the equation, permanently, and there was no way of knowing how my daughter would react. Schoolyard barbs echoed in my head. *And he fucked her sister, too!*

There were several reasons that I ultimately drained my last drink and lay quietly in the dark. Killing myself would be contrary to the teachings of the Church and only bring further shame to Cathy. Torso, the Butcher, and Jennifer would all have a macabre victory, too, if the cops found me cold and blue when I failed to show up for court.

But the true motivation for determining to live, to put one tentative foot in front of the other, was because I could not do to Molly what my father had done to me. No matter the jury's verdict, no matter my punishment, I would be there for my daughter until they slipped an icy needle into my vein.

42

The morning came too early, and I banged down a cup of coffee, interspersed with several spoonfuls of yogurt, before trotting out to Jack's waiting car.

"You doin' okay?" he asked, even though he knew the answer.

"Slept like hell. All this shit . . . lots of rotten dreams last night. The Butcher, Jennifer. And Bernie, hell, had to be him who tipped off Flanagan about me and Martha. I've known him since we were kids, and he does that to me."

"I can ask him point blank if you want."

"Let me think about it; not sure it even matters, now." Bernie had written me out of his life, that was for sure, and then some.

"All I know is you picked a helluva combo for a twofer." Jack flashed a wild grin as he backed down the driveway. "Never saw that comin', that's for sure."

He made me smile in spite of everything, and I wished we could just motor away—New York, Toronto. "I'm gonna miss you, man."

Grunting, he shifted into drive. "I talked to the guy in California again. He's still making calls, workin' his sources."

"Yeah, but it's been months, and what's he got to show for it?" I pictured more dollar bills fluttering out the window. "Tell him to give it a rest."

"Serious?"

"I'm askin' you to do it for me, Jack. Just stop. There's nothin' in California. Mary's not gonna walk through the courthouse door and testify that she told Jennifer where Frank was. No one's going to put Jennifer at the scene. Just tell your guy in San Diego to send a final bill."

We were silent for a spell, just two men in a car. When we pulled onto the Shoreway, I stared out the window, across Edgewater Park, to the lake shimmering in the morning sun. Now that was the way to go, not a lethal injection—just slide beneath the surface of the cool water and watch the sunlight fade to a cold, shadowy black.

Jack accelerated, checking his rearview mirror and then looking back to me. His voice took on an odd, gentle quality. "Sorry it didn't work out."

"Nothin' worked out, Jack. Not a thing in my life."

"Well, I'm startin' to think we don't have to worry about Torso so much." He cleared his throat. "That's one thing."

I could see what he was doing. He was letting me know that he'd be okay, that there was no need to worry about the Torso Murderer getting to him. "He wouldn't stand a chance against you, Jack. For me, not sure it makes a difference if the jury comes back like I expect."

He gave me a wry smile. "Well, which way would you rather go? A quick needle, or . . . "

"Fuck you!" I laughed aloud. "But you're right; I'm getting the better deal."

"Just pointin' out that you're a man with options." Jack glanced away, out the window. "Cathy called me last night. Says she's not coming back to court anymore."

I nodded but didn't say anything.

"Her decision, Johnny."

There are things we can't control—that was the message Jack was sending me. We parked in the usual spot and walked into the courthouse.

The old bastard had lightened my load. They might strap me in shackles in no time, but I would never forget Jack Corrigan, a true friend.

Jennifer was already seated in the gallery when we walked into the courtroom, and her presence was legit, given that all of the testimony had been concluded. She had every right to focus her hazel eyes on my back. Flanagan was across the room, coiled and ready to pounce. Because the prosecutor has the burden of proof, he would speak to the jury initially, followed by Arlene. Flanagan would also be the last one to face the jury box and deliver the final argument in the case.

When the judge summoned him to begin, Flanagan took center stage and seemed to own the jury before he uttered a word, before he ran a hand through his thick hair or adjusted his dark tailored suit coat. His tie was a blaze of red and blue. Softly, he said, "What do you do when a man asks you to trust him, to believe in him? You must fairly ask: what has this man done to convince me that he's telling the truth?"

He turned to me, and sixteen sets of eyes, jurors and alternates, followed his penetrating gaze. I was a creature on display, at the zoo, and I fixed my eyes on his barrel chest as beads of perspiration gathered on my forehead.

"The defendant here wants you to believe him." Flanagan's voice was louder now. "What has he done to earn your trust? The man sitting at that table is an admitted adulterer who had the watch that Frank Frederickson wore—a gift from his father, his retirement watch—thirty-five thousand dollars, and a bloody knife concealed in the wheel well of his car."

Flanagan discredited my testimony with inflection alone. I watched the jury as he paraded in front of them, working without notes and never breaking eye contact. "And he slept with Jennifer Browning's sister, the deceased daughter of her murdered father. He claims that his infidelity was a *mistake*, and that he made the same *mistake* later, when he seduced Jennifer."

He froze in place for a moment, before pivoting sharply. "At the least, there's no mistake that Mr. Coleman earned the title of double-adulterer, is there? Maybe there's a special name for a man who seduces *two* sisters, but frankly, I don't know what it is. What you must do when you deliberate, however, is to ask yourself this: Can you trust a man like that?"

More than a couple of them nodded in agreement with Flanagan. If there had been a towel in my hand, I might have just tossed it at his feet. He was relentless, reviewing the police reports and the pertinent testimony, rehashing the fingerprint analysis.

"Counsel for the defendant raised some questions about the fingerprints—might this have happened, could this have occurred? But her questions fail to explain away the defendant's prints on the knife that the testimony indisputably shows is consistent with the weapon used to slit Frank Frederickson's throat. Only the defendant's own testimony—his claim that he must have handled the knife at Jennifer's apartment—could explain how his prints were left on the knife, other than when that sharp blade was used to brutally kill another human being."

Flanagan held the evidence bag aloft, as though the murder weapon were a trophy.

"And that's *if* you conclude that someone else—Jennifer, a Mexican gang, whatever it is they are claiming—used the same knife to commit the murder, or dipped a similar knife in a dead man's blood to frame the defendant. But before you can dismiss the fingerprints on this knife, which you *must* do if you attempt to find this defendant not guilty, you have to ask yourself whether you can trust this man."

Flanagan prowled about the room and built toward a climax that would impress the jurors and remain fresh in their minds during deliberations.

"Frank Frederickson had, in many ways, a sad life. He watched a mother and a sister die, suffered through the brutal murder of his father, and he battled his own demons. But he was able to live and breathe and laugh and cry and go about his life every single day— until the night the defendant claims to have stumbled upon his body in a pool of blood. He can't tell his sister all of the things he would have liked to say, he can't cry out for justice, he can't tell us what happened the night someone ripped a steel blade across his throat. Now, only you can speak for Frank Frederickson."

Flanagan wheeled toward me and leveled a finger in my direction, his face a mask of revulsion. He had used my name sparingly, but now spat out all three syllables, each one dripping with venom. "*John Coleman*. Only you can find him guilty as charged!"

The courtroom was silent, except for the muted whirr of the camera. Resisting the urge to grip the table for support, I feared that the jury might burst into applause.

The judge looked at Arlene and gestured that it was her turn. As she rose, I stole a glance at Jennifer. She was a picture of calm and composure, a fine mist clouding her beautiful eyes. She caught me looking and, ever so slightly, smiled.

43

Arlene was fluid persuasion in court, her hair perfectly coifed and her scarlet dress projecting a regal authority. She chiseled away at every chip she'd made in the prosecution's case and bolstered any hint of doubt. "And it is the prosecutor who bears the burden of proof, the weight of convincing you that Mr. Coleman is guilty beyond a reasonable doubt. And it *is* a reasonable doubt when fingerprints are smudged, when a knife cannot be positively identified as a murder weapon, when . . . "

Her lyrical voice faltered a bit when she addressed my credibility, making sure the jury understood that even she found my behavior offensive.

"I'm not asking you to like my client. Frankly, I don't. He lied and cheated on his wife. And sleeping with Ms. Browning's sister? Some, including me, would call his behavior immoral and crude. But people are funny when it comes to adultery. They lie about it and hide it and deny it. They don't talk about it. That doesn't make any of it right, but we don't punish them by finding them guilty of something they didn't do. And John Coleman did not murder Frank Frederickson."

Arlene did her best to spin every bit of evidence in my favor. When she had completed a summary that was as convincing as anything I could hope for, she stood completely still, a pillar in the middle of the courtroom. "The prosecuting attorney asked you to think about Frank Frederickson, and I request that you do the same—a young man who was murdered, his life snuffed out too soon. That is, by anyone's definition, a terrible wrong. But we don't make that *wrong* worse by sending the *wrong* man to prison. I didn't know Frank Frederickson and neither did you, but I'm betting that he wouldn't want an innocent man punished for this crime. Let society punish John Coleman for what we know he did, but that cannot include the crime of murder."

She walked slowly back to our table, the jurors' eyes locked on her, the courtroom still. Flanagan rose to make his rebuttal, a boxer eager for the next round. He could have stepped from the pages of GQ magazine: a shellacked and glittering shell concealing a ruthless heart.

"I commend my opposing counsel for her noble efforts to create some doubt in your mind. But there will always be some doubt, because none of us was there that fateful night. Do a few smeared fingerprints make you doubt? So a threatening gang was looking for Frank Frederickson—does that instill doubt? How about the notion that Jennifer Browning might have killed her own brother—any doubt there?"

He stepped away, his forehead furrowed and his fingertips pressed together. "The question is whether any of that doubt is reasonable. Is it reasonable, in light of Frank Frederickson's blood on a knife consistent with the murder weapon, hidden in the trunk of John Coleman's car? Is it reasonable, in light of the money stashed away in that very same vehicle? The watch?"

Flanagan stepped forward and leaned against the beech railing of the jury box, his arms spread wide. "We all know the answer. And we know something else. John Coleman is a liar." He turned and pointed at me again, backing away from the jury, his voice breaking. "Do not let Frank Frederickson's killer go unpunished!"

Damn. But tears glimmered in those green eyes. Even I had to admit that the brevity of his comments made the entire case seem open and shut. The jury remained fixed on him until he took his seat, then turned their attention to the judge. In a stiff monotone, Seidelson somberly read the jury instructions, and the courtroom seemed funereal. There would be no heroic last-minute save this time, no armed cops storming down the basement stairs.

The judge completed his recitation just after five o'clock and recessed for the day. Jack dropped me at home, as usual, and I soon found myself with a glass of whiskey on the living room couch, eyeing cheery family photos still lined up on the mantel, below the crucifix. Our wedding picture, me in a tuxedo with comically wide lapels, and Cathy in a lacy white wedding gown, just the two of us, enclosed in a faux gold frame. No matter how Jennifer had urged me on, I could never reach the decision to end my marriage. And, in that basement, I'd wanted nothing more than a fresh start with Cathy.

What the Butcher had slashed away could not compare with what Jennifer had done. I thought of her, of what she'd said and done and touched, every minute of every day. Her charms had ensnared me, and I'd obliviously staggered from one bad decision to another. And tomorrow, when that earnest jury filed into the courtroom, I knew Jennifer would emerge the victor. She had dismembered me in ways not even the Torso Murderer could match.

I drained my whiskey and held the glass up to the light, enjoying, for just a moment, the glittering refraction. Jennifer's hair—her blonde tresses shimmered in the light like that. I heaved the glass into the fireplace and watched the shards and slivers scatter against the brick.

The next morning, Arlene and I retreated to a vacant deliberation room, while the jury debated my fate in another. The swivel chairs squeaked, and the off-white walls closed in on me. Arlene, on the opposite side of the long, rectangular table, rubbed her eyes. Every bit of her seemed exhausted, from her unusually haggard appearance to her plain brown suit. "If the jury rules against you, we need to revisit the issue of mitigating circumstances, see how we can persuade them that the death penalty isn't warranted."

"So you're thinking there's no chance this might go my way?" I recalled too clearly Arlene's earlier explanation that, following a guilty verdict, the panel's next task would be to consider the death penalty.

She ignored my question. "If they convict and you testify during the mitigation phase, they'll want to hear you confess, accept responsibility, beg for mercy."

"Arlene . . . " Picturing every one of the jurors' faces, I rubbed my tie. Molly had given it to me as a St. Pat's present, and I was desperate enough to hope that neckwear the color of key lime pie might bring me luck.

She held up a hand. "You've made it clear you won't do that. I'm willing to put up people to vouch that you're a good guy, but Flanagan will rip into them on cross simply by showing that none of them were aware of your affair with Jennifer. Or Martha, or anyone else you forgot to tell me about. The jury will wonder how well anyone knew you, John."

And I knew that was exactly what Cathy wondered, when she curled up alone in a twin bed in her sister's guest room. I wasn't going to respond to Arlene's crack about Martha, or others. "We discussed Father McGraw."

"Like I told you, we put him on, you waive any privilege. All those counseling sessions will be fair game for Flanagan. Unless you told Father McGraw about your extramarital escapades, Flanagan will enjoy pointing out that you lied to a priest."

"There's still my secretary, Marilyn. She could at least say that I never cheated any clients."

"After what came out in court, would the jury believe she really knew, John?" Arlene pursed her lips. "I want you to reconsider letting me ask Cathy to testify. She could acknowledge your faults but point out the positive. How you held a job, never abused her or Molly—right? Things like that."

"I never hurt her, never touched Molly."

"The jury will feel sorry for her and might cut you a break because of that."

I thought of Flanagan doing to Cathy what he'd done to me. "Let's leave her alone, Arlene. Just you argue. I maintain my innocence. Make them think about sending an innocent man to his death."

She gave me a stony stare.

"Please, Arlene, let's leave her the fuck alone."

"You're not getting this. The jury—"

There was a rap on the door, and Jack entered without waiting for an invitation. His face was red, and he was breathing hard, as if he'd been rushing. He said, "The guy from California wants to talk."

Arlene looked incredulous. "Jesus, Jack. Now?"

"Gotta be something. Not even six out there. Bailiff got us a speaker phone."

"I said to cut him off, get a final bill."

"And I heard you. But he told me he was still followin' up leads. If you're pissed about his bill, I'll pay it myself."

I almost didn't care what the California guy knew; what mattered was that Jack had gone the last mile for me.

Arlene put a hand on my arm. "John, odds are we can't do a thing, even if he's got something. Proofs are closed."

I nodded. Jack had retrieved a scrap of paper from his pocket and was punching in a number. A raspy voice picked up immediately, and Jack introduced us to Fred Haskins, retired officer from the San Diego police force.

"I had to bust my hump to put this together, Corrigan." Haskins sounded as though he were gargling stones. "You should get charged a premium."

"Premium my ass. Whaddya got?" I expected that Haskins could have been Jack's twin, but if they went toe-to-toe, my money was on Jack.

"It's no wonder I was getting the runaround. That import/export outfit Browning worked for was a front; he was DEA. An old buddy of mine put me in touch with an agent from way back who knows the inside score."

"Which is?" Arlene said.

"Browning was under an internal affairs investigation; they think he was passing information to a gang in Tijuana."

"Yeah, but how's that help us?" Jack had slipped off his jacket, loosened his brown woolen tie, and braced against the table, his legs splayed beneath him.

"Because good wifey Jennifer was working with him."

Our night at Dino's came back in a rush. *And I volunteer, English as a second language.*

"There's more. DEA was about to nail Browning when that truck smacked into him. No one down there buys the hit-and-run bullshit. Timing was perfect for his loving wife, because she still got full death benefits. And with him out of the way, there wasn't enough to pin anything on her."

Arlene leaned in toward the speaker. "That's hardly proof she had anything to do with his death."

"The bet in San Diego is that Jennifer set him up. The driver of that truck sure as hell knew where Robert Browning would be and when he'd be there."

"Frank tried telling me it was all bullshit, the hit-and-run, the import/export . . . " I remembered the photo of Robert in Jennifer's apartment. Was it on display to mislead me, or was the photograph her trophy?

Haskins went on. "But here's the meat. Her brother had been staying with them for a while, maybe breaking into the business. He left right after the husband was killed. The house was still under surveillance, and he stormed out one day, got in his piece-of-shit beater, and drove off."

"Frank wanted me to know something about Jennifer." I recalled the picture of Jennifer and her brother, the Coronado Bridge in the background. His words to me had been urgent and intense: *I should tell you some things about sweet little Jennifer . . . You have no idea what she's capable of.* "He must have known that she helped kill her husband."

Haskins's gravelly voice crackled over the speaker. "They figure she knew she was being looked at and took off before it got too hot."

"So Jennifer ran," Jack said. "Home to Mommy and Daddy."

"Sorry." Arlene looked at me. "Not enough. Suspicion that she killed her husband . . . "

"How about if I tell you they have surveillance video of Jennifer and the late hubby talking to gang members?" Haskins uttered the words as though he'd just hit the trifecta.

"The Andar Feo," I said, the circle closing in my mind. Jennifer had devised a win-win scheme for herself. With Frank out of the way, not only would she inherit the entire estate, but Frank would be silenced forever. Jesus. Jennifer and the Andar Feo.

"Bingo, sport. And she didn't just fuck over the DEA and her hubby. They suspect she passed on info about rival gangs to give the Andar Feo a leg up. She was in deep."

"Will your source give an affidavit?" Arlene said.

"Said he'll do whatever it takes. They lost some solid undercover guys 'cause of what Browning did."

"And I'll need one from you, why we're just finding out."

Haskins's voice bristled. "Tell the judge this undercover stuff isn't exactly public record. I got this info last night, one o'clock in the fucking morning your time, which is why you're hearin' it now."

"And I'll pay your premium." I stood up, and for the first time in days, my legs felt solid beneath me.

"Fuck that. Just tell me how it turns out." Haskins rang off.

Arlene fished her cell from her purse. "Calling Flanagan."

Jack gave me a wide, shit-eating grin and stuck out his hand. I grasped his meaty palm and pulled him in for a hug. He actually let me embrace him for, maybe, two full seconds.

45

Judge Seidelson recessed the jury and gave us twenty-four hours to make our case for reopening the trial. Haskins sent us the affidavits, surveillance photos, and some DEA memos. Jack, Arlene, and I worked late into the night, compiling the motion. On the way home, Jack and I jabbered like giddy high school kids at an after-prom party. When we finally pulled into my driveway, it was after ten o'clock.

Jack shifted into park and grabbed me by the shoulder, his grip firm. "Well, boyo, not a bad fuckin' day."

The dashboard provided some dim light and I could see that he was grinning. "Jesus, Jack, I don't know what to say. If you hadn't kept it going in California . . . "

"Save it until you can buy me a drink." He dropped his hand from my shoulder. "Now get the hell outta my car. It's way past my bedtime."

"Yeah, yeah." I reached for the handle. "But I mean it. Thanks."

"My thanks will be when I get my ass home and kiss some Kessler's goodnight."

I chuckled and got out of the car, then watched Jack's Fiesta until he'd driven at least halfway down the street. Once inside, the events of the day caught up with me and I fell asleep easily. When I awakened, early in the morning, I felt rested for the first time in months. I even allowed myself a tie with a bit more splash of color than usual. After draining a cup of coffee and polishing off a peach yogurt, I headed for the door, knowing that Jack would be there at the usual time.

The driveway was empty.

Jack was late. *Tardiness* was not in his vocabulary.

I knew there was probably a reasonable explanation: flat tire, traffic jam. But Jack didn't pick up his home phone or his cell. My mind locked on the Torso Murderer. Grabbing my jacket, I trotted to the garage, because arriving late for the hearing would be disastrous.

My thoughts drilled down to the one person to call: Bernie. Even though he had screwed me over, he would check on Jack right away, no question. His phone rolled into voice mail, though, so I left a message.

A bleary-eyed Arlene turned in her chair when I hustled into the courtroom, barely on time. I braced myself with one hand on the table, my other hand on the back of her chair, and whispered, "Jack never showed up."

"Block it out." Her jawline was rigid and her eyes never wavered from mine. "Stay focused. Could be a lot of reasons."

"It's not like him. The Torso Murderer—"

"Jack Corrigan can take care of himself. Sit down. Right now, it's all about you." Arlene aligned the edges of her copies of the motion and affidavits on the table. "The brief came together well. Just promise me, Johnny, that you didn't sleep with anyone in the San Diego DEA."

I thought I glimpsed a twinkle in her eye.

Flanagan walked in just as the hearing was about to begin; he didn't look pleased. He gave Arlene a curt nod, but those emerald eyes avoided mine. Jennifer was a no-show.

We all rose at the bailiff's instructions as Judge Seidelson took the bench and surveyed the courtroom. "Mr. Flanagan, I made it clear that

Jennifer Browning was to be here, in the event that the court or the defense wish to question her about these developments."

Flanagan stood and smoothed the front of his suit coat. "Your Honor, we spoke with Ms. Browning yesterday and explained the order."

Seidelson was plainly irritated. "Try calling her."

"We have, Your Honor, several times. She hasn't answered." The confident edge to Flanagan's voice had vanished, and I silently treasured that fact.

The exchange prompted some tittering among the spectators. The unusual motion hearing had attracted the media, and Vanessa Edwards pivoted toward her cameraman. I dreaded the thought that Jennifer might swing the double doors open and saunter into the courtroom. She'd bat those hazel beauties at the judge and explain everything away. *What, Johnny, had your little hopes up?*

Seidelson raised his eyebrows. "We'll proceed with argument then. I've reviewed the briefs and attachments that were filed earlier this morning. Mr. Flanagan, now that you've had the opportunity to examine the material submitted by Ms. Johnson, could you summarize the basis of the state's objection?"

"In a few words, Your Honor, too little and too late. There is no justification to reopen this trial. Even according Ms. Johnson's brief full weight, there is nothing to prove that the State's witness illegally passed information to the Andar Feo or had anything to do with her husband's demise. In fact, there's nothing to prove that whatever happened in San Diego has even a remote connection to this case. Indeed, had Ms. Johnson attempted to put this so-called evidence on during her case-in-chief, I would have objected that it was irrelevant."

Judge Seidelson folded his hands. "And I would have overruled the objection. Counsel's point is that she doesn't need to prove anything. Evidence of contact between Ms. Browning and the Andar Feo—photos, even—could be evaluated by the jury to make any inferences they deem appropriate in determining whether reasonable doubt exists to acquit Mr. Coleman."

"But, Your Honor, the proofs are closed, and the jury's begun deliberating." Flanagan waved his arms in the air and then abruptly pointed at our table. "The State is clearly prejudiced by the defendant's tardiness in producing this so-called new evidence."

"May I, Your Honor?" Arlene rose, and Seidelson nodded for her to continue. "I hope counsel is not inferring that we were less than diligent in our efforts to adduce facts that would be helpful to Mr. Coleman. I've filed an affidavit detailing the steps we've taken. And, Your Honor, both the interests of justice and judicial economy warrant reopening this trial. Based on this evidence, we will certainly file a motion for a new trial if the jury reaches a verdict that is adverse to my client. If the Court were inclined to grant the motion at that time, we'd have to impanel a new jury and start the entire case over. In the meantime, Mr. Coleman could be incarcerated for a crime he did not commit."

"Your Honor, this—"

Judge Seidelson waved aside Flanagan's objections and reviewed his notes. "The Court has read the briefs submitted by the parties and finds the position taken by the defendant persuasive. The affidavit filed by Mr. Haskins from California establishes that his efforts were diligent, and the fact that this new information was uncovered after proofs were closed should not deprive Mr. Coleman of the opportunity to present a full and fair defense . . . "

Seidelson kept talking, about depositions or plane flights from the West Coast, and I wanted to wrap my arms around Arlene and tell her that, yes, indeed, she was a magician. But even her wizardry would have been for nothing if not for Jack, the persistent old bastard who just wouldn't give up on the California angle when all signs pointed to a dead end.

As the judge left the bench, Flanagan gathered his papers and looked at Arlene as if she had kicked him in the balls. His eyes radiated anger, but he stuffed the documents in his slick brown briefcase and strode away without saying a word. The press closed in, and I heard him mutter something about "procedural gamesmanship" before he passed into the hallway.

Arlene and I slipped out the side door to avoid the media and took the elevator down.

"Jesus, Arlene, I feel like I'm reborn. We have a chance now, a real chance, right?"

"No more surprises?"

"None. Promise."

"Then we have a real chance."

I was going to buy Jack Corrigan the best steak dinner in town, at least the best I could afford. I'd approach Father McGraw about talking to Cathy. And Molly. Jesus, I could see my daughter, watch her grow up.

My sense of optimism shriveled when we entered the garage. Bernie was there, pacing. Arlene placed her hand on my arm. "Don't bring up your case. He could wind up testifying again."

We came to a halt steps away from him, and I said nothing, not even hello, and waited for him to speak. Bernie had the same distressed look on his face as the day we'd found Oyster. "I came down to tell you in person. EMTs found him on his kitchen floor."

I grabbed a concrete pillar and held tight. "Torso?"

"Heart attack, and he was lyin' there for a while."

It took me a moment to process what he was saying. Jack had been energized by the new developments, and he'd pushed himself, working the phones with Haskins in California, drafting affidavits for Arlene to review. "It's my fault, him workin' all fucking night."

Arlene rested a hand on my shoulder. "You can't blame yourself."

"Things are turning my way now, and Jack . . . "

"He's at Fairview intensive care, but it doesn't look good." Bernie shrugged. "What can I tell you? They're calling the family."

"I am sorry for you, John," Arlene said. She would never be able to set aside Jack's old-school racism, but he'd done his job, and she knew how I felt about him.

"Think they'll let me see him? I'm not really family . . . "

"Taken care of," Bernie said. He'd written me off and screwed me over, but he'd put all of that bullshit in a box, at least for a little while, to come down and tell me himself about Jack. "He's conscious, and there's something he wants to tell you. Alone."

46

A nurse led me into the intensive care unit and then left me in a close and uncomfortable room of glimmering monitors, tangled rubber tubes, and the stench of an old man. I had considered smuggling in a pint of Kessler's but expected that Jack was long past the point of appreciating even a sip of his favorite tonic.

"Hey," I said, sitting in the plastic chair wedged between the wall and his bed. "Let's get the hell out of here and head over to the Tam."

Jack gave me a weak grin and a slight nod. "Got somethin' to tell you, another reason why I stuck my nose into all this, besides watchin' your back."

His voice was faint, so I leaned in close and rested my hand on the bed rail. "Okay, and good to see you, too."

"Tellin' you, but you gotta keep it close." His breath was stale. "Only you."

Nodding, I hoped that I had misunderstood him. The burden of another man's secrets, even Jack's, was the last thing I needed.

"Remember his letter? What Torso said about knowin' what really happened in 1950?" His gaze drifted away, and he coughed so weakly that his head barely moved. Then he looked at me again, his eyes rheumy.

Damn, he was barely hanging on, and his mind was fixated on something that had happened sixty-plus years ago. "I don't need to hear anything, Jack. You saved my ass."

He tried to lift his head, and his steely eyes narrowed in evident pain. "Shut. The. Fuck. Up." He let his head fall back on the pillow, and I raised my hands in surrender.

Jack's gaze drifted toward the ceiling. "I lied."

I sat there, silent.

He wheezed and sucked in a deep breath, twisting his head sideways. I thought he might stop talking, but he turned back to me after a moment. I leaned in even closer. "Dark in the lumberyard, and me and my partner split up . . . Big motherfucker, but I knew what I was doin'. I waded in . . . got knocked on my ass . . . *one punch*."

"You were doing your job, Jack."

He looked at me like I didn't get it. "Slammed me into the fence."

I raised an eyebrow and waited for him to continue. His voice had become so delicate that I was concerned he wasn't getting enough oxygen.

He raised his head slightly, trying to edge closer to me, and I saw the pain register in his eyes. "Fought with everything I had . . . he was chokin' me, and I was dyin'."

His eyes beseeched me, and I wanted to say that it didn't matter. He deserved the benefit of every doubt. There was no better man than Jack, and no one who would have fought harder.

"Bastard dropped me, run off when my partner started yellin'. But it was too dark for him to know, right? I ran into the street . . . fell on purpose . . . said I twisted my leg. Fuck, I was *big Jack Corrigan,* understand?"

I nodded, almost imperceptibly, wanting this to be the end of whatever he was confessing to me.

"I lied . . . the chief . . . the paper, everyone . . . "

Maybe that explained why he'd beat the shit out of anyone who crossed into Lakewood who he felt didn't belong there. Showing all his cop buddies how tough he was. Trying to prove it to himself, again and again.

I pulled my chair as close as I could. "Jack—"

"Never told no one, not even in confession." He shook his head. "Got my ass beat, covered it up." He inhaled deeply, gathering his strength, and said, loudly and clearly, "*The difficulty in life is the choice. Wrong choice . . . fuckin' kill ya.*"

"You taught me that, Jack."

He waved weakly, his hand trembling. Quoting George Moore on his deathbed. He reached over and placed his shaking hand on mine.

I'd like to say that Jack passed away surrounded by his family, at peace at last. But he died that night, around three in the morning, all alone with his monitors and his tubes and the choices that clawed at him all the way to heaven or hell. Arlene had been wrong. None of us gets away with what we've done.

47

Marilyn's had been the only congratulatory phone call after my acquittal, and even then, our conversation had been terse and awkward. I knew that she had to see me as a walking asshole, just not a murderous one. Reporters had phoned, but I'd referred all of them to Arlene.

The one person I burned to hear from didn't call. I forced myself to wait a full day after my acquittal before dialing her number. From the table in the kitchen, where we used to chat over coffee, my hand wavered as I gripped the cell. I desperately wanted Cathy to pick up and not, when she noted the caller ID, simply hand the phone to her Valkyrie sister. Cathy did answer, after two rings, and I began yammering before she had a chance to change her mind. "Please don't hang up. We need to talk about Molly; that's all."

There was an uncomfortable silence. "Congratulations on the verdict."

"Thanks." I might as well have been talking with a stranger. "You hear about Jack?"

"Yes, and I'm sorry. The obituary was nice."

I remembered Jack growling at me, *Your wife and kid had to see that shit.* "He always liked you."

"That was mutual."

"Molly, too."

"I know that."

"Yeah." I swallowed, cleared my throat. "Cathy, please. I need to see her."

That uncomfortable silence swarmed back over the line, and then Cathy said, "Her sister, too, John?"

"I wish you hadn't been in court."

"Wouldn't have mattered. The newspaper made a headline of it. Molly read it."

"I'll talk to her, tell her what an idiot I was."

"I think she knows that." She sighed. "Most of the city does."

I deserved the crack. Nothing she might say would be out of bounds. "I don't expect you to ever forgive me, Cathy. That's not why I'm calling. But I need to see Molly."

"Do you think that's what she needs, John?"

"This will be on your terms. I'll come over there, sit with both of you."

"She got into another fight when the kids piled on about your intriguing sex life. They suspended her. The principal said she was sorry, but they'd already reprimanded her and didn't have a choice."

"Was . . . was she hurt?"

"Physically, she's fine." Cathy exhaled sharply. "I'm seeing a counselor, someone the lawyer recommended, a fresh perspective from Father McGraw's. Molly's going with me next time."

"No argument." Her words made me recall Arlene's stolid handshake after the jury had pronounced me not guilty. *Don't forget about professional counseling. I think you need it.*

"That's big of you, John."

"Please, don't make this any harder than it is. Can you just ask her if she'll see me?"

"I've discussed this with my lawyer. You've got rights, but I'm asking you not to push visitation now. She's pretty mixed up, and you need to give her time."

"I would rather have lost the trial than lose her."

"A tad late to don the shining armor." Cathy paused, as though choosing her words carefully. "If she wants to meet, will you quit the booze, completely?"

"You know—"

"Answer the question, John."

"Yes, anything." That was all I could say, and there was nothing more to discuss. "I'm sorry, Cathy."

Her voice broke. "I'll let you know."

The call was over; bright icons filled the screen on my cell. The clock above the sink read nearly two o'clock. I supposed that there would be plenty of lame sitcoms and old movie reruns on television. I strolled to the counter by the sink and looked out the window at the bright sunshine and green grass. A couple of yards over, kids were kicking around a soccer ball while a Labrador gave frantic chase. My eyes wandered to the clock again.

Fuck it. I could not spend the rest of my life avoiding the public and worrying about a serial killer lurking in my basement.

The Tam O'Shanter would be a comfortable place to initially show my face, to gauge the reaction of Timmy and Karen when they saw me stroll through the door. And it was as good a place as any to begin keeping the promise that I'd just made to Cathy.

I cruised down Detroit, my front windows down and the warm spring breeze tickling my hair. The street seemed somehow refreshed: the restored façade of the INA building, the colorful pennants strung through the parking lot of St. James Church, the new coffee shop where the hardware store had been for about a hundred years. I breathed deeply of the fresh air and searched for a parking spot near the bar.

Tim and Karen were stocking shelves, preparing for the after-work regulars, when I came in from the light and entered the time capsule that was the Tam O'Shanter. Posters still lined the wall, the Wurlitzer pumped out some Pink Floyd, and the long wooden bar gleamed. Tim was crouched, unloading a case of liquor on the floor. He straightened upon seeing me and nudged Karen. "Hey, look who's back."

Karen, wearing a clingy blue top and a delicate golden chain, smiled. She didn't come around the bar for an embrace, but she did reach for a mug to draw a beer.

I waved her off. "Just a Coke."

"Really?" She froze for a moment and then grabbed a glass from behind the bar and a can from the cooler. "That's on us."

I wanted to believe that they were glad to see me, but the complimentary drink seemed about as far as they were willing to go. Sliding onto my seat, my gaze drifted to Oyster's vacant one.

Tim turned and leaned on the bar. "So are you . . . the case is over, right?"

"The prosecutor could appeal, but my lawyer says we're in good shape. All that stuff that came out at the end, about Jennifer."

"That was pretty wild." He nodded and looked at the TV, then back at me. "So what do they think happened, you know, to her?"

I shrugged. "Everyone suspects that Jennifer had a backup plan, with the Andar Feo. If things ever backfired—which they did—she could certainly pay whatever they demanded to get her out of the country. Drug cartels have the best smuggling ops in the world."

"Jesus, her own brother." Karen stood and pretended to arrange bottles on the bar back, but the labels were already facing out, just the way she liked. "How's your daughter handling everything?"

They had to know that Cathy and I were Splitsville, so they didn't ask about that. And her question was delicate. She probably wanted to use more direct phrasing: *How'd your teenage daughter handle the situation when she found out you'd screwed two sisters, a live one and a dead one? I mean, I know she was alive when you . . .*

Months ago, I would have poured my heart out to her then sympathetic ear. Now, her question seemed to be simply about an object of curiosity: me. "We have to work things out, now that the case is over."

"How old is she?"

"Thirteen, fourteen pretty soon."

"Grow up before you know it, right?"

"Right."

We were all quiet, and I took a gulp of pop. Karen held up a menu, which I declined. Tim finally broke the silence. "You going back into practice?"

"Not sure. I'll have to figure something out." There was no reason to mention that the bar association would probably yank my license for sleeping with a client.

"Well, good luck, whatever you do."

"Thanks." I took another swallow and shoved the glass away, not wanting to be at the Tam anymore and not even caring to finish the Coke. Even though Karen had said the drink was on the house, I left a couple of bucks on the bar. "We're good," I insisted, when they began to protest.

After a couple of steps, I stopped short, thinking again of Karen screaming in the alley. Without saying anything, I turned for the back door. Tim nodded, then looked away, but neither of them said a word.

The Dumpster was in the same place, shoved tight against the chipped brick wall. Exactly in this tight and littered lane, my life had begun to unravel. The days of tipping a cold one with Bernie Salvatore were over. No more gruff and lifesaving bullshit from Jack Corrigan. The aroma of Cathy's chicken casserole would never welcome me home, and I might even lose the pleasure of Molly's endearing smile.

The difficulty in life is the choice, Jack had said. I'd made some dumbass choices, no question. But I had not clawed my way past the Butcher and Jennifer and weathered a trial with my life on the line, for nothing. Jennifer could not be permitted to define me, to allow the despicable and desperate man in that courtroom to shape anyone's lasting memory of John Coleman. That much, I owed my Molly.

I turned and kicked a stone along the asphalt, considering whether to seek some closure and head to Great Lakes, maybe even make a pilgrimage to the alley where I'd been bushwhacked. The gray rock clattered along the littered asphalt before coming to rest against the brick wall, and then my cell buzzed. Cathy had texted me. *She still skates Thursdays at 5:30. Pick her up and take her to the park for a couple of hours, okay?*

I floated all the way to my Buick.

48

On Wednesday night, someone flicked on the lamp on my night table. I was lying on my side, facing away from the light, and sensed a presence behind me. The bedcovers were pulled tight against my chin and I found it impossible to move them. My heart was pounding, and beads of clammy sweat gathered on my brow.

"Hello, John."

I would recognize that voice anywhere.

She had invaded my home.

Raw anger sparked me to cast aside the blankets and roll over. I gripped the sheets and braced myself on one clenched hand. A glance at the alarm clock told me that it was three in the morning.

"Miss me?" Jennifer wore jeans and a sweatshirt, plain gray. She was smiling that smile of hers, the one that I had never been able to resist. A rugged man who wasn't smiling stood near her, closer to the foot of the bed. I thought I recognized him as one of the Andar Feo guys who'd been outside the Alley.

I drew myself to a sitting position and folded my arms across my chest. "Get the hell out of my house."

Jennifer shrugged, then turned and sat on the side of the bed. She adjusted her position on the blanket so that she faced me, one leg on the floor and the other tucked beneath her. "Comfy mattress. Don't mind, do you?"

"I'll call the police." I eyed the phone on the nightstand. Could I make it through 9-1-1 before the guy slipped a knife in me?

She spoke, over her shoulder, to her companion. "*Dice que va a llamar a la policia, Pedro.*"

The man she'd called Pedro stalked to the foot of the bed and glowered. I didn't reach for the phone.

"That's better." Jennifer spun fully onto the bed and crossed her legs. No more than three feet apart, we studied each other across the bed. Pedro remained at the foot, like the apex of a triangle. "We only want to talk."

"I have nothing to say to you."

"Just a few questions, John. Be polite."

I calculated the distance between us, wondering whether I would be able to lock a chokehold on her before Pedro could intervene. "You ruined my life."

She laughed, raucously, looking from the still unsmiling Pedro to me. When she quieted, and the room was again still, her face grew serious, and she said, "No. Let's be clear. You ruined your life."

"Jesus, Jennifer. We had a one-night stand. What you did to me—"

"You had more than a one-night stand with Martha."

Perhaps I should have been at least somewhat surprised, but I wasn't. Jennifer had played me before we even met. *I spent all the time I could with Martha . . . we were so close . . .* "You knew all along."

"I knew everything. You did ruin her life. Killed her."

I shifted closer to the headboard. "Oh, for . . . it was cancer."

"Stress causes cancer, John, or didn't you care?"

"You've got this all wrong." She was as looney as the Butcher. "It was just . . ."

"No, I think I've got it pretty much right." She leaned back and braced herself with her arms. "What you did was the main reason

I chose you, you know." Her lips pursed, then teased into a wicked smirk. "Once a cheater, always a cheater. No challenge, really."

I tried to swallow, but my throat was parched. "To think that I cared about you. When they found that girl, I called, scared that it might have been you. Those photos you showed me, after Frank was killed . . . I was worried."

She chuckled. "Oh, those! Not a bad photographer, am I? And slipping one of me into the packet was a damn shrewd move, don't you think?"

She'd played us all for suckers. Me, the cops, all of us concerned that the big, bad Andar Feo might play crisscross on Jennifer's face. "Your own brother, Jennifer?"

"C'mon, Mister Lawyer. You think I'm going to confess, fall on my knees, beg forgiveness?" She flashed that big, pearly smile. "Of course, you did like me on my knees."

We'd all been puppets, dangling from strands of her vicious web. I thought of little Mary, the *dreg*. "You forced that waitress to tell you where Frank was, then had her killed, too. After that, you just needed to wait for me to meet with him, to walk into your fucking trap."

"My, aren't we the chatty one." Her hazel eyes twinkled. "You probably would have done fine in prison, you know. Some young stud might have even found you some whipped cream."

I stared, wanting nothing more than to smack her smirk into the wall. Pedro cleared his throat and shifted his weight from one foot to the other. I glanced from him to Jennifer and said, "What the hell do you want from me?"

"Just a few answers, John." Languorously, she hinged her upper body forward and rested her elbows on her knees. "By the way, is this the side of the bed where Cathy used to sleep?"

She then spoke in Spanish to Pedro; she must have repeated what she'd said to me, because he grinned, exposing a row of stained teeth. I glared at him, my eyes mere slits. But said nothing.

"We've read the court file. Nice website, very user friendly." She intertwined her fingers. "What else did your investigators find, John? I have some nervous friends."

So that's what her visit was all about. I shook my head. "We gave everything we had to the judge. My life was on the line, remember?"

"Quite well, in fact." She looked at Pedro, then back to me. "Are you positive, John? Nothing more?"

"I swear." I watched Pedro focus on Jennifer, as if waiting for a signal from her. Then he shifted his weight again.

Jennifer pursed her lips and then said, "And what about me? If they try to tie me to what happened to Frank . . . you wouldn't help them, would you?"

"For Christ's . . . " I took a deep breath. "Why haven't you just killed me?"

She unlaced her fingers and sat up straight, her hands on her thighs. "We had that discussion, but I persuaded them not to. I don't think you're going to cause any problems for us, John. And who knows? I might need you someday, to do something for me or my friends."

"No fucking way."

Jennifer tilted her head. "Are you sure about that?"

"I'd burn in hell before I helped you."

She turned to Pedro and said, "*El photo.*"

Never taking his eyes off of me, he reached into his back pocket and then extended his arm in my direction. Pinched between his thumb and forefinger was a picture of Molly. Someone had used bright-red ink to draw markings that resembled fish gills on her cheeks. The words *Andar Feo* were scrawled across her forehead, and an *x* had been drawn over her left eye.

My head swiveled toward Jennifer. "You wouldn't."

"Of course, I wouldn't. But they would."

I looked down at the plain maroon blanket and rubbed the palm of my hand across my forehead.

"The way this works is pretty simple," Jennifer said. "We don't want to hear that you're helping the authorities, and we never want to see you on a witness stand. Ever. Understand?"

I dropped my hand from my forehead and nodded, not looking at her.

"Good. And if I ever ask you for anything, anything at all, you had better think very carefully about your answer." Her weight shifted as she slid off the bed. She turned and rested one hand on her hip. "I remember reading about your father, how the Butcher had described him as hapless. Must be genetic."

My fists gripped the blanket so firmly that my arms quivered. "If you ever touch my daughter, I swear to God . . . "

"Oh, I know, John. You'd hunt me down and kill me and all of that." She nodded to Pedro, who stuffed the photo back into his pocket. "By the way, we already cut the phone line to your house. I'll need your cell, just in case you decide to do something stupid."

For some reason, I thought about the letter from the Butcher, shelved in the bureau against the wall behind them. "Charging, in the kitchen."

"Mind if we take a couple of bottles for the road? Where's your liquor?"

She was provoking me to tell her to get fucked, which I knew was exactly what she wanted. No doubt, she would enjoy watching Pedro knock me around. I managed to swallow and said, "Upper cabinet, by the sink."

She walked to the foot of the bed, near Pedro and bit her lower lip. With a nod to him, they both turned toward the door. Then she paused and rested her hand on the doorknob. "Just so you know, your buddy, Oyster, my dear old dad, molested me when I was a kid. He started when I was four."

And then she was gone, their footsteps pattering down the stairs. I wormed down in the bed, my head sinking into the pillow. I thought about Frank and Oyster, his melancholy eyes. Mostly, though, my mind was laser-focused on the threat to my Molly. Several minutes passed before I staggered into the bathroom and threw up.

49

I called Bernie Salvatore first thing in the morning, from a pay phone at a Dairy Mart a couple of blocks from my house. There had been no point in calling the night before, as I'd known nothing about their vehicle, their destination, or anything that would have been remotely helpful to the police.

And, maybe, I'd simply been too afraid for my daughter to make the call.

Bernie pulled into the driveway only minutes after I'd returned from the convenience store. With a curt nod, he brushed past me and checked the doors and windows. Helping me out, just like the days on the playground or the football field.

"No sign of forced entry." He led the way from the back door into the living room and sagged onto the couch. "Either a damn good lock picker or she has a key."

"Jesus." Another consequence of dropping my key chain on the shelf in her apartment. I dropped into the chair across from Bernie. "She could have made an impression."

"Change the locks, John." He raised his hands, palms up. "Unless you want her to drop by again . . . "

My head snapped back, surprised. "Hey, c'mon."

"Sorry. Too soon." He lowered his arms. "I understand her concern about a new investigation into Frank. No doubt, she's at least an accessory, but proving it . . . "

"What if they make a case and subpoena me?" My eyes drifted to some photos framed on the fireplace mantel, one of Molly just after the adoption. "What about my little girl, Bernie?"

"Don't know what to tell you." He rubbed his chin. "Not what you wanna hear, but nobody can watch anybody twenty-four/seven. But I really don't think you gotta worry too much."

"If you'd seen that photo." I cupped my hands and breathed into them, then leaned back in the chair. "I'm supposed to take her skateboarding after school. I've been looking forward to that, still am, but now . . . "

I shuddered.

Bernie gave me a moment before he said, "They sent you a message, okay? And if there's nothing else you have to tell us, anyway . . . "

He held my gaze. I shook my head.

"I don't think you're on their radar screen anymore. The Andar Feo knows that the DEA, and their friends across the border, will take a fresh look at everything now. Frankly, it's Jennifer who should be worried."

"Why?" I couldn't imagine the ice maiden fretting about anything.

"We know who she is. If the DEA boys find her and she rolls over and tries to cut a deal for herself . . . she's a helluva bigger threat to the Andar Feo than you."

"But she has ties with them, way back."

"That's not how they think, John. Odds are good they'll make her wire transfer her fortune into one of their accounts, and pretty little Jennifer will just disappear. Which, you ask me, is how it should be."

"Maybe so." I pictured a knife slicing into that sweet face. "But I don't see it. She's damn smart."

"And they're damn brutal."

"But if she lives, Bernie, and calls me? Tells me to do something?"

Bernie crossed his legs and stretched an arm along the back of the sofa. "There's only one right answer, John. You get ahold of me."

"But—"

"You call me right away." He spoke very calmly, firmly. "If I have to drive Molly to Saskatchewan myself to protect her, I will. Don't try to play Lone Ranger; you saw how that worked out."

"If anything ever happened to her . . . "

"It won't. I won't let it." Bernie swung his arm away from the sofa and leaned forward, elbows on his knees. "On the phone, you told me that Jennifer knew about you and her sister."

"She never let on." I pressed my finger into the coffee table glass and traced a meaningless pattern. "When that came out in court, you know, I blamed you."

He mulled that over for a minute. "Suppose I can see how you might. But I never knew for sure and didn't see how it mattered. A rumor was all I'd heard."

"I'm sorry about that, Bernie. Sorry about a lot of shit."

"Yeah." He stared at the coffee table, as though he were imagining the figurines bursting to life. Then he ran a knotty hand over his face and turned his attention to me. "I was going to call you anyway. I've got some good news. You'll wanna tell Cathy."

"I could use some."

He reached inside his jacket and handed me a folded piece of paper. "This came in yesterday, and it's been authenticated. You deserve to see it before we release it to the press."

I unfolded the paper and recognized the handwriting immediately.

For one of Cleveland's finest, it was disarmingly easy to pay a visit to Mr. Corrigan's shabby little home. Someone should have counseled him about his Irish taste for cheap swill. Kessler's—how cliché.

I pictured Jack, a mere shadow, curled in that tight hospital crib.

We'd busted our asses late into the night after we'd talked to Haskins in San Diego and learned the truth. Jack had promised to "kiss some Kessler's" before going to bed.

"It was postmarked a couple of days after Jack died," Bernie said. "Read the rest."

You should know that I've now won the game 108 times, beginning with my thirteenth birthday when I first confirmed that my power over cats and dogs extended to people. Poison is not as satisfying as the protocol I used to follow, but we must all adapt with age. Give Mr. Coleman my congratulations. He won his little case, and I'm going to allow him to live a long and miserable life. I'll beat you, all of you, and I'll see you in Hell.

"The bastard." I tossed the letter on the table.

"'I'll see you in hell'—talk about a cliché." Bernie folded the letter and tucked it back into his jacket pocket.

"Jack suffered at the end, Bernie. It's not right." I wished that Torso had poisoned my bottles instead. Let Jennifer choke on the liquor she took from me.

"Course it ain't right."

"Without him . . . they'd have found me guilty, Bernie. Jack, he . . . " My throat was so husky that I could barely speak.

"At least you're in the clear. That's something."

"Jack said you can't figure these sick fucks out. What if it's a trick, to get me to let my guard down?"

"Whaddya gonna do? Jump off a bridge? If he wanted you dead, you'd be dead." Bernie leaned back into the sofa. "Focus on seeing your daughter tonight. Guess Cathy's getting some counseling?"

"Yeah."

He looked around the living room as if to check that everything was as he remembered it and then abruptly stood. "Take care of yourself."

"Bernie . . . I appreciate you comin' over. I really do."

"What I do, I do for Cathy and Molly." He bobbed his head a few times and then said, "You fucked up too much."

"I never wanted this to happen. Ever since we got Molly, I tried to change."

"Guess you shoulda tried harder, John." He headed for the door.

"Bernie, wait a minute." I stood and walked after him. "Can we get together sometime, just to talk?"

He opened the door, hesitated, and turned to face me. "I gotta think about it, John."

I followed him outside and stood on the stoop as he backed out of the driveway, without a glance at me. I stepped back inside the quiet house, turned my gaze to the crucifix on the mantle, and mouthed a silent prayer for Jack.

And for me.

50

I made sure to pick up Molly at five thirty on the dot. Cathy stood behind her, holding open the aluminum screen door as Molly sidled out. She clutched her pink skateboard and looked like she'd just bitten into a sour apple. Cathy followed her, circling around to the driver's side, while Molly dropped her board in back and clambered into the passenger seat. I reached for my daughter, and a perfunctory embrace was my reward.

Cathy ran a hand through her hair. "They just ran a special about that letter from the Torso Murderer. Thanks for calling me."

"We'll be able to sleep a lot better. And I promise to start focusing on our . . . situation." *Situation* seemed like such a convenient word.

"We should wrap things up with the lawyers. Have her back around seven thirty, all right?" She reached for her ear.

"Promise." I shifted into reverse.

"Mom told me about Mr. Corrigan," Molly said as I drove away. "He was always nice to me."

"I'll miss him. And boy, did I miss you."

Her voice was soft, nearly a whisper, as though she were fighting back tears. "It won't ever be the same again, will it?"

My little girl, cutting right to the chase. "No, honey, it won't, not between your mom and me. It doesn't have to be different for us, though."

"But it will. Mom says you'll have to sell the house. Uncle Carl says we can stay as long as we want, but Mom's been looking for an apartment for a while. I'll be going back and forth."

"You'll be loved wherever you are, Molly. That's what matters. We both still love you." I prayed that my choice of words was correct and wished for a damn script to follow. There was one question I was afraid to ask, but it had to be done. "Do you still love me?"

Her fingers toyed with a strand of hair, and she stared through the windshield. "You're my dad. But you hurt Mom, real bad."

"I know that, Molly. I'm trying . . . I am changing."

"Don't people always say that when they've done something wrong?" She looked away from me, out the passenger side window. "That's what they taught us at church."

"But I mean it. There comes a time—"

"Can we just go to the park?" She folded her arms and sank into the seat. "I need to think."

I tightened my grip on the steering wheel and fixed my eyes on the pavement. We soon turned into the traffic circle, just inside the park entrance, and looped past a serpentine stone wall to the parking lot nearest the skateboard run. Molly popped out, grabbed her board, and sprinted away. A couple of other kids were gliding around the ramps, and she joined in seamlessly. I sank onto the lowest tier of the bleachers. My intended heartfelt discussion was taking a backseat to a pink skateboard.

Most of her companions had departed by half past six. With only a couple skateboarders left on the skateboard run, Molly finally allowed herself a water break. While she took a long slurp from her bottle, I said, "We need to talk some more, you know. I promised your mom we'd be back by seven thirty."

She puffed out some air. "I need the practice."

"C'mon. Five minutes, then you're back out there."

Resigned, she took a seat and leaned her board against the bench between us. I thought about Jack, being direct, and dove in.

"Mom said you're going to see a counselor with her. That's a good decision. You remember I had to do that, after what happened with my dad."

"Yeah, but it seems weird. Talking to a stranger about private stuff."

"That's okay. They can step back and take a fresh look at everything." I didn't tell her that some of my counselors had been decent, some for shit, and too many had been eager to dispense medications. "What about school? I know about the suspension, the fighting."

She clasped her hands between her knee guards. "It's better, now that the trial's over. But some kids say you got away with it."

There were surely adults who wondered the same thing. "You have to ignore people like that, Molly. There're always people out there who want to upset you."

"I guess."

"We're all going to move on from this. Whatever you've heard, whatever people say, just give me the chance to prove to you that I can still be a good dad. That's all I ask."

"Some kids, after their parents' divorce, say their dads don't see them when they should."

"That won't be me, Molly. I'll be there for you, promise." I wanted to say so much more, and I really needed a hug. But I sensed that she was beginning to feel pushed, and when that happened, she and her pink skateboard would vanish in the other direction. I simply said, "Okay?"

"Okay." She stood up and grinned. "Now, can I go skate?"

"You sure you don't wanna go home? It's getting chilly." The wind had picked up, and we heard the gathering waves crashing against the break wall.

"I'm fine out there." She nodded toward the run and then paused and eyed me. "But if you want to leave . . . "

"Lemme grab a coffee, and I can hold out for a while. Want something?"

"I'm good," she said, already wheeling toward the ramps.

I strolled over to the refreshment stand fashioned of rough-hewn planks and situated between the tennis courts and the pool. An uninspired coffee cost about a dollar more than it was worth, but at least it was warm. I held the Styrofoam cup between both hands and turned from the booth. Molly was nowhere to be seen. I hurried around the tennis courts for a clearer view, but stared at an empty skateboard run and a chain link fence. I tossed the cup onto the lawn and broke into a sprint.

My daughter's pink skateboard had rolled to the edge of the sidewalk.

She was gone.

51

Maybe she had spotted a friend and run off. Or perhaps she was playing a game of hide-and-seek with me. If she had scampered toward
the parking lot, I would have seen her on my way to the refreshment
stand. The only way that Molly would have been out of my line of
sight was if she had bolted through the gate to the old access road that
twisted into the woods on the other side of the fence. I rushed ahead,
toward the undeveloped copse of oaks and honey locusts.

As I charged along the uneven dirt and into the trees, I tore out
my cell phone and frantically dialed 911.

"What's your emergency?"

"At Lakewood Park. My daughter's missing." The words tumbled out.

"Calm down, sir. How old is she?"

"Why? Thirteen, but—"

"Sometimes teenagers—"

"Damn it! Send a car now, the old road along the fence, down to
the lake."

I clicked off, then punched in Bernie's number and held the
phone to my ear, stumbled, but managed to catch my balance. His

voice mail picked up and I left a message, imploring him to somehow help, then shoved the phone into my pocket.

Dirt footpaths snaked away from the road and disappeared in the trees and shrubs. The wind continued to build, whistling through the branches, and I was so near the lake that the crashing waves were deafening.

With each footfall, the image of that abandoned pink skateboard stalked me. Molly wasn't playing some innocent game, hadn't run off to meet some playground buddy. The only conceivable explanation was that the Andar Feo had abducted my daughter. Goddamn it, I'd done nothing to cause it. I had not crossed Jennifer, had not given her any reason to touch Molly. None.

I screamed Molly's name. There was no reply.

The cratered dirt road led to the groundskeeper's dilapidated wooden garage and a shabby storage shed. I paused, gasping for air. Parked tight against a weathered wall of the shed was a late model white van that struck me as completely out of place. I again cried aloud for Molly and, through the wind, her feeble voice carried to me.

"Daddy!"

I pivoted toward the sound of my daughter's frightened cry.

And froze.

A huge old man stood in the shadow of the oaks and clutched Molly to him with one massive arm. He wore a light-blue windbreaker and jeans—just another kind, elderly face, out for a stroll in the park. But I knew, with an unwavering certainty that made me weak, exactly who he was.

"I trust we need no introduction, Mr. Coleman." The Torso Murderer's voice resonated above the thunderous waves that cascaded into the shale cliff below.

My daughter's eyes were wide, frightened.

"You'll be okay, Molly." My tone was shrill and rushed.

"Quite a fighter, this one, but you are an inherently scrappy people." He tightened his grip as Molly struggled to break free. "I should have used a stronger dose. Pity how difficult it has become to subdue even a child."

"What did you do to her, you son of a bitch?"

"Profanity, Mr. Coleman, is the effort of a weak mind to express itself. No need to worry; she inhaled a simple mixture of chloroform, diazepam, and a few of my special ingredients. I don't expect that you'd comprehend the chemistry. A different formula was blended with your dear friend's Kessler's, by the way. I do expect that my concoction actually improved the taste."

"If you hurt her, I swear to God, I'll kill you."

He made a raspy chuckling sound. "I don't fear God, and I surely don't fear you."

"Just let her go, please."

"Threats, then begging. The usual course. Next, you'll offer to exchange yourself for her."

"You said that you'd let me live. I can't live without her. No one will know about this. Just walk away."

He cackled. "In fact, my promise was for a long and miserable life, which you will surely have when I terminate the existence of your precious daughter."

With Molly gone, I'd follow in my father's footsteps. My daughter could not die. Bernie needed to come racing around the bend, Jack had to come back from the dead. "I called the police."

"Of course you did, Mr. Coleman. Everyone has a cell phone these days. That device would have complicated things for me when I tormented poor Mr. Ness. But we'll have time."

"Just give her to me. You can still get away, the van—"

"How delicious." He shifted his grip on Molly, and she grimaced as his forearm wrenched her neck. "But getting away was never my plan."

Whatever he intended, I had to stop him. I stepped forward. "Damn you, let her go."

"Or what? Are you going to charge me, mount an heroic bid to rescue her? I can snap her neck before you take a step."

"She doesn't deserve this."

"I've seen the shattered parents before, you know. The child who disappears at the communal swimming pool. The one who vanishes from the shopping mall. Those people never recover—you lost your daughter on your watch, Mr. Coleman. Live with that."

"She had nothing to do with the Butcher. That was me."

"But it's only fair—a daughter for a daughter. A wonderful symmetry, won't you agree?"

He stepped back, dragging Molly with him, toward a nearby break in the trees. I followed, gradually narrowing the distance. A numbing wind lashed in from the lake and chilled the air. Molly tried to wrench free, but Torso's grip never budged as he kept shuffling backward to the jagged bluff. Yet his breathing was labored; the exertion was taking a toll.

"With my son and daughter gone, what do I care anymore? The day has come to end my grand game, Mr. Coleman, and with my usual dramatic flair. Think about it: hurling myself into the lake with my final victim cradled in my arms, all while her loving father watches."

He was no more than ten feet from the precipice. I had lived near that shoreline my entire life and witnessed maelstroms buffet forty-foot powerboats, toss sailing dinghies and catamarans about like flotsam. There was no chance that Molly would survive a fall into the waves that hammered relentlessly into a shoreline of jagged rocks.

"The game ends on my terms. Delicious." Torso took another backward step toward the promontory. His voice had weakened; I had trouble hearing him over the wind and the waves. He stepped on a fallen branch and nearly stumbled.

Molly reacted immediately, thrusting an elbow into his stomach and twisting, ducking under his arm. His big mitt pawed the air, and he lurched after her as she darted away. I plunged forward, dropping my head and ramming my shoulder into his waist. My arms locked around his legs. *Drive, drive, drive.* Torso pummeled me in the back, but I would not quit. My legs churned. This was for Molly and Cathy,

Jack, me, my father. And for the 108 human beings Torso had slaughtered. The game would not end on his terms.

At the lip of the cliff face, his great body tottered. I dropped to the ground and jerked his feet toward me. As he tumbled backward, I released my grip and rolled away. I rose to my knees and watched his long arms whirl, those tender eyes gleaming in disbelief as he toppled over the edge. I stood and stumbled to the edge of the precipice, catching a glimpse of the Torso Murderer as he plummeted into the churning, white-capped swell far below.

Then my Molly was there, running to me, and I swept her into my arms. She was weeping, clutching me, shivering from the cold. Looking up, the chill rain striking my face, I held her to me and thanked God.

52

"I'm here because Cathy asked, okay?" Bernie faced me across the coffee table, reminding me of the day we'd read Torso's letter about Jack. "Molly's beggin' her to give you one more chance. Cathy's willing, but not if it's gonna be a waste of time."

"What do you mean?"

"Pretty simple, John." He rested his elbows on his knees. "She won't take a chance about your drinking. I've gotten other guys into a program, so she wants me to talk to you."

"I haven't had a drink since my acquittal. Cathy knows that."

"She's pulling for you, John, we all are. But . . . we've been around the block before, know people who've quit, then fallen back into it. She doesn't wanna get burned, understand?"

I pictured myself sitting on a folding chair in a church basement, raising my hand and telling my story to an earnest circle of strangers. "It's a big step, Bernie."

He extended his arms. "You kiddin' me? Do you want to grow old with or without your little girl? Easy choice, isn't it?"

I glanced around the room, remembering when Molly and

Cathy had been with me. "I'm not denying that I went overboard, plenty of times. But—"

"The fact is that the booze makes you do shit like wind up with Jennifer Browning. You never could handle it. Even back in high school, some of the stuff you'd come up with when you were drunk. Jesus." He grinned and wagged a finger at me. "Like that bullshit about balling Ellen O'Donnell."

I was aware that my mouth popped open. "You knew?"

He chuckled. "Look, you're a great guy when you're sober. Stay that way. I know a good group, can set you up with a sponsor."

I glanced from the figurines to the Bible to the cross mounted on the wall. If that's what Cathy wanted, and it would keep Molly in my life, it was a small price to pay. "Let's talk."

"Good decision."

I focused on my hazy reflection in the glass top of the coffee table. "What about . . . hell, I'll sleep better when they find the bastard."

"It's been two days. He'll wash up, no doubt about it, or some fisherman will run over him. A floater, with his eyeballs nibbled away by the fish. Serves him right."

"Any clues in the van?"

"ID number was ground off. Duct tape and ties in the back, a couple of blankets." Bernie interlocked his fingers and leaned forward. "Some knives, too. And a hacksaw. My guess is he had other plans for Molly, if you didn't get there when you did."

"You shoulda seen her, Bernie. She never quit. A fighter, he called her."

"I always said she had the balls in the family. Well, her and Cathy."

"Fuck you." I couldn't help but smile. This was Bernie, my friend.

He leaned forward, his eyes twinkling. "What, you worried he's still alive and people will stop treatin' you like some kind of hero?"

I grinned. "Yeah, somethin' like that."

"So you knocked a hundred-year-old guy off a cliff. You want a medal?"

"Anyone gets a medal, it's Molly."

"No argument. C'mon, let's grab lunch. I'm buyin'." He walked pointedly toward the door and turned to face me. "For the record, I did nail Ellen O'Donnell, senior year, after the South High game."

The son of a bitch laughed aloud, and I followed him outside, bracing myself for one hell of a lecture.

Bernie told me that a couple of hikers found a charred body in the desert outside of Nogales, Arizona. The lower half of the face had been chopped off, and the body was too badly burned and decomposed to be identified. The dimensions, however, matched Jennifer's build. Maybe the Andar Feo had concluded that she was too much of a potential liability and solved the problem with some knife work and a can of gasoline.

Or maybe Jennifer was sunning on a tropical island, sipping strawberry daiquiris as a bevy of tanned and strapping young men attends to her every need. Sometimes, the thought of that possibility makes me jump whenever the phone rings.

As for me, my license was suspended, but I did find work as a paralegal with a large law firm. I answer to a crew of very accomplished lawyers, many half my age. No complaints, though, because my license will be restored if I stay out of trouble. I've talked to Marilyn, who says the guy she now works for is a stiff who doesn't even comment on her earrings. She'll sign on again with John R. Coleman, Attorney at Law, in a flash.

Cathy and I are dating, regularly. I've been sober for months, and we are even talking about remarrying. Molly is back in my life on a regular, frequent basis. For them, I'm keeping every promise that I made and doing Jack proud. This time, I made the right choice.

And the Torso Murderer?

They never did find his body.

ACKNOWLEDGMENTS

The most difficult part about writing an acknowledgment is the regrettable fact that I will fail to name everyone who encouraged me over the years. There are, however, certain people whose unflagging support is particularly memorable.

First and foremost, my wife, Linda, was always willing to be my sounding board, sage critic, and constant source of encouragement. Without her, there would be no novel. My good friend and judge, the Honorable Dick Ambrose, provided an invaluable step-by-step account of the intricacies of a murder case. David and Carol Rollins, Alex and Kathy Hahn, Sean Halicanin, Lynn Larson, John Schiller, and Molly Schroeder all digested early drafts and offered thoughtful suggestions for revisions. Mary Ellen French faithfully read every draft and was generous with her editorial skills and ideas. Last but not least, the real-life John Coleman, my longtime friend, shared with me what it was like growing up in Cleveland as a member of the terrific Irish community. John has little in common with the troubled character in my book!

And a heartfelt thanks to everyone else along the way—teachers, editors, authors, Roop & Co., Greenleaf Book Group, Mad Jackal Media, friends, and family—who shared of their time, talent, and experience to make this novel a reality.

1. John continually insists that he has his emotions under control and does not need to seek assistance. As the killings continue, this becomes less and less true. What is the breaking point for John? When did he need to seek help? In this context, discuss his relationship with Jack Corrigan.

2. Was John truly only interested in Jennifer's well-being before her betrayal, or did he have ulterior motives from the beginning?

3. Discuss the dynamics of John and Cathy's relationship. Was their separation inevitable? Was Jennifer just a catalyst to John pulling away from his family? Would they have even still been together if they didn't have a child?

4. What was your process of elimination for suspects in Frank's death? Who did you think did it and why? What cleared others of suspicion?

5. How does John's alcoholism fuel his need to be involved in the case?

6. Molly seems to be the biggest hit to John's conscience. Discuss her role in his life. Does he use her as a way of reminding himself what he is throwing away with his reckless actions? It doesn't seem to be enough to actually stop him from making

bad choices. Does he worry about the impact on his relation-ship with her? Does he think to himself, *I have to think about Molly* because that is what he "should" be thinking?

7. Did the identity of any killer come as a shock? Did you find any clues leading to their identity?

8. Is John responsible for what happens to him? Do you think the Butcher was always going to come for him no matter what steps he took to avoid her or go after the truth?

9. What is the more important or compelling storyline: the Butcher, the circumstances of Frank's death, or the Torso Mur-derer's quest for vengeance?

10. Does John deserve a second chance with his family?

11. What are John's biggest shortcomings and how do they influ-ence the plot?

12. Whether he listens to their advice or not, many characters have great impact on John's life and decisions. Discuss which char-acters have the most impact on John and the plot. Why does he value relationships with individuals like Bernie Salvatore and Jack Corrigan?

13. Family relationships are a prevalent idea explored throughout the novel. How is this shown and how does it work into the plot?

14. What are some other main themes present in the story? How do they come through?

15. Did the Torso Murderer survive? Will he come back to finish what he started? Why or why not?

AUTHOR Q&A

Was any part of this story based on actual events?

Yes, the entire story line involving the Torso Murderer and Eliot Ness actually occurred. The depiction of those events in *The Company of Demons* is historically accurate.

What kind of research did you do to prepare for this novel?

I read nonfiction sources on the Torso Murderer, reviewed contemporary newspaper accounts, and researched psychological studies of serial killers. I also reviewed manuscript details with a detective, a judge, and several attorneys regarding police procedural matters, defense and prosecutorial practices, and jury issues in murder trial cases.

Who is your favorite character?

John Coleman. Few things are more gratifying than watching a deeply flawed character confront his weaknesses and, ultimately, become a better person.

What is your writing process like?

I like to devote several hours at a time to focus on a new chapter or chapters. Typically, I'll then set those chapters aside and review and revise earlier sections of the manuscript. I have found that revisions are stronger if material rests for a while and is then approached with a fresh perspective.

Aside from the tertiary killer, the Torso Murderer, the main criminals in your story are women. Was this a conscious choice?

Yes. I developed the Butcher's character as a woman precisely because female serial killers are rare. Further, my choice was driven by an interesting twist in the investigation of the Torso Murderer. When Cleveland police visited the site of a similar killing in Pennsylvania, they learned that the imprint of a woman's high heel shoe was found in the blood. But I balanced the dark characters of the Butcher/Jennifer against the strong female roles of Cathy, Arlene, and even Molly. Given John's character, I felt that his relationships with the various women who impacted his life helped drive the story.

What is the hardest thing about writing a thriller?

Finding the right pace for the story—one that will keep the reader engaged, but not exhausted. The reader needs the opportunity to digest what has happened, consider the clues as to what might happen next, and wonder how the characters will respond to developments in the plot.

What was your favorite scene to write?

The basement scene, when the Butcher has John totally helpless and he must reflect on his conduct, the consequences, and how high the personal price has been.

Where did you find inspiration for your story?

I found the real-life murders by the Torso Murderer fascinating. The fact that he eluded Eliot Ness and then disappeared without a trace is gripping history. I asked the simple question: What if he is still lurking out there and, someday, returned?

How has your real-world legal experience helped you in your writing process?

It was invaluable, because I am familiar with the complex relationships between clients, attorneys, and judges. I have also personally conducted several jury trials and understand the dynamics of a courtroom.

Mysteries and thrillers often reach the climax with the revelation of the killer. Here, you've revealed the Butcher in the middle and revealed the presence of another killer to continue the story. It's a refreshing twist on the classic plotline. What made you write it this way?

History was my motivation. The fact that the Torso Murderer terrorized a major urban area for years, and then simply vanished, is fascinating. I could not ruin that historical reality by making up an identity. Far better, I believe, for the reader to wonder: Who was the Torso Murderer? That same question has perplexed law enforcement officials and amateur sleuths for years.

What are you working on now?

My next project is a WWII thriller set in the United States involving a plot by highly skilled Axis agents to sabotage projects that are critical to the war effort.

 Michael Jordan obtained his undergraduate degree from Ohio Wesleyan University with highest honors and his law degree from George Washington University, where he was a member of the Law Review. A trial lawyer and arbitrator for over three decades, he has been recognized as an Ohio Super Lawyer® and named to Best Lawyers in America®. *The Company of Demons* is his first novel.

A native of Saginaw, Michigan, Michael and his wife, Linda Gross Brown, a soft pastel artist, divide their time between homes in Rocky River, Ohio, and Longboat Key, Florida. They enjoy traveling, pleasure boating, and very cold martinis.